THE DEVIL'S HATBAND

THE DEVIL'S HATBAND

ROBERT O. GREER

THE MYSTERIOUS PRESS

Published by Warner Books

A Time Warner Company

Mysterious Press books are published by Warner Books, Inc., 1271 Avenue of the Americas, New York, NY 10020.

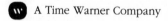 A Time Warner Company

The Mysterious Press name and logo are registered trademarks of Warner Books, Inc.

Printed in the United States of America

First Printing: March 1996

10 9 8 7 6 5 4 3 2

Library of Congress Cataloging-in-Publication Data
Greer, Robert O.
    The devil's hatband / Robert O. Greer.
       p. cm.
    ISBN 0-89296-634-3 (hardcover)
    1. Afro-American men—Colorado—Denver—Fiction.
2. Environmentalists—Colorado—Denver—Fiction. 3. Bail bondsmen—Colorado—Denver—Fiction. 4. Denver (Colo.)—Fiction. I. Title.
PS3557.R3997D48 1996
813'.54—dc20
                                        95-41994
                                        CIP

For Phyllis—The Light and Love of My Life

Acknowledgments

Several people associated with the genesis of this book deserve my heartfelt thanks. Nat Sobel, for believing that there was an audience for my ideas and for giving my efforts visibility, support, and direction. Laura Griffith, for advising me on the need to pause and reflect and for challenging me to take no shortcuts. For bringing a calmness and a true sense of synthesis to the editorial process I thank Sara Ann Freed. Thomas E. Vandermee, Division Chief, Englewood, Colorado, Police Department, answered every question put to him about the technical aspects of police work, no matter how inane they became. Any errors in translating this procedural information into the work that follows are clearly the author's. I thank Connie Oehring for her keen, professional copy-editing eye. Finally, I am grateful to Kathleen Hoernig, secretary without peer, who generously gave of her time beyond the call of duty and who toiled with massive accumulations of handwritten copy, dictation, and unending drafts to finally give *The Devil's Hatband* its typescript life.

Author's Note

The characters, events, and places that are depicted in *The Devil's Hatband* are spawned from the author's imagination. Certain Denver and Western locales are used fictitiously, and any resemblance between the novel's fictional inhabitants and actual persons living or dead is purely coincidental.

Barley-corn, barley-corn, Injun-meal shorts,
Spunk water, spunk water, swaller these warts.

—Tom Sawyer

THE DEVIL'S
HATBAND

One

Her allergies always peaked just as the bright green aspen leaves of summer started to turn Colorado high country autumn gold. No one had ever been able to tell her exactly what triggered the cycle. The allergies had simply always been there. One doctor had told her she had a rare hypersensitivity to decaying plants and exotic molds. Another had claimed the allergies were the result of irreversible family genetics. Etiologies notwithstanding, she had learned to put up with the aggravation, never letting the allergies slow her down.

She was walking through a large flat forest of aspen. She stopped, suppressed the urge to sneeze, and continued on. The aspen were mature and tall. Their slender white trunks reached skyward until their branches formed a translucent canopy that filtered the sunlight into geometric beams that danced around through the forest like light from a strobe. The forest was unseasonably dry. The trees swayed in rhythmic cadence from the push of a gentle upslope chinook wind. The crunch of roots and twigs snapping beneath her feet and the screechy crow-like caw of the pesky birds known as camp robbers were the only sounds she heard.

She often walked in the woods alone. It was her private time, moments stolen for herself. Time away from the pressures of her passion to balance the ecological scales. She tried not to think about the sales job she was going to have to do to rekindle support for her cause.

The West she loved was a land of exaggeration in geography, climate, humor, history, and folklore, with a tradition of violence and boom and bust, and a cattle-culture history she desperately wanted to change. She knew she could. She was a manipulator who could be aggressive and intimidating one minute, coquettish and childlike the next—warm and fuzzy or rock-ice cold. Above all, she knew how to use her considerable persuasive charms.

She came out of the aspen and into the midmorning sun. She stopped, sniffled, then blew her nose, before continuing down toward the valley below. Her swollen red eyes didn't alter the beauty of her dark exotic face. The partitioned sunlight accentuated her tall delicate figure, highlighting the fact that she was black. She would soon turn twenty-nine.

The woman glanced back at the swaying aspen, searching for the peace the forest always seemed to provide. Above the aspen was a two-thousand-foot-wide belt of Engelmann spruce and alpine fir. Higher still, unforested tundra rose another thousand feet. She stood next to a U.S. Geological Survey marker from 1912. The corroded brass cap had been stamped "8,000 ft." To her left Coyote

Creek bubbled off onto a lush green subirrigated mesa before it started undulating its way downhill.

The creek originated from a collection of crystal-clear alpine lakes just above the timberline, then worked its way along the edge of the aspen forest to define the eastern border of the ranching valley below, which was known as Twenty-Mile Park. The flat-topped wilderness, boasting the oldest mountains in the state, formed the border of the valley to the north.

The woman followed Coyote Creek as it switchbacked down gentle slopes toward the white frame house she called home. She had often thought it ironic that a stream carrying the lifeblood of the West could have been named after a predator the ranchers so uniformly despised. Coyote Creek was a superb trout stream. In the East, where she had been raised, she had often fished with her father for lake trout and bass. When she was in college she had dated a man with a passion for the sport. But now she saw fishing as insensitive, uncaring, and cruel and fishermen as killers who operated in a vacuum of self-serving arrogance and pride.

The topography of the land changed dramatically at 7,500 feet, where a shattered rock ridge formed by pressure, glaciation, and centuries of continuous melt and freeze formed a thirty-foot-high shelf of coal. The fracture seam ran above the valley for several miles. Recently, strip-mining had reared its ugly head; not on her side of the valley but to the east. During the long warm days of summer she had heard blasting that she knew was loosening the precious overburden of earth above the seam of coal. Too often the blasting had interrupted her quiet times in the forest.

She thought about why she did what she did. She

hadn't started out to become the leader of a cause. The calling had come to her suddenly, as effortlessly as breathing, as instinctively as making love. Now she couldn't change. She had been called a renegade carpetbagger and a psycho by cattlemen in Colorado and four adjoining states. She was known as the Sidewinder Bitch by the ranchers of Twenty-Mile Park. Their insults and rhetoric rolled off her like a marble on glass. She was resilient, case-hardened by the cultural armor of being black.

The twenty acres immediately surrounding her house turned into irrigated pasture and rolling hills of chickweed and sage. Near the corner of the house willows outlined Coyote Creek's path as it headed west. She checked her watch. Her four-mile walk from the depths of the aspen forest to the fence line that marked the twenty acres around her house had taken her an hour and a half.

She walked through the back door of the house and hung her sweater on a nail in the mudroom.

"Is anyone back?" she called out.

No one answered. She had sent two of her people to town for peat moss and rock chips so they could plant a windbreak of spruce in the stubborn clay soil around the house.

She decided to make some tea. She stepped into the kitchen and pulled an antique kettle from one of the cabinets. She filled it with water and turned on the stove. She thought she heard a noise from the pantry. When she turned to take a look, her Siamese cat, Laramie, scurried across the room toward the front door.

"You must want out," she said. Laramie was waiting for her, posed by the door like a ceramic figurine. She opened the door, and they both stepped out on the porch. Down the lane from the house a couple of red-tailed hawks circled the sagebrush flats between Coyote Creek and the county road.

She knew they were hunting for ground squirrels. One hawk soared toward the ground. Two feet above the purple sage, the hawk shot back skyward. She was amazed at the hawk's ability to change direction so fast. She shaded her eyes and continued watching the sky. One hawk swooped toward the ground again. She didn't see the ground squirrel in its talons until the bird was back level with her eyes.

A sudden gust of wind carried a knot of sagebrush across the lane. The woman and her cat went back inside the house. The tea kettle was whistling. She was surprised that no one had come back from town yet. She looked around for Laramie, but he had scampered away. She dropped a teabag into a large coffee mug and covered it with boiling water to the brim. Steam rose from the mug. She dunked the teabag in and out of the water several times. Soon the rich orange pekoe aroma filled the room. Her stuffy nose wouldn't let her enjoy the smell.

Later that morning, eighty miles north, in the depths of the Wyoming wilderness, she would begin the final stages of her plan, a plan designed to eradicate a ranching culture that for too many years had raped the land. She pulled a stool from beneath the kitchen counter and sat down to enjoy her tea.

She was just about to take her first relaxing sip when a thin shadow looped in front of her eyes, and she felt a series of sharp stings bite into her neck. Her mug fell to the floor and shattered. Laramie ran under a table from his perch on the frayed arm of the living room couch. The woman grabbed at her throat, laboring to breathe, gasping for air. She elbowed at the amorphous human form behind her, an involuntary reflex that screamed *I want to live*. She clawed at the death instrument cutting into her long, elegantly proportioned neck. She tugged at it, lacerating her fingers and bloodying her palms. She struggled violently for her life in the shadows of the late morning sun. She kicked and lunged and wheezed, coughing up laryngeal cartilage, mucus, and blood—carrying the weight of the person behind her across every square foot of the room. She tried to get a look at her attacker, but the pain and lack of oxygen wouldn't let her turn her head far enough to see who it was. As she became weaker she thought about her aspen forest. For almost three minutes she struggled, but in the end her life was slowly choked away, squeezed from her like water from a sponge.

Exactly one week and a day before her twenty-ninth birthday, the woman that Twenty-Mile Park ranchers called Sidewinder B was strangled in the kitchen of her modest white frame ranch house in a remote Colorado mountain valley twenty-eight miles southwest of the Continental Divide.

The wide mountain valleys and imposing thirteen-thousand-foot peaks of Twenty-Mile Park can carry the sound of an elk crossing a hay meadow as far as a mile. In such a setting the scratchy police band radio that the woman tuned in the first thing every morning seemed especially out of place. The radio had been silent all morning long. But, as she lay sprawled lifeless on the kitchen floor, the battered old radio announced, as it had dozens of times before, that the Routt County sheriff and his new deputy were on their way to question her about recent fence cuttings that had scattered over a hundred head of a neighboring rancher's mother cows, leaving ten of them dead. Doing his best Claude Raines impression, the deputy joked across the police band airwaves, "We're on our way out to the Sidewinder's place to round up the usual suspects." The sheriff was not amused.

Thirty minutes would have been plenty of time to cover up the crime. Time enough for the killer to drive to the preselected long-abandoned silver mine shaft and dispose of her body for good. Thirty minutes should have been time enough to inspect the house properly and police the murder scene. But when the greenhorn overeager sheriff's deputy announced to central dispatch in Steamboat Springs, "We're turning onto County Road 27," five minutes was all the killer had.

When the sheriff and his deputy pulled onto the lane leading up to the white frame house, they didn't see the pickup truck drop out of sight just over the hill that local ranchers called Hayden Divide. They had no way of gauging the truck's eighty-miles-per-hour speed. And because the county had sprayed the gravel road with calcium chlorite the day before, there was no customary fantail of dust rising behind the truck.

TWO

Bail Bondsman's Row is a block-long assemblage of six aging turn-of-the-century buildings affectionately known as Painted Ladies. The unlikely but enduring cluster of once proud Victorian houses lines the west side of Delaware Street as it turns toward downtown Denver from 13th Avenue North. Darkness never descends on Bondsman's Row. Brightly lit neon signs jut from the ornate fascia above weathered wraparound porches, yelling freedom to the prisoners across Delaware Street in the Denver County Jail. Blue, red, yellow, and green neon tubes shaped to spell OPEN 24 HOURS, BAIL BONDS ANYTIME, and NEVER CLOSED flash gaudy promises of freedom not only to the inmates but to the prisoners' families and friends.

CJ Floyd had come to work on the row in 1971, freshly separated from three years in the navy. He was six months and twenty-one days on the good side of the war in Vietnam and three months past the salvation of a marriage he wanted to save but couldn't. CJ went to work for his uncle as a runner, the lowest job on Bondsman's Row.

His two tours in Vietnam had been spent as a gunner's mate aboard a 125-foot navy swift boat patrolling the twisted creeks, dense jungle, and humid swamps of the Mekong Delta. Official navy jargon called it riverine warfare. CJ called his tours missions to test his soul. Two years of CJ trying to prove that someone just past being a gang-banging black kid could be a man was all his wife, DeeAnn, could take. She left him, knowing that for all his outward thrill-seeking bravado, he was as fragile as Depression glass.

Some people claim you can tell a lot about a man by what he reads. Perhaps. You could learn more about a man like CJ Floyd by taking inventory of the things he discarded and the things he saved. CJ saved ticket stubs from movies and every manner of game. He had section 34, row 8, seats 11 and 12 ticket stubs from the Broncos' inaugural 1977 Super Bowl appearance, in the Superdome in New Orleans. CJ had two tickets to the Los Angeles opening of the movie Lady Sings the Blues that he had gotten from a client but never used because his marriage had been on its last legs and DeeAnn had refused to go. His apartment above his office was cluttered with coffee cans full of cat's-eye marbles and jumbos. There were cigar boxes of steelies too. In the basement of the building CJ had stacks of mint-condition records, 78s and 45s, stored in tomato crates gathering dust. He had amassed hundreds of tobacco tins and inkwells from around the world, along with maps that seemed to document every place CJ had ever been. But CJ was a collector in the old-fashioned sense; no hoarder like Silas Marner or warehouser of superfluous gaudy late-twentieth-century junk. CJ collected because he liked to. For CJ, everything he collected represented a trail to the important things he wanted to remember from his past.

Conspicuously missing from CJ's collectibles were report cards and the family-oriented board games that meant interacting with other people instead of going it alone. There were no albums filled with Little League pictures or photographs of grade-school field trips to the zoo. No yearbooks or kindergarten finger paintings. No team sports letter jackets or souvenirs from the prom. CJ's collectibles were the treasures of a loner, artifacts assembled by someone who had raised himself.

CJ's collection of antique license plates was a collector's equivalent of the Nobel Prize. The license plates said more about him than any other collection he had. He had started the collection during his teenage years, when his uncle's drinking had reached its peak, and street rods and low-riders had taken the place of family in his life. The pride of his collection were a 1916 Alaska plate and his prized 1915 Denver municipal tag. Both had been fabricated using the long-abandoned process of overlaying porcelain onto iron. Although the collection was impressive, it remained incomplete, and DeeAnn, one of the few people who had ever seen the entire collection, suspected that, like CJ, it would never be whole.

CJ had once told DeeAnn that he eventually hoped to have a first-issue plate from every state and every Colorado municipality license plate issued before World War I. Before 1916 license plates had been issued by cities, not states. The process grew out of issuing license plates for bicycles and mushroomed from there. Eventually his complete collection would hover around 110. The collection currently numbered sixty-five. The only state license plates he still lacked were Minnesota and Tennessee. CJ wouldn't accept any addition unless it was in absolutely mint condition, and he only collected the rarest of the rare.

When CJ was on a full-tilt hunt for plates, he had been known to run on nothing but coffee and donuts for more than a week and to crisscross Colorado, New Mexico, and Wyoming, logging thousands of miles. He didn't begin a license plate odyssey unless he expected a legitimate find somewhere along the way. But he hadn't zeroed in on a mint-condition municipal plate in close to a year. CJ subscribed to a dozen antique trade papers and scoured them daily. He hunted garage sales and swap meets, flea markets and antique guilds. All of those places teemed with women almost to the exclusion of men. The women seemed to be lonely, and they always gravitated toward CJ. True to form, CJ made the encounters brief. A hurried conversation about license plates over a cup of coffee and toast. At the most a one-night stand. Never more. CJ liked to savor his collecting without distractions, influence, or help.

Back from Vietnam, CJ went from runner to bondsman in a matter of months, covering for his uncle when the old man was drunk, posting bond without a license, coming up with what he liked to call "magic money" in the space of an hour. He once put three liens on his car, using a counterfeit title, and extracted money from three separate banks. For two years he ran numbers on the side. When his uncle died, CJ inherited the business from the old man who had raised him, primarily because, as his uncle's sister Til put it, no one else in the family "wanted to deal with trash." He told DeeAnn, who was still on speaking terms with him, that the business came to him the only three ways anything had come to him in life: through divorce, default, or death.

CJ spent the next ten years writing $5,000 and $10,000 bonds, called nickel-and-dime paper on the street. By the mid-1980s he was doing a little bounty-hunting on the side, running down local bond skippers and bringing them back to the halls of justice downtown. In early 1989 he apprehended a skipper who had jumped a $50,000 bond in Denver—a man who had been charged with racketeering, possession of drugs, and assault. CJ tackled the jumper at the United Airlines ticket counter at Stapleton Airport in full view of a local TV crew there on assignment to cover a machinists' strike. The story made the ten o'clock news. CJ's name and face flashed across the Denver airwaves for two full days. When the local and parochial newshounds learned that the linebacking bondsman, as he was called, was a Denverite by birth and that he had served two tours in Vietnam, the story kept its momentum. It lasted three more days when the bond jumper was identified as a relative of the Colorado Assembly's speaker of the house.

For a few months CJ's bonding and bounty-hunting business boomed. He brought in bond-jumping muggers, robbers, even counterfeiters on the lam. His minor-celebrity status earned him special seating at sporting events and one invitation to a black-tie affair. But the notoriety was fleeting and within six months CJ was back to just trying to make ends meet.

When DeeAnn called one day to congratulate him on tracking down a mugger who had most of northeast Denver scared to death, he surprised her by saying that his latest triumph had been just another double, when he was really hoping to hit one over the fence. Three weeks later, six days before his forty-fifth birthday, CJ would have a chance to step back up to the plate.

He was sitting at his desk beneath his portrait gallery of more than seventy-five bond jumpers he had brought in. His wiry hair was graying at the temples, and another patch of gray had recently sprouted near the front. CJ was wearing one of his trademark jet black riverboat gambler's vests, rolling an unlit cheroot from side to side in his mouth. It was Indian summer in Denver, October 18, and the daytime highs had hovered around 75 degrees for three straight days. CJ wasn't thinking about turning forty-five; he was just daydreaming about the luck of the extended warm spell, hoping it would last a little longer before the jet stream made its final trek south, bringing with it a blanket of cold Canadian air. Maybe when winter hit he would work on losing those extra fifteen pounds, which had been ten last year and five the year before. CJ's rhythmic breathing tugged at the bottom of his vest. He knew the first thing he would cut out would be his daily slice of sweet potato pie. He slipped the cheroot back in his pocket.

It was eleven-thirty, always a slow time of the day, when the two men appeared. Both men were black and they were each wearing expensively tailored charcoal gray pinstriped suits. The shorter man's was double-breasted, making him look even shorter than he was. The other man stood well over six feet and looked athletically trim. A briefcase tugged at his right arm.

CJ's secretary, Julie Madrid, had already left for lunch, so CJ had to greet the men himself. As the short man closed the door behind them, CJ wished Julie had taken a later lunch.

"Can I help you?" asked CJ. "My secretary's out."

"CJ Floyd?" asked the tall man, staring intently at CJ through sunglasses he hadn't removed.

"That's me."

The two men exchanged a glance—the kind people exchange when they have inside dope. The tall man removed his sunglasses and put them away.

They could be attorneys, thought CJ. He was used to lawyers running in and out, yo-yoing his day.

"We understand you're the kind of bondsman who will do a job well and keep it quiet," said the taller of the two.

"I offer a professional service, if that's what you mean," said CJ.

CJ prided himself on keeping his business dealings close to the vest. In his twenty years as a bondsman, he had never let any of his confidential dealings spring a leak.

Both men seemed a bit uncomfortable, standing in the middle of the sparsely furnished room, its twelve-foot coffered ceiling echoing their every word.

"I'm Lucius Womack," said the tall man.

"Peter Spence," said the other man, extending his hand toward CJ.

"Good to meet you," said CJ. He shook Spence's hand. It was fleshy and moist. Womack never offered his.

"Can we pull up chairs?" asked Womack.

CJ nodded. Both men retrieved chairs from the corner of the room and rolled them up to CJ's desk. The chairs' squeaky casters echoed off the walls.

CJ slipped into the high-backed red chair behind his desk. From his vantage point both men were below the level of his eyes. CJ's uncle had sawed two inches off the legs of the chairs decades ago. "When you're negotiating business, always keep the advantage, especially when it comes to height," the old man once told CJ.

Spence cleared his throat. "Actually, a bondsman only meets half our needs." He glanced at Womack as if he expected him to say something. When he didn't, Spence continued.

"Have you ever heard of PlanetFirst, Mr. Floyd?"

CJ had, but he wanted to keep the two men guessing about anything that would allow them to size him up.

"Can't say that I have."

"They're a radical environmental group," said Spence.

"Like save the bunnies, save the trees. Give a hoot, don't pollute?" asked CJ, with a grin.

"It's not funny, Mr. Floyd. They think they're supposed to save the world. People who see themselves as saviors can be a troublesome lot. These are radical environmentalists who would rather see *you* skinned than an elk or bear. They would rather live in a concrete geodesic dome than harm a single leaf on a tree. Some are willing to die for what they believe," said Spence.

"I see," said CJ.

"PlanetFirst has a splinter group that they support financially here in Colorado. They call themselves the Grand River Tribe. They named themselves after the original name of the Colorado River."

"So they're into history," said CJ, with a smile.

Womack spoke up, ignoring CJ's attempt at humor. He wanted to get to the point. "They have two things we want back, a woman and a document." The word "document" seemed to stick in his throat.

"Whose document is it—yours or hers?" asked CJ, ignoring Womack's rush to the point.

"The document is ours. It was stolen. The woman's their brainwashed leader."

"We can't prove she stole the papers," said Spence, eyeing Womack like a parent eyeing a child who has just spoken out of turn.

"There's proof enough," said Womack, a hint of spite in his voice.

"Sounds to me like you don't need a bondsman. You need the law. Who the hell but the law wants a thief?" said CJ, probing for more information.

"I'll get to that," said Womack, before adding, "You're more than a bail bondsman, Mr. Floyd. We all know that."

CJ eased back in his chair, pulled the cheroot from his shirt pocket, and lit it up. He took two long puffs. The cherry aroma of the sweet-smelling smoke quickly enveloped the room.

"Smoke doesn't bother you two, does it?" asked CJ.

Both men shook their heads, but when CJ took a second drag and blew a short puff of smoke into the air, Spence quickly rolled his chair upwind.

"Kidnappers and thieves. Like I said, you need the law," said CJ, tapping cigar ash into an ashtray at his side.

Spence inched his chair forward, directly in front of CJ. His knees crowded the desk. "There are ten of them we know of. Eight are hard-core, as tough as nails. Two of them have outstanding warrants for tree spiking and criminal trespass up in Oregon. One of them, Albert Copley, racked himself up a couple of aggravated assault warrants over on a Nevada ranch and another one,

Thomas Deere, set fire to a four-hundred-ton stack of hay."

"Could be a case of misguided youth," said CJ.

"They've been at it for seven and a half years," said Spence. "Even adolescence doesn't last that long."

"You got any proof these Grand River people set the fire? And tree spiking in Oregon, that's a hell of a long way from here," said CJ.

Spence looked at Womack. He could tell he wasn't getting very far.

Knowing that he needed the business, CJ decided to give Spence some negotiating room. "So what do you want me to do, go out and round up the lot?"

"No, just bring back the woman."

"And the papers you mentioned, what about them?"

"She has the papers. Find one and you'll find the other," said Spence.

"Your tiger lady got any outstanding warrants?" asked CJ.

"Just criminal trespass," said Spence.

"Flimsy," said CJ. "You're talking a two-hundred-dollar fine and a slap on the wrist." He leaned back and blew a puff of smoke in the air. "Where do these groupies hang out? Colorado's a pretty big state."

"We don't know where they are now, Mr. Floyd," said Spence. "That's one reason we need you. The last we heard they were up in the northwest part of the state, outside of Craig."

"Half of that country's desert, and the other half's nothing but chickweed and sage. Not a hell of a lot of places to hide."

CJ's information caused Spence and Womack to ex-

change a look that said maybe they should start out after
the woman themselves.

"Lots of rattlesnakes in that country; mostly prairie
rattlers, but a few timber rattlers too. A man wouldn't like
to travel in it unless he knew what he was doing, and it's
a good distance to Craig. More than halfway across the
state."

"Are you searching for a high-water mark on your
fee, Mr. Floyd?" asked Spence.

"No, city boy, just giving you a little insight into
what goes into a bonding agent's job out West."

CJ tapped the ash from his cheroot, then leaned
back in his chair and slipped his hands behind his head.
"How many people did you say were in that gang?"

"Ten," responded Spence. "And they're not a gang.
'Gang' implies that they're thugs. She wouldn't link up
with thugs."

"They're thugs to me," said CJ, noting Spence's
chivalrous defense. "Decent folk don't rack up those
kinds of warrants. You could have me running down a
fucking pyromaniac. And aggravated assault, that's just a
gateway crime. The next time your boys, Copley and
Deere, may decide to crack a few skulls."

"I don't think we are dealing with that here," said
Spence.

"Like I said, you don't know what goes into a bonding agent's job," said CJ.

Frustration showed in Spence's eyes. He looked at
Womack for support. "You're a bounty hunter, Mr. Floyd.
Let's not mince words," said Womack. "Here's the deal:
we need this issue solved in less than forty-five days. It's
more than marginally important to our firm. You've been

recommended, but I am certain that there are others who can handle the job."

Black men offering jobs and decked out in $900 tailor-made suits didn't show up in CJ's office every day. Womack and Spence were a long way from CJ's normal clients. Even with a reputation for getting things done, CJ was still just another black man selling nickel-and-dime bonds who scratched out part of his living bounty-hunting on the side and struggled to make it every day.

The white bondsmen on the row never seemed to have to break CJ's kind of sweat and because they didn't, CJ had always felt like a plow horse among quarter horse studs. The big bonds always seemed to steer clear of him. While CJ was busy trying to collect $50 on the $500 bonds he posted to keep drunk and disorderly wife-beaters out of jail, the other bondsmen on the street were writing $50,000 bonds for white-collar criminals, gangsters, and Denver's politically corrupt. CJ got stiffed on 20 percent of the bonds he wrote and because half of his clients were people he had known all of his life, more often than not he ended up letting them pay when they could. No one else on Bondsman's Row was as softhearted or softheaded. CJ would never admit it, but he resented the way the bail-bonding game seemed to be rigged against bondsmen who were black.

He took a long hard look at Womack and Spence and decided that they just might represent the big payday he had been waiting on for years. And to top it off, maybe he could end up with a few bragging rights on the row. Although the job would involve a hunt, and there was always the chance he could come back without any game, CJ knew right then he would take the job.

But experience told him that people like Womack and Spence needed to be milked a little more.

CJ crushed out the cheroot and leaned forward in his chair. "Who's the woman?"

"Brenda Mathison," said Spence, with a knee-jerk response.

"Name doesn't ring a bell," said CJ.

"There's no way it should," said Spence. His tone of voice was condescending. "She's the daughter of a federal judge."

Spence pulled a photograph from his coat pocket and handed it across the desk to CJ. CJ held the picture up to the light. Only the word "June" had been penciled on the back. A polo-shirted Brenda Mathison was standing beside a 1965 fire-engine-red Mustang convertible. Her arms were folded across her chest. The camera had caught her at the peak of a halfhearted smile. She was pretty enough, but CJ didn't like the smile. Too obligatory. It was one of those thank-you-but-please-go-away kind of smiles CJ used to get from his ex-wife. The kind that became more common when things were on their final downhill course. CJ handed the photo back to Spence.

"She's black. Her father's a federal judge, she's in with some loony cult, and she has a document you two junior G-men just happen to want." CJ stroked his chin and sat back hard in his chair. "You brothers must be pulling my leg," he said, wondering how in the shit he was supposed to find the girl, bring her back, short of kidnapping her, and hand her over to two pinstripe-suited East Coast bozos who probably didn't know that Denver was still east of the Continental Divide. "You guys want a PI, go out and hire yourselves Sam Spade."

"I can assure you we are not pulling your leg," said Spence.

"What about the cult?" asked CJ.

"It's not a cult," said Spence, clearly exasperated.

"Cult, gang, tribe, mob, I don't give a rat's ass what you call 'em, she's in with the wrong frigging crew. I can read between the lines. You want me to pack her back to sweet old daddy the judge on your say-so. My ass. I call that kidnapping, gentlemen, and it's one hell of a stretch down the road from what I do every day."

The room was suddenly quiet except for the low-pitched hum of the ceiling fan above their heads. After a minute of silence Womack stood up, then motioned for Spence to do the same. "You'll be paid one hundred and fifty dollars per day plus expenses. Bring back Brenda and our papers in less than thirty days and there'll be a bonus. We'll be in Denver until tomorrow." He pulled a card from his wallet, slid it across the desk to CJ, and turned to leave. They were almost out the door when CJ asked where they were staying.

"The Brown Palace. Call me with an answer by four," said Womack.

CJ looked down at the card and studied it for a moment. There were six lines of type:

Carson Technologies, Inc.
Lucius Womack, Director
Veterinary Research Division
Boston, Massachusetts 02135
614-277-4693
Boston • New York • Dallas

When CJ looked back up, they were gone.

Three

A patch of gray-white popcorn clouds was blocking the sun when CJ stepped out into the lunch hour rush. CJ checked his watch. It was twelve twenty-five. The Carson Technologies men had been there longer than he thought. He had strung them along for nearly an hour, feigning disinterest in the Grand River job. In his experience, an hour's worth of denial with company men like Womack and Spence almost certainly meant a job.

There was no way CJ was about to trust two window-dressing company niggers in flashy suits. But he had learned over the years that the easiest way to scare off a potential client was by voicing your suspicions of them. His uncle, who had been a con man before turning bondsman, had often told CJ that no matter what the game—war to tiddlywinks—you had to know when to challenge your mark.

CJ already had a pocketful of reasons for wondering

if Womack and Spence were on the up-and-up. If the important papers they wanted so badly had been stolen, why hire a bail bondsman or a bounty hunter when a smart lawyer or a mediocre PI could probably get the job done?

It also looked like his two corporate carpetbaggers from Boston wanted to keep everyone involved black, as they tap-danced around calling in the law. And he thought he knew why. No matter how rarefied the air was up in the lofty chambers of a black federal judge, CJ knew that in the end His Honor couldn't afford to trust anybody white. One wrong move to protect a daughter who might have stolen some white man's precious documents could turn somebody like Judge Mathison into just another black fool. CJ had no doubt that the judge had checked him out and decided that he was good enough to be his house nigger for a while. Probably because CJ wasn't tied into the black upper-class pipeline and he knew how to keep his mouth shut. Paying for an errand boy on a leash made sense. That's how the Irish boys and Italians did it. Let some dumb fresh-off-the-boat Sicilian or South Boston type still harboring a brogue do your dirty work. Black folks were always slow to catch on.

CJ also suspected that Brenda Mathison was a lot less valuable than the papers she supposedly had. Unfortunately, that made her expendable and that's what worried him most. He knew that good money chased bad people all the time, but a smart bounty hunter never got caught up in a chase like that without looking for the oncoming train—no matter how good the money was.

One final thing bothered him. The two hamhocks from Boston had far too much information about Brenda and the Grand River Tribe's movements for it to be just a coincidence. CJ wondered if they had been tracking her themselves. There was one predictable thing about black corporate lackeys like Womack and Spence. When they begin to build up a little nest egg in the white man's pension fund, they all somehow start to take on that characteristic wet dog white man's smell. The odor coming from Womack and Spence had been amazingly strong.

A light breeze from the west quickly evaporated the beads of perspiration on CJ's forearms and brow. He made a mental note to trash his antique ceiling fan before next summer's heat. Maybe taking the Mathison job would allow him the luxury of what his uncle used to call refrigerated air.

By the time CJ reached his car the cloud bank had drifted away, and he could feel the full authority of the mile-high noonday sun. The white-capped Rockies rose from behind Denver's foothills to the west. The foothills were turning a golden autumn blaze. The September colors were reaching their peak. In two weeks the weather would start an irreversible downhill slide. Because CJ hated the cold, he quickly calculated his chances of finding the Mathison girl before it snowed. At thirty days, he had a chance of wrapping up the job before the mountain weather changed to its six-month cycle of snow. If it took sixty days to find her, CJ knew he was going to end up cold. He shivered at the thought.

There were only a handful of cars in the lot where CJ parked his pride and joy, a showroom-clean, pampered '57 Chevrolet Bel Air. He only drove the car during the summer and early fall. The tires had never suffered the indignity of being touched by a single flake of snow. The paint job was a couple of years old and exactly matched the original factory two-tone red on cream. CJ

knew everything there was to know about a '57 Bel Air,
down to the last knob and bolt. He knew how many cars
were sold that year. Thirteen thousand seven hundred
sixty-seven. Which state had sold the most. Michigan.
How many original colors there had been. Sixteen solid
and fifteen two-tones. The engine power. Two hundred
seventy horses. He could spout statistics about the Bel
Air for hours.

CJ had wanted a '57 Chevy Bel Air since he was six
years old and his uncle came into one as collateral on a
bond skipper's $5,000 bond. CJ would sit in the driver's
seat for hours, pretending to drive, his eyes barely level
with the dash, his hands firmly gripping the wheel.
Sometimes after a hard night of drinking, his uncle would
stumble home and pass out in the Bel Air's back seat,
with CJ at the wheel. The next morning they would both
wake up groggy, his uncle hungover, CJ still dizzy from
make-believe driving halfway into the night.

His uncle sold the Chevy the year CJ finished junior
high. CJ never got to drive that Bel Air. Through all his
troubled high school years he promised himself that one
day he would have a '57 Bel Air. The bond-jumping rela-
tive of the Colorado speaker of the house had afforded
CJ the money and his chance. He bought the car in Du-
rango from a rancher who had stored it in his barn for almost twenty years. CJ brought the car to Denver and had
his friend Roosevelt Weaks revive it from the ground up.
Only the paint job was done out of CJ's and Roosevelt's
sight, and even then they both stood around pestering
the help for most of the four days it took the people at
Ken's Autobody to repaint the car. CJ still took the car
over to Roosevelt's Garage and Car Emporium once a

month for a grease job, filter change, and eight fresh quarts of 10W40 Quaker State oil.

CJ cruised down Speer Boulevard, speedometer pegged at 35. His straw Stetson rested in the passenger seat. It was Tuesday and traffic was light, not like a Friday when the rush for the mountains started at noon. To CJ summertime traffic always seemed the worst.

The only nonstock modification to the Bel Air that CJ allowed himself was a tape deck so he could enjoy his sounds. CJ loved music, almost any kind, but he was partial to the blues and old-time rock and roll. He turned north onto Broadway and popped in one of his favorite tapes by B.B. King. A few seconds of static and B.B. was on. "The Thrill Is Gone" filled the front speakers of the car.

CJ wondered what thrills start to leave a man between forty and forty-five. The thrill of making love to a woman? Perhaps. The excitement of watching your child start to blossom? He'd never have an answer for that. For CJ, the thrill had always been the excitement of the game—basketball in high school, Vietnam, bounty-hunting for twenty-five years. Chasing down the Mathison woman might as well usher in a forty-fifth-birthday thrill. She might not want to come home to daddy straight off, but CJ had run enough street bluffs to know that if he was still as good at the bounty-hunting game as the judge had probably been told, then he could deliver the little black brat on a platter, separate her from the mysterious papers she was carrying, and collect a whole lot more than $200 before passing Go. If he couldn't still run a little bounty-hunting chase like that, then maybe forty-five was the age to hang it up. He didn't like the setup of having two corporate Oreos like Womack and Spence yanking his chain, but he had sidestepped suck-asses like them before, and he figured he had one thing in his favor. He would really be working for a job-conscious judge who didn't want any Negro shit to rub off on him.

CJ decided right then to sign on for the hunt. He made a mental note to call Womack right after lunch. By the time CJ parked his car near Mae's Louisiana Kitchen, B.B. King had started another song.

Denver has three neighborhoods that are considered predominantly black: Park Hill, Montbello, and Five Points. In terms of history, place, attitude, and race, only Five Points really qualifies. Five Points is in truth only a landmark, an intersection formed by the confluence of 27th, Welton, and Washington streets and 26th Avenue. It had been the core of Denver's black community since early in the twentieth century. In addition to its homes, churches, shops, and schools, Five Points had one historically famous nightclub, the Rossonian. During the 1930s, 1940s, and 1950s the Rossonian was to Denver what the Cotton Club was to Harlem. Since the 1950s the club had fallen into decline, a boarded-up relic of the past. But Mae's Louisiana Kitchen, its next-door neighbor, had endured, a restaurant and neighborhood gathering place since 1937, run by the same family for more than fifty years.

The restaurant itself was an understated plain brown wrapper of a place, squeezed between the Rossonian Club and Benny Prillerman's Trophy and Badge. In true Louisiana tradition, the restaurant was nothing more than a long narrow box, reminiscent of a New Orleans shotgun house. The entryway was tunnel-like and narrow, with barely enough room for three people to stand. At the back of the entry a hostess, usually Mae's daughter,

Mavis Sundee, greeted people at a mahogany pulpit that had belonged to her preacher grandfather but had long since been modified for more pedestrian use. Fifteen tables covered with checkerboard wax cloth hugged both walls. Most tables seated only two people, but a few jutted out to accommodate as many as six, so the central aisle down the middle of the restaurant undulated in and out, increasing and decreasing in size. A spotless modern kitchen sat behind swinging doors opposite the restaurant's shotgun entry. The restaurant's only concessions to extravagance were its Colorado marble floors and ceilings of ornate tin.

CJ didn't stop at the pulpit; instead he sauntered directly inside. The smell of high-cholesterol, high-fat, mouth-wateringly-delicious Southern fried food hung in the air. The promise of a meal of deep-fried Louisiana-style catfish always made CJ feel sure-enough, down-home BLACK. Half the tables were occupied. All the faces but one were black. A couple of people he knew looked up, nodded, and quickly went back to their conversations or food. CJ tossed his Stetson at a five-point elk antler rack on the wall. The Stetson's brim glanced off an antler and fell, crown inverted, to the floor.

CJ stooped to pick up his hat. From halfway down the center aisle a husky female voice challenged, "Missed again." Mavis Sundee was carrying two catfish specials in her hands. "Hot plate," she said. She placed the lunch plates down at table six in front of a couple holding hands. "Enjoy." She wiped one hand on her apron and motioned with the other for CJ to have a seat.

CJ straddled a chair at table two. "So they've got you delivering groceries today," he said.

"Thelma's out with the stomach flu and Shirley's helping in the back. I'm third choice."

"You look pretty choice to me," CJ said. He pulled an unwrapped cheroot from his vest pocket, put it in his mouth, and did his best imitation of Groucho Marx.

"Your eyebrows don't move up and down enough; besides, you know my daddy's rules. Sweet-talk one daughter and you have to take all three."

Mavis had two sisters. One was a lawyer, the other a civil engineer. Mavis was a Boston University–educated accountant. Because of that training, she had drawn the "come home and run the business" short straw right out of school.

At thirty-nine Mavis still had an old-fashioned wholesome down-to-earth kind of attractiveness that seemed to be getting rarer in women every day. Her flawless skin was a deep rich cocoa brown, and because she kept her naturally curly coal black hair trimmed so short, her face always seemed to beam.

"What'll it be, CJ?" She pulled a handful of food order tickets from her apron pocket.

"Got you so giddy you can't do your job? You really need all six of them tickets just for me?" asked CJ.

"Don't start with me, Calvin Floyd," she said. "Bounty-hunting bondsmen just aren't my cup of tea. They lack what some might call a stable life. We've been down that road before." Her voice had increased an octave.

The couple that had been holding hands looked up.

"I'm turning forty-five pretty quick here," CJ said. "A man has to have something to look forward to after that, don't you think?"

The couple at table six had stopped eating. They

were looking directly at Mavis and CJ, waiting to see what path their conversation would ultimately take.

"Forty-five's not so old, for some."

CJ smiled. He sensed an opening and was about to speak when Mavis cut him off.

"But it's ancient for an airline-ticket-counter-leaping rogue hunter who's already had his war. I care about you, CJ, but I care just as much about me. You may not believe it, but sometimes the rogues actually win. Have you ever thought that the people you track down just might have pictures of bounty hunters on their walls?"

CJ decided not to push his luck. He could tell that Mavis was in the kind of mood that would soon have her rehashing five other reasons for their failed relationship. "Like I said, you're still pretty choice," his voice now almost a whisper. "Better let me have the same thing those two ordered," he said, staring directly at the couple at table six, "and I'll take a glass of milk."

"Sure thing. I'll have daddy bring it out," said Mavis.

The couple at table six watched Mavis head toward the kitchen. By the time she reached the swinging doors, they were back to holding hands.

A few minutes later, Willis Sundee, square-shouldered and straight, looking more like a man of sixty than seventy-nine, Mavis's father, headed down the aisle with CJ's order. The second son of a Baptist preacher and a midwife, he had been born in one of four experimental colony settlements established in Colorado between 1892 and 1911. Willis still had a full head of hair and stood just over six foot three. He greeted CJ with the same broad smile he had offered when they first met twenty-five years earlier, when CJ had asked if he could cut Willis's lawn.

"You got our last catfish plate, CJ. I was saving it for myself." He set the plate down along with a brimming sixteen-ounce glass of milk.

CJ knew neither statement was true, but as always he played along.

"You're welcome to half."

"No, you young people need your strength. After the noon rush is gone, I'll just have myself some pork and beans."

"You gotta watch out for those beans, Mr. S. They have a tendency to end up talking back."

They both laughed, enjoying the same luncheon greeting they had shared, no matter the fare, for more than a decade.

"Truth is, CJ, Mavis didn't want to come back out." He shook his head in mock disgust. "After all these years you two are still beating your sticks at the margins of the thicket, when it's inside you'll always find the game."

CJ offered a halfhearted smile, sprinkled hot sauce on his catfish, and immediately started to eat.

Willis knew it was time to change the subject. "Have you been over to Roosevelt's to see that new engine dynamometer of his? The thing has got more bells and whistles than a moon rocket."

"No, I haven't," said CJ.

"Better get over there fast and let him do some work on your Bel Air before his first payment is due on that beast."

CJ finished off a piece of his catfish and washed it down with two huge swallows of milk. "I may have business over on the Western Slope pretty quick here," said CJ. "Guess I should take the Bel Air over to Rosie's be-

fore I start that job. I'll check out his new gizmo then." CJ
finished the rest of his milk in one giant gulp.

"Good," said Willis, happy to see he had the conversation headed down another track.

"Is your Western Slope business a bounty job or routine?" asked Willis.

"Don't really know yet, but believe it or not it may
involve someone you know. That is, if you still have your
pipeline to America's black bourgeoisie."

Willis Sundee's eyes widened with delight. Unlike
Mavis, he liked the excitement associated with CJ's
bounty-hunting jobs.

"Have you got a name?" asked Willis.

"Mathison, and he is a judge."

Willis had to think for a moment before the name
registered. "Yes, yes. I don't know him, but I knew his
folks. East Coast people, out of Philadelphia. Branford
Mathison, that's the man I knew. He married a girl from
Texas. Way back I did some United Negro College Fund
charity work with his wife. Brenda Pierce, that was her
maiden name. I had heard their son was a federal judge.
I also heard that he left his wife six months after he got
his federal seat, and that he was involved in an illegal
bauxite deal, the stuff they make aluminum from, with
some Jamaicans who ended up doing time."

"Judge Slickass has a daughter who may have gotten
herself out on a limb. Seems she's in with a bunch of environmental kooks and I think daddy wants her out. A
couple of her playmates have been out West here moon-
ing the law. Two of the judge's errand boys want me to
separate the wheat from the chaff."

"I see," said Willis. "Well, that's everything about the
Mathisons I know."

"Interesting fodder," said CJ, pushing back his chair to leave. "Who gets the tip?" he asked.

"Leave it on the table, CJ, then maybe I can afford a beer to wash down my pork and beans."

CJ patted him on the shoulder, knowing that he'd give the tip to his head cook, and headed toward the door. He looked back over his shoulder toward the kitchen. Mavis had never come back out.

When CJ got back to his office Julie was busy at her word processor screening bond-skip files. CJ was chewing on an unlit cheroot, something he only did when he was deep in thought or upset. He stopped at Julie's desk and dropped Womack's business card on top. "Put this card in your Rolodex and make a file. We might have some hound-dogging business on the way."

She gave CJ a quick nod, hardly looking up from her screen. Through gritted teeth she added, "Herman's in the back."

Herman Currothers was a little bug-eyed weasel of a man who owned AAA Bonding Services three doors north. Julie hated his guts. Herman disliked most people, especially minorities, cops, and gays. When he thought he could get away with it, he pinched women's behinds. He had once attempted one of his maneuvers on Julie, who had tried to break his hand with a paperweight and would have if Herman hadn't been so quick. He chewed Red Man tobacco and carried around a Dr Pepper can as a spittoon. Every time something in his building went wrong he came running CJ's way. CJ figured it was because Herman thought all black people had a special set of janitorial genes.

Denver was no different from Sparta, Mississippi.

The bail-bonding business on Delaware Street broke down along racial lines. Herman made sure that all the blue-collar, white criminal action came his way, by greasing the right palms and denigrating the skills of the other bail bondsmen on the street. Cicero Vickers pulled down the bigger white-collar bonds and Ricky Perez scarfed up all the Chicano and Latino action. CJ was left writing bonds for black people, half of whom couldn't pay.

Before CJ could close the door to his office, Herman was in his face, his head bobbing back and forth like a boxer's, his voice half a decibel below a shout.

"They're going to shut us down, CJ. Goddamn preservationists are going to close our doors. Like bondsmen ain't got honest-to-goodness lives. I've got a mortgage, I've got bills. Elitist sons of bitches don't have a clue. Every one of their granddaddies probably stole like shit, and now they're all sweet butter and cream, wanting to salvage the goddamn past. They'll close us down, CJ. We'd better do something fast."

Herman's tirade had caught CJ off guard. He stood motionless, backed up against the door.

"What the hell are you talking about, Herman?"

Herman's head was still bobbing, even though his harangue had stopped. He stepped to the side, suddenly sensing his proximity to the six-foot-two, 220-pound CJ, then backed up and sat down in one of the chairs across the room.

He started again, this time in a lower gear.

"Remember those restoration people, the ones all of us on the block got a letter from about six months ago?"

"Vaguely," said CJ.

"Well it turns out they're historical preservationists bent on restoring Delaware Street to its original genteel charm. They're going to make an offer on every Painted Lady on the block. I got my offer first. It came registered mail. They must have money because I've never seen an appraiser on the street, and I know they've never been inside my place. So they have to be shooting their dollars into the wind."

"I haven't gotten a thing," said CJ.

"That's because they're picking us off one by one. They've already hit Vickers and Perez, and you know the bonehead leasing Dorfmann's two houses doesn't give a damn. Dorfmann's widow is an idiot, she'll sell the place for a song. You're the only contact they haven't made."

"You talk like they're thieves, Herman. They haven't stolen shit."

"Steal, shmeal. This is a fight, CJ, we've got to counter their punch. I set up a meeting for Friday noon. Me, you, Vickers, and Perez. We've got to strategize, come up with a plan."

"I might be out of town," said CJ.

Herman's eyes ballooned. "Hell, man, rearrange your plans. You people put too many fucking things on hold. In case you haven't noticed, the bond business ain't one bit different from selling things in a mall. We need foot traffic to succeed. Take a look out your window at your bread and butter, that county jail across the street. I knew your uncle, CJ, he sweated to buy this building, and I never heard him mention a plan to move his business out with the rich folks in Cherry Hills. We need you at that meeting. Tell that looker of a secretary of yours to put it on your book."

"Sorry bossman," said CJ sarcastically, checking his temper and bypassing an urge to punch Herman out. He knew that one day he was going to end up ripping Herman's tongue from its roots.

Herman was back up in high gear, the same one he was in when CJ came in from lunch. He was out of the chair and through the door before CJ could finish saying "I'll see what I can do."

CJ sat quietly at his desk for a few minutes, trying to erase Herman's intrusion from his mind. Finally, he buzzed Julie and asked her for the number of the Brown Palace. He placed the call himself. Neither Womack nor Spence was in, but the hotel clerk informed CJ that Womack had left an envelope for him at the front desk and would like to meet him in the lobby later that evening, at nine. Womack knew CJ was hungry.

It was close to nine when CJ arrived at the Brown Palace. The ornate six-story-high lobby was quiet except for three men in tuxedos huddled in a corner near the 17th Avenue entrance. One man was telling the other two an off-color joke.

CJ picked up his envelope at the desk. When he opened it, he thought he caught a whiff of perfume. Inside was a note from Womack on Carson Technologies letterhead. Their embossed red corporate logo blazed at the top. A circle inside a diamond inside a square seemed to jump at CJ off the page. Along with a note saying that he expected to complete negotiations on the Grand River job with CJ that evening, Womack had included Brenda's photo, photos of two white men, and a map of Colorado. The men's pictures were copies of official police photographs. Both were a little grainy and gray but the likenesses were good enough for CJ's needs.

Both men looked to be in their early thirties. They

were clean-shaven, each with a head of tousled blond hair that gave them a California surfer look. One had a square face and a dimple in his chin. The other man's face was an elongated egg. It struck CJ that the man's nose was too broad for his face. The broad-nosed man looked to be the more boyish of the two, as if he couldn't have grown a whisker if he tried. Their names were on the backs of the prints: Albert Copley and Thomas Deere. The one with the dimple was Deere. Someone had scribbled the words "torcher and assault" on the back of Deere's photo. Except for his name, the back of Copley's photo was blank. CJ was about to unfold the map when Spence and Womack walked up.

"You've a beautiful city here, Mr. Floyd. Beautiful indeed," said Womack. "We've had dinner and a stroll. We've hit home runs two nights in a row. Your Denver restaurants are first-rate." Womack seemed a different man at night, almost gregarious.

Spence stood to CJ's right, in the shadow of a Tiffany floor lamp.

"I see you've gotten to my map. Have you checked the route?" asked Womack.

"Not yet," said CJ, folding the map out in his lap.

"Well, take a look and just follow the Yellow Brick Road. It'll take you to where you will eventually want to be."

CJ caught a sudden whiff of Womack's breath and suspected that Womack's newfound giddiness had more to do with liquor than a personality remake.

"The yellow highlighted lines give you your routes. The red X's are where we think the Grand River people might be," said Womack, pointing at the map. Spence nodded in agreement.

It still didn't make sense to CJ that two corporate lapdogs from Boston, who probably hadn't read a map since they were second-class Boy Scouts, would have a map that pinpointed the Grand River Tribe's Colorado and Wyoming operations as if they had been sighted in by a bombardier. CJ reminded himself one more time to watch out for the two ass-kissers to his right.

He wanted to tell Womack that he didn't need the yellow lines, that he knew how to find his way to the other side of the state, but he didn't. The X's were all CJ needed to see. One X, the closest to Denver, was just south of Steamboat Springs, the second X was near Craig, and the most distant X was just across the state line at Baggs, Wyoming. He tried to guess which spot might be the most likely one to find the Mathison woman and the papers and decided on the place outside of Steamboat in Twenty-Mile Park.

"What's the Grand River Tribe scamming at your X's?" asked CJ, his index finger covering Baggs.

"The one near Steamboat Springs is a twenty-acre plot with a house," said Womack. "We think it's where they indoctrinate new recruits. I don't know a thing about the other two."

CJ couldn't tell if he was lying or not. He scanned the map again and knew that he would have to travel a few back-country roads to get to each of the places Womack had marked.

"I have an exact address here in an envelope for their Steamboat Springs place, along with outstanding warrants for Copley and Deere, and a cash advance. But you don't get any of it until we have an agreement." Womack's tone of voice was almost playful.

"We're still at a hundred and fifty dollars per day,

and of course we will cover your expenses. I have the first two weeks' payment right here." He patted his coat pocket, then looked over at Spence.

When Spence realized Womack was looking at him for support, he added, "That's right."

"One fifty won't cut it, Jack. Two hundred, or I keep my ass right here in Denver. And what about the thirty-day bonus for bringing back your Dead Sea Scrolls and the Mathison woman in one month?"

Womack looked a little peeved. "I've got instructions not to budge," he said. CJ made a mental note that it was the first time either man had admitted that someone pulled their strings.

"The bonus?" added CJ, in a more demanding tone of voice.

"Twenty-five hundred," said Womack.

"Make it three thousand," said CJ, folding up the map.

"I will not," Womack said with a snap.

All three men were quiet for a moment. Spence broke the silence. "We can go the three," he said, moving out of the shadow of the Tiffany lamp and into the light. "Let's close the deal."

Womack looked confused and a little crushed. He fumbled in his pocket for the envelope, added several hundreds, and reluctantly handed it over to CJ.

"We've given you everything we have. Call us as soon as you have something, Mr. Floyd," said Spence. "After tomorrow we will both be at the number on the card Lucius gave you earlier. We'd like to have the papers and Brenda here in Denver before it starts to snow. Call us if you have a problem getting her to agree. Hope you don't have to chase them all the way back up to the Oregon coast." Spence looked over at Womack, who now had vengeance in his eyes.

"I think we had better call it a night, Lucius," said Spence.

Womack started briskly toward the elevator bank. Spence followed, two steps behind. Unlike their meeting in CJ's office, no one shook hands.

CJ watched them walk away and again thought about how in hell he would get Brenda back if she didn't want to come along. But he knew for sure right then that the whole thing was about the papers and not the girl. She was just the baggage that came along. He headed for the hotel lobby gift shop to buy a pack of cheroots. On the way he glanced back over his shoulder toward the elevators and saw Spence steady Womack by the arm. As he watched the two of them enter the elevator, CJ couldn't help but wonder if they were riding up to their rooms comparing notes on him.

Inside the teak-paneled elevator Womack and Spence rode in silence until the third floor. Three floors seemed to be enough to fully charge Womack's anger. He looked at Spence and said, "Brenda and her little white boyfriend pulled off their fucking shit on your watch, then tripped away under your nose. If it hadn't happened in my division's shop, I'd let your ass hang out to dry."

Spence countered, nonchalantly, "Her father's on Carson's board," as if he expected the fact to save his hide.

"That should tell you which monkeys are going to be left swinging bare-assed in the breeze if this whole thing explodes," said Womack. "I know they have you watching me," he added. "But guess what, I'm doing the same for you. We can go down together, one by one, or ride this thing out." He looked at his partner for a response, but all he got was a widening of Spence's eyes.

"Carson's bottom line has always been money," said Womack. "For them it's the only thing that counts. They're not communists or Nazis, racists or fascists. Just a bunch of white folks who like the color green. Did you know that over the past ten years our dear employer has been in court two dozen times on twenty counts of patent infringement alone? Or that they made more than seven million dollars last year on one antihistamine drug from a formula they stole from some poor chemistry instructor at a community college in Ohio who didn't know how to fight back on his own? I've put in twenty years with these leeches and in a few more I plan to quietly fade away. Screw God, country, and a solid gold watch. I'll take my annuity and tell them to kiss my black ass. I don't want your little screwup sinking my ship." Again he looked at Spence for a response.

"They've got you watching me?" said Spence, as though he hadn't heard any other word that Womack had just said.

Womack shook his head in disgust. "Since the day after Brenda and Deere disappeared with the vaccine. The boys up top don't know if you were in on it too. And I'm saddened to say that after twenty years of devoted and inspirational service, they still don't trust me."

"Shit," said Spence. "What would make them think I was in on the theft?"

"The little itch in your crotch, Mr. Spence. They know Brenda let you keep it wet. And for all they know, you planned the whole damn thing."

Womack's last statement deflated Spence like a punctured hot air balloon. His pudgy cheeks even seemed to collapse. Nervously, without realizing it, he began grinding his teeth. He wanted to tell someone at Carson who counted that they were wrong, that Brenda had just been a bad decision. He wanted to scream that he did his job professionally and judiciously every day. He wanted to shout: I'm a good decent middle-class black man whose parents sacrificed to send him to a first-rate Ivy League school. He wanted to plead his case and tell someone that he was proud to be a member of the Carson team. But the only person he had to say any of this to was Womack. Spence leaned back against the rear wall of the elevator and sighed.

"We're small potatoes, man," said Womack. "A window-dressing division head and a chief of security who's still wet behind the ears. Carson can hire dime-a-dozen spooks like us all day long. But there's one thing they can't replace at the drop of a hat, and that's their nigger-in-the-woodpile board member, the judge. They made a mistake when they let him in the henhouse. He's got political savvy, influence, and worst of all for them, he knows how Carson really works. Whoever's calling the shots right now, probably some headquarters VP for finance, is weighing whether to go after Brenda full-tilt or call in the FBI, FDA, and the cops. We had better come up with a win-win solution to this whole mess in the six-week window they're giving us to work or you, me, and Daddy Dearest are going to be out in the cold."

"Don't you think Judge Mathison can hold them off any longer?" asked Spence.

"Fuck no," said Womack. "If I know they're busy manipulating research, faking their data, and fixing the prices on dozens of drugs, you can bet Mathison knows a whole lot more. They would love to see him gone. Besides, he's never been Mr. Clean. A few years ago, a couple of his international trade deals almost got him disbarred. He's a liability if things get rough."

Womack could tell that he was finally getting his point across. "If we give the judge back his daughter and Carson back their vaccine we're heroes, a credit to our race," mocked Womack. He glanced again at his watch.

Spence thought for a few moments before responding. "Answer one thing for me," he said to Womack. "Why did we drop everything in the lap of some ne'er-do-well bail bondsman like CJ Floyd? If he screws up, they chop off our heads."

"The judge wanted Floyd. Somebody the judge knows knew Floyd in Vietnam—said that Floyd could get the job done real clean. If Mathison thinks he can, who are we to quibble? What do we care if Floyd takes all the risk? We just want our asses to come out looking good in the end. He's the bounty hunter. As long as we get Brenda and Carson's property back and not necessarily in that order, I don't care if he gets his goddamned self killed."

"What's his scam?" It was the first time Spence had shown any real interest in CJ.

"He's a street nigger retread—a whole lot more like me than you," said Womack. "The word I got on him is that he's made over two thousand arrests and that he is slick. I've dealt with people like him before. No question he can find Brenda for us."

Spence was surprised at Womack's knowledge. "How did you get all your inside dope?"

"The same way I found out you were told to keep an eye on me," Womack said, with a smile.

Womack's answer scared Spence. Spence thought

about whether, after all was said and done, he was going to be just another unemployed black man on the streets. And he wondered who the people were that Womack had keeping an eye on him. He wasn't like CJ, a retread off the streets, and he certainly wasn't like Womack, some faceless overachiever from the 'hood. He wanted to kick himself for ever learning Brenda Mathison's name.

The elevator doors opened. Womack and Spence headed down the tenth-floor corridor past subdued turn-of-the-century lights toward their suite without exchanging another word.

CJ tucked a pack of official Brown Palace Hotel gift shop cheroots that cost a dollar more than at any other place downtown in his shirt pocket and headed out into a postcard-perfect 65-degree mile-high summer night. On his way to the Bel Air he opened the envelope Womack had given him and counted out twenty-eight hundred-dollar bills. He folded the envelope over and slipped it into the right pocket of his vest. The money made him think about just why Mavis continually held him at bay. But he would never fully understand why Mavis was so intimidated by what he did. Then he thought about the role reversal that had just taken place between a tipsy Womack and a gunner like Spence. Mavis had once told CJ that the people he dealt with were always dangerous and more than a little bit weird. Maybe she had a point.

He patted the envelope, pulled out a cheroot, and stopped to light up. The sweet smell of the tobacco and the crisp night air made him feel at home. The Bel Air was still a block away. CJ was in no hurry to get to the car. Womack was right, Denver was a beautiful city, and he had a delightful mid-October night to enjoy.

Four

All summer long and into the early fall Denver's two daily newspapers, the *Denver Post* and the *Rocky Mountain News,* had been busy trying to outscream each other, copycatting the Eastern press, labeling Denver's recent gang wars a summer of violence. The gangs had finally been moved from the front pages by an unprecedented early October wave of heat that broke two days before Womack and Spence showed up at CJ's office.

Denver's barrel of gang-banging rotten apples were busy smelling up the black and Hispanic sections of the city, Five Points, Montbello, the West 38th Avenue corridor, and Curtis Park. The white neighborhoods still wouldn't tolerate gangs. The police department had more than its share of iron-muscled, thick-necked, six-foot-five would-be cowboys who were born and raised in those neighborhoods. These cops were called roosters by gang members because it was said that they loved to crack gang members' heads and strut their stuff, and they would just as soon snap the neck of some piss-and-vinegar black or Chicano hoodlum cruising the wrong turf as go to a Broncos game and chug down a six-pack of beer. The so-called summer of violence had hit Five Points the hardest. Gang members had been busy infecting any Five Points kid who was having trouble trying to find some direction in life. Willis Sundee liked to say that all of the apples weren't yet rotten, but the bad ones were clearly raising a stench.

The two high-profile black gangs of Five Points were the 26th Avenue Blades and the Henchmen. The Blades, as the former preferred to be called because their leader, Raymond Hicks, claimed that 26th Avenue restricted their scope, were the more organized, intimidating, and vicious. They were a gang of drug traffickers and hard-core teenage criminals and one member was in jail for killing a cop. The Henchmen were more along the lines of 1950s loud-mouthed punks who liked to get drunk, beat up their girlfriends, and steal a few cars.

Hicks was known on the streets as Razor Dog because he carried a pearl-handled straight razor in a custom-made pocket inside his left shoe. At eighteen Razor D, the name Hicks preferred, had lost his big toe and the two adjoining toes to poor peripheral circulation, juvenile-onset diabetes, and gangrene. He liked to tell rival gang members that he didn't give a witch's tit about offing them because, with sugar in his blood and the way he liked to drink, he would probably be dead before he was thirty-five. Razor D was twenty-one. He was mean enough to hurt you if you pushed him, hospitalize you if you pushed again, and kill you if you ever made him lose face. His photograph was displayed prominently in

CJ's rogues' gallery, right next to that of a statuesque raven-haired Puerto Rican bunco artist whom CJ had chased for two years before tracking her down. When he finally caught up with her in the high New Mexico desert just outside of Santa Fe, they ended up making love in the bed of her pickup. It didn't help her cause. He still brought her back.

Razor D had been a recent addition to CJ's gallery, but he was a rogues' gallery exclusive. CJ hadn't received a bounty for bringing him in. Razor D's photograph was there for one reason alone. He had threatened Mavis Sundee.

Razor D's rap sheet was three pages long. For years the Denver police kept him in a revolving door between his gaudily furnished condo, financed with an illegal federal loan, juvenile hall, and the county jail. But nothing associated with Razor D's gang activities, his suspected dealings in the sale of the .25 caliber handgun favored by gang members and called the Raven, or his known affinity for violence had enabled the police or the district attorney to assemble anything that resulted in Razor D serving any serious time in jail until he crossed Mavis.

Mavis was hosing off the sidewalk in front of Mae's one lazy September morning just after Razor D and three of his entourage had parked themselves in front of her restaurant in Razor D's candy-apple-red BMW convertible—the eight boom-box speakers turned on high. They were playing loud gangsta rap and cursing out anyone who had enough nerve to walk by. Mavis, who had never had any difficulty standing her ground, had just told them to move their profanity, ignorance, and shaved heads from in front of her restaurant when CJ and Rosie Weaks came out. Razor D threatened Mavis, saying that he would smack her high yellow ass into the middle of next week. But when he saw CJ and Rosie, two men he knew might be armed, he decided to move his act further down the street.

CJ decided that the police and the Denver DA were too busy looking at Razor D's shell. He promised Mavis he was going to take a closer look, largely because Razor D still owed him for posting a $10,000 bond. With his secretary Julie's help, CJ decided to examine the lavish way Razor D lived. Julie, with her jailhouse lawyer's knowledge, street smarts, and three years' worth of community college prelaw credits, ultimately zeroed in on Razor D's Achilles heel, a HUD loan for his condo. CJ knew there was no way that a thug like Razor D could qualify for a loan without at least one visible source of income. He suspected that Razor D's loan had been an inside deal.

He turned out to be correct. Someone at Denver's only black-owned bank had put in the fix. Once CJ found that out, he turned up the heat on Razor D. Mavis knew that CJ was enjoying the chase too much, but she couldn't warn him off. She knew Razor D would eventually react like a wounded animal being stalked. When she told CJ that he had gone to a lot of trouble to make an enemy over losing a thousand dollars, he told her he could tolerate everyday brothers who had a hard time paying for their bonds but not scum like Razor D. Besides, CJ added, it was bad for business. CJ ultimately traced an illegal $80,000 loan and the low-level web of deceit to one of the loan officers at the bank. The fact that the whole incident coincided with S&L investigations and scandals involving the Resolution Trust didn't hurt CJ's cause. CJ knew that if the government was going to

the kind of deep singsong voice that comes from saying the same things day after day for thirty-two years.

Razor D didn't respond. He was too busy looking back into the courtroom, counting the number of Blades and congratulating himself for the beefed-up security in the room. Bodine nudged Razor D's left foot with his own. The look that Razor D gave Bodine bubbled with contempt.

"Yeah," he said, turning to give the judge a similar look.

Bodine knew not to push Tannenbaum too far. "Mr. Hicks wishes to plead not guilty, Your Honor." He spit the words out so fast they sounded almost like one.

All the Blades in the courtroom began stomping their feet. Judge Tannenbaum slammed his gavel down hard. Once, then twice. Two additional police officers had been assigned to the courtroom because two days' worth of gang-war headlines had been served up by the press. The officers eased their hands toward their guns. Razor D nodded his head once, and the foot stomping stopped.

"I'll only ask for order this once," said the judge. "The next time the courtroom will be cleared." There was more than frustration in the judge's voice.

Bodine realized that Tannenbaum was suffering from seeing justice take too many wrong turns. He knew the judge was tired of handling the likes of Razor Dog Hicks. He wanted Razor D's bond set quickly, and he wanted out of the stuffy room.

The seasoned old white judge looked out at the courtroom of black faces, awash in a sea of gang colors of purple and green. Three-quarters of the people looked to him to be in their middle teens. Tannenbaum wondered what it was that made a man who was nearly twenty-two thrive on manipulating fifteen-year-old kids. After more than three decades he still didn't understand how self-destructive personalities like Razor Dog Hicks could attract the kind of people that now filled his court. He didn't understand it, but he knew that whether it was politics, a Detroit assembly line, his own profession, or gangs, the key that most often turned the latch on followers was the sheer ability of their leaders to impose their will. Razor D was no different.

The judge looked Razor D squarely in the eyes. "You've amassed quite a résumé in five years, Mr. Hicks." He held up the complaint and Razor D's rap sheet for Razor D to see. Razor D decided to stare the judge down.

Tannenbaum finally turned and looked at Bodine. Using the only club he had left, and realizing that he might be overridden in the end, he said, "Bond will be set at fifty thousand dollars." Almost immediately a bailiff began ushering Razor D toward the prisoner's exit at one side of the courtroom.

"Fifty grand. That ain't right," said Razor Dog to Bodine. "You said twenty, maybe twenty-five, tops."

"I'll get it lowered," said Bodine, looking first at Razor Dog, then back up at the judge.

Razor Dog stomped his foot. The rest of the Blades chimed in. Some courtroom spectators, seemingly satisfied that the show was over, had started to clog the exit. One of the police officers pushed them ahead.

Herman Currothers had made his way to the front of the room. He was trying to get Bodine's attention.

"I can't handle no fifty," shouted Razor D back at Currothers. "You're my bondsman, get the number down."

The bailiff was holding Razor Dog in check, waiting for the jailer responsible for transferring prisoners to take Razor D back to his cell.

Razor D called one last instruction back to Currothers before he was hustled away. "You can tell that grinning Uncle Remus motherfucking next-door neighbor of yours, CJ Floyd, we gonna plant his ass on the other side of life. Now finish up with that skinny lawyer of mine and arrange my goddamn bail." The Blades in the courtroom continued stomping their feet again.

True to his word, Judge Tannenbaum slammed down his gavel and had the courtroom cleared.

Five

Any of the three routes from Denver to Steamboat Springs mandates crossing the Continental Divide, not once but twice. CJ decided to take the fastest route, I70 through the Eisenhower Tunnel, up the Blue River Highway, and finally over Rabbit Ears Pass and into Steamboat. It was not the route that Womack had highlighted on the map.

An hour and forty minutes out of Denver, CJ decided to stop in the little town of Kremmling for gas. It was a warm, breezy 72 degrees when CJ turned off the Blue River Highway into town.

CJ ran through a mental list of potential loose ends back in Denver as he filled his Jeep up with gas. The Bel Air was at Rosie's for service and a diamond coral wax. Julie had been left to dig up everything she could on Carson Technologies and its errand boys, Womack and Spence. CJ had stonewalled Currothers and the other bondsmen on the row, saying he wouldn't meet with anyone, preservationist threats or not, until he received a letter like theirs. CJ also had Julie researching Judge Mathison, as far back as she could. If the judge was dirty, CJ knew that Julie, with her penchant for identifying loose threads, would find the dirt. The thing that troubled CJ most was knowing so little about Brenda Mathison and the Grand River Tribe and knowing virtually nothing about Copley and Deere. Their photographs made them look like beach boys gone sour, but neither appeared as if they could pass muster for even a temporary assignment to CJ's rogues' gallery wall. CJ had the bond-skip warrants for the two of them in the glove compartment of the Jeep. Perhaps Copley and Deere were surfer boys gone bad, but CJ still hadn't dreamed up a reason for Brenda being in the Tribe. The pump clicked off at $10.88. In less than three minutes CJ was back on the road.

The thirty-five-mile stretch of U.S. Highway 40 between Kremmling and the foot of Rabbit Ears Pass crosses a vast expanse of high plains grassland ranches peppered with rock piñon and sage. Hay meadows fill the acres in between. Irrigated pastures shoulder icy creeks that snake their way down out of the mountains to the west. Emerald green table mesas occasionally pop up on the horizon from the high plains floor. Somewhere at each mesa's edge some engineering-minded rancher had banked in an irrigation ditch that slid in the winter and fouled with mud in the spring. A ditch the rancher swore at after it had been cattle-tramped from a summer's worth of grazing and had to be repaired all fall, but a superhighway watershed for raising hay that no cattleman could do without.

Looking out on the hay and alfalfa meadows, CJ

couldn't help but appreciate the tenacity of people like Mavis's grandfather, who wrestled so openly with the land, hoping to reap their tiny share of the infinite riches of the West.

The Jeep clipped along at sixty-five, nosing into a slight breeze out of the west. There wasn't a cloud in the ice-blue Colorado sky. An endless chain of four-strand barbed wire fence ran along the highway's edge. Periodically, cross fences jetted off at 90 degrees, speaking the language of ownership to every passerby. Sections of newly stretched barbed wire stood out from their rusting neighbor strands and glistened like quicksilver in the afternoon sun.

Barbed wire facilitated the settling of the West, although initially the cowhands and the ranchers they worked for resented the wire because it injured their livestock and limited their previously unimpeded movement across the plains. In consternation, old-time cattlemen dubbed the new restrictive fencing "the devil's hatband." But barbed wire endured, and eventually the devil's hatband became a signature of the West.

CJ started up Rabbit Ears Pass and downshifted into low. He spent the better part of the next twenty-six miles shifting gears, engaging his clutch, and tapping his brakes until, at mile 27, the Jeep made its final descent into Routt County and the Yampa Valley below.

Steamboat Springs sits at the westerly base of Rabbit Ears Pass in a bend in the Yampa River. The area is filled with a hodgepodge of natural mineral springs. The most famous spring gave Steamboat its name: a spring that was said to spout water in the air and make a chugging noise that mimicked the sound of the huge paddles on the steamboats that served the big rivers of the Midwest and East.

Steamboat, a city of six thousand, is known as Ski-town USA, and although it remains the county seat in a valley dominated by ranching, over the past decade the Denver media had begun to suggest that Steamboat has become a haven for the California and Texas millionaires who don't want to pay the billionaire prices in Aspen and Vail.

CJ cruised along Route 40, Steamboat's main street, at less than 25, watching a conga line of summer tourists stream down the sidewalks at his side. Near the edge of town he eased over to the curb and pulled out Womack's map. The property he was looking for was twenty-five miles southwest. The route was all on pavement except for a secondary country road the last three miles. CJ hoped everything would go quickly. He decided he would case the property first, then come back after he had figured out how to separate Brenda and her documents from Copley and Deere. CJ didn't expect any of the Grand River Tribe to know anything about him, so he felt secure in making his initial contact with them straightforward and fast. Before beginning a job CJ always calculated his chances of success on a scale of one to ten, ten being a certain success. He notched this one in his mind as a nine.

County Road 27 was a dusty, lightly traveled gravel country access road just two steps above a path, checkered with enough potholes and tire ruts to make CJ downshift to second and ride along at less than 15 miles per hour. He had checked his odometer when he turned off the pavement. Exactly three miles later, CJ saw the house. It was a small white frame building sitting in the middle of twenty acres of irrigated land. Sagebrush and scrub oak mushroomed into rugged hillsides that rose abruptly along the sides and back of the house. CJ turned off the county road onto a lane that led up to the house. He didn't see the Routt County sheriff's cruiser parked near the porch until he crested a small rise halfway up the lane. CJ swallowed hard.

CJ pulled the Jeep to within fifteen feet of the front door and hopped out. No one came out to meet him, so he took six quick steps up onto the small porch and walked to the door.

A young, curly-headed sheriff's deputy wearing black logger's boots and sprouting a poor attempt at a mustache was standing near the back of the living room reeling in a metal tape. The room was filled with clutter. Dirty dishes were scattered everywhere, on tables, stacked on cardboard boxes, and piled up against the walls. Reading material was jammed in every available nook and cranny in the room. Hardcover books, paperbacks, magazines, and newspapers were stacked on top of one another or wedged against something to prevent them from tumbling to the floor. CJ stepped over a mound of books into the center of the room, his hand extended toward the deputy.

"CJ Floyd," he announced in a firm voice, hoping the deputy wouldn't ease him directly back out the door. "I'm looking for Brenda Mathison; maybe you are too," he added.

The deputy looked a little surprised but shook CJ's hand and pumped it once.

"Better step in there and talk with the sheriff," he said, nodding CJ in the direction of one of two doorways that had yellow tape stretched across them. CJ recognized the crime scene tape and knew that a new set of complications had weaved their way into his simple plan.

Sheriff Carlton Pritchard wore neither a snappy wide-brimmed Stetson nor spit-shined Western boots. Though he talked with an exaggerated accent, it was a Tennessee drawl, a tribute to Southern rather than Western roots. His uniform hung baggy at the shoulders and in the seat, the result of a recent six-week battle with Hepatitis A. He was the kind of man who could ride an illness, a person, or himself into the ground. His doctor had told him he was lucky he hadn't ended up in the hospital for three months, flat on his back. Pritchard dismissed the doctor like a runner walking off a cramp and went on with his job.

"Come on across the tape," he said to CJ. "Just pin it back in place."

Surprised at how accommodating the sheriff was being, CJ stepped into a cramped musty area of the kitchen that he suspected served as both a pantry and a mudroom. Empty shelves lined the walls; dozens of canned goods, irrigation boots, and several shovels were scattered across the floor. A woman's body was stretched facedown across the middle of the floor.

"She must have put up one country bull of a struggle, Mr. . . . ?" The sheriff paused for CJ to give his name.

"CJ Floyd."

The sheriff looked intently at CJ, then back down to the body on the floor. He looked up again, this time with a hint of recognition in his eyes.

"You're that bounty hunter out of Denver. Yeah, you're him all right. Seen you on TV," he added, as if he were making two entries in a ledger instead of one.

"What have we got up here in Routt County that draws you four hours away from home?"

"I was hoping to locate Brenda Mathison," said CJ, looking down at the body.

"That's her," said the sheriff, with a nod at the floor.

Brenda's body looked for all the world like a department store mannequin being readied for display. Her arms and legs pointed in every direction. During his life CJ had seen scores of dead bodies, but he had never been able to come to grips with staring at a dead woman. Somehow it always struck a sensitive chord, reminding CJ of the motherless void in his own life. Brenda looked like a gangly child who had taken a tumble. He remembered Womack's charge: bring back both Brenda and the papers. All Womack had told him was that there were "papers." He wouldn't be bringing Brenda back, so he scanned the room for anything resembling a packet of documents. There was nothing. CJ knew he would have to find a time to look closer when the sheriff wasn't around.

"What went down?" asked CJ, staring back at Brenda's slender lifeless form.

"Don't know. We came out here on a complaint from one of the ranchers up valley about somebody cutting his fences and scattering his cattle into the marshes. Cattle don't gain much weight when they're hung up in muck."

"Why'd you decide to make a stop over here?" asked CJ.

The sheriff looked at CJ and smiled. It was the kind of smile that said they both knew a little more than they were letting on. "Same reason as you probably, Mr.

Floyd. The best place to look for the beginning of a river is to find its source."

He walked over to Brenda's body. "Awful way to die, plain awful way to die." He shook his head. Her face was a mass of bruises from forehead to chin. Her eyes were bulging. The thing that riveted CJ's attention was her tongue, pushed out along the right corner of her mouth and twice its normal size.

The sheriff pulled back a towel he had loosely draped around Brenda's neck. A three-foot section of barbed wire had been twisted tightly around her neck.

"Can't cut the barbed wire off until I get some photo and print boys out here," said the sheriff. "Feel bad about that. I called for them just before you drove up. Saw your car out the window and wondered who you would be. Things move a little slower out here than in Denver. Those boys might not be here for a while. You better find yourself a seat."

CJ looked back through the doorway. The young deputy was standing within a foot of the threshold on the other side of the crime scene tape. CJ realized that he had been standing there all along. It wasn't until the sheriff nodded at the deputy that the deputy dropped his hand away from the butt of his holstered gun.

CJ pulled up an old-fashioned milking stool from the corner of the room and shifted his weight down onto it. Suddenly he remembered his own office and the sawed-off legs of his chairs. "Think I'll stand," he said, dusting off the seat of his pants.

A parent can never predict what path their child will take, or, for that matter, how any child will turn out. CJ was glad he wouldn't have to suffer the burden of Judge Mathison's grief. He remembered a boy he had gone to

high school with, Madison Rowe. Madison's father was a
doctor, and his mother had taught CJ at Smally Junior
High. Growing up, Madison had been a dreamsicle of a
child. A Little League star, an Eagle Scout, always at the
top of the honor roll at school. At sixteen Madison com-
pletely changed. He struggled through the last two years
of high school and dropped out of college twice. From
eighteen until he died attempting to rob a liquor store at
age twenty-eight, Madison was a jug of sweet apple cider
slowly going sour. No one forced Madison Rowe down
the path he took. There were no parents to fault, no per-
sonality-altering childhood blow. Madison went rotten on
his own. CJ wondered what had caused Brenda Mathison
to choose the path she took. He suspected she had been
a lot like Madison Rowe.

He also wondered if he hadn't just stepped into the
kind of manure pile his uncle used to like to call "home-
grown cornbread Negro shit." Like most black people, CJ
had spent a good part of his life looking in the rearview
mirror, making certain that his ass wasn't hanging out un-
protected in a white man's world. Now he was standing
two steps from a dead black woman, flanked by two
raw-boned white country cops, on a failed rescue mission that had blown up in his face. To top it all off, there
wasn't a damn thing that remotely resembled important
papers or documents anywhere in the room. CJ was beginning to think that maybe Womack and Spence had set
him up.

He watched the sheriff step off the distance between
Brenda's head and the pantry door. The sheriff didn't say
one word as he did, and he never looked up at CJ. CJ
watched him, and thought maybe the whole dirty deal
came down to someone hoping that he would get busted

for Brenda's death. Maybe the sheriff had arrived just a little bit sooner than had been planned. All the maybes were bothering CJ so much, he didn't realize it when suddenly he mumbled, "Damn."

"What?" asked the sheriff.

"Nothing," said CJ. He pulled out his last cheroot and started chewing on the end. Womack and Spence had left him hanging bare-assed, nuts swinging in the breeze. He reminded himself to mention it to them the next time they met—in the kind of unsanitized black man's language that he knew; Oreos or not, they'd both understand. He searched his pockets for a match, then thought better of lighting up, and went on chomping on the end of his cigar and thinking about the big payday that had seemed so certain an hour ago going up in smoke.

CJ had to follow the sheriff into Steamboat to make a statement about why he had stumbled onto a murder scene, and because of that he caught a break. The sheriff had compiled two years' worth of information on the Grand River Tribe, which he kept in an orange crate behind his desk. The word "Tribe" had been spray-painted in red three-inch block letters on the crate's side. Data on Brenda Mathison made up three-quarters of the file. CJ sneaked a look at the file when the sheriff left him for about five minutes to help his new deputy book a drunk. From what CJ could gain in his five-minute peek, Brenda Mathison had been a fairy princess of a daughter most of her life. She had graduated from Baylor with honors and a degree in molecular biology. She completed a master's degree in cellular genetics two years later at MIT. Brenda had linked up with the PlanetFirst movement and Thomas Deere during her two years in Boston at MIT.

From what CJ could piece together, Deere had been a Ph.D. student at Harvard at the time. Sheriff Pritchard had no additional information on Deere except that Deere was from Oregon, not California. Brenda and Deere had surfaced along with Albert Copley in Bozeman, Montana, five years earlier. The three of them, along with several other hard-core PlanetFirst people, were involved in brushes with the law in Montana during most of the rest of that year. Charges leveled against the three of them included tree spiking, destruction of private property, suspected arson, and assault. The arson charge, setting fire to four hundred tons of hay on the Cedar Creek Ranch, was a crime that Montana authorities decided to press. All the evidence they had pointed to Deere as the arsonist. At Deere's arraignment, the judge had set bond at $20,000. In less than a week Brenda, Copley, Deere, and the rest of the Grand River Tribe had disappeared.

They all surfaced in Routt County late the same year. Sheriff Pritchard had never actually seen Deere, so he couldn't execute the outstanding Montana bail-jumping warrant, and he didn't have enough on Brenda and the rest of the Tribe to do anything but ride their asses.

CJ suspected that Deere either flew into and out of Steamboat at will or that he played musical chairs between the Tribe's three parcels of land, because the sheriff's Grand River file contained a memo to four other county sheriffs and the Steamboat Springs airport alerting them to watch out for Deere.

The sheriff was walking CJ to the front door when a man with rough Naugahyde-textured skin, testimony to too many years of working in the sun, strolled into the County Municipal Building's foyer. The man was tall and limber and appeared to CJ to be in his midsixties. He was wearing a $250 7X Beaver Resistol cowboy hat and oiled leather work boots. His hat was gunmetal gray, and he wore it tipped forward on his head, just enough to fully shade his eyes. He acknowledged CJ and the sheriff by touching the brim before finally locking eyes with the sheriff.

"Hear you got a murder on your hands, Carlton."

Sheriff Pritchard tugged up his shirt sleeve and looked at his watch. "Almost six hours to the minute since we called it in to dispatch. I guess bad news around here still travels fast."

"Any news about that little witch and her crew of turds turns a pretty quick ear," said the man.

The sheriff knew that, left unchecked, Boone Cantrell could deliver a two-hour fire-and-brimstone sermon condemning the Grand River Tribe. He decided to try and cut the sermon short.

"I don't expect you know CJ Floyd," said the sheriff. "He's out of Denver. Bail bonding's his game."

"No, I don't." He poked a meaty hand at CJ. It was the largest hand CJ had ever seen on a man as wiry as Cantrell.

"Hope you're not up here to bond out any of them Grand River turds," said Cantrell.

"No way. Just looking for the Mathison woman."

"Guess you found her," Cantrell said, curtly. He shot the sheriff a glance. "Did one of her own people kill her? Wouldn't surprise me in the least if they did."

"I don't know the answer to that, Boone, and I wouldn't tell you if I did," said Sheriff Pritchard.

Cantrell smiled. He knew the sheriff wouldn't volunteer a thing. Keeping information about a murder case close to his vest wasn't just one of Pritchard's law enforcement rules. It was also Colorado ranch country courtesy. In Routt County people with loose lips weren't held in very high esteem.

Cantrell was ranching stock through and through. He bought his original 250-acre parcel of land and named it the Coyote Creek Ranch just after coming home from the Korean War in 1953. He liked to remind people that he bought the place back when that much land could still be leveraged by a common man like him. The first year he owned Coyote Creek he had stocked it with two heifers and a bull. The ranch was now fifty-five hundred acres, and Cantrell ran six hundred head of mother cows.

Cantrell knew that the old animal-centered agricultural ranch he had built from scratch was a thing of the past. Modern ranches were becoming no more than machines for feeding cows. He also knew that Western environmental extremists like Brenda Mathison and her Grand River Tribe heard voices telling them to save the planet, and he realized that the Tribe and others like them weren't going to go away.

He had once confided in Sheriff Pritchard that he and ranchers like him were like the aging water buffalo on the African savanna, trapped in the springtime mud of American politics by environmental fanatics like Brenda Mathison and the Grand River Tribe and forced to watch their ranchland culture fade like ripples in a stream. During the same conversation he had proclaimed that, unlike the trapped African beast, he had the power to fight back. He had told Pritchard that he would have no qualms about mounting Brenda's head next to one of the trophy elk heads in his den.

Cantrell knew that although the sheriff wouldn't talk about Brenda Mathison's murder, he was obligated to tell him about any of the Grand River Tribe's lawbreaking that directly affected him. So he turned the conversation that way. "Find out anything about who cut my fences and scattered my cows?"

"No more than I knew yesterday when you made your complaint," said the sheriff.

CJ followed the conversation, hoping to hear something that might help him explain what had happened to Brenda.

"Think I did her in?" asked Cantrell.

"Nope," said the sheriff. "You're too cantankerous, too claustrophobic, and too married to that land of yours to risk spending the rest of your life in jail."

"What do you think?" asked Cantrell, directing the question to CJ.

Surprised at the straightforwardness of the question, CJ responded as neutrally as he could. "You'd need a motive."

"Hell, I could give you five or ten, but let me settle on just one." He didn't seem to care that Sheriff Pritchard was standing right there. "You know what a sidewinder bull is, Mr. Floyd?"

"No," said CJ, and he wanted to add, And I don't give a shit, but he figured that the haggard old rancher might toss out a nugget or two that might help him with the case, so he checked his response.

"Well, I'll just fill you in then," said Cantrell. "They're what vets like to call surgically altered bulls. Nowadays we use sidewinders to identify cows in heat because dollar-wise it is just too risky to send a regular bull out in the pasture with the cows and let nature take its course. The profit margin's become way too small. If a regular bull misses impregnating too many cows, the bank just might

end up owning all your land. Nowadays, we do everything by artificial insemination." Cantrell reached down
and grabbed his crotch.

"Sidewinders have their member rerouted by a vet
so it comes out through their side. When the bull gets
aroused in front of a bunch of cows it does what any
other bull would do. But because its member is sticking
out its side, the bull doesn't get to stick anything into the
cow he mounts. The sidewinder leaves a colored dye on
the cow's rump from a marker that we hang around his
chin. That way we know which cows are in heat and
which ones to inseminate by hand."

"And . . ." said CJ, waiting for Cantrell to make his
point.

"A while back I took to calling that Mathison girl
Sidewinder B. I thought it was downright courteous of
me to use the letter B instead of calling her what she
was, a bitch. Believe it or not, my little pet name for
Brenda made the papers. A California reporter looking
for a story to fuel the flames of the cow culture–environ-
mentalist wars came out to the ranch to talk to me, asking me why I had taken to calling the Mathison girl that
name. I told him straight off, it was because in the end
she was going to end up fucking us all. The damn reporter gave the quote to the Associated Press, and it
ended up making the *L.A. Times*. From then on out the
Mathison girl, her tribe of noodles, and me went at it
heads up. I'll tell you right now, I could have killed the
stringy little witch, and not just because she was black. I
like a lot of you people."

There was a long pause before Cantrell added,
"What would you do if somebody tried to take away

your way of life—steal the pick and shovel you used to make a living right out of your hands?"

CJ thought for a moment. "Don't know if I can answer that." CJ's lack of an answer seemed to spur Cantrell on.

"She and those cow turds of hers, the Tribe, had half the ranchers in the county scared shitless. But they didn't scare me. They've been running around screaming that the earth wasn't meant to support a billion cows. Like they've counted every one on the planet. She said cattlemen were wreaking havoc on the West, destroying habitats all over the world, and killing off the rain forests. The thing about her ravings that hurt me the most was that she was trying to turn kids around here against the ranching way of life. She had schoolchildren giving me funny looks. One twelve-year-old right here in Steamboat whose daddy manages a hotel told me that my cattle were keeping him from enjoying the land. That witch had wormed her way into giving talks at the schools. So I fought back. I organized a bunch of ranchers who plan to bring the Grand River Tribe's message to a halt—make people get back in touch—use some common sense." He looked at CJ for some sign of support.

The sheriff knew just how to cut him off. "You're digging yourself a hole, Boone. You're starting to sound less like a rancher and more like a suspect. If I were you I'd zip it up."

Cantrell could have kept going, but he respected the sheriff. He knew that Pritchard had a job to do, and if it meant questioning him about the murder he would do just that. He still didn't know which way CJ leaned on the subject of the environment, but he decided to take the sheriff's advice.

"You know where you can find me, Carlton. When you get around to figuring out who scattered my cows, let me know."

"Nice to meet you," he said to CJ. He turned to leave the room. But before he did, he couldn't help but take one more swipe at the Tribe. "Economic warfare. That's where we're headed next," he said. "I wonder if those Grand River Tribe cow turds have the stomach for that." A gust of wind blew through the doorway as he left. The door slammed shut.

"He's one of a kind," said Sheriff Pritchard.

"The killing kind? He sounded awful angry," said CJ.

"I don't think so, but I've been fooled before." Sheriff Pritchard held the door open. As CJ walked out into the blustery high country wind the sheriff said, "Routt County and Denver aren't that far apart."

CJ expected that sooner or later he and Pritchard would meet again.

Six

Wyoming state Highway 70 originates in Baggs, a lonesome remnant of an old cow town with a population of 403. From there it gradually rises into the Sierra Madre mountains until, thirty miles east of Baggs, the road peaks at Battle Pass. The highway then descends into the Platte River Valley, ending at Encampment, an old copper mining town and a favorite Platte River fly-fishing haunt.

The first twenty miles of the route, from Baggs to the tiny hamlet of Savery, runs along the Little Snake River through a pastoral lush green valley of fifth-generation family ranches that start in the valley floor and work their way halfway up the surrounding peaks. Soon after the idyllic ranches end, hundreds of Forest Service roads, limited-access Jeep trails, and cowpaths split off Route 70 and into the Medicine Bow National Forest. The Grand River Tribe was bivouacked in a clump of shaggy firs in the shadow of the forest's eleven-thousand-foot Bridger Peak.

Three days earlier Albert Copley had guided the Tribe into the heart of the Sierra Madre on a treacherously narrow, dangerously steep, old logging trail. Copley had grown up on a ranch just outside of Savery, and although he may have looked like a surfer in the grainy photograph CJ had seen, Copley's personality, outlook, and demeanor were at the exact opposite end of the pole. He hated the ocean, California, the movies, fast cars, and the sun. Even more, he disliked what those things seemed to attract. People. Especially people with views different from his own.

Growing up in a town of fourteen people during the 1970s, with nothing more than a post office and miles of surrounding cattle range, had turned Copley into a moody, self-reliant, opinionated cuss. Most of the time he was as inflexible as a mule. His obstinate nature had made him leave the harsh ranching life behind, that and the fact that raising cattle had been his father's dream, not his. Although Copley had been a standout horseman during high school, even to the point of taking the Wyoming Little Britches rodeo calf-roping honors his junior and senior high school years, he left Savery for the marines a week after graduation and had never returned.

The marines packaged Copley into a rigid, by-the-book platoon leader with all the flexibility of steel. During his second tour of duty at the Quantico marine base, just south of Washington, D.C., the Marine Corps survival school had instructed Copley in survivalist tactics that included cooking rattlesnake, when to amputate your leg if you had to, and how to live without water in 115-degree

desert heat. Copley had finally found his niche. He became a survivalist freak.

He left the marines after Quantico and bounced
around in the security industry for a while, selling alarm
systems and deadbolt locks. He met Brenda Mathison
and Thomas Deere at a Las Vegas security convention
during one of his company's western swings. Brenda
convinced Deere that they could use someone with Copley's ranching background and paramilitary skills; and
eventually Brenda convinced Copley to sign on. When
Brenda asked Copley why he had joined the Grand River
Tribe, he told her it had been because of two things: he
liked the Tribe's size and maneuverability—never more
than twelve members in one place at a time—and he rel-
ished the fact that they were going to let him put his survivalist training to use. When she had probed further,
trying to size up Copley's environmental views, he told
her the land belonged to whoever had the biggest stick.

It was half past seven, and the sun had already set.
Six Nordic Army mountain brigade tents were arranged
in an open semicircle with the mountains at their back.
Lanterns glowed inside. Thirty-mile-per-hour gusts of
wind had the tents undulating in and out. Two pack
mules and seven horses were captured in sturdy buck-
fence corrals that had recently been fabricated from
aspen and fir. The mules were sniffing the ground in
search of Indian summer's last blades of grass. The more
pampered horses were gathered in one corner, waiting
for someone to deliver their hay.

The sky was clear, and the air was ice-chest cold.
The inside walls of the tent that Copley and Deere shared
were covered with frost. Thomas Deere had just wolfed
down half a bowl of lumpy oatmeal and he was flexing

his feet back and forth in his boots, trying to keep them warm while he thought about the future. Unlike Copley, Deere was a man who hated isolation. He despised the Grand River Tribe's annual three-week backwoods autumn trek, and he hated the fact that Brenda Mathison mandated the retreats for every member in the Tribe but herself. While he usually froze his ass off for twenty-one straight days, she commuted back and forth between their mountain campsite and their place on Coyote Creek. Deere didn't relish the idea of being trapped in the woods, and the fact that ten other people were there too didn't make him feel any more secure. Each year by the end of the first week in the high country tundra, Deere would begin to second-guess his commitment to the Tribe, but somehow he always stuck it out. Brenda had initiated their retreats to pacify Copley and to send a message to ranchers that the Tribe was resilient and tough. Deere had always gone along because Brenda had been the one who laid out their original successful anti-rancher guerrilla warfare plan. But for him the mountain bivouac had turned into a stale idea. An ex-marine survivalist leading them on harebrained trips into the woods while their base of financial support was withering in the wind made no sense to Deere at all.

The Tribe's objective was what mattered to Deere, and to his displeasure, Brenda had defined the Tribe's Colorado mission as one of incessant harassment—ever-present instigators who would peck away at cattle ranchers by scattering their cattle, cutting their fences, and stealing their hay; pests who would wreck their irrigation ditches and divert their water to make them lose their crops. Brenda's premise was that the Tribe would keep the ranchers off balance long enough to pick them off one by one. Deere knew that Brenda's methods were childishly naive. He wanted a more permanent solution, and fast. But because of her father's connections Brenda had been able to position the Grand River Tribe at the head of the anti-cattle environmental movement's money trough and the Tribe became the darling of the movement, feasting from their money coffers because Brenda was a beautiful superb saleswoman and well connected. The Environmental Protective Fund, the Range Conservancy, and the New Forestry Alliance had spent three years tripping over one another trying to give the Tribe as much money as they could. Brenda knew how to make them feel good, and on top of it, she was a three-in-one bargain: black, female, and a leader of their kind of cause. Brenda once bragged to Deere that the anti-beef environmental gurus funded people like the Tribe because they liked to turn on the ten o'clock news and have some talking head confirm that they were politically correct. Her statement confirmed for Deere that Brenda was more into glamorous causes than the war.

The whole Grand River Tribe, anti-cattle, anti-beef, save-the-grasslands movement had its gestation when, tired of graduate school, and bored with life, Brenda decided to prove to her daddy that she wasn't just another black trophy debutante daughter with egg batter for brains, but a woman who could be a mover and shaker on her own. She decided that returning America's grasslands to the people was as good a cause as any, and her East Coast mentality told her that Western cattle ranchers were a special-interest group that the world could do without. But her decision to kick the cattle industry in the head wasn't made overnight. Her pro-environmental, animal-rights, save-the-planet mind-set had been germinating since college, when she hooked up with a group of white rich-bitch sorority sisters out to save the whales. In the years that followed Brenda became more distant from her family and more militant about animal rights and environmental causes, until her father worried that she needed psychological help. By that time she had fully wound herself into her save-the-planet coil, and Thomas Deere had surfaced as not only a love interest but as someone who would egg her on.

It didn't matter to Brenda or Deere that cattlemen had tamed the land, fenced it, and turned Western drylands lush and green. Other people's past had no meaning or importance for either of them. Deere was out for one big bang of recognition, and Brenda had flipped to pretending that she hadn't been rocked in the cradle of America's black bourgeoisie. Brenda saw the ecomovement as a way to be somebody and at the same time balance the scales of justice against her money-grubbing, graft-taking old man. Deere was out to settle a score. He was a man who could only visualize things in terms of black and white. You were for him or against him and there was no in between. Any perceived slight could set him off. Once at a meeting with a Tribe supporter in Billings, Montana, Brenda had failed to introduce him as Dr. Deere. In the tirade that followed, Deere spent ten minutes cursing, spitting, stomping, and acting for all the world like he had the DTs. The next day Deere went back out to the man's two-acre exotic-fish pond and laced it with fifty gallons of benzene to show Brenda who was in charge.

Brenda's guerilla warfare plan against ranchers had always been simple. Supported by their well-heeled anti–cattle industry benefactors, the Tribe would buy strategic plots of land. Land that was always within five or ten thousand acres of productive cattle range. Then the Tribe would peck away at ranchers from what Brenda liked to call the field of play. For three years, aided by tapping into her father's political connections, she had finessed enough people with fat wallets and a guilty conscience, or a need to dodge taxes, to give the Tribe the money to accumulate two small parcels of land in Montana, two on Colorado's Western Slope, and one in Wyoming.

But the Tribe had recently run into a problem. They were no longer the grassroots darlings they had been at first. They had adversaries within the environmental movement itself who questioned the anti-cattle sincerity of a small band of scruffy dropouts and roughnecks, led by two left-wing egghead wackos and an ex-marine. Old-school adversaries who liked to turn the tables on Brenda and point out that she was not only a woman but also black. They didn't like the Tribe having an inside money track and they were busy calling the Tribe's methods ineffective, a waste of money, and nothing more than college pranks.

The competition for money and recognition inside the ecomovement had Thomas Deere working on a plan that he hoped would rock the Western cattle industry on its heels and produce a new stream of dollars from the kind of environmental movement backers who wanted to see a range war that shed a little blood. Deere knew the Tribe needed a big score to keep their part of the eco-movement going. His plan was to put two dozen Twenty-Mile Park ranchers out of business within the space of a summer, and he didn't mind killing a few.

Albert Copley pulled back the entry flap on the tent

and stepped inside. A rush of cold air filled the tent. He had just finished feeding the horses alfalfa and hay. He closed the flap.

"It's an iceberg in here," complained Deere.

Copley checked the thermometer that hung from one of the aluminum supports. "Fifty-two degrees. Hell, you've got a heat wave in here. If you want, I'll switch with you. You can take care of the horses and mules for a change." Copley knew the way to stick it to Deere. Deere didn't know a quarter horse from an Arabian, a Tennessee walker from a plug. Deere didn't like the odors, the noises, or the messes that animals made. Any animal larger than a dog made him nervous. Just working around 1,200-pound mother cows chewing their cud made Deere break out in a sweat.

Deere ignored Copley, set his bowl down, and started flipping through a sheaf of papers next to his cot.

"You got us a foolproof plan yet?" asked Copley.

"We're just about there," said Deere.

"I hope so," said Copley. "I'm ready to head back to Baggs."

Deere was surprised that Copley wanted to head back to their headquarters. He had expected Copley to drag his heels about having to break camp, as usual. Copley's response bothered Deere because survivalist guru or not, he had never been sure of Copley's reasons for linking up with the Tribe in the first place. Deere didn't trust Copley. He had told Brenda more than once that Copley was a country redneck and a man they shouldn't trust. Brenda always downplayed his concerns and told Deere that he was just afraid that a real cowboy might steal his thunder.

"What's your hurry to head out?" Deere asked, in a

voice meant to challenge Copley's commitment to the
Grand River cause.

"It's not your concern," said Copley. He sat down on
his cot and began taking off his boots.

"We can't leave until I gauge just how long it takes
to infect these cows," said Deere.

"Never thought I'd live to see somebody try to
knock off their own herd," said Copley.

"Ten animals don't make a herd," said Deere.

"My old man started out with two," said Copley.

"Then I guess a herd's different for you and me,"
said Deere.

Copley didn't respond. He eased his manure-
splattered boots underneath his cot. He was rubbing both
of his feet, trying to warm them up, when a skinny, dark-
eyed man with a mop of unruly black hair pulled back
the flap on the tent and stepped inside. He looked at
Deere and said, "We got two dead cows. Been dead at
least fifteen minutes."

Copley could tell that the man had something else to
say, but Deere cut him off in disgust. "Why didn't you
come get me as soon as they died?"

" 'Cause we got bigger problems than that," said the
man, who was known simply as Lutts in the Tribe. "Billis
and Whittacre just got back from Steamboat." The man
paused briefly, then, looking straight at Deere, said,
"Brenda's dead."

Deere was silent. Copley kept rubbing his feet. After
a minute or so Deere stood up. Copley watched his eyes.
They didn't reflect sorrow or surprise.

"What happened?" said Deere.

"Somebody strangled her out at our place on Coyote
Creek. When we got back from Steamboat with the ab-

solute alcohol and the other chemicals you wanted and some rocks Brenda said she needed for planting trees, the sheriff's new deputy was there. He said she died a little before noon. He took our statements and we headed straight up here."

"Shit," Deere said, the way you would if you stubbed your toe. "Any suspects?"

"None as far as I know," said Lutts.

Copley knew that Thomas Deere had never liked playing second fiddle to Brenda's first. Deere tolerated the situation because he needed Brenda just as much as she needed him. But now that Deere had two dead cows to his credit, he knew he had something to sell. Something he could use to make himself rich.

"There was some guy who stumbled upon the murder scene, though," said Lutts. "Some colored bounty hunter out of Denver. We got his name out of the sheriff's big-mouthed deputy. CJ Floyd."

"Why would a bounty hunter out of Denver be traipsing around up here?" asked Deere.

"Maybe he's looking to start up a herd," Copley said, sarcastically.

Deere ignored Copley's remark. "Find out a little bit more about him," he said to Lutts.

Copley noticed how quickly Deere had put himself in charge and he resented it, so he decided to put Deere on the defensive and needle him a little bit. "You were gone most of the afternoon, Thomas. It's not but two hours back to Steamboat. I don't suppose it was you who took her out."

Copley knew that because of Deere's volatility Brenda always kept him on a short leash and he knew Deere hated it. He also knew that in addition to being one of the smoothest liars he had ever met, Brenda had a way of using men up. During their stay in Montana, Copley and Brenda had had a brief affair right under Deere's love-blind, intellectual nose. Just after the Tribe solidified their operations in Colorado, Deere found out about Copley and Brenda's Montana fling. He never said a thing about Brenda's infidelity. But when Copley found four chunky, twelve-inch-long baby rattlesnakes sharing his bed one evening, filled with enough unspent venom to kill a two-hundred-pound man, he knew Deere had found out. From then on, Copley always checked every tool, utensil, bed roll, or morsel of food that he suspected Deere might have touched, and he made it a point to never let Deere approach him from behind.

Copley doubted that Brenda would have been capable of investing fully in the deadly scientific domino game that Deere was plotting, because she knew that no matter how Deere sugarcoated it, the plan would lead to murder in the end. Now, with Brenda dead, Deere was free to make sure that things played out his way, and Copley knew that Deere's mind was tilted just far enough off-center for him to delight in watching every single domino fall.

Deere gave Copley a hateful look and lay back on his cot. Deere had his own ideas about who had killed Brenda. He suspected that one of the Twenty-Mile Park ranchers had finally gotten their fill of her and decided to put a stop to their losses. He shot Copley a second bitter look and said, "I need you right now, Albert, so I won't respond to your shit. But soon enough I'll finish my business around here and you know what? You just might end up like one of my special cows."

"I'll chance it," said Copley, unintimidated.

Deere turned his attention to Lutts. "Get a line on that bounty hunter, Floyd. I want to know why he turned up. I don't need some bounty hunter gumming up the works. I want somebody tracking his ass."

Then he gave Copley a knowing look. "Could be that some of our Montana sins are finally starting to catch up." What Deere didn't say was that in Montana he had killed a man. A drunken Blackfoot Indian ranch hand had died in one of Deere's haystack fires. Everyone, including the investigating sheriff, thought the man had died trying to put out the fire. The sheriff suspected that Deere had set the fire, but he had no way of knowing, much less proving, that Deere had smothered the half-stupefied Indian with a seat cushion and tossed him into the blaze when the man threatened to turn him in to the cops.

In the Wyoming mountains, sixty-mile-per-hour winter winds can drive along deadly high country blizzards that can freeze an animal in a matter of minutes. The howling wind outside the tent reminded Albert Copley that winter was on its way. He expected that now that Brenda was dead and Deere had the answer to how long his specially treated cows could live, they would be moving back down to lower ground within the week. He felt a strange uneasiness about Brenda's death, but no sadness or regret. For him, Brenda had been nothing more than a facilitator, someone who enabled him to exist in isolation, flex his muscles, taste a little danger, and keep his survivalist skills intact.

He had watched Brenda use her charm and her brains to finagle money out of people in order to keep her little band of environmental zealots in business chipping away at the very foundation of the kind of life that he had been born into and left. He had admired her powers of persuasion as she had kept so many people galvanized behind her cause. Copley had never known what demons drove Brenda, and he never understood why she had chosen to fight the cattle industry tooth and nail. But he remembered her saying over and over that the earth couldn't save itself, so it needed disciples like the Tribe. Copley figured that her passion for the earth and her disdain for cattlemen was what had gotten her killed, so he suspected Boone Cantrell as well as Thomas Deere.

Copley wondered if Deere had finally decided it was time to pay Brenda back for her infidelity. Although Brenda had always thought she was the switch engine that maneuvered Deere down the track, Copley knew she had been wrong. He knew that within the environmental movement's radical right, Deere had supporters of his own—anti-government PlanetFirst people with the kind of money necessary to fuel Deere's version of an ecological holy war. People who wanted to eliminate not just ranchers but the government entirely—nuts who needed more bang for their buck than Brenda had ever been willing to give. He also knew that Deere had been tapped into the power train of the anti-cattle ecomovement long before Brenda had come along. She had simply been his meal ticket to move along the power train gears.

Deere had his own plans, plans that included increasing the Tribe's numbers into the hundreds and duplicating their Colorado activities in ten Western states. Deere's current experiments on a newborn calf and cow in the icy Wyoming wilderness were designed to move those plans along.

Copley walked over to the thermometer and gave it a tap. "Down to fifty in here." He looked at Deere for a response.

"Funny," said Deere. "I'm not as cold as I was before." He turned to Lutts. "Put a woman on Floyd. She'll attract less notice."

"Sure thing," said Lutts.

"We'll stay here another ten days, then move back down to our place in Baggs. I should have everything lined up by then," said Deere.

Copley knew that if Deere could gain support for the Tribe from the most radical factions within the Western anti-cattle environmental movement, it would be the same as if he had planted rabid dogs within their midst. But to gain their loyalty, Copley realized Deere would have to put on one hell of a show. Copley didn't know much about the specifics of what Deere was planning, but he knew that in America when it came to showtime, what sold was sizzle.

Deere got up from his cot, oatmeal in hand, and began pacing back and forth. After a dozen trips between his cot and the tent's entrance, he stopped and looked back directly into Copley's eyes. "We have to do more than scare people now," he said, before breaking into a jack-o'-lantern grin. Then he opened the tent flap and tossed his cold, congealed oatmeal out into the snow.

Copley shrugged his shoulders and nodded in agreement, deciding that for the moment he might as well just go with the flow. Copley knew that anyone who really faced survival would never toss aside a daily ration so easily. He sat back down and stretched out on his cot, fully aware that Deere was capable of tossing people aside just as easily as he had disposed of his meal.

Seven

CJ returned to Denver from Steamboat Springs on secondary roads, through Oak Creek, Phippsburg, and State Bridge, needing a little more time to think than he did on his way up. He spent a scant forty minutes on I70, only because he had to, and eased back into Denver late in the evening, driving through a massive early fall caddis hatch in Clear Creek Canyon that plastered his windshield with the aquatic bugs.

By the time CJ hit the city limits the sun had already set. He marveled at how quickly the Denver air took on a frosty bite once the sun finished its slow dance west. CJ headed straight for the office. Julie's outer office smelled musty, and the scent of Mexican salsa hung in the stale evening air. CJ knew that Julie had eaten dinner at her desk, a certain sign that she had too many things to do. CJ started to light up a cheroot but remembered the poor ventilation in the building and thought how unappealing cigar smoke mixed with salsa would smell the next morning at eight o'clock. He tucked the cheroot away.

Stacks of mail were arranged in two neat piles on his desk. One pile had a yellow sticky note that read "UR-GENT." The other had a note that read "NOT; SEE YOU MONDAY—J." CJ sifted through the NOT mail first. Two envelopes were bills. CJ pushed them off to the side. The third envelope was a notice from his dentist informing him that his teeth needed cleaning and that he was two months overdue. The final envelope contained a letter with a plea for his continued moral and financial support of the Denver Police Athletic League.

The URGENT pile contained two installment checks, both for $100. The checks were from the mothers of two young rival gang members that CJ had had to bond out of jail. The checks made him remember Razor D's threat. The mothers had nothing of value to use as collateral for their $3,000 bonds, so CJ had set up a monthly payment schedule at Julie's urging, a procedure that was totally against his office rules. The two checks represented the second payments of three. CJ slipped the checks under his desk blotter.

A certified letter rested at the bottom of the pile. The return address was in Bethesda, Maryland. In letters twice the size of the city and state, the return street address screamed LANDMARK RESTORATION AND PRESERVA-TION SOCIETY, U.S.A.

"Shit," said CJ, his voice resonating around the empty room.

Along the margin of the envelope Julie had written: "Call Currothers, Monday A.M." Before CJ could say shit again, he had unwrapped a cheroot and lit it up.

He crumpled up the cigar wrapper to toss into the

trash and noticed a third yellow sticky just below the week-at-a-glance calendar he kept on his desk. Julie had scrawled: "Rosie Weaks wants you to call him. Message on machine." A message from Big Red was the only thing in either of the two piles that CJ himself would have defined as urgent. He played back his answering machine tape.

"It's me, Red. When you get back see me first thing, I've got a problem with parts for the Bel Air."

The message didn't strike CJ as too urgent, not at eight-thirty at night. Not after two nights of fitful sleeping in an unfamiliar motel, eating what CJ liked to call chicken-fried food, and walking in on the scene of a murder. Big Red and the rest of the world's problems would have to wait. CJ sat down behind his desk in the dimly lit room and decided to finish off his cheroot. The smell of salsa and stale tobacco smoke would be a problem for tomorrow. His smoke drifted up toward the high Victorian ceilings, then disappeared into CJ's apartment above.

After a terrible night's sleep and a short stack of pancakes and two and a half cups of coffee at Mae's, CJ walked over to Rosie's garage. He felt rest-broken, as if he had just stepped off a red-eye flight. A three-thirty call from Womack had jackknifed CJ straight up in his bed. Womack was livid. He spent fifteen minutes blaming everyone from the PlanetFirst movement to the Routt County sheriff's office for Brenda Mathison's death, and he didn't exclude CJ. After CJ calmed Womack down, Womack surprised him with the news that Judge Mathison wanted CJ to track down Brenda's killer, probably Copley or Deere. The judge had snorted, "Before that hillbilly sheriff, the Colorado cops, or any-fucking-body else." At the peak of their conversation, Womack asked CJ if he had found the missing documents. After CJ explained that he had unexpectedly walked in on the murder scene, and that he had probably been a brief suspect himself, Womack said that he would take up the matter of the papers with Sheriff Pritchard when he talked to him later that day. Womack ended the conversation as abruptly as it began, saying that the judge had approved an additional $5,000 bonus for CJ when and if he found Brenda's murderer, and $5,000 more if he could bring in the missing papers without causing anyone to notice. CJ was about to tell Womack that Sheriff Pritchard had a well-chronicled Grand River file and that he wasn't as dumb as he might sound on the phone, but before he could, Womack hung up. CJ had remained upright in bed for another fifteen minutes, thinking about how sweet Womack's mention of $10,000 had sounded.

Rosie's garage had been located in Five Points at the corner of 26th and Welton since 1972. Roosevelt Weaks and his wife, Etta Lee, had started the business three months after Roosevelt finished Denver Diesel Mechanics School, with nothing more than two aging Conoco gas pumps, an unpaved gravel drive, and a lean-to service hut for oil changes and lubes. Some local people said the business had succeeded on the strength of Etta Lee's brains and Roosevelt's back. In truth, each of them had contributed both ingredients and more to the success of the business. Like CJ, Roosevelt had been a car lover all his life. CJ had always admired automotive beauty, engineering, and style. Roosevelt did CJ one better: he understood what made cars run.

In two decades, Rosie's garage had grown from a run-down eyesore to a Five Points business success. The always spotless concrete drives sported three service islands with six Conoco pumps. All six pumps were the same 1940s variety that came with the place when Rosie and Etta Lee originally signed on. The tall, stately pumps with their white enamel globes had become Denver landmarks. The original lean-to garage with its grease-monkey pit had been replaced by a modern garage with three service bays, a small business office, and a huge storage room in the back. Whenever Denver politicians wanted to catalogue the black community's business successes, they never failed to single out Rosie's garage.

Every pump at Rosie's was full-service. The attendants, usually local college kids going to Metro State, still cleaned your windshield, checked the oil, and made sure that the pressure in your tires was even all the way around. If they didn't, they knew they would have Rosie or Etta Lee to contend with in the end, and no employee wanted that. Etta Lee was a petite, light-skinned woman with a high-pitched voice that could sting like a rivet gun when she wanted to dress a person down. Only CJ and Willis Sundee were allowed to call Roosevelt Weaks, Big Red, a nickname he had earned in high school because he liked his hamburgers almost raw. Rosie was six foot four with an enormous head, no neck, and shoulders that made it appear he was always wearing football pads. He was even-tempered and slow to anger, but he could intimidate almost anyone with one of his legendary ice-dagger looks.

Rosie's, like Mae's Louisiana Kitchen, was a long-established community gathering place. But over the years the garage had become much more. Locals called the back storage room "the den." At the den you could gamble, play the numbers, buy liquor on Sundays (still against Colorado law), or, if you had a mind to, just hang around all day and shoot the breeze. Rosie didn't mind local Five Points people loitering, since they accounted for a large portion of his business, but if he caught them cursing in front of a female customer, or if one of their poker games turned sour and ended up in a fight, he sent everyone packing. Local politicians never made mention of what everyone knew went on in Rosie's back room.

Rosie was handing a customer the change from $20 when CJ walked in. After counting out the change he told the customer the same thing CJ had heard him say after every sale for over twenty years: "Come see us again, now."

When Rosie saw CJ a genuine smile of long-term friendship crossed his face. "How was your trip, home-boy?" asked Rosie, sliding the twenty-dollar bill into the till.

"Ran face first into a murder," said CJ.

"No shit! Wasn't nobody from around here, was it?"

"Nah. A pretty little high yellow girl from back East."

"A murder, you say. That's bad, any day of the week." But Rosie had his own bad news. Rubbing his chin, he stepped from behind the cash register and walked to within a couple of feet of CJ. "How long we been friends, CJ?"

CJ squinted at Rosie, the way he did when one of his clients couldn't come up with collateral for a bond. He knew Rosie was building up to either telling a tale or making a point.

"All our lives," said CJ.

"Good thing you remembered, 'cause I got some unsettling news that's gonna test that bond."

"Stop your dancing, Red, go on and sing your song."

"Okay, but it's gonna slam you pretty hard." He rubbed his chin again. "Somebody broke in here the night before last. They stole a bunch of auto parts and tools and it looks like, just for the hell of it, they decided to trash the Bel Air."

CJ grimaced. His left eye started to twitch. He gritted his teeth, then unclenched them and ran his tongue around the inside of his mouth. The Bel Air was more than just a car. It was CJ's link to the past. A tie to childhood memories and his uncle, an alcoholic bumbler, but the only real family CJ had ever known. For CJ, attacking his Bel Air was the same as attacking his family. He immediately suspected Razor D and the Blades and knew that this was only the first skirmish in what would probably escalate into an all-out war.

"I know it pains you, CJ. If it's any consolation, I had the Bel Air parked inside like always, locked up in one of the bays. I'm sorry."

"What's the damage?" asked CJ, staring at the floor.

"Bad, real bad. They broke out all your windows, spread transmission oil all over the inside of the car, and poured sugar in your gas. And, if that wasn't enough, they started her up and ran her for a while. What's left of your engine wouldn't get you from here to the end of the street. Might as well come take a look." He headed for the service bays. CJ followed.

The first bay was empty and the stock shelves around it had been stripped bare. There wasn't a hose, fan belt, air filter, or even a quart of oil to be found. The Bel Air was in the next bay. It looked like an abandoned junker. Every window was missing, the tires were flat, the headlights smashed. Both the trunk and hood had been ripped from the car's frame.

CJ shook his head. Near the rear bumper, he stepped into a trail of white granular powder that crunched under his feet. When CJ realized it was sugar, the only word he could muster was "Damn."

"Your power plant's a goner," Rosie reiterated.

Suddenly CJ wasn't thinking about the Bel Air. He was staring trancelike at the wall, running through his head the names of every bond skipper and thug he had ever brought in; Razor D kept coming up at the top of the list.

Rosie had seen the look before, once back in high school, when a rival player had tried to undercut CJ as he made a hard drive to the basket on one of the neighborhood courts. Rosie had seen the same cold detached look almost every day the first six months after CJ's return from Vietnam. The last time Rosie remembered CJ drifting off into what Rosie called his fog was when CJ was still married to DeeAnn. A thug named Jake Ishley had threatened to kill CJ and DeeAnn when CJ had gone after the only thing of value Jake had in the world, $1,500 worth of plumber's tools, after Jake defaulted on a bond. CJ and DeeAnn lived in an apartment above a bakery, at the head of two flights of stairs. One evening after Jake had been drinking, he came after CJ and DeeAnn at their home. Rosie had been the one to warn CJ that Jake was on his way. CJ waited for Jake in the doorway of his apartment, facing the stairwell just outside. CJ was standing in the doorway, eyes as big as quarters, staring straight ahead, when Jake's right foot hit the top landing that night. Catlike, CJ stepped out of the doorway and pushed Jake backward down the stairs. Jake broke both collarbones and fractured his skull.

Rosie hadn't seen CJ's foggy look in years. It made him a little nervous to see it again. "I can fix the Bel Air up, good as new, but it'll take me a while to round up an engine and parts."

"How long?" asked CJ, still staring off into space.

"The better part of a month," said Rosie.

"Shit," said CJ.

"I'm sorry," said Rosie. "I feel like it's my fault."

"It's nobody's fault but the shit-ass that did it. Sooner or later we'll settle up," said CJ.

CJ turned his back to Rosie and stared out the big service bay windows for a while. When he turned around again, his foggy look was gone.

Julie was used to CJ showing up at the office early, so she was more than a little anxious when CJ didn't arrive from Rosie's until close to noon. "Ten minutes more and I would have put out an APB," she said.

"Sorry. I had to deal with a major problem."

"Hope you got it solved, because there's going to be one here if that Spence character calls again. He's called twice and both times he was class-A rude. And he didn't want anything. Just called to check and see if you were working on the Mathison case. One more of his belligerent calls and I'm going to wrap this phone cord around his throat." Julie demonstrated her technique, then added, "Currothers has been down here from his office twice, pacing up and down in front of the building. I guess he knew you weren't here. At least he had enough sense not to bring his lecherous low-life self inside."

"Anything else?" said CJ.

"Nothing, except somebody called here three times and hung up."

"Not even a grunt?" asked CJ.

"Nothing," said Julie. "Just silence, and then they slammed down the phone. Maybe it was Spence."

"Strange." CJ pulled out a cheroot and wet down the tip. "I'll run over to see Currothers and hose him down. Why don't you go on to lunch."

"I almost forgot," said Julie, in the middle of locking up her desk. "Mavis called to say she was sorry to hear about the Bel Air. Me too. Had to be some real kooks to do a thing like that."

"No different from the ones we get in here every day," said CJ.

"Guess so." Julie swung her purse across her shoulder. "Want me to bring you back a slice of sweet potato pie? I'm headed over to Mae's."

CJ patted his stomach twice and started to chew on his cheroot. "No. I've got to get this thing back to being flat."

"Suit yourself," Julie said, as she headed out the door.

CJ gazed slowly around Julie's little office. The walls seemed closer to him than they ever had. He was divorced, forty-five, and getting fat. Someone had damned near destroyed his precious Bel Air, and he was looking for a murderer with no clear idea of where to start. CJ had never believed in midlife crises, adolescent crises, or, for that matter, crises that may have taken place in the womb. But he was beginning to wonder if perhaps he might not suddenly be staring at a midlife crisis wall. Until recently, Mavis Sundee had always been the one person who could help him keep his life's compass straight. Someone feminine and genuine—someone soft. Always there when CJ felt the need to escape from the bottom feeders he dealt with all day long. Mavis enabled CJ to touch the simple pleasures of a normal life. But now she was moving further away, saying that it was becoming too difficult to be the only stabilizing force in his lone-wolf, high-risk, predatory world. Her exact words to him had been that he was just too high-maintenance. Maybe Mavis was right. Maybe he was turning into an aging high-maintenance collector's item just like his Bel Air.

CJ glanced at the message from Herman Currothers on Julie's desk and shook his head in disgust. Might as well head down the street to Currothers's office and fan that flame, he thought. He lit up his cheroot, locked the outer office door, and left.

Herman Currothers operated AAA Bonding out of an egg-yolk-yellow Painted Lady three houses down the street from CJ. Of all the houses on the row, Herman's property was the least well maintained. The sidewalks in front of the house were cracking, buckled, or both. A rusting wrought iron fence, coming apart at every soldered joint, surrounded a house that had been painted without proper preparation so many times that paint actually bubbled up along every corner and clapboard seam. The house needed to be meticulously sanded down before anyone ever applied another coat of paint. Herman Currothers, as tight as he was, would never stand for that.

A couple of handbills were still lying on Herman's sagging front porch when CJ walked up. Herman had mounted an old-fashioned key-chime doorbell on the front door. CJ ignored the doorbell and walked right in. He stepped into a little alcove similar to the one he'd enlarged into Julie's office. Herman's entryway had never been tampered with and remained exactly as it had been constructed in 1899, a dimly lit passage that opened on either side into the heart of the house.

CJ could hear voices coming from behind the stairway at the end of the hall. The stairs led up to a second floor that had been sealed off for years. He walked around the stairs into a Victorian living room–dining room that now served as the business offices for AAA Bonding. The large, once airy room had been partitioned off into three cubicles using 1940s-style wooden partitions set on casters. One work station was a payment area complete with a cashier's cage and a mini-bar.

Herman, Cicero Vickers, and Ricky Perez were crowded into the largest of the three work areas, the one that served as Herman's office, engaged in heated conversation that stopped immediately when CJ entered the room.

"Grab a chair and get over here," called Herman.

CJ took a metal folding chair from one of the other cublicles and carried it with him into Herman's office. He scooted into an opening between Vickers and Perez and folded out the chair. Both men nodded at him at the same time.

Cicero Vickers had been a bail bondsman for thirty-five years; twenty-five of them had been spent on Bondsman's Row. He was rail thin, with coarse salt-and-pepper hair, short knife-edge sideburns, and grainy oily skin. Cicero never spoke to anyone, regardless of how well he knew them, unless the other person spoke first. He had been married twice, both times to women nearly twice his size. Cicero liked to gamble, and he loved to drink.

He had lost his license to drive so many times that some of his friends had nicknamed him DUI. His teeth had yellowed from smoking two and a half packs of Camels a day. To mask the smell of smoke that emanated from his pores, Cicero constantly sucked on Sen-Sen. As a result he always smelled like a drunk trying to mask his breath.

Cicero was an old-time bondsman. Cutting bail bonds for criminals was all that he did. He didn't bounty-hunt like CJ, nor did he run a string of portable hot dog stands to make a living on the side like Ricky Perez. Cicero was what bail bondsmen had been long ago, loan-sharking entrepreneurs who had more to gain if a person defaulted on their bond than if they paid it off. Cicero had no colleagues and very few friends. To Cicero, CJ, Currothers, and Perez were no more than acquaintances who happened to work on the same street.

Ricky Perez was a rotund pear-shaped ex–minor league baseball player with half a dozen kids. He looked much older than his forty-three years, largely because he was almost totally bald. In addition to being a bondsman and a street vendor, Ricky sold silk-screened T-shirts on the side. Ricky was always looking for that one big score and CJ expected that one day money would be his Achilles heel. His most recent successful scam had been to silk-screen a thousand Colorado Rockies T-shirts with the team's official major league logo emblazoned across the chest. He did this all a month before the team logo was officially announced. The Rockies management screamed foul, but by then Ricky had sold every shirt he had. The Rockies' inside leak was never found.

The only common theme among the four Delaware Street bondsmen was that they were all in the same business, they tolerated one another as best they could, and every one of them but CJ always carried a gun.

"You working banker's hours today, CJ?" Herman asked.

"No, just got a late start."

"I know you got your letter, Julie said you did," said Herman, quickly getting to the point.

"Got it right here, but I haven't read it yet." CJ pulled the letter from the Landmark Restoration and Preservation Society, U.S.A. out of his back pocket.

"It'll read the same as ours," said Vickers.

CJ quickly read the letter.

September 15

The Landmark Restoration and Preservation
Society, U.S.A.
1250 S. Wicker Way
Bethesda, Maryland 20001

Dear Mr. Floyd:

Few of us will have the opportunity in life to pursue our American Heritage and at the same time achieve financial security and business success. You, Mr. Floyd, are fortunate to be among that select few.

Our goal at Landmark is to accommodate those lucky citizens who own renovatable historical real estate by compensating them in a manner that enables them to allow that real estate to be transformed into an American treasure that can be enjoyed by us all.

Your property at 210 Delaware Street can become part of that dream. Our experienced appraisers recently site-assessed the property, considered its location, and projected a new-use restoration profile for your home. They have urged us to discuss with you the possibility of its sale. I am prepared to discuss this matter with you at your convenience. I may be reached directly at the toll-free number listed below or by telefax. I await your response.

Sincerely,

Roland J. Lawson
Vice President, Acquisitions
Phone: 301-326-5512   Telefax: 301-227-4911

"Sounds to me like they're blowing smoke," said CJ.

"It's a scam," said Perez, twisting uneasily in his chair. "Besides, even with their pot of gold we'd all lose our main calling card—proximity to the fucking jail."

"Scam sham, who the hell cares, it won't cost us a damn thing to call their offices and check them out," said Vickers.

"Sure, call 'em up and sell us out," said Currothers. "What do you care about those of us left with faces to feed, Cicero. You've got the first fucking nickel you ever made."

Vickers gave Currothers a hard-edged stare. Then reassessing the source, he rolled his eyes and shook his head.

Vickers's reckless eyeballing didn't slow Currothers down. "I'm telling you, if they get one person to sell, those East Coast shysters will come in here and buy up the whole goddamn block. Delaware Street will end up nothing but a bunch of Molly Brown museums, boutiques, and foo-foo shops run by fags. Then ten years from now they'll sell all their dolled-up Painted Ladies for ten dollars on our dime."

"You watch too much television, Currothers, it's warped your mind," said Perez. "You better hope that there's someone out there dumb enough to come in here and buy up these old wrecks. I say we string them out. Get a few offers in writing, then cool our heels and up the ante a bit."

CJ leaned his chair up into Currothers's desk. His feet dangled above the floor, and his pants rode halfway up his boots. "No harm in flushing Daddy Warbucks out," said CJ.

"I figured you for more backbone than that, CJ. You're spitting on your uncle's grave. Sometimes you people amaze the fuck out of me," said Currothers.

CJ ignored the remark and the urge to crack open Currothers's head. "Since Herman's hell-bent to lop off these people's balls, let him check out what they're all about."

Vickers, who hadn't looked up from the floor since Currothers called him cheap, nodded in agreement. Then he went back to staring at the floor.

Perez shrugged his shoulders. "Okay by me," he said.

"Sure, you boneheads want me to take the point,"

said Currothers. He thought a few seconds, suddenly at a loss for words, then added, "Okay, sure, I'll see what the slimy sons of bitches are all about. But if I find any of you dealing behind my back, I'll figure out a sure enough way to cut off your nuts."

"Let's give Mr. Big here all his lines," said Vickers. "If we don't he'll ad-lib us all into the poorhouse or jail."

"How about just calling them up and asking them to send out a bid on one of our places?" said Currothers. "Then we can compare it with what some local appraiser gives us from right here in town. It'll be easy enough to see if these preservationists are for real or smoking a rope."

"Sounds good to me," said CJ. "But we'll need some sound numbers on every one of these barns. You got my okay to have an appraiser come in and look at my place."

"And what if they're on the up and up? You gonna sell?" asked Currothers.

"If they come up with the right numbers, I'll throw in my wife," said Perez, answering the question before CJ could respond.

"I'd expect that from a wetback like you, Perez. You'd sell your mother on the street for the right price," said Currothers. "Should I contact Dorfmann's widow about her places too?" he added. For the first time in the conversation he sounded like he truly didn't know the answer before the question was asked.

"Might as well," said CJ.

"That old bag has shit for brains. It'll take me half a day to explain to her what this whole damn thing is all about."

"Did she get a letter?" asked Vickers.

"As far as I know," said Currothers.

"Then like CJ said, she has to be in," said Vickers.

Currothers looked at Vickers, then at CJ. He poked out his lower lip, suddenly sensing that he had been ganged up on. "Just remember, in all of this, I'll be looking out for my own ass first."

"You always do," said Vickers, getting up from his chair. "I've got to be in Aurora by one o'clock, so if that's it, I'm out of here."

CJ leaned forward, and his chair clunked against the hardwood floor. CJ and Perez stood up at the same time.

"Haven't seen you very much in the past two weeks," said Perez. "What you got cooking, CJ?"

"Same old same old," said CJ. "What about you?"

"Nothing much but putting a bunch of gang-bangers back on the streets. The little suckers are like vermin. These liberal judges need to be setting ten times the bond they do, if you ask me," said Perez.

"I hear you," said CJ, thinking of his Bel Air. "None of your little angels have been out trashing cars, have they?"

"Don't think so," said Perez. "Why?"

"Just wondering," said CJ, turning his attention to Currothers. "What about your boy Razor D, Herman? Has he been out thumping any cars?"

"He doesn't live with me," said Currothers. "Besides, you're his soul brother. Ask him your goddamn self."

CJ decided that soon enough he would.

Vickers was already gone when Currothers started ushering Perez and CJ toward the door. "Move it boys. This ain't no bar. You can do your jawing outside. I've got to be somewhere myself."

Outside on Delaware Street a police cruiser rolled

slowly past. The temperature had dropped 15 degrees. A stiff westerly wind kicked a couple of fast-food wrappers across Currothers's water-starved lawn, trapping them in a thicket of weeds sprouting along the porch.

"Looks like we have some weather on the way," said Perez.

Currothers brushed past CJ without speaking and slammed his rickety one-hinged gate. Perez was already halfway up the street.

CJ shaded his eyes from a sudden gust and looked out toward the west. The mountains were shrouded in clouds. CJ thought about the other business at hand. He knew that in order to find Brenda's killer, the Rockies were where he would have to head. Bad weather was already there.

He would have to start back in Routt County, at the little ranch house where the trail began. In order to find the papers he was after and the killer, CJ also knew he would have to track down the two men in the surfer boy photos, Copley and Deere. He hoped he hadn't let the trail get too cold.

Eight

CJ's Jeep was the first motorized vehicle of the day to venture down Routt County Road 27. The mountain weather was more like midwinter than early fall. The temperature hovered at 33 degrees. Six inches of fresh snow had filled the road's tire ruts with a fine granular snow that skiers called Rocky Mountain champagne powder. Deer tracks peppered the drifts.

The central Rockies' first major storm of the season had come in quickly from the southwest. As rapidly as the storm had materialized, it was gone. The sky had turned icy blue. CJ hoped that the absence of cloud cover would be a blessing and that the temperature might still make it up to 50 before the end of the day.

In his haste to get back on the trail of the Grand River Tribe, CJ had rushed to the mountains like an out-of-state flatlander hunter chasing a wounded deer. He had grabbed Julie's just-completed file on Judge Mathison and the Grand River Tribe, then called Womack to tell him where he was headed and assure him that he would check back when he had some kind of lead. He also told Womack to tell Spence that he was on the job, and to quit calling his office.

CJ had made sure that Rosie had placed an order for the parts for the Bel Air. He had warned Mavis to watch out for Razor D, and asked Julie to find out all she could about the restoration people who were trying to buy up his block. He had started a diet the very same day, promising himself that after he came back from the mountains he would take every meal at Mae's for a month. He persuaded Mavis into agreeing that she would monitor his daily intake of fat and banish him from the fried-food side of the menu. For a month, he was going to become a black coffee and salad man, and above all he was going to keep his hands away from anything that resembled sweet potato pie. CJ wasn't about to admit it, but the grim middle-age reaper actually had him concerned.

When CJ left Denver it was 65 degrees. He expected the trip to be a quick turnaround, nothing more than a couple of days. In his haste to leave, he had absentmindedly left the duffel bag with his parka and Colorado high country gear behind. Since the beat-up leather suitcase in the back of the Jeep contained nothing to battle the elements but summer clothes and an old Boston University sweatshirt that Mavis had given him eight years before, CJ was hoping the weather wouldn't get any worse.

CJ tugged at the fraying sleeve of the shirt he was wearing and turned the Jeep's heater up a notch. The white frame house where Brenda Mathison had been killed was nearly invisible against the freshly fallen snow. CJ hoped that one of the sheriff's people had left the heat turned on, but when he stepped over the yellow crime scene tape, picked the front door lock, and walked inside the house the warm air from his lungs frosted out like a megaphone in front of his face.

All the books and clutter were gone. CJ opened a curtain to let in some light. Half a dozen moths fluttered out into the room. He scanned the room, then checked out the bedrooms at the back of the house, rooms he hadn't had the opportunity to examine the first time he was there. They were bare except for a couple of Hollywood bed frames and several chewing gum wrappers scattered across the floor. CJ made his way back to the pantry where Brenda's body had been found. Two small packing cartons filled with books and magazines had been left behind. CJ kneeled down and started pulling the contents out one by one. The titles were a parade of anti–cattle industry hits: *Public Land, Private Profit; Beyond Beef; Tropical Deforestation and Pasture Development; Acid Rain: A Critical Review of Monitoring Baselines and Analyses; Slaughtering America's Forest.*

Inside the *Green Lifestyle Handbook*, CJ found a two-year-old letter from Brenda Mathison to her father. The letter was full of clichés. In it she complained bitterly about his lack of respect for her "view of the world." She argued that if you're not part of the solution, you're part of the problem, and said that she had finally found her purpose in life. She had signed the letter, "Somebody now, Brenda," and added a postscript that at Thanksgiving she planned to be home to work things out. There was no evidence that the note had ever been sent, and CJ had no way of knowing if Brenda had ever shared its contents with the judge. All CJ knew was that two years earlier there had been friction between a father and his daughter and that possible reconciliation had been in the wind. The whole thing sounded like it belonged on *Oprah* to him. He pocketed the note.

The room turned dark as a bank of clouds momentarily blotted out the sun. The sudden loss of light made CJ realize that he was cold. He shivered and patted his arms. A field mouse darted out from behind one of the cabinets and scampered across the room.

CJ walked back out to the Jeep to get his Routt County map. The temperature had dropped a few degrees. He studied the three circled tracts of Grand River Tribe land, tracts that Julie's research had revealed the Tribe called their reservation land. CJ was standing directly in the middle of the first parcel, freezing his hide. He looked around at the poor-quality, snow-covered pasture, the cold drafty farmhouse without a barn or one piece of equipment, and twenty acres of useless chickweed and sage. If the property really was a reservation, like the reservations of the past, the Grand River Tribe had gotten the short end of the stick.

Back inside the house, CJ spread his map out across the floor. The Tribe's second twenty-acre parcel was located outside Craig, thirty miles to the northwest. The topography would be pretty much the same. CJ had circled the Craig parcel and Womack's X in red. The third piece of land was at Baggs, Wyoming, high desert country just across the Colorado border. That parcel consisted of 320 deeded acres, an entire half-section of land, and a lease on 1,200 acres of what Julie had told CJ was Bureau of Land Management land. What the Grand River Tribe would want with BLM grazing land puzzled CJ. If you didn't graze cattle on it every year, you lost your lease. The Tribe had leased the land three straight years. A cattle-grazing lease owned by an anti-cattle environmental group was a bit like Abraham Lincoln owning slaves. CJ checked every room in the house once again, then decided it was time to head for Craig.

The temperature had dropped from 38 to 22 degrees when CJ reached the outskirts of Craig thirty minutes later. Craig was a small ranching and mining community that had seen boom times during the 1980s oil shale craze. But since 1986, the town had suffered an extended bust. For CJ, the most important thing about Craig was that it was the epicenter of northwestern Colorado's big-game country, and there were sporting goods stores all over town. When CJ walked into Alpine Sports, the toasty warmth hit head-on and he knew instantly that he was going to feel better fast. The store carried a wide assortment of hunting clothes lined up on racks, row after row. CJ bought a blaze-orange hunter's jacket and a pair of leather stockman's gloves. At the checkout counter a cache of tobacco products from around the world was on display. He couldn't resist a box of overpriced Virginia cheroots. He slipped into his new jacket and walked out the door with two dollars and eighteen cents remaining from a hundred-dollar bill. On his way back to the Jeep he lit up a cheroot and thought of how he was going to weave his purchases into the per diem charges he would eventually present to Womack.

On his drive to the Tribe's second place, CJ puzzled over who might have wanted Brenda Mathison dead, and why. From what the old rancher Boone Cantrell had said, she had rubbed enough Twenty-Mile Park ranchers' faces in their own cowshit to make everyone in the valley a suspect—and Cantrell headed CJ's list. Her two surfboard cronies, Copley and Deere, probably had reasons to kill her too, but CJ couldn't come up with a cast iron murder motive for either one of them, except for the missing papers. Could be the documents said things about Copley or Deere that neither man wanted to see the light of day. And two men and one woman always made jealousy an angle to explore. Finally, the two corporate lapdogs who had hired him couldn't be overlooked. Womack was an aging blowhard looking for retirement cover and Spence was an Oreo Bumpy who acted like he had gone in for an oil change and had his blackness drained. It didn't make sense for either of them to want the woman they had been sent to rescue dead, but CJ figured he didn't know the whole story. CJ thought back on what his uncle had once told him about the bounty-hunting game: "Never trust a man who hires you to run down another. You may go into it thinkin' you're the fucker and come out of it bein' the fuckee."

The road to the Grand River Tribe's second reservation was a recently paved secondary highway that went directly past the property's gate. Three-inch-diameter oil-rigging pipe formed an archway at the entrance about thirty yards off the road. The gravel road beyond the archway wound through a graveyard of antique tillage and hay machinery and more than a dozen half-century-old cars. Undulating snowdrifts rose up into the wheel wells of most of the rusting hulks so that they appeared trapped in a sea of white sand. The only improvement on the property was an imposing but deteriorating open-sided hay shed that rose twenty feet into the air and ran 150 feet long. A persistent wind snaked in between the fifty-foot-wide hand-hewn wooden rafters and what remained of a corrugated tin roof, producing a high-pitched whine that reminded CJ of the engine whistle on the old Santa Fe *Chief.*

CJ walked inside the hay shed and out of the wind.

Once inside he made a complete 360-degree turn, checking things above, below, inside, and out. There wasn't a single sign of life around except a lone red-tailed hawk perched on a sagging fence brace thirty yards from the back of the shed. The hawk seemed unperturbed by CJ's presence, as if he had seen every move CJ made hundreds of times before.

As far as CJ was concerned, the Grand River Tribe had struck out twice. Their second reservation was worse than the first. He wondered where the two surfers could be. If any of the Tribe members were still in Colorado they must have turned themselves into snow.

CJ stomped his boots hard a couple of times before retreating to the warmth of his Jeep. As he backed down the driveway to find a turnaround spot and head back out, he thought he noticed an old 1960s-style Volkswagen bus cruise slowly by the arch at the front. But when he got back to the entryway there was nothing to greet him but a blast of alabaster Colorado champagne powder and a stiff twenty-mile-per-hour wind.

The road to Baggs was built from crushed Wyoming clinker, red cinder rock created when coal is burned underground. Clinker turns into an ice rink when it's wet. CJ drove the forty miles from Craig to Baggs locked in four-wheel-drive. He had experienced wet clinker roads before.

Most of Baggs's inhabitants are ranchers who can trace their roots in Wyoming back more than a hundred years. The town itself is cradled in a bend of the Little Snake River and remains pretty much isolated from any Wyoming town of prominent size. There's nothing to the south except Colorado and Craig. It's an hour's drive to I80 and the Great Divide Basin, and there's nothing west of Baggs for a hundred miles until you reach the Flaming Gorge.

In the old days, Baggs's isolation made it a sought-out destination for the likes of Butch Cassidy and the Sundance Kid. CJ knew Baggs was just as infamous for being a hideout for one of the West's most notorious black outlaws, Isom Dart. In 1883 Cassidy and his band, the Wild Bunch, took over Baggs after a robbery in Winnemucca, Nevada, that netted them $35,000. It's said that the people of Baggs, being more visionary and entrepreneurial than Butch and his friends, were able to fast-talk the gang, dodge a few bullets, and get the outlaws to spend almost all of their money in Baggs on a party that lasted the better part of a month. Back then, Baggs was a rustic cow town with one way in and one way out. CJ drove in on one of two recently completed divided highways that had destroyed the Old West atmosphere and left a quiet, forlorn little place severed by two overimproved government pork-barrel roads.

It was seven-thirty in the evening by the time CJ pulled up to the B&B Motel. He had left the clouds behind in Colorado and the first post-harvest moon resembled a giant white fluorescent globe against the pale blue Wyoming sky. CJ jumped out of the Jeep, stretched, and slammed the door. A cluster of icicles fell from the top of the wheel well, tinkling to the ground like off-key musical notes.

The motel was a simple extended ranch with two wings, four units to a side, and an office in the middle. The neon vacancy sign had fewer than half its letters lit. It buzzed like a bug zapper, flashing VAC. CJ grabbed his suitcase from the back of the Jeep and walked into a comfortable, brightly lit office filled with Western knickknacks, a rack of Wyoming tourist information, and a huge potbelly stove. The man behind the reception desk was balding and about CJ's height, with sun-leathered skin, muttonchop sideburns, and droopy hound-dog eyes. He wore a blue and white pin-striped chambray shirt framed by double-wide red fireman's suspenders that pulled his pants up too tight in the crotch.

"Help you?" he asked, looking up from his cross-word puzzle at CJ.

"Sure can," said CJ, stopping to rub his hands to-gether above the stove. "I need a room."

"We can help you there," said the clerk. "We've got plenty of those. Smoking or not?"

CJ's surprise at the question showed on his face.

"My wife makes me ask," said the man apologeti-cally. "She says that in this day and age, it's only right for people to know what they're sucking into their lungs. Wouldn't matter to me one damned bit. But you'd be sur-prised at some of the responses I get to that question every day."

"Smoking," said CJ.

"Smoking it'll be," he said, pulling a key out from beneath the countertop. "One night or more?"

"One night should do it," said CJ, still rubbing his hands together above the stove. "I'll bet this old clunker has seen a few fires."

"I'll wager it's older than you and me together. It be-longed to my wife's father. He started ranching on the Snake back in 1882." The clerk slid a registration card across the countertop to CJ. Then abruptly, as if he had forgotten, he asked, "Cash, MasterCard, or Visa? Sorry, we don't take no others, and we don't take checks."

"Cash," said CJ, filling out the registration card.

"Twenty-eight even," said the clerk. "You can pay now or in the A.M."

CJ handed the card back along with three ten-dollar bills.

"By the way, I am Ernest Devine," the clerk said, extending his hand. His grip was bone-crushing firm.

He handed CJ his change and the key to his room. "Four B, last room on the wing to your left, Mr. Floyd. Out of Denver, I see. You just drive up today?"

"Yes."

"Bad day for travel. Yesterday would have been the day to pull in. It was in the sixties all day long."

CJ looked at the old stove and smiled. "I know," he said.

"What are we doing for you here in Baggs?" asked Devine.

The man's directness caught CJ off guard. But he didn't want to head out in the next morning's chill without at least some advantage on his side, so he answered, "I'm looking for a group of people who call themselves the Grand River Tribe."

"Indians?" asked Devine.

"Not these flakes. They just call themselves that. They've got a piece of land, about a thousand acres or so, east of Baggs on County Road 9." CJ pulled Womack's map from his back pocket, walked over to the counter, and spread it out.

Ernest Devine put his finger immediately on Baggs, as if a force from the center of the universe had drawn his finger in. "This here's County Road 9," he said, slipping his finger along a crease in the map. "It's about six miles east of here. Runs just along the foot of the Sierra Madre range."

"My secretary tells me the place I'm looking for is what used to be called the V-Bar Ranch," said CJ.

"Now *that* I've heard of," said Devine. "Never heard

of that Grand River Tribe though. The old V-Bar Ranch sets right in the spot you have highlighted here in yellow." He tapped the spot with his index finger for emphasis.

"I'd guess them Grand River people you're looking for and the V-Bar owners must be one and the same. But if there's any confusion about where the place is, or who owns what, I'd ask old Billy DeLong. He'd know for sure. He ran the V-Bar for more than twenty years."

"How do I find him?" asked CJ.

"Easy enough," said Devine. "He lives in an old cabin in the foothills just before you turn off into the mountains off Route 9. This map of yours ain't detailed enough to show you how to go. Let me draw you up the way," said Devine.

For the first time all day CJ was warm. He realized that he still had his hunting jacket buttoned up all the way to his neck. He slipped out of the coat while Devine drew the map.

"Old Billy is pretty much a legend around here," said Devine. "He was one hell of a bronc rider in his day. I'd say he was, and you know what," said Devine, looking CJ straight in the eye, "he's a colored fellow too."

It was the second day of Wyoming elk-hunting season, so most locals would not have questioned the sound of high-powered rifle shots ringing out just after dawn. But what sounded to CJ like two loud thunderclaps caused him to arch straight up in his sagging motel bed the next morning. He had been dreaming about trying to land a thirty-inch Snake River rainbow. He had heard for years that trout that big still inhabited the waters of the Little Snake River just down the bluff from where he slept, but he suspected that landing a trout that size would always be a dream.

CJ got out of bed and walked over to the window. A curtain of mist hung over the river bottom below. Every car in the parking lot was covered with dew. But ribbons of sunlight peeking out from a thin layer of clouds that hugged the valley floor told CJ the weather was going to be a lot better than the day before. He pinched his sides with both hands, and thought about his diet, wondering if there was a restaurant anywhere in the state of Wyoming that served a breakfast of red beans and rice, red-eye gravy, hush puppies, and grits. He was thinking about what to do about breakfast when three loud raps sounded on his door. The voice outside called, "Mr. Floyd, Mr. Floyd."

"I'm comin'," said CJ. He walked over to get his pants from the chair he had draped them across the night before and slipped them on. Through the peephole, he saw Ernest Devine nervously rocking from side to side. When CJ opened the door, Devine exploded into the room. At first he looked like he didn't know what to say. After looking at CJ, who was puzzled, shirtless, and shoeless, Devine blurted out, "Better come with me and have a look out front."

CJ slipped on his shoes and a shirt. The door to his room was standing wide open and a beam of sunlight had started to work its way up the front. Still, CJ could feel the morning chill. He grabbed his coat from the closet on the way out and followed Devine.

Devine hurried toward the motel's business office, where CJ had left his Jeep. He shook his head back and forth all the way. When they reached the Jeep, Devine folded his arm out, MC style, as if he were introducing an act. "Take a look," he said defensively, sounding as if CJ had brought a pox upon the land.

CJ walked around the vehicle. At first he didn't see the windshield damage. He was too busy checking out the doors, trying to see if anyone had broken in. Eventually his eyes wandered up to the windshield and he saw the two driver's-side bullet holes, three inches apart. The holes were surrounded by concentric impact spiderwebs in the glass. CJ frowned, trying to see inside the Jeep through the shattered glass and window fog.

"Go on, have a look inside," Devine prodded.

CJ walked around to the driver's side of the Jeep. He could see where the door had been jimmied. He wiped the window off with his coat sleeve and looked inside. Someone had propped a life-sized cardboard cutout of a man in the driver's seat, the kind that police used for target practice on firing ranges. The silhouette's face had been painted black. The impact from the shots had caused the cutout to list to the right. The cardboard head had two bullet holes: one in the middle of the neck, the other just below the left eye. CJ folded the silhouette forward. One bullet had ripped into the seat back, splitting the fabric for more than a foot. CJ couldn't see the path of the other bullet.

"Took one hell of a marksman to do that," said Devine. "I'd say the shots came from the mountains above my place." He pointed to three snow-capped camel humps behind the motel. "You must have really pissed someone off."

CJ stopped searching for the second bullet and looked up at the hills. "Can I get up there?" he asked Devine.

"Not without climbing gear or a mule," said Devine.

"Somebody's mountain goat did," said CJ, realizing

that someone had also been close enough to put the cardboard dummy in his Jeep. It bothered him that he hadn't heard a thing. The long-distance shot and the dummy seemed to be a message: We can take you wherever and whenever we want.

"If they did, they came down from the Sierra Madres, then slipped back up," said Devine, as if to confirm CJ's thoughts.

CJ stood for a moment gazing up at the three humps. The mountains didn't look all that imposing, but he knew that beneath the four-foot-deep snow crust there were jagged, razor-sharp rocks and an unsteady snow pack that could come tumbling down on anyone foolish enough to try and climb along their freshly covered rocky faces so early in the fall. He thought about who might have set up the little charade. He didn't think that any of the gangbangers, dopers, wife-beaters, or petty thieves he usually dealt with would set foot in Wyoming, much less travel to Baggs. But he couldn't help but remember Razor D's threat. He bent back into the car and felt around the seats for the missing bullet. Devine stood and watched. After a few minutes, CJ found it. The bullet had been stopped by a metal support between the back seat and the trunk. The slug was twice its original size, flattened out to the diameter of a nickel. CJ rolled the spent bullet around in the palm of his hand. It felt unusually heavy.

"Maybe those Grand River people you were asking me about wanted to send you a message," said Devine.

CJ flipped the slug up and down a couple of times, playing heads or tails. It still felt heavy. Finally he slipped the bullet into his pocket. He looked at Devine and said, "Maybe the little pissants did."

Nine

Few people knew just how Billy DeLong happened to come to the high desert country of southwest Wyoming, with its tiers of decaying homestead cabins hanging off the mountainsides like box seats at the opera. According to Devine, his arrival had something to do with an unfortunate first marriage to a white woman in North Carolina. As the story went, Billy was forced to leave that wife and two children one humid summer evening when a contingent of baseball-bat-wielding white men discovered that he wasn't a former diplomat from French Guiana but simply a wily black man from Hemphill. A second story that circulated through Baggs was a little more sympathetic. Billy had supposedly lost his farm outside Dublin, Ohio, to a shifty tax assessor. The two stories were probably a mixture of fact and fiction with the truth somewhere in between. According to Ernest Devine, if someone really wanted to know, all they had to do was ask Billy, but no one ever did.

Billy drank heavily and had one glass eye. Long ago, he had lost his real eye to diabetes and Ron Rico rum. He was a little man with thick, curly black hair and a squared-off mustache that stopped right at the corners of his mouth. Though he was sixty years old, his cinnamon-colored skin was barely wrinkled, even with all his drinking, and he had a heavy West Indian accent that caught most people off guard. Devine said that only his bronc riding and his Caribbean roots had kept all the rum from shriveling him up like a prune.

CJ headed out for Billy DeLong's place at ten o'clock that morning. Devine told him that if he wanted to get a straight story out of Billy it had to be before noon, which meant before Billy had finished his first pint of 151-proof.

DeLong's cabin wasn't much of a home, just an old split-log house dug into a hillside of river rock and shale, supported on the front end by four gigantic lodge-pole pines. The road up to the cabin wound back on itself twice up a 9 percent car-killing grade. CJ kicked up a trail of mud and river rock, and the Jeep bottomed out twice before he made it to the little two-acre mesa that was Billy DeLong's domain. From the only patch of level ground for miles, CJ could see the entire Snake River Valley.

It was 15 degrees warmer than the day before. The snow had started to melt, and a drip line from the cabin's sheet-metal roof formed a shallow trench around the house.

Billy DeLong was sitting in a rocker on his porch, wrapped in an old army blanket. A sawed-off shotgun lay at his side. CJ called to him from twenty yards away. "I'm looking for Billy DeLong, and I'm sure hoping you're him, 'cause I don't want to head back down Pork Chop Hill," said CJ.

"I'm him," said DeLong, kicking the barrel of his shotgun straight at CJ. "Get on up here where I can see whether you're a friend or foe."

"Friend," said CJ. He couldn't help but admire De-Long's guard-dog stance. It reminded him of the way his uncle used to take on the world. He liked Billy right off.

"I'll be the judge of that," said DeLong.

By the time CJ got to the porch, Billy was standing with his shotgun at port arms across his chest. CJ paused at the bottom of the steps.

"I'll be damned," said DeLong. "They've sent a buffalo soldier to drag me down off this hill."

"Afraid not," said CJ. "I'm a navy man."

CJ noticed an uncapped pint of rum sitting on the rotting cedar-plank floor just to the right of the rocker. The bottle was two-thirds full.

"Mind if I come on up?" asked CJ.

"You one of them new equal-opportunity deputy sheriffs I've heard about?" said Billy, tightening the grip on his gun.

"Not in this lifetime," said CJ.

"Well, if you're not a soldier, and not a cop, then what the hell are you doing here?"

"Looking for you and some folks I'm hoping you know," said CJ.

"You some kind of government man?" asked Billy.

"Shit no. Do I look like some pencil-pushing nerd?" A light breeze pushed the scent of alcohol into CJ's face. He inhaled the sweet sick smell of rum, and memories of his uncle surfaced. He took a step back.

"Guess I missed on all three counts about why

you're here. You fanned me fair and square," said Billy, dropping the butt of his shotgun to the cedar-plank floor with a thump but holding on to the end of the barrel. "Come on up."

"You've got yourself one hell of a colored man's view here," said CJ, glancing back down the hill, thinking about what the motel keeper Devine had said the night before.

"It keeps me thinking. About where I've been and where I ain't. Without something to think about a man might as well be dead." With that, Billy put his shotgun back in its original position on the floor.

"Beats the view in Denver," said CJ.

"I reckon it does," said Billy. "You out of there?"

"Yeah. CJ Floyd," he said, extending his hand.

Billy DeLong's grip was as strong as Ernest Devine's. CJ wondered if every sixty-year-old man in Wyoming had a grip like theirs.

"Pull up a chair," said DeLong.

CJ pulled up an old straight-backed, cane-seated chair and sat down. He looked out over the valley below and guessed which treeline along the river might have served as the route Butch Cassidy and his gang had followed on the final leg of their trip from Nevada to Baggs.

"Hear you used to run the V-Bar Ranch," said CJ, turning his concentration back to Billy from the valley below.

"For nineteen years if you're countin'," said Billy.

"Why'd you pack it in?"

"I didn't. Got put out to stud," said Billy, smiling, revealing a half-inch gap between two splayed top front teeth. "Left the place after some new people bought it a few years back. I ran it for them for a couple of years after they bought it, but in the end me and the new owners didn't see eye-to-eye. So we parted ways."

"Did they call themselves the Grand River Tribe?"

Billy poured two fingers of rum into a plastic cup and gulped it down straight. "Hand me that canteen over there, would you."

CJ handed Billy a Boy Scout canteen. It was in the original canvas carrying case, complete with a faded Boy Scout emblem and a frayed shoulder strap. Billy took two big gulps from the canteen and set it aside.

"It's only water," said Billy. "You don't think I'd drink that stuff straight?"

CJ didn't answer.

Billy finally answered CJ's question. "Yeah, that's what they called themselves all right. The Grand River Tribe. Still do for that matter. It's an insult to Indians if you ask me," said Billy. "Most people around here think they're nothing but a bunch of warmed-over self-righteous hippies out playing cowboy games. But they ain't. They're dangerous—as a coiled rattler," Billy added with emphasis. "They've got a little bit of money behind 'em too. Every one of 'em's holier-than-thou, and they don't give one tinker's damn about our ranching way of life."

"How did a woman named Brenda Mathison fit in?" asked CJ, remembering Ernest Devine's advice from the night before and hoping to get all his answers before noon.

Billy DeLong's eyes narrowed, and the muscles tightened around his lower jaw. "She was the queen fucking bee, a pampered little witch. If it wasn't for her, I might still be managing the V-Bar."

CJ didn't ask what happened. He moved the conversation along.

"She's dead," said CJ. "Somebody strangled her with a three-foot strand of barbed wire last week, over near Steamboat Springs."

"I'll be," said Billy, rocking back in his chair. His locked jaw was back to normal, but he was still squinting hard. He reached for his pint and poured rum into his cup until the pint was just below the halfway mark.

"What's your angle in all this?" he said, looking CJ square in the eye.

"I was hired to get her away from the Tribe. Now I'm looking for whoever killed her."

"You wouldn't have made much headway getting her out of the Tribe. Brenda lived for manipulating them simple bastards' lives. You're better off looking for who done her in."

"How about a couple of beach boy types named Copley and Deere? Know much about them?" asked CJ.

"Sure do. Suck-asses all the way. But in addition to being a kiss-ass, that Copley could be mean as a strapped-up bucking horse. I think Brenda wanted him that way."

"Meaning?" asked CJ.

"Copley kept people at their distance, off Brenda's back. I always got the feeling that there was someone else telling Brenda what to do. Copley seemed to be the strongarm between Brenda and whoever it was."

"What about Deere?" asked CJ.

"He was Brenda's pet. I think he wanted to be more, but she kept him on a leash and reeled him in and out whenever the need arose. But I always had the feeling he was slicker than she thought. He wasn't no country boy like Copley. Deere was citified, real book-smart, and slick as snot."

"How smart?" asked CJ.

"About a year after they bought the place, Deere switched to an artificial insemination breeding program and computerized the whole ranch operation to boot. That's when we fell out. I'd been breeding all my life, the old-fashioned way, turning the bulls in when it was their time. But Deere said he wouldn't be doing things that way no more. I argued with him about it more than once, but after I saw Brenda was on his side, I held my tongue. It didn't matter though; after my run-in with Deere, everything between me and the whole Tribe went downhill."

"Think either one of them was capable of murdering her?" asked CJ.

"Yeah, knowing Brenda, she could have provoked either one. I know she was screwin' them both. And them two didn't have the temperament for being played like that for too long, especially Deere."

Billy's impression didn't surprise CJ. "How many people are in the Tribe now?"

Billy stroked his chin and poured himself another drink. "Can't tell you about now. I've lost touch. But back when I was running the V-Bar, fifteen, maybe twenty people were constantly in and out."

"Were they old, young, ranching types, businessmen, anybody that really stuck out?" asked CJ.

"Like I said, most of 'em looked like hippies to me, and the whole damned lot probably couldn't spell the word 'ranch.' The only other one that sticks in my mind was Holly Beckwith."

CJ could see that the mention of Holly Beckwith's name lit a spark in Billy DeLong. "What made her so special?"

"She liked the spirits," said Billy, tapping his nearly empty pint on the floor. "So me and her hit it off good. She told me that until she joined the Tribe, she didn't feel like she had a home. Joining up made her feel proud. She said the Tribe was going to make a difference in the world, and according to Holly it was going to be real soon. I was off the job before she talked about just what that difference might be."

"Are they out at the V-Bar now?" asked CJ.

"Not this time of year, they ain't. From mid-October to about Halloween they head back into the hills. They call it a retreat. You'd have a hell of a time trying to find them unless maybe you're part bloodhound and part mountain goat."

"What's their retreat about?"

"Hell if I know. Maybe they go into the woods to talk to the bears. All I know is you'd have one hell of a time flushing them out. I know, I tried. One other thing that's strange, when they load up for the hills they take off on horseback with pack mules, plenty of water and food, some cows, and a bunch of guns."

CJ thought about the black-faced silhouette with the two bullet holes before saying, "Then no one's at the V-Bar now?"

"Probably not since the middle of last week," said Billy. "Even Brenda would have been there by now. She usually only joined up with them the last week of the retreat, and that chafed the hell out of Deere."

"How about going over there with me to have a look?" asked CJ, finally realizing why Brenda hadn't been in the mountains with the Tribe, and becoming even more suspicious of Deere.

Billy picked up his pint of rum and finished it off.

The twinkle in his good eye said that Billy was up to set-tling an old score. "You know, I'm feeling pretty good today, think I just might do that." He capped the empty bottle and slipped it up next to the butt of his shotgun. "You better drive though, I'm not in the mood," he said, giving CJ one of his gap-toothed grins.

CJ looked down at the narrow winding road with its 9 percent grade. At the bottom of the hill a landing of river rock and shale sparkled in the sun. He wondered if it would be easier going down than it had been coming up. It wasn't.

The V-Bar Ranch, unlike the Grand River Tribe's Col-orado property, was anything but run-down and old. If the Tribe had been land-snookered in Steamboat and Craig, they had found their pot of gold in Baggs. The ranch was a replica of a Kentucky colonel's horse farm, with three hundred acres of alfalfa meadow and hay sur-rounded by snow-white four-rail polyvinyl fence. Rolling grasslands spotted with drifts of snow blended into the Sierra Madre foothills to the west. A California ranch-style house sat at the head of the hay meadows, about two hundred yards from the road. An imposing Amish-style red cedar barn cast a shadow across the house. Oil-drilling pipe had been used to fabricate a maze of adja-cent corrals. The corrals had been painted a lacquered bronze and built to stand a hundred years.

Two gleaming silver, bomb-shaped liquid nitrogen tanks the size of a compact car sat along the side of the barn closest to the house. CJ decided to inspect them first.

"We call those AI tubes," said Billy. "They're for holding frozen sperm."

"Takes all the fun away, doesn't it."

"And it costs to beat the band," said Billy. "But the university folks over in Laramie and even the county extension people say that sooner or later it's the way all the cattle business in America's gonna go."

CJ and Billy were shouting at each other over the howl of a Wyoming wind that had pushed three-foot-high snowdrifts into a shaded area against the barn.

CJ waded into one of the drifts, dragging his size twelve bootprints through the snow. "Let's look inside."

"Guess it ain't trespassing if we don't get caught," said Billy.

CJ slid the barn door back along a ball-bearing track as smooth as glass. The barn was empty. A dozen pristine, freshly painted metal stalls lined the walls. Each stall was filled with a bed of eight-inch-thick hay.

CJ was ten steps into the barn before Billy shut the door. "Turn on a light," he shouted back to Billy, forgetting that he was inside, out of the howl of the wind. "I want to see what's out back." He walked down the center aisle toward the rear of the barn. The lights flashed on. "Damn," said CJ. "What's that smell?"

Billy caught up with him at the rear barn door. CJ rolled the door back and stumbled into a bloated five-hundred-pound steer.

"This little piggy didn't make it to market," said CJ, stopping in his tracks.

"It's a Gelbvieh," said Billy, kicking the carcass. "And it's been dead awhile."

"Think they left it here on purpose?" asked CJ.

"Probably not. My guess is that it got weaned from its momma, turned out to pasture, and was left behind by mistake. The only other possibility is it ain't theirs. Could be a stray. Let's turn him over and take a look at the brand."

The carcass was as stiff as steel. CJ jumped back when he saw the steer's face turn up straight. "What the hell's that on its face?" asked CJ.

"Looks to me like a wart. One ugly cauliflower hump of a wart," said Billy, looking at the softball-sized knot just above the cow's right eye.

"Do cows get those little presents all the time?" asked CJ.

"No, they're pretty rare. Usually they grow on a mother cow's teat. I ain't never seen one this big."

CJ's eyes had gone past the wart and zeroed in on the brand on the steer's rump. "Is that the brand the Grand River people run?" he asked, dusting the calf's hindquarter off with his hand.

"Sure is," said Billy.

CJ bent down to get a better look at the brand. He wanted to make sure he wasn't seeing double or reading the brand upside down.

"What do they call it?" asked CJ.

"Box O Diamond is the registered name," said Billy. "All it is is a circle inside a diamond inside a square." Billy drew the brand in the snow with the toe of his boot. It was identical to the Carson Technologies logo on the letterhead Lucius Womack had given CJ.

CJ stepped back, gazing at the carcass, and thought about who to go after first, the Grand River Tribe or Womack and Spence. From what Billy DeLong had said, tracking the Grand River Tribe would be a job and a half. At least he knew where to find Womack and Spence.

"I know some other people that run this brand," he said to Billy, erasing the snow brand with the sole of his boot. "I think I need to give the lying bastards a call." Then he pulled a knife out of his pocket, kneeled down over the dead steer and cut off a half-dollar-sized hunk of wart.

Back at Billy's place he plopped the specimen into a mason jar filled with grain alcohol that Billy claimed he kept around for medicinal purposes. Before CJ headed back down Billy's hill, he asked the old cowboy if he would help him by keeping an eye out for the Tribe's return and running a close tab on Copley and Deere.

When Billy said okay, CJ saw a grin of enthusiasm for the hunt spread across his weathered face. Right then CJ knew that he and Billy DeLong were two of a kind.

Ten

CJ didn't have to call Womack or Spence. They were waiting for him in his office along with a dour-faced Judge Lewis Mathison the next morning in Denver at eight o'clock—the day CJ turned forty-five. They were an odd trio, resembling an uneasy group of Third World diplomats assembled against their will, each man eyeing the other, hoping that hostilities wouldn't break out. Julie had them drinking herbal tea from her cache of twenty-four-ounce 7-Eleven Styrofoam cups. CJ walked through the door, and made a beeline for Womack and Spence. He was within a foot of them, close enough to see Womack cringe and the light-skinned Spence start to turn red, before he stopped and gave them an icy stare.

"Have you two cornbread heads ever heard of coming clean? It's a term gangsters used in Grade-B 1930s films. Usually just before they got shot," said CJ. "I'm big on coming clean. Lots of times it keeps me from traipsing off to the mountains on wild-goose chases and freezing my ass."

Julie cleared her throat and nodded toward the judge. CJ was so focused on Womack and Spence that he still hadn't noticed Judge Mathison sitting in the only comfortable chair in the outer office, in the far corner of the room, eyes glued to the floor. When Julie cleared her throat a second time, still nodding conspicuously in the judge's direction, CJ finally got the hint.

"Whatever the confusion, they were on orders from me," said the judge, slowly raising his head.

CJ turned toward the judge. "And you are, General?" he said sarcastically.

"Lewis Mathison. Brenda's dad."

The word "dad" and the way he said it caught CJ off guard. Mathison hadn't said "father" in the authoritarian manner CJ had imagined he might. He hadn't bellowed the word. He said "dad" softly, sadly, his voice trailing off at the end. Despite CJ's conjured images of the man, Lewis Mathison seemed to be just another balding, grieving, overweight father who had just lost his child.

CJ disliked the bitter taste of Julie's tea, and he hated drinking from Styrofoam cups. But he wanted to size up the judge a little more so he decided it might as well be teatime for him too. "Think I'll have some of that tea," said CJ, catching Julie by surprise. "We can talk in my office," he added, swinging back the door. All three men followed him in.

The office was cold. CJ had remembered to fire up the furnace two weeks before, but he had forgotten to open the heating vents before he left for the mountains, and the old Painted Lady didn't heat up well without warm air circulating evenly through her veins. The chilly office reminded CJ of his trip to Craig, and he had the urge to present Womack with the bill for his new coat. He resisted the impulse, deciding there would be a better time. Instead he walked around the room flipping open vents.

"Anyone cold?" CJ asked as he dusted off his hands. "I can crank up the heat."

"No," said Womack. Spence and the judge remained silent.

CJ walked over to the room's oversized bay window and directly into the warming rays of the early morning sun. "Where, old faithful NAACP brothers, should we begin?"

After a moment of silence Judge Mathison spoke up. "I've lost my daughter in this mess," he said, looking directly at Womack and Spence.

"I understand," said CJ. "But maybe if your two Roto-Rooter men in suits had told me the truth from the start we could have avoided it coming to that." He looked at Womack and Spence. "I get sent off on some college kid snipe hunt looking for Brenda and a band of save-the-planet loose wires, and no one bothers to tell me that the people I'm working for are swimming in the same environmental-kook cesspool and smelling like shit. Any of you three credit-to-his-race weasels want to tell me about the real tie-in between Carson Technologies and the Grand River Tribe?"

Womack and Spence both looked at Judge Mathison. He was still staring at the floor, slouched down in one of CJ's low-profile chairs. It took a few seconds for the judge to realize that everyone was waiting for him to speak. He cleared his throat and sat up straight. When he did, his entire demeanor changed. He looked self-assured, as though he had suddenly been asked to listen to testimony in a trial. The sadness CJ had seen earlier was gone.

"A few years ago I was asked to serve on the Carson Technologies board of directors for a three-year term. I'm afraid that's what set this whole sad affair on its course."

"Hold it. Before we go any further, how about telling me what the hell Carson Technologies does?" said CJ, directing his question squarely at the judge. He wanted to measure the judge's response against what Julie's background check had uncovered, to see if he was lying.

"They're a biotechnology firm that produces everything from operating room suture material to man-made genes," said the judge.

"That's covering the waterfront," said CJ, still enjoying the warmth of the sun. "And your two less-than-candid homeboy disciples here? I know they have fancy titles, but for the record, besides grinning and shuffling for you, what the fuck do they do?" CJ glanced over at Womack and Spence. Both men looked like unprepared schoolchildren suddenly asked to recite before the entire class.

"They're part of Carson's Veterinary Research and Security divisions," said the judge.

"Industrial cops. I should have known," said CJ.

"Not quite. Why don't you tell him what you do, yourselves," said the judge, tired of playing intermediary.

"I'm a patent attorney," said Womack, "and Spence here's an electrical engineer."

"I see," said CJ, "educated industrial cops." He moved away from the bay window and took a seat on the edge of his desk. "Does Carson have a barbed wire fence strung around their plant?" asked CJ, looking directly at Spence.

"Certainly not," Spence said indignantly, recognizing CJ's attempt to link Carson to Brenda's death. "Our surveillance is electronic. We don't run a prison camp or one of your Colorado farms."

"Just for the record, we call them ranches out here," said CJ. He turned back toward the judge. "So you have the A-Team here running back and forth across the country trying to beam your daughter up. They hire me to help. And just coincidentally they also want me to bring them back some papers she's packing along. Sounds to me like she was carrying around something pretty damned important. Maybe it got her killed."

"I'd say," said Womack.

"Please, Lucius," said the judge.

Embarrassed, Womack eased down in his seat.

The judge continued, each new sentence sounding more and more like testimony from a trial. "Nine months after I took my seat on Carson's board, Brenda came to me and asked if I could help get her a job. She said that she and Carson would be a perfect fit. And they would have been," he said defensively, "if the job request had been for Brenda alone. But she wanted to drag along Thomas Deere. Like any father, I wanted to help, so I spent almost two months lining them both up with jobs. Good-paying jobs too. I didn't know anything bad about Deere. He had all the tickets. A Harvard Ph.D., good references, a string of publications a page and a half long." The judge's voice hardened. He slammed his fist into his open palm. "How was I to know he was a jackal in disguise?"

"Deere's the link to Brenda's death," Womack

chimed in. "I've said that from the start. He stole the plasmids and the prototype vaccine. Murder's not beyond the man."

"Slow down," said CJ. "You lost me with the plasmids. Do you guys make blood products too?"

"Not plasma—plasmids," said Womack, visibly appalled by CJ's lack of familiarity with scientific terms. He stood up and started pacing the floor. "Plasmids are molecular probes, the self-replicating elements of a cell. Little pieces of DNA that scientists use to take a close look at genes. They're worth their weight in gold."

"How much gold?" asked CJ.

"In the long run? The ones we need to get back are worth seven figures, easily, maybe as high as eight," said Womack.

"And Deere just whisked them out from under your noses?" asked CJ.

"He stole them," said Womack, upset with CJ's description of the crime. "Stole," he emphasized again. "He ripped off bovine papillomavirus plasmids that we had been working on for years."

"Run that by me again."

Womack's frustration with CJ was mounting. He started talking very slowly, stretching out his words. "Bovine papillomavirus, Mr. Floyd. A year ago he stole tumor-producing plasmids, known in our industry as molecular probes. And along with them he took a newborn genetically engineered calf, and an irreplaceable vaccine. We delayed going right after him, and the judge stalled action by the board because Brenda was involved. But finally we had to move. With what Deere's got he can choose to either infect or immunize every cow from here to Texas and every calf from Wyoming clear up to the Oregon coast. The scientific term for the tumor the virus produces is a papilloma. But you'd call them warts."

CJ wanted to say *you're kidding,* but decided he had better not. "So what's the big deal about a cow with warts?" he asked, feigning surprise, hoping that none of the three men were aware of the specifics of his trip to the Grand River compound in Baggs.

"You don't know very much about the cattle industry, do you Mr. Floyd," said Womack.

"I've eaten one or two Big Macs," said CJ.

"So you have," Womack quipped. "Well, aside from that part of your immense knowledge about beef, you should also know that in terms of dollars and cents, the cattle business in America is right up there with IBM, General Motors, GE, and Ford."

"You don't say," said CJ sarcastically, holding back an itch to remind Womack that he had lived in Colorado since he was two.

"I'm afraid it's too big a business for the lunatics in the PlanetFirst movement and holier-than-thou pseudo-scientists like Thomas Deere," said Womack. He was about to include Brenda's name too but thought better of it when he glanced over at the judge. "Deere and his Grand River people claim that their goal is to get cattle off federal lands, but what they really want is to put the American cattle industry out of business. And above all, Deere wants to show that he has the balls and brains to bring an American industry to its knees."

"Sounds like Deere's a nut case with an inferiority complex to me," said CJ.

"Nuts or not, Deere has a virus capable of wiping out the cattle business overnight," said Womack. "A virus that can produce GI tract tumors capable of killing an animal in a week. He also has *our* vaccine."

"Sounds to me like Deere and Brenda did what they were paid to do," said CJ. "Seems like the screwup was in your security shop. Somebody forgot to close the door and the mice ran away with the cheese."

Spence spoke up defensively, as if he expected a challenge from either Womack or the judge. "There's more to it than that."

"It's water under the bridge now," said Judge Mathison, looking at Spence. "Brenda's dead."

"Let's just say Brenda charmed Mr. Spence here into letting her come in and out of our heavily secured industrial facility at will," said Womack.

"So she stole your silver bullet. Why not just make up a new batch of vaccine and cut your losses?" asked CJ.

Womack shook his head in disgust.

Spence broke in. "You don't get it, Mr. Floyd. It wasn't the vaccine they wanted. It was the plasmid they were after. They wanted the purified, tumor-producing, viral DNA. They don't want to vaccinate cows. They want to kill them." He looked at Judge Mathison as if he expected him to respond. When he didn't, Spence added, "We didn't know it then, but Deere never finished his Ph.D. They booted him out of Harvard for fudging research results and assaulting a dean. He wants to prove that the world's wrong about him and rub a little shit in our faces too. Unfortunately, Carson gave him a perfect little setup for doing just that."

"How much of your precious plasmid did they take? A thimbleful or enough to tank up a DC-10?" asked CJ.

"Like Spence said, there's more to it than that. It's

not the amount that counts," said Womack. "They have the protocol for amplifying the tumor-viral DNA. With the proper chemicals and a surprisingly small amount of laboratory equipment, they can make as much tumor-producing viral DNA as they want. And, during his time at Carson, Deere made himself a necessary member of several of our research teams. Before he took off, he not only took the protocols for producing the plasmid and the vaccine, he also altered, deleted, or damaged enough data to keep us working on duplicating his experiments for years."

Spence interrupted. "Go on and tell him the rest. You might as well."

Womack seemed to enjoy what he said next. "We found out after the fact that Deere completed a few gene-rearrangement studies that he didn't fully inform us about. The bottom line is that in addition to making the bovine tumor plasmids, Deere was working on how to link them up with plasmids that were human. It seems that while Brenda was busy romancing the stone, our Mr. Spence here, Thomas Deere was trying to make a plasmid capable of infecting not just cows but humans as well."

CJ thought about Billy DeLong's assessment of Thomas Deere. The words "real book-smart, and slick as snot" repeated themselves in CJ's head.

Womack continued. "We think Deere and Brenda had been field-testing the virus on cows before she was killed."

"Deere was using her," said the judge.

Womack ignored the remark. "If they had somebody giving the stuff out free, palming it off as a vaccine, they would have ranchers lined up for miles."

"And humans?" asked CJ. "How many of us could your boy Deere potentially knock off?"

"We don't know," Womack said matter-of-factly.

Womack's answer stunned CJ. He had run across nuts before. In Vietnam there had been plenty. Guys who wanted to see every tiny village go up in flames, and more than a few psychos who got their kicks from spraying Agent Orange, even some generals who wanted to unleash the bomb. But that was war. You have to rub shoulders with one or two lunatics during a war. In fact, during Vietnam, the lunatics had been CJ's yardstick for remaining sane. He knew that the day he started to act like them, he would be dangerously close to the edge. Deere sounded as if he had raced to jump over the edge. The idea of infecting cows with a virus that caused killer warts had seemed a little comical to CJ at first. A bit like some college prank thought up by a group of self-righteous bored little white boys and girls out to save the planet from belched cow gas that was supposedly destroying the ozone. Womack hadn't convinced CJ that the situation was anything more than that until he substituted the word "humans" for "cows." The idea that some lunatic was on the loose in the Colorado mountains, working on perfecting a virus that could kill people at will, shifted the entire Grand River problem for CJ, from comical to sadistically sick. The whole scenario made the muscles in CJ's face go stiff.

"What do you think he'll do now?" asked CJ.

"For real, or what do I hope?" asked Womack.

CJ lost his cool. "For real, you window-dressing Uncle Tom, or do you think this is some kind of game?"

"I think he'll punish everyone he can. He wants revenge for people screwing up his roadmap to success,"

Womack shot back. "I think that's why he probably killed Brenda."

"You're sure of that," said CJ. "You know Deere that well?"

"I know people like him, and people like you too, for that matter."

"Forget me," said CJ. "I'm interested in Deere's problem with the world, Mr. Freud."

"I'm not a psychiatrist," said Womack, defensively. "But I think the bottom line is that Deere's just a spaced-out egghead who wants to prove he can do what somebody probably said he couldn't."

"I don't buy it," said CJ. "He could have stayed at Carson making cow vaccine for the rest of his life, with everyone there kissing his ass and the worldwide cattle industry snuggled up to him like he was some kind of god."

"You don't seem to get it," said Womack. "For Deere, Carson Technologies and the cattle industry were just the two toys he needed to help him prove a point. After Harvard bounced him out on his ear, and trashed his self-respect, he needed to feel like he was somebody again. I think he'd kill you or me to get back that self-respect."

Womack's remarks made CJ recall the letter from Brenda to her father that he had found in the Tribe's house outside of Steamboat Springs. The letter she had signed, *Somebody now*. It made him suspect that maybe Deere and Brenda had been suffering from the same kind of inner demons.

Judge Mathison turned toward CJ and Womack. "I don't give a damn about Deere's motives," he said. "I want the man who killed my daughter to answer for what he did."

"We don't even know that Deere's the murderer. What about Copley?" said CJ. "And just for the record, what about Brenda's role in planning to kill off more than just a few cows?"

"I won't dignify that with an answer," said the judge, vengeance burning in his eyes. "Let's get back to the real matter. I want you to bring Deere back to me, Mr. Floyd. Tied in chains if you have to. But I want a crack at him before he gets to the law."

"Rough talk for a judge," said CJ, remembering that Mathison's reputation wasn't totally pristine.

"Do you have any children, Mr. Floyd?"

"No," said CJ.

"Then save your criticism for when you do," said Mathison. He stood up from his chair and walked over to the window, turning his back on everyone in the room.

CJ watched him for a moment, then turned back to Womack. "Have you called in the cops?"

Spence answered instead. "Security is still my area, and no, we haven't."

"Are you crazy? With that virus out there on the loose?" said CJ.

"We still expect to handle this in-house. There isn't anything to suggest that the virus has gotten out of hand, and above all, we have to think about the Carson vaccine," said Spence.

"I'll be a goat-roped dog," said CJ. "What you chowderheads want is the vaccine—you're the white men's puppets to the end."

"There are other considerations," said Spence.

CJ shook his head. The words "you're a sorry fucking lot" were about to explode from his mouth, but he held them back. He looked over at the judge and saw a man who wanted vengeance instead of justice. CJ wasn't sure he would have blamed the man on the street for wanting to have a few minutes alone with a tire iron and the man who killed his daughter, but somehow he expected a little more from a federal judge. He glanced briefly at Womack and Spence, two corporate lackeys dancing on a string, and realized that they were no more than well-groomed, articulate, ass-kissing, middle-management thugs.

CJ decided it was time to fully define his role. He turned to Spence. "Tell you what I'll do. See that jail across the street," he said, pointing in the direction of the Denver County Jail. "I'll bring Deere and whoever's linked up in this mess with him back on their outstanding warrants, so they can bunk across the street for a while. And, if I can, I'll round up the missing papers and your vaccine. As for any other fantasies the three of you might have about getting even, shipping the vaccine back east to Carson, cracking open heads, preaching the gospel, or for that matter transporting nerve gas to Timbuktu, you're on your own."

"Then you can't help us very much, Mr. Floyd," said the judge, turning around to face CJ.

"Maybe I can't, but I can sure as hell call the FBI and follow that up with a call to the FDA. Based on what you've told me, they'd both sure have great big ears right about now," said CJ.

Womack and Spence reacted as if they had just been sentenced to hang. They looked at the judge for support. The judge paced back and forth for nearly a minute. Finally he responded. "Fine, we'll keep our agreement just like it was from the start. But I want my daughter's killer in chains before Thanksgiving, along with the protocol for the vaccine."

CJ thought the judge's answer sounded too pat, but he decided to play along. "Good. I've got someone helping me up in Baggs on the Grand River end. If it doesn't snow us out, I think I can still have Deere and any of his playmates who might have been involved in Brenda's murder sitting in the clubhouse across the street by the end of the month. If he has the papers on your renegade virus with him, I'll convince him, very nicely of course, that he should give them back. But my involvement with this mess ends right there. You three frat brothers better figure out how to get that virus genie of yours back in the jar real fast, because if you don't, when Deere and whoever's involved in this with him have to start cooling their heels in jail, I think they'll hum a tune that's more than just an old Negro spiritual, and the three of you'll be sharing space with them quicker than a mosquito bite in a swamp."

Nothing CJ had said seemed to bother Womack, Spence, or the judge. They all sat in silence for a moment. Finally Spence spoke up. "Once you find Deere, how are you going to get him back here to Denver?"

"Let me worry about that. Just remember that bringing him and the papers back is as far as I go. By the way," added CJ, "what happens if you touch one of those warts?"

"We aren't sure. But we do know that the more times you get exposed the greater your risk. Why? Are you planning to go French-kiss some cows?" asked Spence.

To keep from planting Spence on his ass, CJ thought back to his trip to Baggs and the steer carcass in the Grand River Tribe's corral. He remembered kicking the steer and erasing the brand out of the snow with the toe of his boot. And he remembered cutting off a piece of the cow's grotesque wart. He rubbed his hands together as if he were washing them with an imaginary bar of soap. Then he looked again at the trio of men. For the second time that morning, he held back on what he really wanted to call all three.

Eleven

Womack, Spence, and Judge Mathison left CJ's office just before ten. As soon as the door had closed behind them, CJ turned to Julie, frowning. "Kind of leave behind that artificial sweetener bad aftertaste, don't they?"

Julie nodded in agreement and went back to work.

CJ could see that there was something bothering her. But he decided for the moment not to pursue it. He walked back into his office and pulled out the mason jar with the wart from his bottom file drawer. He fished the piece of tissue out of the alcohol with a pair of tweezers and transferred it to a second smaller jar of formalin that he had had Julie pick up from a pharmacy on her way in to work.

The pungent fumes from the formalin, a formaldehyde derivative, stung CJ's eyes. He quickly capped both bottles and slipped them back into the file drawer.

On his way back out to Julie's alcove he realized that his office had the unpleasant smell of a morgue.

Julie was still sitting at her desk, looking unusually stiff. Her face was expressionless and she didn't look up. CJ wondered what was going on.

"See if you can get Henry Bales for me, over at C.U.," he said, flustered.

Julie flipped through her Rolodex to the P's. Henry Bales was a University of Colorado pathologist. His card was filed by his profession instead of his name. Dr. Bales and CJ had served together in Vietnam and Julie had always liked him. She was just enough of a romantic to have a soft spot for a genuine Colorado cowboy sawbones like Henry.

CJ stepped back into his office. The smell of offensive embalming fluid was gone. He was leaning against a bank of file cabinets formulating his next move on the Mathison case when Julie stepped in. "Dr. Bales is out of town for five days," she said.

"At his brother's ranch?" asked CJ.

"His secretary didn't say."

Five days was a long time to have to wait for the information he needed, and CJ knew that the trio that just left his office had their impatient corporate and judicial meters ticking. But he wasn't about to trust any pathologist but Henry Bales with his specimen. After what Womack had said, the cow wart was very likely the key to the whole Mathison case.

"Call him back and leave a message," said CJ, sensing that Julie was still peeved. "Ask his secretary to have him call me as soon as he gets back. Tell her it's urgent."

As Julie walked away, CJ thought, What can a few days matter? Brenda's already dead. His thoughts were interrupted when Julie marched back into his office, rolled her eyes, pointed at his desk, and said, "Didn't you see the flowers I left?"

The golden-colored mums were partially hidden by a stack of files. CJ picked up the card lying next to the flowers. It read: "Happy 4 and a half, Julie."

CJ was at a loss for words. Two flunkies for a shady pharmaceutical company, a grieving irrational judge, a formalin cocktail containing a cow wart instead of an olive, and a pathologist who was out of town when he needed him most had caused CJ to forget it was his birthday. He looked at Julie. An apologetic look crossed his face. "Thanks," he said humbly. "I'm sorry I didn't notice."

"But you did," said Julie, reluctantly letting him off the hook.

Julie had been CJ's secretary for nearly seven years. She had taken the job shortly after CJ brought her bond-skipping, physically abusive husband in on an outstanding domestic violence warrant. She was twenty-three, with an eight-month-old asthmatic son, and swimming in the kind of self-pity and low esteem that manipulators like her husband seemed to thrive on. When she came to post bond for her husband CJ had initially dismissed the petite, frail, dark-haired, exotic-looking Puerto Rican woman as just another unfortunate female trapped in the hellish cycle of domestic violence. But CJ changed his mind when Julie insisted that under no circumstances was the collateral for her husband's bond going to be their house. As intimidated as she might have been by her husband, she had the strength to insist that if CJ was going to bond him out of jail, his low-rider Pontiac Bonneville would have to serve as collateral.

CJ had never been able to explain why later that

day, as Julie stood in the drafty Denver County Jail looking embarrassed, shivering and clutching her son, waiting
for them to bring her husband down from lockup, he
had said, "You need to put as much room between you
and that husband of yours as you can." CJ had no idea
that the reluctant smile that he saw on Julie's face in response meant that she had finally broken her husband's
spell. Weeks later, when Julie answered his ad for a secretary, CJ hired her on a two-week trial.

CJ's office had always been a disorganized mess. His
record system consisted of stuffing every document there
was on a case into a Pendaflex folder and wrapping it
with a rubber band. As the file grew, CJ would simply in-
crease the size of the rubber band.

Her first day on the job, Julie found files that dated
back twenty years, stacked like little mountains around
the outer office wall. By the end of the day she was
pleading with CJ to buy some filing cabinets and a reception desk. He only agreed to the purchases several days
later, after Julie accused him of being an outdated hiber-
nating bear. Within three weeks she had the office organized and fifteen years of records codified and filed
away. When CJ complained that he didn't like the idea of
having to walk all the way down to the basement to retrieve a file, Julie told him that computers had been in-
vented for people just like him.

Getting CJ to spring for an office computer system
took Julie another three months. By the time the system
arrived, Julie had become an indispensable part of CJ's
business and by then she had also left her husband, Maurice. Soon after the split, Maurice showed up at her
house drunk and began dismantling furniture against the
floors and punching holes in the wall. Julie stayed clear

of him and managed to lock herself in the bedroom, where she called CJ and the police. When CJ arrived two policemen were dragging Maurice across the lawn toward an awaiting Denver black-and-white while he shouted obscenities back at Julie and claimed he would be back to even the score.

CJ spent the next several nights on surveillance, parked in his Bel Air across the street from Julie's, waiting for Maurice to make an appearance. Maurice showed up in his low-rider on the third night. When he opened the door to the Bonneville to get out, CJ jumped in the front seat next to him and slammed him back against the seat. When CJ reminded him that Julie had a restraining order, Maurice called CJ a cock hound and accused him of screwing his wife. CJ grabbed him by the hair, slammed his head back into the headrest as hard as he could, and told him that in addition to being a worthless aging punk, he had far too dirty a mind. He left Maurice holding his throbbing head, with the warning that if he ever summoned up the nerve to bother Julie again, he also should imagine what his head would feel like banging off the porcelain walls inside a toilet. Maurice never surfaced again.

In the years that followed, not only had Julie succeeded in giving CJ's office a professional look and a much needed feminine touch, she and CJ had developed the kind of rock-solid friendship that evolves between two people when they have shared the same kinds of desolate childhood experiences.

The flowers touched CJ. Like most loners, deep inside, he was happy that someone cared. He knew that Julie's concern was genuine and he had almost ignored it. He felt a knot rise in the back of his throat. "I owe you for reminding me that someone thinks I'm special," he said. "And because you reminded me of it, I'm taking the rest of the day off. I'll be out looking for license plates." The words came slowly as if they had been locked deep inside him for a very long time.

"It's your day," said Julie. "You should do what you like."

CJ surprised Julie with a hug, thanked her for the flowers again, then walked back into his office and closed the door.

A week earlier CJ had heard from a Five Points numbers runner who spent most of his days at Rosie's and all of his nights at the den that an old pink-faced white man in north Denver had some antique license plates he wanted to sell. The numbers man knew CJ collected antique license plates, so he passed the information on, knowing that one day he might need CJ to cut a bond and the favor might help lower the fee. He didn't know the north Denver man's name or his address, but the word on the street was that his plates were pretty much mint. CJ called a few of his contacts around town, and they told him the same thing. But the only license plate collector that CJ knew of up north was a disbarred lawyer who was neither pink-faced nor old.

CJ spent the better part of the afternoon trying to locate his man. By late afternoon he had talked with the disbarred lawyer and knew that the pink-faced man was Mario Satoni. Satoni was a seventy-year-old curmudgeon who had run a secondhand furniture store in north Denver for nearly forty-five years. Some people claimed he had connections to what there was of the so-called Denver mob. The lawyer had told CJ not to deal with the old man. Satoni wanted a fortune for his plates, and the lawyer warned CJ that he would end up wasting his time. "The old cuss is worse than a peep-show MC. He'll let you look, but in the end he won't sell you a thing," had been his exact words.

CJ caught up with Satoni as he was locking up his store for the day. He was gnawing on the butt of a cigar and struggling with a wad of keys when CJ walked up and asked if he was the guy who collected license plates. The old man ignored him and walked away. CJ trailed him through the parking lot, explaining that he was looking for a 1913 Deer Trail municipal plate, that it had to be mint, and that he'd pay top dollar, in cash. When Satoni realized that CJ wasn't going to leave and that he wasn't a robber or the law, he grunted, "Follow me."

CJ followed as Satoni drove his showroom-clean 1953 Buick Roadmaster ten miles through some of the roughest neighborhoods in Denver to his house, a drab brown 1930s-vintage stucco bungalow wedged between two brand-new warehouse complexes that hugged the frontage road along I25. Inside Satoni's house, the smell of sour cabbage and sausage emanated from the walls. The old man led CJ to a cellar that was stacked almost floor to ceiling with boxes of license plates, vintage movie posters, thousands of occupied-Japan ceramics, baseball cards, and first-edition books. When Satoni asked CJ if he collected books too, CJ said no. The old man eyed him disapprovingly and told him he should start.

Running headfirst into a dozen mint-condition municipal plates would be enough to make any serious collector recount the story of the find for years. Coming face-to-face with ten shoeboxes of almost virgin plates made CJ start chewing on his lower lip. Satoni had amassed a collection of more than 250 municipal plates from all over the United States, dating back to 1913. Every plate CJ saw was in excellent or mint condition. CJ found the Deer Trail plate he was after as he flipped through the contents of a shoebox labeled simply "Colorado #4." The license plate was white porcelain on metal and just over a foot long. The number 33 was set in high relief in the center, with "Deer Trail, Colorado," spelled out below.

Satoni stood back chewing his cigar as he savored CJ's astonishment. He let CJ look the plate over for a good five minutes. When CJ finally summoned the courage to ask the old man for a price, Satoni looked at him and said, "What'll you give?"

Without hesitating, CJ said, "Five hundred," knowing the license plate was worth eight.

Satoni said he would sell it for six hundred to a collector, then, almost as an afterthought, he added that it had been appraised for nine. CJ looked a little embarrassed. But he quickly reached in his coat pocket and counted out six hundred-dollar bills. When CJ asked Satoni why he was selling such a rare municipal plate so cheaply, Satoni gave him two reasons. "I'm old, and I don't want my merchandise going to my asshole disbarred lawyer nephew who tells people I'm a gangster and spends his afternoons counting the days until I croak."

Satoni wrapped CJ's Deer Trail plate in newspaper and stuffed the $600 in his pocket. "Come back and see me again. Maybe I'll get you started collecting books." Then, as if he had suddenly remembered that he had something to do, the old man looked at his watch and told CJ he had to leave. "I have to take a nap, or that bastard of a nephew of mine might get his wish."

CJ played his good-luck song, "My Girl," over and over all the way home. That evening on the balcony of his apartment, he said to hell with his diet and in the chill of a starless Colorado night, he grilled a twelve-ounce T-bone steak and deep-fried a heaping basket of fries. He washed them both down with half a bottle of Silver Oak cabernet. It was only the second time CJ had fallen off the diet wagon in two weeks. Just before ten o'clock he called Guinella Folks, a quick-witted computer programmer who always made time for him no matter what, and asked her to drop by and share some birthday wine. Their relationship was purely physical, bordering on lust, and Guinella made certain it stayed that way. She showed up close to eleven wearing only a camel's hair overcoat, strapless heels, pantyhose, and a bra. She and CJ managed to finish off a bottle of merlot and a sixty-four-ounce bag of barbecued pork rinds between sweaty thirty-minute sets of lovemaking that lasted until late into the night.

CJ didn't feel guilty about blowing his diet until late the next night, when he sat at Mae's, eyeball-to-eyeball with a bran muffin with a birthday candle and a leafy green tuna salad surprise.

Mavis had just closed Mae's kitchen. It had been an unusually slow evening, and the restaurant was empty except for Mavis, Rosie, and CJ huddled at a table near the back. CJ was picking at his tuna salad with his fork like a finicky seven-year-old being forced to eat something he didn't like.

"A couple of more pounds and this rabbit food can take a hike. It's like eating grass. Besides, it stinks."

"It's good for you, CJ. Etta Lee makes me a salad with my dinner every day," said Rosie.

"My ass," said CJ, stabbing the tuna with his fork. "I know you always get something that sticks to your ribs."

"I sure do," said Rosie. "But I ain't the one that's fat." He punctuated his point with a quick little smile.

CJ went back to twirling his fork around in the bowl.

"You've made it this far, CJ, don't give up now," said Mavis.

CJ bit into a forkful of tuna salad, pinched his nostrils together, and swallowed hard. Visions of T-bone steak and cabernet danced in his head.

"Good boy," said Rosie, patting him on the head.

"You're pushing your luck, Red."

Rosie laughed and slapped his thigh. "Got the engine for the Bel Air today. Thought I'd hold back on the good news until you dove into your meal."

CJ pushed his chair back. His eyes lit up. "All right, when can you have her done?"

"Give me a week and she'll be as good as new," said Rosie.

"Have you heard any more about who broke into the garage?" asked Mavis.

"The word on the street's that it was Razor D. But the cops don't seem convinced. They say I've crossed too many people who might hold a grudge. Could be that somebody just doesn't want to be my friend," said CJ, pushing his salad downwind.

Mavis rolled her eyes and shook her head. "You need to take this thing a whole lot more seriously, CJ. Whoever trashed the Bel Air wasn't playing games."

CJ didn't answer.

"Think I'll have a wedge of your sweet potato pie, Mavis," said Rosie, gesturing toward the dessert case up front. "I'll need something sweet to keep me going all night while I work on skinny man here's car."

Mavis and Rosie stood up in unison and headed toward the front. On the way, Rosie spotted someone at the restaurant's front door.

"Looks like you've got a late customer, Mavis. Maybe he wants a slice of pie too," said Rosie. The person standing in the entryway tapped lightly a couple of times on the glass.

"I'll see who it is," said Rosie.

Mavis slipped a wedge of pie into a Styrofoam container. CJ lit up a cheroot and started blowing smoke rings that expanded to the size of donuts before they broke apart.

"They're closed here," said Rosie, pointing at the sign hanging in the window. The person on the other side motioned for Rosie to open the door.

"Can't," said Rosie, peering through the glass, trying to place whether he had seen the man before. "It's somebody I don't know, Mavis. Better come take a look."

A lanky slump-shouldered white man who looked to be no more than twenty stood at the door. He had a woolen navy watch cap pulled down to the lobes of his ears. A mop of frizzy blond hair sprouted from beneath the cap. Although the temperature hovered at 40 degrees, he was wearing only a short-sleeved summer shirt and faded jeans.

"We're closed," mouthed Mavis through the glass.

"Need to talk to CJ Floyd," he said loudly, rapping once more on the glass.

Rosie and Mavis looked back at CJ. His head was shrouded in a cloud of smoke. Mavis cupped her hands around her mouth. "There's somebody outside who says he needs to see you, CJ." Her words echoed off the empty walls.

"About what?" asked CJ.

"What do you need to see him about?" asked Mavis, shouting back through the glass.

The man was rocking back and forth from one foot to the other, trying to stay warm. "His car," he said.

"He wants to see you about the Bel Air," said Mavis.

CJ stubbed out his cheroot, fanned a cluster of three perfectly symmetrical smoke rings out of his way, and rushed toward the front of the restaurant. His chair tipped over backward on the way. "Let him in, let him in," said CJ.

"At this time of night?" asked Mavis, thinking of the rash of gang violence, robberies, and carjackings that had plagued Five Points for more than a year.

CJ looked at Rosie. "Have you got your piece on you, Red?"

"Sure do," said Rosie, patting the back pocket of his coveralls.

CJ looked back at Mavis. "Just crack the door."

Mavis had been with CJ in similar situations before. They seemed to start out as uneven ripples in an otherwise normal day, but they often turned to violence in the end. Once, during intermission at a black-tie affair for the Children's Hospital, a nonsmoking zealot had called CJ a public menace when he wouldn't put out his cigar. CJ ended up stubbing it out on the sleeve of the man's tux. Almost immediately security arrived, and he and Mavis were escorted out the hotel's front door. There had also been too many arguments over parking spaces that ended in fights. CJ claimed that his knee-jerk reactions were a thing of the past, but Mavis knew they had just been put on hold. CJ's need to place himself in jeopardy was the main reason the two of them had never closed the loop on their cat-and-mouse romance.

Mavis didn't want to argue, so she eased back the deadbolt and opened the door about halfway. Rosie fumbled in his back pocket for his gun.

"Are you CJ Floyd?" the man asked, staring at Rosie through the crack in the door.

"Afraid not," said Rosie.

"I'm Floyd," said CJ, nudging Rosie aside.

"Good," he said. He shot a look at Mavis. "How about letting me in? It's cold out here."

Mavis looked at Rosie, then at CJ. They both nodded that it was okay.

The man stepped around the half-opened door. He was even skinnier than he had appeared outside. His jeans stopped high-water style, six inches above his shoes, and he was chewing on a wad of gum. Mavis caught a whiff of the sweet citrus flavor of Juicy Fruit as he walked past.

"Now that you've ID'd me, let's even things up. Who are you?" asked CJ.

"Derrick James," he said.

"You're on strange turf for a white boy this late at night," said CJ. "You lost?"

"Nope. Just down from Cheyenne."

His answer made CJ wonder even more what a beanpole white kid from Wyoming was doing running around Five Points on a Thursday night.

"A little far south, aren't you, Derrick?" asked CJ.

"I know my way around."

"So you do," said CJ. "Now that we've settled that, what's your beef with me?"

"No beef, I just think I've got some information that might help you out," said Derrick.

"Well twist my nuts. A Good Samaritan who wants to share," said CJ.

"For five hundred bucks," Derrick said boldly.

If there was one thing CJ hated worse than diets, it was being shaken down. He reached around Derrick and slipped the deadbolt on the front door back in place before Derrick had a chance to react. "How about me having Big Red here sit on you while I call the cops?"

"What about four hundred?" asked Derrick, as boldly as before.

CJ looked at Rosie. Mavis had stepped back out of the way.

"I'll tell you what," said CJ, inching forward, and poking his finger into Derrick's chest. "Why don't you just pretend that I'm a priest and you suddenly realized that there was something you desperately needed to confess." He walked Derrick straight back into the door.

Mavis shouted, "CJ!" The alarm in her voice made Derrick fold. He started breathing fast, and before long he was panting in CJ's face.

CJ said, "Now, sonny, what about my car?"

"I saw the people that done it. The whole thing," said Derrick, swallowing hard.

CJ stepped back, but Derrick still wasn't breathing normally.

"Did you see them rip up my garage too?" asked Rosie, easing his hand away from his gun.

"Saw that too," said Derrick.

Rosie gave CJ the same kind of you-take-'em-high, I'll-take-'em-low look that the two of them had been exchanging all their lives. Mavis hated to see them look at each other that way. It always meant trouble in the end.

"Who did it?" asked CJ. "And were they white or black?"

"Don't know their names," said Derrick. "But I can point 'em out to you easy enough—and they were all black."

"How soon do you want to start?" pressed CJ, thinking that Derrick would finger either Razor D or some of the Blades.

"Can't till Saturday night," said Derrick.

"Why not?" asked Rosie, in a huff.

"Because that place of yours, the den, won't be open for no high-stakes gambling until then. And that's where they'll be."

Rosie suddenly realized that he had seen Derrick James before. "You're that white boy who's forever losing his ass at blackjack. I knew I'd seen you before. Hard to recognize you in that silly gangster cap."

Derrick smiled. "I always wear it down here in Five Points at night. Been buying pot down here for a couple of years. Seems like color don't matter when it's green."

Before Derrick had stopped smiling, CJ was questioning him with both barrels. "What time can you be at the den? How many of them were there? Can I handle them alone?" He barely took a breath between questions.

Derrick shot back. "There weren't but two. They're at the den every Saturday night. At least ever since I've been losing my shorts there." He looked at Rosie.

"I don't pick the winners, son," said Rosie. "I just pay the rent."

"You might want to call in the cops on this, just in case," said Derrick.

Rosie laughed. "Somehow I don't think the cops would show."

"How will you tip us off?" asked CJ, wishing that Saturday night had already arrived.

"I'll just pull off my cap," said Derrick, who demonstrated by taking off his cap.

"Sounds good enough to me. But if I were you, I'd wash that filthy thing pretty quick. Looks like rats have been nesting in it. What about the time?" asked CJ.

"Seven-thirty, eight. They usually show up about an hour past dark."

CJ took a few more steps back. With CJ no longer breathing in his face, Derrick relaxed and looked around the room. He spotted the dessert case and walked over to take a closer look. "You got any apple pie in there, ma'am?" he asked Mavis, as politely as an Eagle Scout. Suddenly he seemed a lot more boy than man.

"I believe so," said Mavis.

"I'll take a piece to go," said Derrick.

Mavis walked behind the counter to get the pie. She handed Derrick James his pie and 85 cents change from three one-dollar bills. She already had a bad feeling about Saturday night, but she didn't say a thing. Suggesting to CJ any way of dealing with the people who had vandalized the Bel Air besides confronting them in the back room of a garage after dark would have fallen on deaf ears.

"We're out of here, Mavis," said CJ, opening the front door. The way he was smiling he could have been on a five-cup coffee high.

"No late-night snacks," Mavis said, as she ushered

Rosie and Derrick James toward the door. CJ's stomach growled.

"Are you on a diet?" asked Derrick, tightening his grip on his pie.

"Aren't we all," said CJ, sneaking a final peek back at the pies.

The trio headed up Welton Street, walking briskly into a stiff breeze and frosty 35-degree air. Rosie peeled off at 26th toward the garage. Derrick turned up a side street at 28th, saying that he would see CJ on Saturday night.

CJ had to walk over to the 7-Eleven on Vine Street, where he had left the Jeep earlier that day. He was so busy thinking about Saturday night that he didn't notice the car that had been tagging along behind them ever since they left Mae's.

A giant billboard announcing the pure Rocky Mountain Stream freshness of Coors towered above the 7-Eleven. The sign featured two ski bunnies in skintight ski suits negotiating the Aspen slopes. Cans of Coors Light whizzed past the two beauties like silver bullets.

Earlier in the day there hadn't been a space available in front of the 7-Eleven so CJ had nosed his Jeep into a tight little space between the west side of the building and the alley. The Jeep's front bumper had lightly tapped one of the billboard struts. CJ got out to make sure there was no damage to the Jeep. Then he had glanced up at the two ten-foot-tall Amazonian beauties looking down on him from above. He walked away smiling, thinking no real woman could ever match the fantasy of a billboard.

Now it was dark, and the 7-Eleven parking lot was empty. CJ looked up at the billboard. Two of the six lights that normally highlighted the sign were out. The other four were focused squarely on the two skiers' butts. CJ was trying to decide whether the lighting arrangement was accidental or planned when someone jumped out from behind one of the sign's I-beam supports and tore into his midsection. The man's shoulder caught CJ squarely in the ribs. He struggled to catch his breath and slammed into the side of his Jeep.

The man was big. A ski mask hid his face and he was wearing work gloves to hide the color of his skin. The surprise of the attack kept CJ frozen against the Jeep for a few seconds. The attacker landed a couple of hard rights to CJ's face. CJ felt the man's pinky ring catch the bony socket beneath his right eye. The wetness of blood trickled down his face.

The car that had been following him pulled up behind the Jeep. A man wearing a green surgeon's operating room bonnet and welder's goggles jumped from the passenger's side to help the first man subdue CJ. The driver stayed put.

The first attacker had his hands wrapped around CJ's throat. CJ felt his voice box give. He kneed the man in the groin, and the man relaxed his grip. The second man was smaller and armed with a police baton. He landed three solid blows across CJ's ribs. He had his arm cocked for a fourth, but CJ rolled out of the first man's grip. The baton slammed into the hood of the Jeep with a thump.

The first man, now down on his knes, reached out and pulled CJ's feet out from under him. CJ landed tailbone first. The hard landing sent his head slamming into one of the Jeep's tires. He went lightheaded, remembering what one of his gunnery chiefs had told him when he first got to Vietnam: don't ever let nobody take away your feet from you over here. You do, and you'll sure enough end up dead. The big man gripped CJ by his legs. CJ was dizzy. He felt like he was kicking in a dream. The big man started dragging CJ down the alley while the second man kept kicking CJ with size thirteen Air Jordans. Most of the blows caught CJ in the head or the neck.

The sound of a sixty-pound manhole cover slipping off its metal housing sounded to CJ like locomotive wheels reversing themselves on the track. A second ski-masked man popped up from the manhole. "Get that fucker over here," he said. Only his head and shoulders poked above the street.

"Son of a bitch is strong," huffed the man who had been dragging CJ. "Quit kicking him," he said, looking at the man in the $140 basketball hightops. "You're just making it harder."

"I want the MF dropped down here headfirst," said the guy in the hole. "Be sure and drop him headfirst."

His instructions had barely left his lips when CJ freed a leg and kicked him in the face as hard as he could. Blood rushed from a gash in the man's chin.

"Goddamn it," he shouted, grabbing his chin. "I think the fucker broke my jaw. For that I'm gonna kill your ass nice and slow."

CJ grunted, wiggled, kicked, then screamed as he tried to free his other leg. He pulled the other leg loose just as lights flooded the alley. Suddenly it was as bright as day.

A Colorado Public Service repair truck, the monster kind with a high-rise boom that linemen use to repair downed powerlines, blocked the mouth of the alley. Reflected in the glare of the big rig's headlights, CJ and his attackers looked like toy soldiers from inside the cab. The driver lay on his horn. The man who had been dragging CJ and Mr. Basketball Hightops ran for their car. The other man shot up out of the manhole like a piece of toast and ran down the alley, away from the lights of the truck.

The horn blast ended. The driver and his passenger both started out of the truck toward CJ at the same time.

"You okay, man?" asked the driver, a balding, overweight black man sporting a two-inch-long goatee. By then two of CJ's assailants were in their car. The driver screeched his tires halfway across the 7-Eleven lot, losing a rear hubcap as he bumped out of control across the curb.

CJ tried to sit up, but he couldn't. His ribs felt as if they were about to explode through his skin. He reached back and felt a knot the size of a walnut on the back of his neck. He tasted blood at the corner of his mouth and he felt his right eye begin to close.

"You okay?" repeated the driver. His partner, a young white man, stood over CJ looking dismayed.

"Yeah," CJ said, finally. By then four or five other people had come out of the 7-Eleven to take a look. An old man wearing a grease-stained Colorado Rockies baseball cap said to his woman companion, "I think it's CJ Floyd."

"Damn," she said, looking at CJ's bloody face.

The two Public Service workers helped CJ up. The driver pulled a wadded handkerchief from his back pocket and stuck it under CJ's swollen eye. "Hold on to this," he said. CJ held the handkerchief in place. He could feel the gash beneath it.

"We better call the cops," said the white man. The

people in the crowd, now numbering ten, looked around at one another. Three of them immediately walked away.

"No need," said CJ, steadying himself on the bumper of the Public Service truck. "I'm fine." The last thing CJ or anyone else in the crowd wanted was a bunch of cops peppering away at them like a gaggle of hungry crows. CJ was afraid that the way he was feeling right then, fuzzy, lightheaded, and not in control, might make him say something that he didn't want the cops to know. Not to mention the fact that he might give the cops a lead to his assailants that he didn't want them to have. He planned to settle the score himself. Things still worked like that in Five Points. He had a pretty good idea who to start looking for. As soon as CJ said he was fine, the man in the Rockies hat and his lady friend walked away.

"You sure?" asked the Public Service driver.

CJ took a deep breath. His rib cage screamed. He dabbed the handkerchief at the gash he could feel but couldn't see, then pulled the once white hanky away to take a look. It was soaked with blood.

"Mind if I keep this?" said CJ, squeezing the blood out.

"It's yours," said the driver.

"Don't you think we should call the police?" said the other Public Service man again. The driver gave him an old-time one-room-schoolhouse teacher-to-pupil stare. "You got a lot to learn about Five Points, my man," he said to his partner. "Sometimes people down here don't want nobody calling the cops." The man finally seemed to get the point.

CJ wanted to thank the men for their efforts, but he hurt too badly to utter the word. In addition, he was too busy running through a list of all the people who might want him dead. When the cardboard cutout in blackface had taken two bullets up in Baggs, Copley, Deere, and even the old rancher Boone Cantrell had topped CJ's list. Now, Razor Dog Hicks had leap-frogged over them to the top. Gingerly, inching along in an old man's shuffle, CJ started toward his Jeep. The last three people in the crowd finally dispersed.

The truck driver helped CJ to his Jeep. "I know you ain't gonna call the cops, but at least let a doctor check you out."

"Tomorrow," said CJ, limiting his sentences to one word. His body felt like three separate pieces: an exploding head, a crushed rib cage, and legs that felt like rubber. He eased himself behind the wheel of the Jeep.

"Can you see all right?" asked the truck driver.

CJ nodded that he could. Just as he did, one of the billboard lights above him flickered out. One of the Amazon ski bunnies had lost the light that emphasized her attractive buns. CJ couldn't help but laugh when he thought how much better it was that she had lost her ass instead of him. The laugh immediately turned into a painful sigh. He had forgotten about his ribs.

The Jeep's engine turned over. A puff of smoke cleared the exhaust. It was only then that CJ realized that his right eye was swollen shut, and that he would be driving half blind all the way home.

Twelve

CJ was floating in the groggy no-man's land of Tylenol with codeine when the phone started to ring. At first he thought the ringing was in his head. An hour earlier he had stumbled up the steps to his apartment, barely able to breathe. His ribs had hurt so badly it took him five minutes to get out of his clothes. He shuffled to the medicine cabinet, found half a bottle of pain pills left over from when his wisdom teeth had been extracted, swallowed three without water, and inched his way into bed. When the ringing wouldn't stop CJ reached for the alarm clock by his bed. The stretching motion sent a stabbing pain through the middle of one lung. When he finally realized that the phone was ringing, he groaned. The phone was a foot past his alarm clock. His brain was saying *don't stretch,* but he clenched his teeth and in one painful motion reached for the phone.

"Yeah," he slurred into the mouthpiece.

"CJ, it's Rosie. Red," he repeated, when CJ didn't answer. "Got a problem down here at the jail."

CJ tried to get his eyes to focus but his right eye was frozen in its socket. He eased himself up until he was sitting on the edge of the bed. His sides felt as if they wanted to split.

"You in jail, Red?" asked CJ.

"No. But Monroe is—for receiving stolen goods and some of them was in the trunk of your car." Monroe Garrett was Rosie's chief mechanic. "And I've got a bigger problem than that."

"Somebody hurt?" asked CJ, wondering if Razor D had made a second visit to Rosie's to give his car another hammering or maybe plant some stolen goods. Could be Razor wanted him to take the rap and got Monroe by mistake. But he had the nagging feeling that someone besides Razor D wanted him out of the way. And he suspected it all had to do with Brenda Mathison's murder.

"Wish it was that simple. They hauled Darryl in too."

"Your nephew?" asked CJ.

"None other," said Rosie.

"Oh, shit," said CJ, knowing there was no love lost between Darryl's mother, Charlene, and her brother-in-law, Big Red. She didn't like Darryl playing grease monkey every hour he wasn't in school. But she was no match for a seventeen-year-old with a junker car and an uncle who owned a garage.

"The arraignment's tomorrow morning at ten. I need you to bond them out."

CJ tried to straighten up. His effort resulted in a painful grunt.

"What's with you, man? You on the pot?" asked Rosie.

"No. Just licking my wounds."

"What?" said Rosie.

"I'll tell you tomorrow," said CJ. "Anything else?"

"No."

"Then I'll see you at ten." CJ hung up the phone and eased back down on the bed. He wanted to get up and take another pain pill, but this time his brain won out. He remained motionless, flat on his back. In a few minutes, with one leg still hanging over the edge of the bed, he drifted back to sleep.

CJ couldn't fathom how he remembered Rosie's phone call, or how he had made it downstairs to his office by a quarter of ten. But he was there. When he walked in, Julie took one look at him, started trembling, and said, "Oh my God."

"Look that bad, huh?" said CJ, wheezing each time he took a breath.

"What happened?" asked Julie, rushing from behind her desk to help CJ into a chair.

"A couple of guys tried to Air Jordan the shit out of me."

The look on Julie's face told CJ he hadn't made his point. "I got the shit kicked out of me."

"When?" asked Julie.

"Last night, just down the street from the 7-Eleven over on Vine."

Julie walked back to her desk, pulled her makeup kit from her purse, and handed CJ a small hand mirror and a comb and brush. CJ looked into the mirror. His hair was matted down on one side, still caked with blood.

"Comb your hair while I run in the back and wet down some towels," said Julie.

CJ had been so stiff when he woke up that it had taken most of his energy just to negotiate the back stairs down to his office. A shower and grooming had been out of the question.

Julie's mirror gave CJ his first real chance to assess the damage to his face. The first thing he did, after admitting the fact that the reflection in the mirror was really his, was test the mobility of his front teeth. They all felt secure in their sockets. Satisfied that he would still be able to talk and eat, CJ took a close look at the left side of his face. Except for one small cut it looked normal. But the right side reminded CJ of some distorted image from a funhouse. A purple donut-shaped bruise, an inch in diameter, circled his right eye. His right nostril was swollen shut, and the fleshy area below his cheekbone was the size of an egg. Crusted mucus clung to the corners of his eyes.

Julie came back with three damp towels and started cleaning up CJ's face. The warmth from the towels was the first soothing thing CJ had felt in twelve hours.

CJ had pushed the comb and brush aside, unwilling to risk the painful overhead stretch that would be necessary to brush his hair. Julie went through all three towels without CJ flinching or moving an inch.

"That's better," she said, tossing the last towel aside. "At least you look human."

CJ forced a smile.

"How about that head? Looks like a bird's nest up there," said Julie.

"It'll have to wait, I've got a ten o'clock arraignment for a bond."

"It can wait," said Julie.

"Not this one. The city and county hotel across the street has two of Big Red's boys."

CJ stood up. But not before Julie brushed his hair and made him presentable enough for an arraignment. By then the pain in his ribs had leveled off to somewhere between excruciating and severe. "Hand me a couple of our standard forms."

Julie passed CJ the bond agreement forms. He started to tuck them under his arms but he remembered his ribs and rolled the papers up diploma-style instead.

"If you need me, I'll be across the street. When I'm done I'll come back and maybe let you do my hair again, but only because I know there won't be another seat available at Charles of the Ritz."

Julie smiled, but the smile faded quickly as she watched CJ listing to his right as he walked out the door.

The Denver County Jail had an uncanny resemblance to a tenth-century fort. The four-story stuccoed cinder block building took up a full city block. From outside you had to stare long and hard to find any windows in the building's sterile gray outer shell. The bonding office was tucked away on the first floor at the far end of a maze of brightly lit corridors. CJ entered the building hoping he wouldn't run into anyone he knew. He almost got his wish.

Herman Currothers was walking out of the bonding office with Nugene Turner, one of CJ's former clients. Nugene cut and power-raked lawns for a living. On the side he ran numbers and cheated on his wife. He was the kind of man who enjoyed having more than one ball in the air at a time. Nugene called himself "The Lawn Doctor."

Nugene tried to avoid eye contact with CJ. Six months earlier he had stiffed CJ on a drunk-and-disorderly felony menacing bond that CJ had posted after Nugene beat up his wife. CJ had gone soft on Nugene because of the frantic pleas from his wife, Willa. CJ knew that Nugene was probably there because he had beaten poor Willa's ass once again.

Nugene tried to make it to the door before CJ could ask about his money. But he couldn't help but notice CJ's swollen face, and that stopped him in his tracks.

CJ knew that Herman Currothers never did a bond on a black man without getting his money up front. As a result Herman got few black offenders. CJ was the only one on Bondsman's Row softhearted enough to take on the likes of Nugene Turner without getting paid.

"CJ, my man. You run into a truck?" Nugene grinned. His upper lip puckered, exposing two gold teeth.

The way he was feeling, CJ decided it wasn't worth getting his blood pressure up by arguing about his money with Nugene. And he didn't want a snake oil salesman like Herman knowing that he hadn't been paid. It would be bad for business so CJ decided to keep quiet.

Herman chimed in, "Hope the other guy looks worse."

CJ acknowledged them with a nod.

Nugene urged Herman down the corridor, but Currothers kept looking back at CJ. They were still within earshot when CJ called out, "Nugene, don't you know white men can't jump?"

Nugene ducked his head and continued walking away.

The woman clerk at the counter inside the bonding

office had seen it all, so she barely took notice of CJ's swollen face.

"Monroe Garret et al." said CJ. "Need to bond them out."

"Arraignment's at ten. Right about now," she said, just as Rosie Weaks walked through the door.

When CJ turned around after getting the information, the only word Rosie could muster when he saw CJ's face was, "Shit."

"No jokes, Red. I'll fill you in later. Did you get to the arraignment?"

"Just came down," said Rosie.

"The judge set Monroe's bond at five grand, Darryl's at two. I'll cover Darryl. Monroe's on his own."

CJ was trying to imagine what Monroe might own that was worth $5,000 when Darryl's mother, Charlene Gentry, stormed into the room and headed straight for Rosie. Her right arm was cocked. "You worthless alley mechanic. You reduce my sister to a gas pump jockey, and now you try to suck my baby down the drain."

Rosie stepped aside just as Charlene let loose with a vicious right uppercut for his head. Unperturbed, Charlene spun around, gathered a second full head of steam, and flew into Rosie again, this time landing a couple of blows to his chest. He shoved her aside, and she bounced off CJ. It happened so fast that CJ didn't have time to protect his ribs. Pain shot through his side like a knife.

"Out of my way, CJ, unless you want me to brain you too."

CJ knew she meant it. Charlene was a petite woman, just like her sister, Etta Lee, but she had an iron will. Her husband, a Denver firefighter, had been killed in a suspected insurance fraud arson fire, and for fifteen years she had lavished all of a grief-stricken mother's love on Darryl.

Rosie had managed to move to the far corner of the room. Charlene kept after him. "I lost Freddie. Now you gonna have me lose my Darryl. Big as you are, you still don't amount to no more than a piss-bump on the ass of the world, Rosie Weaks."

Rosie was silent. His 240-pound body was now squeezed into one small corner of the room. CJ knew that Rosie would never go against a woman, even in self-defense, unless his life was on the line. CJ figured that Charlene would wear herself out soon enough.

She landed a blow to Rosie's side. Rosie flinched and moved away. She went after him, flailing away at the tree-trunk-sized arm Rosie had thrown up to ward off her blows. She landed five or six good shots before CJ pulled her away in an adrenaline rush that allowed him to move her aside without his rib cage exploding in pain.

"That's right, save his butt again," said Charlene. During the scuffle her auburn wig had twisted sideways on her head. She rearranged the wig and adjusted her skirt. "Huh," she said, finally calming down. "You better be glad I'm saving something for that lowlife, Monroe Garrett, or else you wouldn't have no eyes, Rosie Weaks."

CJ turned his head and found himself looking directly into the eyes of the front desk clerk. Up close, without the reception desk between them, CJ realized that she was his height and that she was wearing a gun.

"Have you got things under control here?" she said, matter-of-factly.

"Yeah," said CJ, a little out of breath. "How about

asking the boys upstairs to bring the Gentry kid down first?"

"Don't matter who brings what when," said Charlene. "Monroe ain't made of glass, and I know where he lives. Sooner or later I'll settle this score." She walked off in a huff to one of the benches in the back of the room, where she sat down in a ladylike manner, reached into the purse she had tossed there when she stormed in, and pulled out a *People* magazine. She kept her eyes glued to the magazine and didn't look up until they brought Darryl down about forty minutes later. During that time the desk clerk went back to her station, and four or five people shuffled in and out. Rosie and CJ stayed seated as far away from Charlene as possible.

Darryl looked embarrassed to see his mother. She ran up to him and hugged him. "Baby, baby, you okay?"

When Darryl saw CJ and Rosie he looked even more embarrassed. "Sure," he said to Charlene, in a feigned tough-guy kind of voice.

"They treat you all right?"

"I did okay. How come they didn't bring Monroe down with me?" said Darryl, looking to CJ for an answer.

"He's coming," said CJ. "Paperwork around here takes a while. Why don't you and your mom go on up to the desk over there, sign your papers, and head on home?"

Darryl finally caught Rosie's eye. "Monroe says he's sorry about all this, Uncle Rosie."

"I bet he is," said Rosie.

"I think it was a setup. We never even knew the stolen parts were in the garage." Darryl had caught a glimpse of CJ's hammered face the instant he walked into the room, but he hadn't said a word. Finally, he took a long hard look. CJ could feel him staring, but Darryl still didn't say anything. He was still staring when Charlene grabbed his hand and pulled him like a schoolboy to-ward the reception desk. They both signed a couple of papers that the clerk handed them and left carbons on the desktop for CJ. When she and Darryl swept hand in hand out the door, Charlene still hadn't looked back at Rosie or CJ.

It took another hour to bond out Monroe. While they waited, CJ filled Rosie in on what had happened to him behind the 7-Eleven the night before.

During the time it took to complete the paperwork and for CJ to post the bonds, there weren't more than a dozen words spoken between Monroe, Rosie, and CJ. No one said anything about CJ's face until they were all headed out the door. Finally Monroe looked at CJ and asked, "Who fluffed you up?"

"I'll fill you in on the way over to Mae's," said CJ.

Rosie looked at Monroe and shook his head in dis-gust. "And Monroe, your story should be even better."

It was, but Monroe's bottom line was the same as Darryl's. He swore to Rosie that the whole thing had been a frame. Just before they pulled onto Welton Street, Monroe looked at CJ and said, "I think somebody was lookin' to stick it to you. Half the stolen parts were in your trunk, but the dumb-ass cops pinch me and Dar-ryl—give me a fucking break! Besides, that jelly-belly Sergeant Dellems was leading the bust, and as far as he was concerned, all that mattered was that he had treed a couple of coons."

CJ knew that Monroe was probably right and he was already thinking *Razor D.*

The Georgia smokehouse aroma of Poppa Loomis

Kinnard's Bar-B-Q and the delicious spicy smell of fried chicken coming from Lee's Chicken Shack permeated the Five Points air. It was almost noon, and the half-block-long stretch of storefront restaurants along the north side of Welton Street was springing to life. The neighborhood was just starting to sizzle with food and gossip about who was doing what to whom when Rosie and his contingent from the jail pulled up in front of Mae's at a quarter past twelve.

A string of three taxicabs, a police cruiser, and a limo were in a line at the makeshift drive-up window that Poppa Loomis had installed in what had once been the dining room of his house in order to keep pace with the fast-food demands of the times. The business had mushroomed from the kitchen of his house to include the GI Bill crackerbox next door, an art deco eyesore, and finally the old carriage house in back. All three buildings were connected by a series of improvised tacky bridges that gave the complex the appearance of having been constructed from Tinker Toys.

Hickory wood and New Mexico piñon pine were stored in cords in the backyard behind the carriage house. It was in the carriage house that Poppa Loomis's two sons spent hours smoking his famous meat. Sometimes during the long holiday weekends they had been known to go through a thousand pounds of beef.

Poppa Loomis was outside Mae's talking to Willis Sundee when CJ, Monroe, and Rosie piled out of Rosie's car onto Welton Street. When CJ was close enough for him to see, Poppa Loomis took a look at his face and said, "Forty-five looks like it's already been treating you pretty bad."

Everyone else walked on into Mae's, but CJ paused to answer.

"Nah, Poppa, just had one of those bad days at Black Rock kind of days."

"Did you run into the same guys that did the job on your car?" asked Willis.

"Don't know," said CJ, straining to see out of his one good eye. "One thing for sure, somebody out there doesn't like me or my car."

Willis and Poppa Loomis looked at each other and shook their heads. CJ knew what the looks and nods meant. Both men had been friends of CJ's uncle. They had watched CJ grow up. As a teenager, CJ had heard both men tell his uncle more than once, "Give that boy some direction." His uncle's response had always been the same: "Butterflies gotta fly." At forty-five they both thought CJ was still in need of direction. Poppa Loomis called it CJ's killer-diller life. CJ knew the look in both men's aging eyes was one of concern, but the killer-diller life was all he knew. "Catch you later," he said, and walked inside Mae's.

Rosie and the others were already seated at a table near the front. CJ knew Rosie hated being caught in the draft that always swirled around the tables near the door and wondered why Rosie had picked that spot. He found his answer when he spotted Charlene Gentry, Darryl, and Mavis huddled at a table in the rear.

"We already ordered," said Rosie.

CJ remembered his diet. He patted his swollen eye and stared down the room at Mavis, suspecting that sooner or later Mavis would come down the aisle to have a look at his battered face. And though she wouldn't say it, he knew she would be thinking, *you're a wise woman,*

Mavis Sundee, to have steered clear of what sooner or later is going to be one hell of a human wreck.

CJ was thinking about what he would say to Mavis when the waitress slid up beside him to take his order. "You having the same as everybody else?"

"No," said CJ. "Just bring me a quart of orange juice and a hard-boiled egg." He had always heard that vitamin C helped speed the healing of wounds.

"You know we only got OJ in pints," said the waitress.

"Then bring me two," said CJ, feeling his ribs.

On her way to the kitchen the waitress passed Mavis, who had started toward the front. When Mavis reached the tableful of hungry men she smiled at them one by one.

"Boys' night out, I see," Mavis said, when she got to CJ.

CJ suspected that Charlene had given Mavis an earful about how they were conspiring to turn Darryl into either a serial killer, bank robber, or common thug. CJ focused in on Mavis with his good eye. One good eye was all CJ had ever needed to drink Mavis in.

The waitress returned with her hands full and both arms cradling plates. Mavis helped her serve. When she got around to CJ, she served him from his bad-eye side.

"What happened?" she finally asked, trying to erase any hint of criticism from her voice.

"I ran into some Muslim fundamentalists who mistook me for Salman Rushdie."

"You're too old to joke about almost getting yourself killed, CJ. The word about what happened to you last night was up and down both sides of Welton Street before ten this morning."

CJ didn't feel like defending the way he lived his life to Mavis, and he didn't really want to be sitting there in pain, preparing to eat a tasteless hard-boiled egg. He wanted to be up to his neck in a giant whirlpool giving his forty-five-year-old body a soothing rest.

"How about some hot sauce for my egg," said CJ, forgetting his fantasy for the moment.

Mavis handed CJ a bottle of hot sauce from the next table. He sprinkled the two halves of his egg, took a bite from one, and chased it with half a carton of juice.

Everyone else at the table had buried their heads in their plates as they tried to avoid watching two people who cared about each other so deeply pretend that they didn't.

Mavis had her own idea about who one of CJ's assailants had been, and she decided to voice it. "You better watch yourself, CJ. Razor D is the kind of thug that will kill you."

The worried look in Mavis's eyes told CJ that it wasn't a time to joke.

"I'll do that, Mavis." He reached for her hand and squeezed it firmly, holding it long enough for everyone else at the table to steal a look.

The waitress came back with a basket of hot biscuits and honey. Rosie noticed that Darryl and Charlene had slipped quietly out the back. "I better get home and explain this whole damn mess with Darryl to Etta Lee before Charlene does, or I'll be sleeping at the garage. Put the meals on my tab," Rosie said as he got up.

Monroe split the biscuit he was holding in two and sopped up the last bit of gravy from his plate. "All my paperwork straight?" he asked CJ.

"You're square," said CJ. "Just don't skip your bond. I've already got enough skippers on my list."

"No sweat," said Monroe.

As they all clogged up the entryway on their way out, CJ looked back and noticed Mavis talking with the waitress. He wondered what they were saying. Maybe Mavis's promise to herself to never let CJ wiggle his way back into her life was going to be a promise she couldn't keep. CJ wanted to think Mavis still cared. He wanted her feelings to be the same as his.

CJ spent the better part of the afternoon in bed licking his wounds. Judge Mathison woke him from a restless sleep about five o'clock to press him about where he was with finding Brenda's murderer. When CJ tried to respond, the judge told him to turn up the heat on Copley and Deere. CJ wondered if the judge kept the same open mind about who was guilty in his judicial cases.

The rest of that evening CJ combed Five Points trying to locate Razor D. Every time he took a deep breath or slipped out of his Jeep to run down a tip about Razor D's whereabouts, his ribs shouted *ease up*. The pain made him think about how easy it would be to keep a loud-mouthed black slug like Razor D from continuing to infect the whole Five Points community with one well-placed shot. In the shadowy half-light of a first-quarter moon, it scared CJ a little to realize that he was actually contemplating killing Razor D. By midnight CJ had flushed out a half-dozen piss-and-vinegar Blades and a couple of Henchmen from their usual Five Points haunts, shelled out $40 for leads on Razor D, and listened to B.B. King tapes until he was into repeats, but he still hadn't turned up Razor D. He worried that Razor D's next move would be to go after Mavis and he knew that if Razor D

did, he'd end up killing the little slope-headed toeless di-
abetic for sure. Just before one o'clock CJ gave up his
search and decided that he might have better luck tracing
Razor D through his lawyer, Clyde Bodine. He made a
mental note to drop by and see Bodine the next day.
Then he slipped a scratchy-sounding John Lee Hooker
tune that he had taped from one of his uncle's vintage
blues 78s into the Jeep's tape deck, and hummed along
with John Lee all the way home.

Thirteen

Dr. Henry Bales called CJ the next morning to ask him if the five-day-old message on his desk was still urgent.

"As a bitch in heat," said CJ, easing out of bed.

"Then meet me at my lab at nine and leave any horny dogs you have at home," said Bales.

CJ laughed. "Nine sharp, and I promise no dogs." He marveled at how easily their friendship could swing back into high gear even when they didn't see each other for months at a time.

CJ was in such a hurry to get his biopsy specimen from the Grand River Tribe's dead steer over to the laboratory that he walked into his office after a quick breakfast at Mae's and passed Julie with barely a hello. He didn't notice the woman standing in the corner. After two days of recuperating, CJ was still a sack of soreness, but at least he could breathe without constant pain and his eye had opened back up. He had been diagnosed with severely bruised ribs and a concussion, and the doctor had him wearing an Ace bandage that felt like a girdle. CJ had promised himself that it would be the last day for the bandage.

The first camera flash froze CJ in his tracks. On the second flash, he barked at Julie, "What's going on?"

Before Julie could answer, a middle-aged woman's overly made-up face popped up from behind the camera. "We'll need a shot of every room. Landmark Restoration here to serve and preserve." The words shot rapid-fire from her mouth like a television ad for the marines.

CJ looked at Julie for an explanation. Julie shrugged her shoulders. "She was standing on the porch with Currothers this morning when I unlocked the door. Currothers said you had given your okay."

"I thought that nitwit was gonna get a local appraiser to give the place the once-over first," said CJ, throwing his hands up in the air.

"Afraid not," said the woman, swinging her camera up for another shot. "Landmark Restoration and Preservation always gets to cue up first."

Exasperated, CJ responded, "Who the hell are you?"

"Abby Lindel. Pleased to meet," she said, dropping the word "you" and snapping another shot.

CJ shook his head.

"Currothers wants to see you before you take off," said Julie.

"For what? Looks like that lizard's moving along okay on his own," said CJ, looking across the room at Abby Lindel.

"Something about Mrs. Dorfmann, he said."

"Can't it wait? I've got to get this damn Mathison murder put to bed." He reached in his coat pocket, pulled out his specimen bottle, and set it on the edge of Julie's desk. The cauliflower-sized mass of tissue bobbed up and down inside.

Abby dropped her camera to her side, and her eyes widened as she looked at the bottle's contents.

CJ wanted to laugh. "We deal in bad deeds here, Ms. Lindel. Didn't your renovation people tell you that?"

"No, they didn't," she said, regaining her composure.

"I need a label for this." CJ picked up the bottle and swirled the tumor mass around. "And call Currothers and tell him I am on my way. I'll give him ten minutes to plead his case."

Julie handed CJ a label from the top drawer of her desk, then picked up the phone and dialed Herman's number.

"Nice meeting you, Ms. Lindel, take as many pictures as you like. Look the place over good." CJ tucked the specimen container and the label into his coat and rushed out the door. As he did, his sore ribs reminded him to slow down.

Shaking her head, Abby Lindel looked at Julie. "Is he always so intense?"

"Usually not," said Julie.

"Well, I hope not. It's enough to spin-dry your brain." She stepped back and took aim with her camera, capturing Julie in the middle of the frame.

Herman was standing on his front porch talking to Ricky Perez. The conversation was animated. Herman's arms were fanning the breeze.

"Come on up," he shouted once CJ was within earshot. "I don't want to repeat myself."

"He's on a roll," said Perez, greeting CJ with a nod

before he said, "You look a hell of a lot better than earlier this week."

Herman didn't comment on CJ's health. Instead, he went straight to the problem at hand. "The old bag can't make up her mind. One day she's going to sell the places. The next day she's not. I think the old witch has Alzheimer's."

"Mrs. Dorfmann, you mean?" asked CJ.

"Who do you think I mean, Mother Teresa?"

CJ ignored Currothers and turned to Perez. "What difference does it make if she sells or not?"

"Seems there's a new glitch. The renovation people want every building on the block," said Perez.

"That's right. It's all or none, CJ. You ever played that game?" asked Currothers.

CJ thought back to a couple of sticky all-or-nothing situations he had found himself in in Vietnam. He knew it would be pointless to try to explain to Currothers what all or none meant when your life was on the line, so he shrugged his shoulders and said, "Not recently."

"I've been telling Perez here that the way to go is to buy the old bag out and sell the places right back to the preservation people," said Currothers.

"I already told you, I'm not in the market for more buildings," said Perez. "It's a struggle every month for me to pay for that white elephant down there." He pointed toward his own building down the street.

"Well, if we don't make some kind of move, and quick, the restoration birds are going to fly away," said Currothers.

"They can't fly too soon," said CJ. "They're just now getting around to appraising my place." He paused for a moment and looked at Currothers. "I thought you were going to let me know when the appraiser was coming by."

"You want me to do everything?" Currothers shot back in self-defense. "How about me coming by and wiping your ass after your morning dump? I gave the job of setting up all the appraisals to Perez."

CJ looked at Perez for confirmation.

"He did," Perez said reluctantly. "I've just been a little slow getting things done."

"Next time give me some notice," said CJ.

"Sure thing," said Perez.

"What's our move now?" asked CJ, directing his question back to Currothers.

"If Ricky here won't go for buying old lady Dorf-mann out, I guess we wait for the appraisals and see what the old barns bring."

"Sounds okay to me," said CJ. "I'm in no rush."

"Me either," said Perez.

"The whole thing is back on you," said CJ, smiling at Currothers.

"As usual," said Currothers.

"I've got to run," said CJ, giving the bottle in his coat pocket a pat.

"Where are you headed?" asked Perez.

"Off to see a man about a cow," responded CJ.

Perez and Currothers looked at each other and shrugged. Before they could comment, CJ was down the steps and halfway to the gate.

Fourteen

The University of Colorado Health Sciences Center is a sprawling forty-acre health care giant located almost directly in the geographic center of the Mile High City. UCHSC, as it is known, is the only comprehensive academic health center in the state. Henry Bales had been with the university for twenty-one years, and he could trace his Rocky Mountain roots back to the 1830s, long before Colorado became a state. On his father's side he was one-quarter Cherokee and one-quarter Cheyenne. His mother had been French Canadian. Henry jokingly called himself a paleskin to friends like CJ, but to his white colleagues and the rest of the world he was Dr. Bales.

Bales had served with CJ in Vietnam. He had been a soil conservation biologist in 1969 when his lottery number came up in the low teens. He joined the navy instead of becoming a foot soldier, and the navy decided that the best use they could make of a soil conservation biologist with no ROTC background who refused to go OCS, was

to turn Bales into a corpsman and to assign him to the
42nd River Patrol Group at Can Tho. He and CJ linked
up there. Every night for the entire year that they served
together, Henry would say the same two things before he
squeezed into his bunk for the night: "When I get home
I'm never leaving the Rockies again," and, "This war
gives me gas."

When Henry got home he enrolled in medical
school at the University of Colorado within a year. He
had remained at the Health Sciences Center through a
pathology residency and a molecular biology Ph.D. and
currently served as chief of cytopathology and diagnostic
molecular biology. He had a staff of twenty, federal research money to burn, and a space-age research laboratory that he liked to boast would put any Ivy League
institution's research center to shame. True to his Vietnam mantra, Henry hadn't set foot beyond the bound-
aries of Colorado, Wyoming, Utah, or New Mexico more
than half a dozen times in twenty years. Although Henry
and CJ didn't run in the same social circles, over the
years they had remained good friends.

CJ was half an hour late for his appointment with
Henry when he reached the Health Sciences Center. A
scrawny bird-faced parking lot attendant told CJ he
couldn't park in the research building's lot unless he was
faculty or staff. CJ lied and told the man he was Dr.
Floyd, visiting from MIT. He pulled out his wallet and
flashed a photo ID. The man grinned, revealing an assortment of decaying teeth and swollen gums. Then he
let up the gate and waved CJ into the lot. It never ceased
to amaze CJ how well a bogus photo ID worked to open
doors.

During his drive to the university, CJ had tried to

imagine what bizarre alignment of full moons made Thomas Deere and his Grand River people tick. Anyone smart enough to develop a vaccine potentially worth millions for an outfit as big as Carson Technologies had to be savvy enough to know that if he stole the vaccine, the company would come after him with enough muscle, lawyers, and cops to grind him into dust. CJ also found it more than coincidental that there hadn't been one word mentioned about Albert Copley during his conversation with Womack, Spence, and Judge Mathison during their visit earlier in the week. If, as Billy DeLong had said, Copley was the enforcer in the Grand River Tribe, then CJ knew he was going to have to tread lightly or get hammered in his attempt to flush out Deere. His ribs hurt too badly to get hammered again.

If Deere had really killed Brenda, it was a bonehead move. As far as CJ could see, killing Brenda hadn't helped Deere one bit with his plan to pin the cattle industry to the mat. All it had done so far was bring out the corporate troops. Maybe Copley had knocked her off. It wasn't too hard to imagine a love, hate, jealousy triangle among the three. Perhaps Brenda became a problem because she had a sudden change of heart. The whole Grand River business could have gotten out of hand, and Brenda could have told herself it was time to run home to daddy again. If she did have a change of heart, and Deere was concerned about the production details on the genetically engineered plasmid or the formula for the vaccine finding their way back to Carson Technologies, putting Brenda on ice would have been one sure way of making certain that all the information stayed with him.

While he waited for an elevator, CJ stared out of the research building's imposing floor-to-ceiling atrium windows and watched the parking lot attendant argue with a man in a delivery truck. By the time the elevator doors opened, the attendant had waved the man in.

Henry Bales's laboratory was on the seventh floor, and the view was a ski country advertising agency's dream. The entire west side of the building was a wall of glass that offered a spectacular panorama of the entire Rocky Mountain Front Range. Mount Evans glimmered, white-topped, in the distance.

Henry's laboratory was a 2,400-square-foot scientist's ideal gallery for splicing genes. The only thing ordinary about the lab was that it had washable glossy white enamel walls. Five evenly spaced laboratory counters paralleled one another, compartmentalizing the room. Each countertop was overflowing with high-tech biomedical instruments, chemicals, and computer printouts, some stacked a foot high. Bales's private office was nestled in the northeast corner of the laboratory, without a view. CJ watched three technicians hovering around a machine the size of a dishwasher. They seemed to be tethered to the machine by invisible ropes. Henry later told CJ that the instrument was a DNA sequencer that had cost $100,000. CJ walked by the sequencer and watched a dizzying array of numbers flash across a digital display. When CJ stopped to watch the numbers, the pungent smell of acetone filled his nose.

"Over here," said Henry, breaking CJ's trance. He was standing in the doorway to his office, fumbling with a plastic canister and a roll of film. "You'd think they'd make these things big enough to insert the film." He finally snapped a lid on the canister and jammed it into the pocket of his wrinkled lab coat. "How's it hanging, CJ?" No lofty university title, big-ticket salary, or space-age research facility had been able to erase Henry's Colorado straightforwardness. He feigned a punch to CJ's arm, but pulled it just before contact when he noticed the swelling around CJ's still half-closed eye and the healing gash above.

"About half," said CJ, pointing to his face.

Henry knew CJ would get around to telling him what had happened, so he decided to leave the issue for later. "Well, let's see what I can do to fill her up. First off, hit me straight up with your problem."

"It's more of a puzzle than a problem," said CJ.

"Problems are for mathematicians, puzzles are for kids. I'm all ears."

CJ knew that Henry meant what he said. Once, in Vietnam, when their patrol boat had been pinned in a swampy estuary by friendly fire, it was Henry who had found the back door out. Henry was a problem-based learner. He had a knack for putting things together so they just naturally fit, and he did it best when the pressure was on.

"Tell me what you know about papillomaviruses," said CJ. He hesitated. "In humans and cows."

Henry looked surprised. "I'll be Bullwinkle. That's pretty fancy medical jargon you've got dripping from your lips, CJ. Are you enrolled in one of those night school classes the medical school PR people are always trying to get the faculty to give?"

"No way," said CJ, shaking his head. "I picked it up from some folks who were real close to a woman I was looking for on an outstanding warrant. She turned up dead."

"That bail-bonding business you're in seems to be getting nastier every day. Think I better stay put here in academe." Henry paused for a few seconds, then tugged at his ear. "As for those papillomaviruses of yours, they're quirky little fellows, and a little bit schiz. Remember the story about the little girl with the split personality? When she was good she was very very good, but when she was bad, oh boy. Well, some of those viruses of yours can be real real bad."

"How bad?" asked CJ.

"Let me set you straight on the human virus first," said Henry. "And not necessarily because I prefer humans to cows. The acronym we use around here for the human virus is HPV."

CJ nodded, indicating that he knew the acronym.

"There are more than seventy different HPV subtypes. We just give them numbers right now, from one to seventy-two. The bad ones are sixteen, eighteen, thirty-one, thirty-three, thirty-five, forty-two, and forty-five. Stick any one of those little buggers somewhere in the human anatomy where it doesn't belong—let's just say your throat for instance—throw in a lifetime of smoking and booze on top of it," said Henry, clutching his throat, "and you can get cancer anywhere from your Adam's apple up."

"What about cows?" asked CJ.

"Same thing," said Henry. "We just haven't run the numbers up as high as seventy-two. Maybe twenty different subtypes of the bovine virus have been identified, perhaps a few more."

"And the bad ones in cows?" asked CJ, anticipating a list of numbers again.

"Numero uno," said Henry, flashing his index finger in the air like a football player who had just scored. "BPV One. I don't work with it, but I have some friends in the vet school at Colorado State who tell me it's a bastard and a half. They tell me it produces humongous tumors in a cow's gut. How'd you like to have three stomachs all backed up with cancer from A to Z?"

CJ said he wouldn't, then he shifted gears.

"Henry, you grew up on a ranch. What would you say the cattle industry does hard-core dollarwise every year in our fair state?"

"It would be a pretty big number, one with no fewer than nine zeros trailing behind. Billions is the more colloquial term," said Henry with a laugh.

"Suppose I wanted to kill the golden goose. Knock the cattle industry down for the count. Could I do it with one of our little bugs?"

"Maybe, if you could infect enough cows. But that would take too long, and sooner or later some wise guy would come up with a vaccine," said Henry.

CJ's face lit up at the word "vaccine." He knew that if he let Henry keep going he would eventually think the problem through. And when he did, CJ might find a way to proceed with the Mathison case that made some sense.

"If you were the guy with the big bad bug, and you wanted to make sure it really could kill the goose, how would you get it done?" asked CJ.

"I'd produce a hybrid," said Henry. "Hook up the most infectious parts of the viruses from both humans and cows. Then I'd stick it in a lab animal to see what it did. Having a hybrid virus like that, instead of one that just infects a single species, would be like having a neutron bomb instead of TNT."

"Could it be done?" asked CJ.

"If you knew the receptor sites on the gene."

"Run that by me again," said CJ.

"Receptor site. The place where the virus inserts itself into you or me or the cow," said Henry, pointing to himself and then at CJ.

"Suppose the person making up your hypothetical hybrid also had a batch of vaccine," said CJ.

"You have to be kidding," said Henry. A look of surprise crossed his face.

"No. There's a vaccine all right," said CJ.

"Then whoever made the vaccine knows the damn receptor sites already. And I'll tell you, they'd have to be pretty sharp," added Henry.

"Everybody who knows him says he is, and crazy to boot," said CJ.

One of the lab technicians walked over and handed Henry two spreadsheets. Henry scanned them both quickly and gave them back to her with a nod.

"Remember finding the back door out of that friendly-fire drubbing we took back in Vietnam?" asked CJ.

"It surfaces in my memory bank every now and then."

"Think you could back-door this virus deal for me and let me know whether or not the virus I'm after is a hybrid or not? If it is, I'm going to have to call in the law."

"Not without a piece of one of the tumors it's produced. And even with that it's no more than a fifty-fifty shot," said Henry.

CJ fished around in his pocket. "Say no more." He slipped out the jar with the piece of tumor from the Grand River steer and set it on the countertop next to Henry. "Straight from the source."

"You got yourself one hell of a puzzle here, CJ. Is this some kind of terrorist game?"

"Not really," said CJ. "Just a rerun of 1969. White folks out protesting again." CJ remembered the barefooted long-haired war protesters who seemed to be everywhere when he came back from Vietnam. There hadn't been a black face among them. Now twenty-five years later there was a new group of protesters interested in saving the planet instead of protesting the war. The strange thing about the whole Grand River mess, however, was that this time a black woman had been leading the way.

Henry picked up the mason jar and turned it slowly around in his hand. CJ's statement had him thinking back to Vietnam too. "I'm afraid it's a little different this time around. Sounds to me as if the friendly fire's over here," he said as he set the mason jar down on his desk.

CJ spent the next twenty minutes telling Henry Bales the entire Grand River tale and another ten describing his encounter with the three men in the alley behind the 7-Eleven. He explained to Henry that he thought the two things might be linked, and expected that sooner or later he might be up to his neck in FBI agents and cops. When he finished, CJ asked Henry how quickly he thought he could wrap things up on the molecular biology end.

Henry told him that it would take him a couple of weeks to determine whether the virus was a hybrid. When CJ pressed Henry to guess how lethal to humans a hybrid virus might be, Henry answered with the single word, "Very."

CJ left the university and headed for Clyde Bodine's law office for a little powwow about Bodine's client

Razor D and some lunchwagon law. He wanted to see if Bodine was the one keeping Razor D on such a short, low-profile leash. When he got to Bodine's, Monroe Garrett was in the outer office paying the receptionist, and he was beaming.

"We're off the hook," he said to CJ. "Darryl, and most important, me. Turns out the cops didn't have no probable cause to roust us the other night, and they damn sure didn't have no warrant. Bodine said so himself. Best five hundred dollars I ever spent."

"That's good to hear," said CJ.

The receptionist handed Monroe a receipt. Monroe quickly stuffed the receipt in his shirt pocket. Monroe still hadn't paid CJ for posting his bond.

"I'll get to you real soon with the money for that bond," said Monroe, making a beeline for the door.

CJ stepped up to the reception desk, shaking his head. Some things in the bail-bonding game never changed. A vase with droopy-looking columbines three days past their prime partially hid the receptionist's face.

"Is Mr. Bodine in?" asked CJ.

"No. He's stepped out."

"Would you tell him CJ Floyd stopped by?"

The receptionist had already jotted the time on a neon green While-U-Were-Out pad. The iridescent color caught CJ's eye. The receptionist realized that CJ was staring at her message pad. "It's to get their attention," she said, defending the color.

CJ thought about his recent beating in the alley behind the 7-Eleven. He was convinced that the person in the manhole had been Razor D. "How about adding something else to that note?"

"Sure."

"Just say that if Razor D plays jack-in-the-box with me again, I'm gonna cut off his head."

The receptionist looked surprised, but she wrote down exactly what CJ had said. Against the bright green background, CJ's words seemed to leap off the page.

Fifteen

Boone Cantrell, the crusty old rancher CJ had met in Steamboat at the sheriff's office just after Brenda Mathison's murder, stood on the front porch of the clapboard house that had been his home for forty years, surveying the five hundred acres of his Coyote Creek Ranch's hay meadows and thinking how lucky he was that Brenda Mathison was now out of his hair for good. The slugs she ran with would be gone soon too, if he had any say in the matter. He was sipping piping-hot coffee, wearing the same cowboy hat, tipped to shade his eyes, that he had worn the day he had met CJ. Cantrell was waiting for Derrick James. James had been Cantrell's drover boss for almost a year, and before that he had been a high school rodeo star with a small-town bad-boy reputation earned up in Casper, Wyoming. Derrick had helped Cantrell emerge from the protective shell he had worn for twenty-five years following the death of his only child. They were now as close as father and son.

Derrick was late. He didn't arrive until almost ten. By then, Cantrell had been pacing back and forth on his front porch for half an hour. When Cantrell saw how disheveled Derrick looked, he shook his head disapprovingly. Derrick's hair was down to his shoulders—long, oily, and unruly. His jeans were damp with patches of mud. He was wearing a pair of run-over logger's boots and the trademark filthy watch cap he usually only wore in Five Points. To Boone he looked just like what he was pretending to be, a member of the Grand River Tribe, who, aside from a couple of one-day trips to Denver, had been stashed away in the woods with the Tribe for nearly two weeks. He had been able to finagle his previous days away from their camp and now a three-day leave from their mountain bivouac because he had told Deere that his mother, who supposedly had terminal cancer, had finally passed away.

"You're starting to look like one of them," said Cantrell. "Next thing I know you'll be scattering my calves, separating them from their mothers, leaving them in the chickweed to die. If I didn't know better, I'd swear you were one of them Grand River sons of bitches for real." The smile on Cantrell's face and the bear hug he gave Derrick James said otherwise.

"Just make sure that if you go to shoot one of them in the ass, you take a good look first to make sure it ain't me." Derrick was smacking on a wad of gum.

One day before Derrick James came to visit Cantrell, he had learned that the Tribe was in the final stages of a plan that Thomas Deere claimed would put them and their cause on the front page of every newpaper in the country. James had been told that afterward there would be a steady stream of money flowing to the Tribe like water from a broken spigot.

Cantrell and Derrick walked up the dusty driveway to the tackroom that occupied the back quarter of the ranch's landmark three-gabled blood-red barn. Once a horseman's jewel, the tackroom had crumbled over the years to its current neglected state. The room was a fifteen-by-fifteen-foot hot box, connected by a breezeway to a decaying bunkhouse that hadn't been used in twenty years. Yellowing boxcar siding covered the tackroom and bunkhouse walls. Years of spur tracks had bruised every square foot of floor. A hodgepodge of aging saddles hugged rickety sawhorses. Cracked leather bridles looped around wall-braced two-by-fours. A mildewed heap of saddle blankets had been lumped next to the door, and boots lined every wall, some still caked to the heel scallops with dried-out mud.

Derrick sat down sidesaddle on a rickety sawhorse in the middle of the room. "They're planning something big, but I don't know what just yet."

"For here in Twenty-Mile Park?"

"Best I can tell," said Derrick. He walked over to the musty pile of saddle blankets, nudging them with his toe. Then he bent over and started smoothing out a frayed Indian blanket with an intricate zigzag design. His thumb punched through a raveling moth hole.

"All I can do is keep my ear to the ground. Deere and Copley do all the planning, and they're real close-mouthed about what they're up to. With Brenda dead, they pretty much keep the rest of us grunts in the dark. Deere thinks Copley killed her and Copley suspects Deere. They cat-and-mouse around the whole thing a couple of times a day. Sometimes I even wonder who did her in. What do you think? Any chance you or one of the good ol' Twenty-Mile Park boys offed our chocolate-covered Ms. Priss?"

"Do they still have that stash of guns?" asked Cantrell, ignoring Derrick's question.

Derrick knew not to ask again. "Yeah. But mostly just shotguns and thirty-thirtys. Nothing big enough to really go to war. I still say they're just a bunch of flakes trying to make the cover of some slick environmental magazine."

"Flakes or not, they're trying to kill our way of life." Cantrell waved his hand around the room. "I won't let nobody do that."

"Think we need to call for some help from the sheriff?" said Derrick.

"I'll go asking for help when I need it, not before," said Cantrell. "Besides, like you said, there're a few old boys out here in Twenty-Mile Park who'd love to settle things outside the law."

Derrick knew not to argue with Boone when he had his mind made up. He could be as stubborn as a two-thousand-pound bull. Derrick sat back down on the sawhorse and leaned against the wall. All four legs wobbled out of sync, like the legs on a newborn colt.

Cantrell hooked his thumbs in his belt. "You got any more on that bounty hunter, Floyd? Maybe he knows something we don't."

"I met with him the other night. He don't know any more than us. But you know what, something strange happened a few days before we met. I saw some guys beat the hell out of his car. I think they were hoping that maybe Floyd would be inside it," said Derrick. "I'm supposed to meet Floyd Saturday night and point out the guys who trashed his car."

"Why'd you want to do that? Isn't this complicated enough? Suppose the Tribe hears that you're helping the black guy out? Your cover's blown. Sounds to me like you're looking out more for a damn bounty hunter than you are for us."

Derrick looked peeved. "Let me handle it, Boone. It won't hurt to keep Floyd on our side. He's probably working for Brenda's old man, and who knows, he may throw me a bone about what the Grand River people are really up to."

Cantrell thought about the glare-ice winter nights he had slept alone in the calving barn tending a mother cow trying to calve, and he remembered the helpless times he had lost one or both of them before Derrick James had come along. "Do your thing, but watch your front and your back," he said apologetically.

"Don't worry, I know who's working for who," said Derrick, getting up from the sawhorse and stretching his legs.

"You look like a bum," said Cantrell.

"You want me looking like some fancy Dan bucka-roo in silver and cutoff chaps?" said Derrick, pulling his jeans up to his knees to make his point. Both men laughed, knowing that real cowboys never sported silver and wore only full-length chaps.

They walked out the back of the tackroom into a meadow of golden-brown stubble hay. Standing in si-lence, they stared out at the flat-topped mountains in the distance. On the dry stream side of one of the fences that cut across Coyote Creek five mother cows were brushing against one another like sleepy-eyed strangers.

"I don't mind saying I'd kill for this way of life," said Cantrell, taking in the view.

Derrick thought about Brenda Mathison again. He hadn't asked Boone directly if he'd killed her or not. But he had broached the subject, and he did know one thing for certain. Boone Cantrell always meant exactly what he said.

Fifty miles to the north, just across the Colorado state line, still deep in the Wyoming wilderness, Thomas Deere had just injected two five-hundred-pound steers with his new plasmid. Within five minutes both steers dropped to the ground, foaming at the mouth. Two minutes more and they were dead, their soft, gentle eyes bulging from their sockets. Now Deere had a hybrid that even Dr. Henry Bales hadn't imagined. A plasmid that could not only cause tumors but induce anaphylaxis—instant allergic death.

Albert Copley quietly walked inside the Tribe's makeshift corral and up behind Deere. All the while Copley kept staring at the fallen steers. Deere never turned around as Copley approached.

When Copley got to within two feet of Deere he said, "Need to head back down to the ranch pretty quick."

Deere whirled around as if he had been shot. He shoved a syringe full of plasmid to within inches of Copley's face. "Don't ever sneak up on me like that."

Copley eyed the syringe and took a step back. "Looks like you're wanting to kill things quicker and quicker," he said.

Deere didn't answer. Capping the syringe, he walked over to one of the dead steers and kicked its head. Then he turned back to Copley. "We'll move out tomorrow at first light."

Sixteen

CJ knew that Henry Bales's attempt to isolate an obscure hybrid wart virus capable of wiping out every rancher and cow on the Colorado Western Slope wouldn't tell him where to find Thomas Deere. He had Billy DeLong working on that. But CJ had a hunch that when it came right down to it, Deere was only a small part of the entire convoluted Grand River–Carson Technologies web. Womack, Spence, and even the judge had been far too eager for him to go the Grand River case alone, without a thread of assistance from anyone with a badge. In CJ's business that meant they probably had something to gain and almost certainly something to hide. Given their history, CJ also suspected that Carson Technologies had trampled more than a handful of interstate commerce laws in a rush to make money on their papillomavirus vaccine. Henry Bales had told CJ he was sure that Carson couldn't possibly have been in compliance with the FDA, if it had produced a vaccine without

completing what Henry had called Phase III research tri-
als. He assured CJ he hadn't seen a Carson Technologies
Phase III drug research trial or animal vaccine protocol
reported in the Federal Registry in over five years.

CJ was so wrapped up in thinking about his next
move that he nearly sideswiped Julie's Chevette as he
pulled up next to it after lunch. His stomach was growl-
ing, the aftermath of a Mavis-orchestrated, tasteless-as-
cardboard chicken salad meal. He'd only lost one pound
all week, and Mavis, who was still controlling his calo-
ries, seemed puzzled as to why. CJ didn't have the heart
to tell her that he had been eating like a horse since his
encounter at the 7-Eleven. During lunch CJ suggested to
Mavis that her diet was going to end up making him im-
potent. Mavis shot back that she wasn't aware that there
was anyone in Denver who cared. By the time CJ washed
down his last forkful of dog-food-dry chicken salad with
a glass of skim milk, he knew that at least he was a half
hour closer to his evening meeting with the people who
had trashed his car.

When CJ got back to the office Julie had a *Colorado
Peace Officer's Handbook* opened to page 212. Her index
finger inched its way down a paragraph near the bottom
of the page, just beneath the heading "Criminal Conspiracy."

"Studying for the bar?" CJ asked jokingly as he
walked past.

"No. Just trying to see if there's a way to cover your
rear," said Julie, speaking into the handbook without
looking up. Her finger jumped to the top right-hand col-
umn of the next page. "Mrs. Dorfmann's nephew was
here earlier. He said, and I quote, he's going to sue your

ass. The way he spouted off, I thought he was an attorney. But it turns out he is a Lakewood cop."

"Never met him," said CJ.

Julie looked up. "Oh you will, trust me, you will."

"Why does he want to sue?" asked CJ.

Julie tapped the criminal conspiracy heading with her finger a couple of times, then turned the book around so it faced CJ. "Seems he thinks you, Currothers, Perez, and Vickers are conspiring to cheat his aunt out of her house."

CJ bent down, turned Julie's handbook toward him, and started reading aloud from the economy-sized government print: " 'A person commits conspiracy to commit a crime if, with the intent to promote or facilitate its commission, he agrees with another person or persons that they, or one or more of them, will engage in conduct which constitutes a crime or an attempt to commit a crime, or he agrees to aid the other person or persons in the planning or commission of a crime or of an attempt to commit such crime.' "

His head snapped back, and CJ straightened up. "Why the hell am I reading this mumbo jumbo? I know what criminal conspiracy is." He slammed the book shut. "I smell Herman Currothers in this somewhere. Has that SOB screwed up again?"

"What a lucky guess," said Julie, trying to keep a straight face. "You're not going to believe what that lowlife has done this time."

"Try me," said CJ.

"Her nephew claims that Herman got the old lady drunk on rum and Coke and convinced her to sign her buildings over to him. And get this, according to the nephew, Herman tried to get a little nookie on the side."

All CJ could do was shake his head. As far back as he could remember, in order to ward off her rheumatism, Mrs. Dorfmann had eaten a daily quotient of one clove of garlic and chased it with a glass of gin. He tried to imagine Herman cozying up to her.

"Leaves me out," said CJ, emphasizing the word me. "Herman was on his own."

"Not quite," said Julie. "After she sobered up, Mrs. Dorfmann told her nephew that Herman said that signing the buildings over was just a tax dodge to keep her from having to pay big money this year. Herman supposedly told her it was a corporate holding procedure agreed to by the rest of his corporation, consisting of you, Cicero Vickers, and Ricky Perez, and that after the first of the year the corporation would determine how to distribute its proceeds to everyone involved."

"That little snipe didn't," said CJ.

"Afraid so," said Julie.

"That fucking Neanderthal. He'll have us all bunking across the street," said CJ, glancing out his front window in the direction of the Denver County Jail.

"Perez was in here looking for you earlier, so I filled him in on Herman's scam. He said that if he found Herman before you did he was going to wring his neck."

CJ paced back and forth in front of Julie's desk, then charged into his office and slammed the door. A dull pain gripped his still tender ribs.

Julie had left two DUI bail bond cases, properly signed and ready to go, on CJ's desk. They were what CJ liked to call slam dunks. All he had to do was walk across Delaware Street to the bonding office in the jail, hand over the papers, and the bond was guaranteed. In ten or fifteen minutes two drunks would be back on the street, and CJ would end up with $300 for his efforts.

CJ looked at the two files. Both bonds involved clients he had dealt with before, not virgins, as first-time offenders are known in the trade. A half hour more of jail time wouldn't make either of them late for the policeman's ball, so CJ decided to call Billy DeLong. He slid the two DUI folders aside, picked up the phone, and dialed Wyoming. He cradled the phone under his chin and counted the rings while he searched his top drawer for a cheroot. Billy picked up on the fourteenth ring. By that time CJ had lit up.

The conversation was brief. Billy told CJ that no one from the Grand River Tribe had shown up back at their ranch. He assured him that he had checked the place twice a day for a week and admitted to CJ that the Tribe's not showing up right after Halloween was strange. CJ asked him to keep up his surveillance for a few more days and added that if the Grand River people weren't back by the end of the week, he and Billy might have to head into the mountains to track them down. Although CJ didn't think much of the idea, he told himself: *I'm not being paid to sit around and think.* But it seemed like that's all he was doing—thinking about whether Copley, Deere, and the whole pack of Grand River kooks had skipped out in order to stay ahead of a murder investigation that might come nipping at their heels—wondering if Copley and Deere were also at the top of Sheriff Pritchard's list of suspects—and thinking about whether the old baggy-pants sheriff might find the killer before he did. CJ knew that he needed to find Brenda's killer and the missing papers before the sheriff if he expected another payday.

Billy ended their conversation by telling CJ that it had snowed for most of the daylight hours every day that week. "But only enough to make it pretty," he chuckled. "Maybe a foot, maybe two. Just enough to make the road up to my house as slick as shit, and slow down any lead-assed law folks who might be looking for the Tribe and our boys, Copley or Deere."

Two crazy men running around the Wyoming mountains with some kind of killer virus, willing to freeze their asses off while they hunkered down in two feet of snow, was enough to make CJ really worry. They just might be off center enough to kill somebody just to get an adrenaline rush. CJ remembered how deadly accurate the two bullet holes in the cardboard dummy had been up in Baggs. Although he had concluded that most of the members of the Tribe were wide-eyed losers and drifters out for a kick, he suspected that Copley and Deere were two tightly wound springs ready to pop.

CJ decided to give Henry Bales time to come up with as much as he could on the virus and vaccine. He knew that the more information you had about the other guy's game, the stronger your hand, and he figured that he could stall Womack, Spence, and the judge for at least a week. Even with $10,000 as a reward, the thought of having to head into the Rockies in November, and trudge into two or three feet of snow, made CJ shiver. He hoped that Deere, Copley, and the rest of their clan would come back to their ranch and spare him the burden of spending Thanksgiving freezing his butt off tracking them through a Wyoming blizzard.

He turned his attention back to the two DUI files. He never would be able to understand the fascination people had with filling themselves full of liquor, then going out to play Russian roulette with a two-ton car. But for CJ, not understanding something and judging people weren't the same. He never passed judgment on drunks. CJ had seen his uncle drink nearly every day of his life. Even so, the crafty old man had established a successful business, bought and sold real estate, always at a profit, and somehow had taught CJ the difference between right and wrong. When he died in his car in a twilight stupor one freezing February night, he was feeling no pain. CJ reasoned that his uncle's death had to be better than being strangled by barbed wire or dying from inhaling some doomsday virus you couldn't even see.

CJ stubbed out his cheroot, got up from his desk, and walked over to the window. A resilient cluster of black and gold petunias that he and Julie had planted in the late spring were struggling to stay alive in the wake of Denver's first frost. A couple of alcoholic wrecks, Morgan Williams and Dittier Atkins, were busy raking up leaves in the narrow yard along the side of CJ's building. CJ had known the two black ex–rodeo cowboys for years. Every November, Morgan and Dittier came by the office, faithfully looking for the leaf-raking job. One year, when they hadn't shown up by November 22, CJ gave the job to three high school kids. Morgan and Dittier came by CJ's office two days later, saying they had both been deathly ill. CJ knew that they were lying—that they had been on a binge. But he also knew that a portion of the money they would have earned from raking leaves would have gone for a Thanksgiving meal at Mae's. So he paid them $10 apiece to caulk a few windows and sent them on their way. Every November that followed found CJ patiently waiting for Morgan and Dittier to show up, regardless of the date.

CJ stepped out the side entrance into the yard. Morgan and Dittier were just finishing up. The woodsy smell of decaying aspen leaves filled the air. CJ paid the two men with crisp new twenty-dollar bills.

As they were preparing to leave, CJ asked them what they were doing for Thanksgiving. The question just seemed to pop into his head. He knew it was a strange question the instant he asked. "We're going to meet a man," said Morgan, pulling a full, uncapped pint of whiskey from his grease-stained coat pocket and pointing to the picture of Jim Beam.

CJ smiled, went back inside, and grabbed the two DUI folders off his desk. Then he headed back out to the front office. "I'm going to set a couple of butterflies free," said CJ, rippling the folders in the air.

"Any messages you want me to give your conspiracy partners if they show up?" asked Julie.

"I've decided to let that problem take care of itself. Sooner or later Herman'll be down here screaming bloody murder at the top of his lungs. Maybe his screams will be muffled from either Vickers or Perez having their hands wrapped around his stupid neck."

Julie looked at her watch. It was almost two-thirty.

"Are you coming back?" she asked.

CJ glanced out the front window. Morgan and Dittier were halfway up Delaware Street and nearly out of sight. "No. When I finish up with the two DUI's I'm going to meet a man," said CJ.

When Julie looked up at him, puzzled, CJ added, "About the Bel Air. Tonight I've gotta meet a man about who trashed my car."

Seventeen

It was Fat Saturday night in Five Points. A rare full-mooned Saturday that rolled around only once every five years the weekend after Halloween. Rosie's den was packed. Cars lined both sides of Welton Street and 26th Avenue for several blocks to the east and west. CJ had to park three blocks away. On his walk to the den he hurried past everything from Mercedes-Benzes glimmering in the moonlight to twenty-year-old pickups, cluttered with beer cans, drywall scraps, PVC pipe, and broken glass.

All afternoon, dark clouds had been drifting over the front range of the Rockies into Denver. CJ could feel the sharp bite of the first hard early autumn freeze. Five bitter months were on the way. The temperature was in the low 40s, not nearly as cold as it would get. In an hour or two CJ knew that the air would turn perfectly still. An eerie calm would settle, then it would start to snow. It was always the same when a cold front came through. CJ walked into a stiff breeze from the west. The air was filled with the nauseating smell from the Purina rendering plant. From late October until early April, that odor served Denver with a warning that Mother Nature was about to have her way.

CJ watched two street people pushing shopping carts filled with aluminum cans down one of the alleys between Welton and 26th and realized it was Morgan and Dittier. They stopped midway down the alley, and Morgan bent down and flipped a couple of cans into his cart. CJ wondered what doorway would serve as their home for the night.

Fat Saturday at the den almost always produced a few scuffles and at least one all-out fight. It almost had to. There was too much money changing hands, too many people filled with what Rosie liked to call gravedigger brew, and absolutely too many people in too little space. The congestion made everyone hair-triggered as the evening wore on. When their edginess peaked, the skirmishes began.

Whenever CJ entered the den on a Fat Saturday night, the first thing he did was look for the quickest way out. More often than not, the exits would be blocked by knots of people, roulette wheels, poker tables, or liquor stacked by the case. Fat Saturday and New Year's Eve were two nights that even Rosie's, usually off limits to the law, might receive a visit from the police.

The busts never resulted in much more for Rosie than a hefty fine and a slap on the wrist. But CJ liked to make sure he was never around during a gambling bust. He liked to keep his bail-bonding license Ivory Soap clean. It never paid to ruffle the feathers of the Denver police, and although they weren't disciples of the guys who beat Rodney King to a pulp, they could have their moments. CJ didn't want some rookie policeman's need to show who was in charge to ever come at his expense. So he always determined the quickest way out of the den on his way in. CJ eyed the exit next to Rosie's office and decided that in an emergency it would be the way to leave.

The den was no more than the oversized stock room of a gas station and garage, but it sported one of the most elegant bars in the state. The bar had been rescued from a turn-of-the-century Kansas City stockman's saloon. CJ had helped Rosie move the forty-foot semicircular solid mahogany bar the seven hundred miles from Missouri to Denver on a flatbed truck in a near blizzard, just one month after he had come back from Vietnam. In eastern Colorado, Rosie had almost rolled the truck on an invisible plate of black ice outside Limon at two o'clock in the morning. When they stopped, turned sideways across both westbound lanes of the interstate, Rosie was frozen catatonic, his arms rigidly gripping the wheel. For some reason, during the whole spin all CJ could think of was sitting on the deck of the *Cape Star,* on night patrol, shirtless in the 90-degree heat just outside Can Tho, Vietnam. When they stopped, the first words out of CJ's mouth had been, "I knew I wasn't meant to buy it in the fucking snow."

People were lined up two and three deep around the bar. Monroe Garrett was acting as bartender, filling orders as fast as he could. He caught CJ's eye and gave him the kind of nod that said make your order simple, CJ.

"Dos Equis," CJ hollered, above the din. "And in a frosted mug if you've got one around."

Monroe shook his head. "Are you kidding, CJ? A frosted mug, tonight? You might as well ask permission to sleep with the queen." He popped the bottlecap on

CJ's beer, snatched a glass that was still dishwater warm from the rack overhead, and slid them one at a time along the bar into a narrow opening between a man with a gold front tooth that sported a three-pointed ivory star and a rail-thin Ichabod Crane–looking man in a three-piece suit who was carrying a cane. CJ grabbed them and said thanks.

"Settle with me later," said Monroe. The man with the cane rapped it against the bar and demanded another Bud. Monroe's eyes rolled back and shot skyward. Rosie kept all the high-stakes poker tables lined up near the back, out of view of the entrance, just in case someone foolishly decided that he needed to be robbed. CJ knew that he would find Rosie lingering at one of them. He negotiated his way across the crowded room, shaking hands, acknowledging people with a smile, sometimes squeezing an arm or giving a friendly nudge.

The press of people didn't ease up until CJ was almost to the back wall. He caught a glimpse of Rosie's back. Rosie was standing next to Willis Sundee, facing the wall.

"I'll be," said CJ, talking to the back of Willis Sundee's head. "Mavis must have taken her sweetness pills today if she let you out in this mess to try your luck."

Willis looked over his shoulder at CJ and grinned. "A man's got to be able to finance his beans or he's lost," he said, sweeping the tabletop with his poker hand twice, calling for two new cards.

"Red," said CJ, acknowledging Rosie with a slap on the back as he eased his way between the two of them.

"Better not say anything else bad about Mavis, CJ," said Rosie. " 'Cause she's here."

CJ immediately looked around the room. More than two hundred people were crammed into a room meant to hold no more than ninety-five. He couldn't find Mavis in the crowd. It surprised him that she was there. Mavis hadn't made an appearance at Fat Saturday night in five years, not since she had gone with CJ and he ended up breaking a local disc jockey's arm. The arm had been attached to a hand that somehow found its way onto Mavis's behind. The fight between CJ and the disc jockey had been brief, but for Mavis it had been the final straw. The incident made Mavis decide that her relationship with CJ couldn't move ahead. She told him afterward that he was still too wired. In the years that followed, CJ liked to think that he had toned himself down. It made him a little nervous to know that Mavis was somewhere in the room.

"I don't see her," said CJ.

"Don't worry, she'll be back to make sure I haven't lost my shirt," said Willis, examining his cards.

CJ looked at Rosie, who had been constantly scanning the room, his head pivoting back and forth like a surveillance camera in a convenience store. "Have you seen the Wyoming kid? You know, the white boy with the stupid wool gangster cap and the tropical shirt?" asked CJ.

"No. But he'll show," said Rosie. He locked his eyes on a blackjack table near the front of the room. "I think Bobby Lester is skimming on me again," said Red, his eyes glued to the table's dealer.

"I thought you shit-canned him a few months back," said CJ.

"I did, but he came to me with a song and dance

about having to feed his kids. You know, CJ, I think I'm getting soft."

"That's good to know," said CJ. "Maybe you'll ease up on hammering me about what I eat."

Rosie laughed and went back to scanning the room. "Finished up the Bel Air this afternoon. Your baby's as good as new. Didn't test-drive it though. Just ran the engine for a while and took a cruise around the pumps. I figured I would let you have the pleasure of breaking the new engine in."

"All right!" said CJ. "One problem down and one to go."

"Two?" said Rosie, surprised. "I thought our little stoolie from Cheyenne was going to wrap up everything real nice and neat tonight."

"He is," said CJ. "But that's just problem number one. I still haven't figured out who killed that Mathison girl. And believe me, that problem's getting thornier every day."

"Take my advice and leave that one for the cops," said Rosie.

"Afraid I can't. I'm into the case up to here," said CJ, saluting his Adam's apple, then shaking his head. "And I need the coin." He looked around the room for a cowboy hat, with no luck. He recognized a couple of car strippers he had once refused to bond playing blackjack and wondered whether they had memories long enough to make them want to trash the Bel Air. When he assured himself that they didn't he went back to looking for Derrick James.

The room had turned into a congested pillbox full of noise and smoke, packed to the gills with everyone from jackleg preachers to petty thieves. CJ had known most of

them all of his life. There probably were no more than a
handful of people there he couldn't call by name. Sometimes he wondered what made the people in Five Points
stay. There were dozens of other neighborhoods where
black people could live and even flourish; after all, it
wasn't 1945. But the people of Five Points seemed to
linger, as if they were struggling to maintain some fraying
link to the past. He couldn't imagine Five Points being
home to a man like Judge Mathison. He would have
parked his snooty middle-class ass in a suburb or Park
Hill. CJ knew that for the judge places like Five Points
were simply sepia-toned relics from another era. But CJ
reasoned that if the judge had vested himself in a place
like Five Points, his daughter might have had a different
set of values, and she might still be alive.

"Full house," screamed Willis Sundee. "Send that
money over here." The dealer slid five one-hundred-
dollar bills across to Willis.

At the high-stakes poker tables Rosie never used
chips. He liked to watch the joy of winning explode on a
customer's face. And he enjoyed seeing everyday working people rake real money in. He knew that most of the
den's patrons would never have a major financial score.
For most of them, winning five hundred dollars at poker
would be the financial high point of their lives. Willis
was an exception.

Willis handed CJ one of the hundreds. "You brought
me luck, CJ, go get yourself some of those expensive
white folks' beans, that is, after you lose yourself a couple more pounds."

CJ knew not to insult Willis by refusing the hundred.
As soon as he saw that CJ had tucked the money away,
Willis eased up from his chair. "I better find Mavis and

quit while I'm ahead. Love taking your money, Red. Makes me know I'm living right," he said, punching Rosie on the arm before he knifed his way into the crowd.

CJ decided it was time to look for Derrick James in earnest. He threaded his way between two portly fair-skinned women in wide-brimmed hats. He jostled the one who was sipping red wine, smiled at them both, and kept moving. The other woman looked at her friend and whispered, "That's CJ Floyd." All that CJ could muster in the way of a greeting for any of the gamblers at the low-stakes tables was an occasional nod. He knew that they were all too busy trying to count the cards to talk to him about Derrick James. After one rotation around the room, CJ started to wonder if Derrick James was going to show.

CJ checked his watch. Eleven-thirty. "Where the hell is he?" CJ mouthed through clenched teeth. He tapped his fingers impatiently on the face of his watch and decided to have another beer.

He and Mavis arrived at a just-vacated spot at the bar at the same time. In the crush of people they ended up sandwiched together face-to-face. "Dr. Livingstone, I presume," said Mavis.

CJ tried to turn sideways. His chest ended up pressed against Mavis's right arm.

"No, I'm his cousin, CJ Floyd."

A couple inched their way backward away from the bar. CJ and Mavis mushroomed into their space.

"Haven't you heard, it's Fat Saturday. What brings you out?" asked CJ.

"Daddy. I'm watching out for him," said Mavis. "And you? Wait a minute. Don't tell me. You're looking for that guy from Cheyenne."

"Have you seen him?" asked CJ, looking over his shoulder back into the crowd and seeing only a sprinkling of white faces, none belonging to Derrick James.

"I haven't seen him since he left the restaurant with you and Rosie the other night. He's trouble, CJ, mark my words."

"All I want is for him to point me in the direction of whoever it was that operated on my car."

"Then what are you going to do? Make a citizen's arrest?"

CJ thought for a moment before saying, "Nothing."

Mavis hated to see CJ lie. She ordered a chardonnay and CJ nodded at Monroe for another beer.

"Once I know who did it, maybe I'll just pass their names on to one of your lover boys in blue." He was referring to the fact that Mavis had an on-again, off-again relationship with a cop.

Mavis gave CJ an icy stare. "Who are you kidding? We both know how you and Rosie are about settling scores."

Before CJ could respond, Mavis slammed into his side and his beer glass went flying into the air. His injured ribs felt like they had suddenly been caught in a vise. Like falling dominoes, the people at the bar fanned backward into the rest of the crowd. Two poker tables near the front crashed to the floor. Poker chips skipped and cartwheeled across the room. A dozen people filled the space where the poker tables had been. CJ was still looking for the reason for all the fuss when Rondell Burns, a gang member whom Ricky Perez had recently bailed out of jail, careened off Ajax Henderson and slammed into CJ. CJ shoved Ajax, a squat potbellied long-haul trucker, back toward Rondell. Ajax plowed headfirst into Rondell's midsection and pinned him against the bar. He was busy landing overhead chops to the side of Rondell's head when Rosie stepped in to pull them apart.

"You little maggot," said Ajax. "I'll teach you to palm a card." He cocked his arm to deliver another blow.

It took all of Rosie's 240 pounds to pin both men against the bar. Rondell struggled to get free, but each time he had almost wiggled away, Rosie slammed him back into the bar.

"I'll go through you, Rosie, don't matter to me," said Ajax, freeing himself and taking aim at Rosie and Rondell. Most of the den's bar patrons had scattered when the fight began. CJ and Mavis remained trapped at the bar. Ajax primed himself for another charge. Just as he was off his mark, CJ reached out from behind him and grabbed him by the collar of his shirt. His feet flew out from under him, and Ajax slammed tailbone first into the floor.

"Might as well make it even," said CJ, looking down at Ajax. "And you owe me a beer."

In obvious pain, Ajax made two attempts to get up. When he couldn't he propped himself up on his elbows, grimacing in pain. "The little turd cheats," Ajax said, in self-defense.

"We don't allow no cheating in here," said Rosie, still struggling to keep Rondell from getting free.

"I wasn't cheating. That burned-out road jockey's fucking blind," said Rondell.

"Blind, my ass. The SOB was holding an extra eight," said Ajax, struggling to sit all the way up before falling back on his elbows again.

"I want both of your asses out of here right now," said Rosie. "Come back when you get issued brains." He let

Rondell free. Rondell lunged at Ajax, who had finally made it to a jackknife position on the floor. Rosie slammed Rondell back against the wall. "See that exit sign across the room," said Rosie. "I want your narrow behind under it by the time I count to ten. Move!"

Rondell started for the door. "Get up and follow his trail," said Rosie, looking down at Ajax.

"That little peanut cheats," said Ajax, painfully pulling himself up from the floor.

"Tell it to his social worker," said Rosie.

Like a man in leg irons, Ajax hobbled toward the door. Halfway there he looked back across the room. "Nice to see that CJ's still saving your butt, Rosie." He hobbled a little faster for the exit. CJ followed him to the door.

Mavis had made her way across the room to the same exit. She was standing there with her father, shaking her head. Before CJ could say anything in self-defense, Mavis had opened the door for the two brawlers. She and her father followed them out. "Things never change," Mavis said as she left. CJ followed her out the door.

A block down the street, CJ could see the flashing overhead lights from police cruisers and what looked like a vehicle on fire in the middle of the street. Mavis and Willis headed away from the lights, up the street in the opposite direction, toward Mae's.

CJ stepped outside into three inches of freshly fallen snow. Reflected through the curtain of falling snow, the amber and blue lights of the police cruisers reminded CJ of incoming rocket tracers.

When Ajax Henderson shouted back to CJ, calling him a sissified motherfucker with dogshit for brains, CJ decided to trail him a little further up the street toward the police cruisers. Still hurting, Ajax waddled to within thirty yards of the patrol cars before he veered off down 26th and into the night. CJ knew that even though an old interstate drug-trafficking charge hadn't stuck, Ajax still made it a point to steer clear of the police.

Two policemen were standing at the back of one of the cruisers, talking to Morgan Williams and Dittier Atkins, CJ's two street-bum yard men. Just as CJ walked up, the second police car pulled away. CJ recognized the two remaining cops. One was Ralph Dellems. A street-tough, no-love-for-black-folk, white sergeant that CJ had had run-ins with before. The other cop was black, Samuel Glenn. Glenn had little use for bail bondsmen, calling them garbagemen who put society's trash back on the streets, and to make matters worse he had been chasing after Mavis for years. Although Mavis sometimes went out with him, Willis Sundee had once told CJ she called Glenn, Boring Sam. CJ wanted to ask Mavis what she saw in a man who had never made it past patrolman in all his time on the force. But he never did.

CJ could see that the charred hulk with its nose jutting from an alley into the intersection of 26th and Vine had once been a van. The smell of gasoline and burning rubber permeated the midnight air. Welton Street was a two-inch-deep water slick, laced with gasoline and oil. A Fire Battalion pumper truck was sitting forty yards up the street. The firemen on the scene were busy stowing their gear. CJ wondered why he hadn't heard any sirens. Then he remembered the rock concert noise level inside the den.

Glenn was the first person to see CJ. He looked CJ

up and down before he said, "Out for a midnight stroll, or have you been down the alleys looking for clients?"

"No. Just curious. What's up?" CJ had learned long ago to ignore anything Sam Glenn said.

Before Glenn could respond the sergeant walked over and started motioning for CJ to move along. "Move it on, Floyd. This is no business of yours." He looked over at Glenn. "How about taping the area off? We don't want anyone else strolling up."

"Come on, Sarge, what's the deal?" asked CJ.

The sergeant gave CJ a look that said, *I thought I told you to move along,* but he was streetwise enough to know that a midnight crime scene in Five Points probably wouldn't turn up a single witness. It was possible that CJ had seen something that could help him out. So he offered CJ a bone. "Looks like some John Doe bought it trying to torch a van. See anything that might help us out?"

CJ didn't answer the question. Instead, he looked over at Morgan and Dittier. "Why are you holding them? They're just a couple of street people out collecting cans."

"I've got their story. I just haven't given them the okay to leave. Strange, though, they claim the guy inside didn't even try to get out," said the sergeant.

A fire hose snaked its way between CJ's legs on its way back to the pumper truck. CJ skipped out of the hose's way. He felt water squish around inside his shoes and realized that his feet were soaking wet. He turned up the collar on his coat and stomped his feet. His shoes felt as if they weighed twenty pounds.

"How bad's the body burned?" asked CJ.

Irritated by the fact that CJ was still there, and asking

questions to boot, the sergeant snapped, "I've seen worse."

"Mind if I take a look? You never know, I might be able to ID your man," said CJ.

CJ's disregard for authority was outweighed by the sergeant's need for help in identifying the John Doe. Against his better judgment, the sergeant acquiesced. "You can take a quick gander, but all I want is an ID. Don't go snooping around inside."

CJ walked past Morgan and Dittier and said hello. Morgan gave CJ a raised-eyebrow nod that told CJ he knew more than he was willing to tell Sam Glenn. Glenn was busy adding to the statements Morgan and Dittier had given the sergeant. He looked up as CJ walked by, then immediately went back to jotting down notes.

The back doors of the van were sprung open as wide as they could go. Up close CJ recognized that the van was actually an old Volkswagen bus. The glass was missing from the rear doors, which had been baked charcoal black from the fire. The only seats inside were two captain's chairs in the front. A man's body, locked in the fetal position, rested behind the seats on a partially incinerated floor. A few smoldering floorboards supported the body's weight. The first thing CJ noticed was the singed woolen navy watch cap pulled down over the victim's ears.

He climbed up on the rear bumper and looked inside. For a second the nauseatingly sweet smell of burned flesh took him back to Vietnam.

"Well, can you ID our John Doe or not?" called the sergeant, shining his flashlight inside.

CJ reached inside the van to turn the victim's head toward him and when he did half of the man's face disintegrated. But even in semidarkness, with most of his face burned away, CJ could see that the man was white. What was left of the rest of his face looked like a hollowed-out charboiled coconut. The man's upper jaw was burned so badly that CJ could see the roots of his teeth. CJ took a long hard look at what was left of Derrick James.

He nibbled at his lower lip and grimaced as he surveyed the burned-out remains of the bus. Most of what was left, you would expect after a fire. Buckled metal, waterlogged fabric, remnants of plastic, charred pieces of wood. CJ shook his head. As he eased his way off the bumper of the bus he snagged his coat on something tucked discreetly in the far right corner of the van. He felt for the object and pricked the fleshy part of the palm of his hand.

"Shit," he murmured, snatching his hand away. As soon as his feet hit the pavement and before his head was out of the bus, he shouted back to the sergeant to shine his flashlight into the back right-hand corner of the bus. The sergeant's flashlight beam glimmered through the falling snow.

"Over here," said CJ, pointing to where he wanted the light. The arc of the light settled on what looked like a spool. At first CJ thought it might be the kind of spool used to dispense TV cable. But on close inspection, CJ found a blackened heat-fused spool of barbed wire.

"What's that?" asked the sergeant.

"A link to the past and the present—a murder weapon for some," said CJ, fiddling with the puncture wound in his hand.

CJ's mind was racing. There was more than coincidence involved in Derrick James's incineration and a spool of barbed wire in the back of a burned-out VW bus. CJ knew it all tied back into Brenda Mathison's murder somehow.

The sergeant looked at CJ as though he had snapped. "Funny—funny as hell. Now, can you ID our John Doe or not?"

"Your John Doe here is what's left of Derrick James," said CJ. "I was supposed to meet him earlier tonight." Halfway through the sentence, CJ wished he could have taken the words back.

Sergeant Dellems immediately wanted to pat himself on the back. He had let CJ step beyond the bounds of official police procedure, and CJ had not only given him the one piece of missing information he needed, but linked himself to the victim in one slip of the tongue. Dellems grinned at his luck.

CJ crouched down in a deep kneebend and started feeling along the bus's rear bumper. "How about shining your light my way again?" asked CJ.

Still euphoric, Dellems obliged. CJ felt his way along the bumper until he found the blackened remnant of a license plate. He looked it over with the gleam of a collector in his eye. As badly charred as the license plate was, two-inch-high letters, CRT and the number 185 remained readily visible in the light, along with an unmistakable set of smaller letters that spelled out Oregon below.

CJ stood up. Sam Glenn called out to the sergeant, asking him if it was okay to let Morgan and Dittier go.

"You got all their vitals and their statement?" asked Dellems.

"As much as street people can give," said Glenn snidely.

"Then let 'em go. But tell them we may need to talk to them again."

Glenn did as he was told.

CJ suddenly wished he had Henry Bales's knack for making all the pieces of a puzzle join together in a perfect fit. He knew one thing for certain. The VW bus that he thought he had seen the week before outside the Grand River Tribe's place near Craig hadn't been a mirage. The van was right here, staring him in the face, a burned-out coffin for Derrick James. But exactly where Derrick James fit into the whole Grand River jigsaw puzzle had CJ stumped. One thing for sure, Derrick James had to fit.

CJ rubbed the puncture wound in his hand and continued staring at the license plate. When he finally looked up, Sam Glenn was standing at his side.

"Since you were supposed to meet the victim earlier, we'll need a statement, Floyd," said Dellems, his euphoria from CJ's quick victim ID passed. The ring of authority had returned to his voice.

"How about first thing in the morning?" asked CJ.

"Right now," said the sergeant. "As soon as we finish up here." The sergeant's tone made Sam Glenn look especially pleased.

CJ wiggled his toes and felt the water inside his shoes squishing around. The snow had stopped. But he knew it was only a lull. There would be more accumulation by the morning rush. He bent over to reexamine the Oregon plate. CJ ran his injured hand across the face of the plate just once and decided that even with the most skillful repaint job, the plate would never bring more than a dollar and a half.

Eighteen

The District Three police station in Five Points was a musty, echoing, long-span prestressed concrete building that had been the first structure of its kind erected west of the Mississippi after the Korean War. During its construction the building had been front-page news because its basement had been designed to serve the people of Five Points as a civil defense bunker in the event of thermonuclear war.

Like the onslaught of prefabricated governmental buildings that had their birth during the Cold War, the District Three station had failed to serve either the government or the people very well. The basement had become a moldy, rat-infested, frequently flooded nuisance rather than a safe house for the people of Five Points. And it was rumored that the entire building might have to be boarded up because it was filled with enough asbestos to kill most of the people it had been designed to protect.

It was past midnight by the time CJ and Sergeant Dellems sat down across from each other in a small, poorly lit interrogation room that was furnished with only a wobbly 1950s-vintage library table and two institutional gray trash cans.

On their way to the station, CJ had noticed that the sole of his waterlogged left shoe had pulled away from its leather upper. The shoes were $150 cap-toed Florsheims, barely two weeks old. CJ decided he would pass the cost of a new pair of shoes along to the judge. He bent down to stuff the edge of his sock back through the opening in his shoe. When he looked back up, Dellems had a spiral-bound notebook flipped open and a ballpoint pen poised ready to write.

"We're running a set of prints on your Mr. James, just to make certain he's who you say he is. In the meantime, so I have it for the record, what time did you say the two of you were supposed to meet? And, just for the record, why don't you tell me why."

CJ didn't like Dellems's tone. "We were supposed to hook around seven-thirty or eight."

"Where?" pressed Dellems.

CJ didn't want to give Dellems a reason to send out the troops to hammer on Rosie, so he bent back a little corner on the truth. He figured that since Dellems hadn't seen the direction he had come from when he walked up to the Volkswagen bus, then Dellems had no way of knowing that he had come from the den. "At Mae's," said CJ.

"They close at ten," said Dellems. "Seems like somehow a couple of hours just got up and flew away."

"I spent them with friends," said CJ.

"I bet." Dellems jotted something in his book. When

he noticed how intently CJ was watching him, he hunched over and shadowed the notebook with his arm like he was trying to keep CJ from stealing answers off his exam.

"Bet Rosie's is popping tonight," said the sergeant.

CJ knew the sergeant was sniffing for a reason to raid the den, and it bothered him. The best Rosie could gross, even on Fat Saturday, was fifteen or twenty grand. And out of that he had to pay for equipment rental, bartenders, dealers, and croupiers. Not to mention 10 percent to a snake-oil-selling city councilman who peddled black enterprise zones at the same time he sold protection for the den. CJ knew the councilman would sell Rosie out in a second if he could figure out a way to make a hundred dollars more than Rosie paid him to have the police look the other way. When all was said and done, Rosie would barely clear enough to make the down payment on a new car for Etta Lee. CJ was about to tell the sergeant to go join the war on drugs or run out and arrest the president of an S&L when Sam Glenn appeared at the door, rapping on the glass. Glenn had a Cheshire cat smile on his face that made him look like the lead singer in a 1930s musical extravaganza ready to burst into song. Dellems moved from the table toward the door.

"Back in a minute," he said, moving Glenn out of CJ's vision once he was out in the hall. When the sergeant reentered the room, all pretense at courtesy had disappeared. "Looks like our John Doe wasn't the victim of an unlucky car fire at all. Turns out he was killed."

Although Dellems wasn't telling CJ anything he didn't already suspect, CJ tried to look surprised. "Tough world."

Dellems started to lecture CJ in a gravelly monotone. "We can do things real fast around here nowadays, Floyd. It's not like the old days when your uncle was hustling bonds. We're in the computer age now. Our print people made your boy James in half an hour. He's who you said he was all right. And guess what. He's wanted on a couple of outstanding warrants. Bet I really didn't have to tell you that, though."

CJ remained silent, hoping that Dellems would blabber on and fill in a few more blanks on Derrick James.

"We didn't even need to call the pathologist in to add this one to the homicide sheet. It seems that when the morgue wagon boys moved the body they found a couple of rags stuffed down your boy Derrick's throat. And, just for good measure, his windpipe was crushed—probably from a piece of barbed wire they found at the scene. You know, those two things could make it real hard for a man to breathe." Dellems paused, put his foot up on the edge of a chair, and looked at CJ for a response.

CJ had been thinking that maybe Razor D had killed Derrick, but he knew that Razor D liked guns. "What's your point, Dellems?" asked CJ, referring to the sergeant by his name for the first time all night.

"I want to know why you were supposed to meet some white kid at night down in the Points a couple of hours before he's murdered. Sounds a whole lot to me like a drug deal gone sour. Shame on you, Floyd. I always pictured you as a whiskey head, like your uncle. Never figured you for dope."

"You're crazy, Dellems," said CJ, who had been interrogated by policemen a lot more skilled than Dellems would ever be. He knew that the only reason he wasn't being questioned by a homicide detective was because they were all in bed. And he knew that Dellems was still just a slow-thinking patrol cop with good-behavior stripes. If he worked Dellems right, he could leave the interrogation room with the information advantage tilted his way. He decided to string Dellems along, hoping to get a better line on who had been pulling Derrick James's strings.

"I was supposed to meet the James kid about my car. He claimed he knew who trashed it out," said CJ.

"Yeah, I heard somebody did a hammer job on your car, too bad," said Dellems sarcastically. "But you're only singing part of the song. I want the real link between a gas station burglary, that car you baby, and James." Dellems phrased the question as if he already had the answer in hand.

"Don't know," said CJ. "Maybe he just walked in on Rosie's burglary by mistake."

"Nope," said Dellems. "I think the connection is you."

CJ didn't know where Dellems was headed, so all he said was, "Me?"

"Yeah, you, Floyd. And don't act like you don't know what I'm talking about. You know as well as me that cashing in on the outstanding warrants on James could put a guy like you in cigars for a couple of months. Or have you retired from hunting bounties on the side?"

Dellems's assessment was so far off the mark that CJ decided to let his fat-headed ego keep fanning the wrong flames.

"You got a law against what I do?" asked CJ.

"No, but bounty hunters knot my gut," said Dellems.

"Come on, Floyd. Tracking down a nineteen-year-old kid for a couple of out-of-date warrants. I thought you were more in demand than that."

"A job's a job," said CJ, trying to keep a straight face.

Dellems took his foot off the chair and sat down. "Here's the way I see it. I think James probably did see whoever it was that broke into Roosevelt's place and he probably saw who got to your car. The way I figure it, a little white puke like him would stick out like a sore thumb in the Points, unless of course he was moving dope. You know how your people give dope dealers around here a free ride. My guess is that in between dealing his dope, he wanted a little extra cash to supply you with the information about who fucked up your car. When he tried to shake you down, you ran a search for priors on him, and bingo, up popped the outstanding warrants."

"Say you're right," said CJ, playing along. "Who kissed him off?"

"Hell, probably the same people who trashed your car. Dopeheads, gang-bangers, second-rate thugs—maybe Razor D or some of his boys. They wouldn't think more than a second about snuffing some white doper who'd seen them committing a crime."

Some of what Dellems said made sense. But concluding that CJ was after Derrick James to make a profit on a couple of outstanding warrants emphasized why Dellems was still behind the wheel of a patrol car after twenty years.

"Where did you go after you left Mae's?" asked Dellems.

"Over to the Empire Lounge. I had a couple of beers," said CJ, still trying to steer Dellems away from placing him at Rosie's den. CJ knew that if necessary, KK Woodson, the loan-sharking ex-con bartender at the Empire Lounge, would give Dellems a corroborating yarn five minutes long, punctuated with dates, times, what CJ had had to drink, and whether the drink had been with or without a lime.

Dellems made an entry in his notebook and pushed on. "How long had you known James?"

"It's two A.M., Sarge, how about cutting me some slack. I didn't kill your boy," said CJ.

"How long," repeated Dellems.

"I met him once. A few days ago at Mae's. Like I said, he told me that he could finger the people who trashed my car. I never saw him again until I looked inside that VW bus."

Dellems checked his watch. He knew that CJ hadn't killed Derrick James. But he was enjoying playing detective. When he passed his preliminary investigation notes on to the homicide boys, they'd see that he wasn't just another jelly-roll Dunkin' Donuts cop.

Dellems stood up and walked around the table to CJ. He sat on the table's edge a foot from CJ. Hunched over, he leaned into CJ's face. "When I hand over my report, the homicide dickheads are going to get a shot at you. And you know detectives. They'll fill in everything you've left out. The only people on the murder scene were a couple of street people collecting cans, and then you. And the street people didn't know Derrick James. When the homicide boys finish gnawing at your connection to James, you may wish you'd sung your song to me," said Dellems.

CJ wanted to laugh. Dellems sounded like some grade-B actor playing a cop. CJ knew that homicide cops resented being called dickheads. Only criminals used the term. Another cop calling a homicide detective a dick-head was almost a call to arms.

"I'll take my chances," said CJ. He knew it would be a couple of days before anyone from homicide would get around to talking to him. The first people the police would want to talk to would be possible eyewitnesses, and that meant that CJ was going to have to track down Morgan and Dittier before the cops got to them.

Sam Glenn reentered the room, hoping for a chance to gloat. CJ had been countering Glenn's moves with Mavis for so long that he had programmed himself to respond to Glenn in ways that perpetually kept the patrol-man off balance. This time CJ's response was one of his best.

"And tell those dickheads of yours that they can kiss my ass," shouted CJ, springing from his chair. "Now charge me with something or I'll have my lawyer shove his false arrest briefcase down your throat."

Caught off guard by CJ's outburst, Dellems, who still wanted to appear in control, quickly decided that his best strategy would be to do exactly as CJ had asked. "We've had our little chat, Floyd." It was a conversation-ending signal to Glenn that regardless of CJ's bravado it was Dellems who was bringing the interrogation to an end. "But I'll pass your sentiments on to the boys in homicide, and you can count on me not changing a single word."

Sam Glenn flashed an obligatory subordinate smile.

CJ knew he had pushed Dellems to the limit. He was in a police interrogation room with two street cops and no witnesses. He decided he had strung the process far enough along. He looked at Glenn and grumbled, "Done with me?"

Dellems, tired of sparring too, said, "Don't let the door hit you in the ass."

CJ breezed past Glenn and was out the door before Dellems had second thoughts.

It was two-forty in the morning when CJ flipped on the lights in his living room. On his way home he had shoved everything about the Mathison case, Derrick James, and the Grand River Tribe to the back of his mind. All he wanted at the moment were two dry feet and a bed.

Since his divorce, the four-room single-bath apartment above his office had been CJ's home. He had spent sixteen years sharing the apartment with his uncle as a child. Everyone considered CJ a Colorado native, but the first two years of his life had been spent in Ohio. CJ's father had always wanted to be an engineer, but instead he worked for Baldwin Piano in Cincinnati for over thirty years. The factory overlooked the city, neatly pocketed into the side of a hill. His father was a scale design stringer for baby grands. Every day for three and a half decades he would calculate the piano wire tension needed to produce a single perfect note. Everyone called him Keys. He could play a trumpet like Satchmo, but he never chased his dreams. CJ's mother threatened to leave him if he ever did. One day when CJ was almost two, his father decided to take her up on her threat. He was back home in a month, but by then she had dumped CJ in Denver with his uncle on her way to L.A. His mother never surfaced in his life again. His father made sporadic visits to see him until he was ten. After that the visits stopped. CJ didn't know if his father was alive, dead, or just uninterested.

When CJ moved back into the apartment the week

after he and DeeAnn had finally called it quits, the only thing he could remember about the place was that he had hated living there when he was growing up. But strangely, after a few weeks, he started to feel at home. The apartment's ten-foot-high Victorian ceilings, Gothic mountains to CJ as a child, made him feel less closed in as an adult. To enhance the feeling even more, CJ painted every room eggshell white.

All the rooms but the study in the back were furnished with a hodgepodge collection of couches, tables, and chairs that an interior decorator might call eclectic. The study was a pint-sized room, barely ten-by-ten, with a pocket door entry that CJ and Rosie had installed to save space. A woven wicker desk and high-backed wicker chair were shoved against the wall opposite the entry. A matching magazine rack overflowing with copies of *Gray's Sporting Journal, The Antique Trader,* and other collectors' magazines sat alongside the desk. A turn-of-the-century Mormon glider rocker was tucked into the only remaining space in the room. The walls on either side of the desk were lined with license plates, from the ten-inch-high turn-of-the-century baseboard to the ceiling cove. There were thirty-one plates in all, ranging in color from sunshine yellow to mauve. CJ's Deer Trail municipal plate was sitting on the desktop along with a box of drywall push pins, ready to be hung.

CJ tossed his coat onto the rocker and sat down at the desk to take off his shoes. His socks were in that stage between damp and soaking wet. He had one sock off and had started on the second when he looked over at his birthday purchase, the Deer Trail plate he still hadn't hung. For years he had kept a spot for the Deer Trail tag just below a 1915 Denver municipal plate with the number 1. CJ held the license plate up to the empty spot and tacked it onto the wall with the heel of his shoe. He stood back, admiring his latest find. Suddenly it occurred to him that if the deal with the renovation people went through he would have to move. He reached into his shirt pocket for a cheroot. He chewed on the end of the cigar for a few minutes, remembering how difficult each plate had been to find. The moment he lit his cheroot, CJ decided that his apartment and the business below were the only tangible evidence that CJ Floyd had spent some time at life's treacherous wheel. He decided it wasn't the time to sell. He inhaled deeply on the cigar, slumped back into his rocker, and made a couple of mental notes. First thing in the morning he would call Herman Currothers and tell him that the renovation people could take a flying leap. Then he was going to have to find Morgan and Dittier before the cops. CJ pulled his wrinkled coat out from under him and dropped it across his chest. He finished kicking off his other sock. He laid his cigar in the black-lacquered 42nd River Patrol Group's tenth reunion souvenir ashtray on his desk. Before he could make another mental note, he was sound asleep.

Nineteen

The alleys behind the high-rise office buildings downtown were prime locations for Morgan Williams and Dittier Atkins to enjoy a good night's sleep and not have to watch out for the police or for thugs looking to rob them of their last quarter. If they arrived early enough, between six o'clock and seven, they could prop up their cardboard houses in the back doorway of one of the businesses, then stuff the corners with newspapers and rags to block out the wind, pull out their bedrolls, and settle in for the night. There were always easy pickings in the trash Dumpsters too. The business world didn't place the same value on aluminum cans as Morgan and Dittier.

"Come on, Dittier, my cart's half full," said Morgan. "Quit your slow-assing. It's gonna snow."

Morgan was still thinking about stumbling across a burning van and a dead man the night before, when ominous slate-gray snow clouds started gathering in the west.

"Come on, champ," repeated Morgan, a muscular cigar stump of a black man with a shaved head and skin as smooth as a carnival Nubian's. "If we hurry up we'll be early enough to stake out a spot behind First National. We get one of those and shit—in the morning we'll be dry as a bone. Quit your moping. I told you yesterday to let me pull that tooth. Now you're paying the price."

Dittier pulled his empty shopping cart up next to Morgan's.

"Better get to looking harder or the only thing you'll have to show for a day of scarfing is a cartful of snow," joked Morgan.

On their trip down the alley between 16th and 17th avenues, they struck gold. Morgan spotted a man emptying trash. They stepped back into a doorway. Peeking around the corner, they watched the man finish. Then, very deliberately, the two of them approached the Dumpster.

"Keep a lookout, we don't want to get run off," whispered Morgan. He shinned up the side of the eight-foot-high Dumpster and dropped down inside. It was empty except for a corner filled with greasy shopping bags, papers, and a treasure chest of aluminum cans. The wind was already howling through the Dumpster, swirling around the trash inside. A sudden gust filled Morgan's eyes with dust and grit. Winter gnats buzzed around his head. The bottom of the Dumpster was wet and slick. Morgan had to step carefully or risk falling into the ooze that covered the floor. He started tossing cans over the top to Dittier. Some still contained soda or beer. Their contents spilled onto Morgan's hands. He swatted at a bug, missed, and wiped his sticky hands on the front of his coat. When he finished hurling out the last can, he knew they almost had their limit.

Morgan climbed from the Dumpster, smiling. His cart was full. Dittier's was halfway there. Two full carts of cans, at $2 a pound, would bring $12. Since the Safeway up on 13th Avenue had installed a can crusher, Morgan no longer ran the risk of cutting up his hands or jamming a heel from smashing a day's collection of cans. Now he simply dumped them in the crusher and waited for the machine to spit out their money.

The can men made two more sweeps down the alleys behind 14th and 15th. Morgan surged ahead, carefully surveying every possibility. Dittier dragged behind.

"Damn it, you still ain't but half full," said Morgan, dropping back and examining Dittier's cart once again. "One of these days, I'm gonna quit looking out for you. You got me pulling all the load."

Dittier grimaced in pain, then looked sheepishly over at Morgan. Dittier's sad black face was a dry wash of wrinkles from too many years in the sun, his eyes were bloodshot from lack of sleep, and he had a four-day patchy growth of beard.

"I didn't mean that, Dittier. I just want us to beat the weather. If we have to drag these cans over to the Safeway in the snow it'll be too late to get a good spot, and we'll spend the night freezing our asses. Understand?"

Dittier nodded yes.

"Come here, champ, let me take a look at that jaw," said Morgan.

Dittier screwed up his face while Morgan patted his swollen jaw. "Shit, it's twice as big as yesterday, and it's real warm too. Better let me take a look inside."

Dittier opened his mouth wide, like a child showing off a new tooth.

"No wonder it's killing you. There ain't no top part

of that tooth left. The damn thing's broke off down to the gum. You better let me pull it. The pain ain't gonna stop till I give what's left of that sucker some fresh air and sunshine."

Dittier gave Morgan a long questioning look, then nodded okay.

Morgan walked around to his cart and opened up the smaller of two plastic bags he kept attached to the sides. Inside were a few tools, an oily parka, and a blistered leather shaving kit. He pulled out a pair of pliers. Then he walked over to the other bag and rummaged through old boots and shoes until he found some mildewed paper towels. Morgan's house, an old Amana freezer box painted with Thompson's Water Seal, was neatly folded flat and tied to the bottom of the shopping cart. The clothesline holding it down was unraveling. Morgan teased out an extra flap of cardboard from inside the box and tore off a piece the size of a half-dollar. He wrapped two paper towels around the cardboard and handed it to Dittier.

"Hold on to this, champ," said Morgan. He reached into his coat pocket, took out a half-empty pint of Old Crow, and soaked another towel for rubbing down the pliers.

"Now, hold out your towel," he said.

Dittier obliged. Morgan poured half of the remaining whiskey over it.

"You can kill what's left of it, champ." He handed Dittier the bottle.

Dittier swallowed the rest of the whiskey in one gulp and gave the empty bottle back to Morgan. Morgan looked at it for a moment, shook his head, and tossed the bottle aside.

"The things I do for you," said Morgan, mussing Dittier's coarse, matted hair. "When I'm done pulling what's left of that tooth, I want you to bite down on that paper towel, but not too hard, okay?"

Dittier nodded his head up and down rapidly.

"It'll be good for disinfecting the wound, and biting on it will help stop the bleedin'. Now open up."

Dittier opened his mouth with a grunt. Morgan struggled with the tooth for over fifteen minutes, while Dittier stoically endured the pain. Neither of them expected bleeding to become a complication. Morgan always claimed that getting a wound "dirty" was the risk. During their years on the streets every cut, scrape, and gash had always stopped bleeding. This time was different.

"Hell, I can't figure it. I got the rest of that tooth right here," said Morgan, rolling the bloody root between his thumb and forefinger. "Let me take another look. Maybe I can see where the bleedin' is coming from."

Morgan took a makeup compact from his shaving kit, opened it, and held the cracked mirror inside up next to Dittier's thin face.

"Maybe I can get a better look with this." He pushed the mirror as far back into Dittier's mouth as he could. "Try not to breathe, champ, you keep fogging up the mirror."

Dittier took a gulp of air and held his breath.

Morgan angled the mirror around until it was covered with blood. "Beats me. I don't know where the bleedin' is coming from, champ. It don't look real good." He wiped off the mirror with a towel and closed the compact with a snap.

Dittier let out a long warm stream of air and a trail of condensation rose in front of his face.

Still puzzled, Morgan took off his faded cap and

rubbed his forehead. "We better head for Denver General and have somebody there take a look before you bleed out on me like a stuck pig. At least it's on the way to the Safeway. We'll get you patched up and with a little luck still have time to dump our cans and scope out a good spot for the night."

He handed Dittier another paper towel. "Bite down on this. And button your coat up all the way. Ain't summer out here," said Morgan, as they headed for Denver General.

Fifteen blocks north Razor D was huddled with another man beneath the 23rd Street viaduct that bridges Five Points with Denver's Hispanic neighborhoods. Like Dittier's, Razor D's jaw was also throbbing. He was rubbing his hands together, rocking back and forth, trying to stay warm. The other man stood as stiff as one of the rusty steel girders supporting the viaduct. His cheeks were rosy from the cold and he was wearing an old painter's hat. A convoy of gasoline tanker trucks headed for the mountains rumbled overhead. The traffic noise and the pain in his jaw made Razor D's head want to explode. A battery of streetlights along the viaduct flickered on, just as heavy wet flakes of snow started to hit the pavement. Filtered through the light, the snow looked like flecks of silver.

"Sure, I'll kill the motherfucker," mumbled Razor D, through the stainless steel arch bar wires holding his jaw in place. "Look what the son of a bitch did to my jaw." Razor held his hand up to his face. "I think it's infected. You need Floyd offed tonight?"

The other man looked at Razor D and shook his head. "Hold your piss, James Bond. You already screwed up on the deal with his car and Floyd damned near kicked your brains out the other night. How about this time you get it right?"

"Watch your mouth, pussy face. I can numb your nuts too," said Razor D, in a singsongy clenched-teeth voice as he pulled out a .25 Raven and waved it at the man.

The man looked at Razor D as if he knew Razor D wouldn't use the gun unless he pushed a few more of his buttons. "You're talking to me, goofball, not Floyd or one of your cokehead Blades. Put that thing away."

Razor D hesitated a few moments before slipping the gun back into his pocket.

"Floyd's sniffing around too many bushes. Gotta remember he's the kind of junkyard dog who just might figure this whole business out, and cost me a bundle along the way. I want to see his name on the last page of the newspaper by the end of the week," said the man.

Razor D beamed the toothy grin of an acne-faced teenager in braces.

"Take him out in Five Points, not around here," said the man.

"My pleasure," mumbled Razor D.

"And this time don't be sloppy."

It was the second wrong chord he had struck with Razor D. Razor's eyes narrowed and he was just about to spit at the man, when he remembered his mouth was wired shut. He caught himself before he made the mistake. Instead, he mumbled, "Fuck you and your momma too."

Twenty

When CJ heard from Rosie that Razor Dog Hicks had skipped bond, it made his day—for about an hour. CJ wanted an official reason for displaying Hicks's photograph in his gallery of rogues, and technically he didn't have one. Now Hicks met at least one requirement for inclusion: he had skipped his bond. The news also reminded CJ that it had been a week since his ass-stomping at the 7-Eleven. The vision in his right eye had just about returned to normal, and the night before, for the first time since the beating, he had been able to turn on his side and sleep without pain.

When his old friend Vernon Lowe, part-time Five Points mortician and part-time Denver County Morgue assistant, called CJ from Denver General Hospital, where the city morgue was housed, to tell him that early that morning Sergeant Dellems had found Razor D with a .25 caliber bullet hole behind his left ear and an exit wound the size of a quarter above his right eye, CJ felt a sense of victory that lasted only a few seconds. He realized the cops wouldn't work too hard at trying to find the killer of a sociopath like Razor D, but he knew that they'd go through the motions. He also expected that he himself was probably at the top of their list of suspects. There had to be a tie-in between Derrick James's murder and Razor D's. CJ could sense it but he couldn't put his finger on the connection. The fact that Sergeant Dellems had found Razor D's body was a bad sign, because CJ knew it would give Dellems one more reason to lean on him. Razor D had been dumped in with the barbecue piñon pine behind Poppa Loomis's carriage house, left there like a sack of potatoes. CJ wanted to gloat, but Vietnam had taught him that you always lost a part of yourself when you gloated over your enemy's death.

Vernon Lowe joked that since Razor D didn't have a big toe to tie his toe tag to, the tag kept falling off every time someone came in to take a look at the body. "Death tags just won't hang on no little toe," Vernon said. CJ didn't ask him why he didn't change it to the other foot, but he did ask Vernon if Razor D had a gash on his chin.

"Sure did," said Vernon. "And a broken jaw. The cops are looking for one of them Henchmen, but I heard 'em mention your name too. They ain't got no murder weapon though. I know that," he added, as if it was meant to be a warning.

After Vernon hung up, CJ subtracted Razor D's name from the list of people who might like to see him either off the Mathison case or dead. He now knew for sure that Razor D had been the one in the manhole behind the 7-Eleven, but he suspected there was more to the attack than Razor D simply trying to settle a score. He should have felt a sense of relief, but there were at least two dozen more 26th Avenue Blades, and CJ knew that some eager Razor D avenger might want to build his reputation by carrying out the orders of his dead leader's ghost.

CJ stripped Razor D's photograph from the rogues' gallery wall and tore it in half. He sat in silence for a while and thought about life's violent hairpin turns. He thought about his own harsh teenage years and wondered what his chances of ending up like Razor D would be on today's Five Points streets. His thoughts were interrupted by a call from Judge Mathison, who told him to keep pushing on the case. Then the judge surprised CJ by admitting that he was probably the reason Brenda had chosen the out-of-sync life that had gotten her killed. "I pushed her too hard early on to be a man when she was just a girl," he said, before hanging up.

CJ spent the rest of the day trying to track down Morgan and Dittier. Any other time they would have been somewhere crisscrossing Five Points, pushing their shopping carts, scouring the neighborhood for cans. But CJ hadn't been able to locate them. He chalked up their disappearance to six inches of fresh snow, and he never would have known to finally head for Denver General Hospital if Julie hadn't offhandedly mentioned, as she prepared to leave for the day, that Dittier had been complaining of a toothache earlier, when he and Morgan had come to rake leaves.

By late evening CJ had traced the two ex–rodeo cowboys to Denver General, where he talked to the doctor who had treated Dittier. The doctor pointed CJ in the direction the two men had gone when they left.

The time and temperature sign on the Cadillac dealership across the street from the hospital read 15 degrees when CJ rushed back out onto Bannock Street looking for them. The wind was gusting out of the west, and snowdrifts had piled up against any impediment to the wind. When CJ caught a glimpse of the two men digging a couple of shopping carts out of a two-foot snowdrift next to the emergency room wheelchair ramp, he started running toward them.

"Morgan, Dittier, wait up," shouted CJ, struggling to keep his balance on the icy sidewalk.

Dittier kept digging, but Morgan stopped and glanced back. When he realized it was CJ he tapped Dittier on the shoulder and told him to stop.

CJ slid to a stop in front of one of the carts and he braced himself on the handle. "You two are hard to find," he said, out of breath.

"Been all evening getting Dittier patched up. But he's as good as new now," said Morgan.

Dittier wiped a clump of wet snow off the cardboard he had been using to scoop up snow. He was still biting on a wad of gauze. His right cheek was puffed out, so he looked like a child with mumps.

"I think your wheels are frozen to the ground," said Morgan, giving Dittier's cart a kick. "Better get back to digging out."

Dittier returned to the task of freeing his cart.

Morgan set aside the two warped cedar shingles that he had been using to dig out his own cart. "Figured you'd be looking us up after the other night. Too bad about that dead guy. You know, I seen him around Five Points more than once."

"Where?" asked CJ.

"Mostly goin' in and out of Rosie's den. When it comes to what's shaking around the Points, Dittier and me, we got real big eyes. I seen him a couple of times eatin' at the Burger King over on Lafayette and once I ran up on him arguing with a couple of gang-bangers that hang out peddling dope behind the old Rossonian Club."

Derrick James had had a higher profile around Five Points than CJ had suspected. "Have the cops been around to see you yet?" said CJ.

"Not yet. But I expect they will. Bad thing is, we'll probably end up havin' to tell them the truth, that Dittier seen the whole car-torching thing, right from the start," said Morgan.

Dittier finally freed the wheels of his shopping cart from a two-inch-thick chunk of ice. The wheels made a loud clunk. He tapped Morgan on the shoulder, wanting him to take a look.

"Good," said Morgan.

"Think you can get Dittier to fill me in on what went down?" said CJ, watching Dittier roll his cart back and forth.

"Sure," said Morgan. "But first Dittier and me got to find us a spot."

CJ knew that the two can men had dozens of places they hunkered down in during a storm. He also knew that if he let them disappear, he might not find them for a week. "How about getting out of this storm for a while over at the Empire Lounge?" asked CJ. "After that I'll spring for a room at the Ramada over on Colfax." CJ knew the Ramada's price and the motel rules by heart—$37.50 and no disturbing the peace.

"You up for the Empire?" asked CJ, tapping Dittier on the arm. Dittier's head immediately bobbed up and down.

"Slide those carts inside one another and you can

shove them into the back of my Jeep. It'll be a tight squeeze for the three of us up front, but it's only a few blocks," said CJ.

"Beats walking," said Morgan. He motioned Dittier in the direction of CJ's Jeep. "Let's go, Dittier, looks like we're gonna ride this weather out in style."

Dittier froze in his tracks, shook his head no and started pointing at his cart full of cans.

"Damn," said Morgan, realizing why Dittier was being so stubborn. "We'll have to dump our cans out in the back of your Jeep. We ain't leaving 'em here."

"Fine," said CJ, turning into the snow and running to get the Jeep. "I'll be right back."

As soon as CJ pulled his Jeep up next to the carts, he heard the sound of aluminum cans banging on top of one another in the cargo space in the back. It reminded him of small-arms fire against the metal hull of the *Cape Star*. Morgan slipped his shopping cart inside Dittier's and lifted them both into the back on top of the cans.

"Gonna have a sticky snowball back there when we pull our carts and cans out," said Morgan.

The problem hadn't crossed CJ's mind. He was cold and wet. He leaned across the front seat to hold open the passenger door. "Let's go," he said, already anticipating the warmth of the Empire and a beer.

Morgan and Dittier piled into the front seat, bringing the smell of their unwashed bodies with them. CJ took off, fishtailing, leaving a set of wide S-shaped tracks in the freshly fallen snow.

Colfax Avenue is billed as the longest street in the United States. It starts in Aurora, an eastern suburb of Denver, and ends twenty miles later in the foothills to the west. Over the 120 years of its existence Colfax has boasted every imaginable tenant, from gold rush miners to high-profile politicians, from endless cheap motels to Kitty's House of Porn. The Empire Lounge had stood at the southwest corner of Colfax and Race in a blue-collar racially mixed neighborhood for nearly thirty years. If you want Denver's best brain-numbing margarita and a burrito bulging with juicy, sweet Colorado ranch-fed beef, the Empire Lounge is the place to go.

A thirty-mile-per-hour wind gust blew CJ through the lounge's front door with Morgan and Dittier in tow. "Son of a bitch," mumbled CJ. The wind kicked at the door again as CJ forced it shut.

The lounge was divided into two equal squares separated by a row of waist-high wooden planters filled with plastic tropical ferns. The ferns were so dusty that the leaves were sand-colored instead of green. To the right of the planters was a bar, and behind it, counter to ceiling, entryway to exit, were two thirty-foot-long beveled-glass mirrors. In true camera obscura fashion, the mirrors always reflected the movement of everyone in the room. The food service area and kitchen were to the left of the ferns. Patrons placed their orders at the back of the room. When their orders were ready a voice from the kitchen shouted out a name. From there on out it was serve yourself, down to grabbing your own napkin and utensils, condiments, and corrugated cardboard minipackets of pepper and salt. You had to traipse back over to the bar if you wanted a drink. There was no bar service in the room. Whether high noon or midnight, both sides of the lounge were always dark, and the Empire's customers seemed to like it that way.

CJ stopped halfway down the bar, pulled out a stool,

and sat down. He watched his reflection in the mirror. Morgan and Dittier followed his lead.

The bartender was tall and skinny, a long-faced greyhound-looking black man. He was wearing a yellow, black, and green African skullcap. A large gold earring hung from his right ear. Up close it would have been easy to see the pockmarks on his forehead and cheeks, but from CJ's vantage point, ten feet away, his dark brown skin looked unmarred.

"KK," said CJ, tapping his fingers drum-roll fashion on the bar. "How about something to warm us up?"

The bartender eased past his cash register and beyond the only other two people seated at the bar. The cash register area was the only well-lit area in the room. CJ knew the added light was for the benefit of whoever was tending bar, so they could quickly locate the billy club and semiautomatic pistol in the small compartment beneath the till.

CJ watched KK as he loped toward them. He stopped directly in front of CJ and, in what seemed like one fluid motion, retrieved two dirty shot glasses, wiped down the adjacent two-foot length of bar, dealt out three cocktail napkins, and said, "You just missed the cops. And they was singing your name."

"At this time of night?" asked CJ. "You're yanking my chain, KK."

"Not our local variety. These boys was CBI. You must be into something sure enough kinky or Canon City bad to bring those neo-Nazis out." The state penitentiary in Canon City owned a decade of KK's life.

If the Colorado Bureau of Investigation was on his trail, CJ suspected that the papillomavirus cat might be out of the bag. The CBI was Colorado's version of the FBI:

spit-and-polish lawmen who dealt with high-profile law-breakers involved in cross-county crimes. One hundred years earlier they would have been Texas Rangers, vigilantes, or both. Anybody from the governor to a county sheriff could call in the CBI. CJ was hoping that neither one had sicced them on his tail.

"What did they want?" asked CJ.

"Asked me if you were in here the other night." KK smiled. "What could I do? They was cops. I lied."

CJ smiled back. "Those dickheads were running down an alibi I dropped on dimwit Dellems the other night."

"I told them you was in here all right, polishing off Negra Modelos, watching the Nuggets game, and chasing every other beer with a tequila shot if the Nuggets dropped behind."

Dittier laughed. Morgan nudged him lightly on the leg and told him to stop.

CJ realized that he hadn't told KK what they all wanted to drink. "Set Dittier and Morgan here up," said CJ. "Anything they'd like."

"CC and 7," said Morgan. "Same for Dittier."

"Those CBI boys say anything else?" asked CJ.

"Nah. After they asked about you and I said my piece, they just looked the place over like they was health inspectors or something. The kitchen, the eating area in the other room, and finally behind the bar. Guess when they didn't find no cockroaches around they decided to leave."

"Any District Three cops drop in to chew the fat?" asked CJ, wondering if Dellems had also made the rounds.

"Not a one," said KK. "But I heard somebody

dropped a dime on Razor D and the cops is lookin' to see if you're carrying that kind of change."

"Wasn't me," said CJ, sensing that something wasn't right. CBI types wouldn't be after him unless they were playing gofer for the FBI, cooperating with a neighboring state on a case, or knitting together the goods on a multi-county Colorado crime. He reflected a moment, and reasoned that the only honey strong enough to draw flies like the CBI might just be a federal judge. He debated whether to call Judge Mathison or one of his two flunkies right then, but decided that for the moment, the CBI would have to play second-fiddle to Morgan and Dittier. He still needed to know exactly what Dittier had seen when Derrick James was killed on Saturday night. CJ spun his stool around toward Morgan. "How about filling me in on the van fire the other night?"

"The whole damn thing was weird," said Morgan, nursing his CC and 7 as if it might very well be his last.

"Why?" asked CJ.

" 'Cause when Dittier and me first started watching what was goin' down, the guy who got killed and the man he was with was acting as thick as thieves. Ain't that right, Dittier?"

Dittier nodded in agreement before stuffing his mouth full of bite-sized pretzels that KK had placed on the bar. Morgan gave him a look that said *slow down*.

"Dittier was the one who got me to lookin' at them close. Somethin' about the champ here, he ain't never been one to miss a wounded stray or people with bad intentions. He can pretty much spot them both right off. Anyway, real quick Dittier is nudgin' me and doin' one of his little dances he does when trouble's in the wind. Then he starts pointin', and through the windshield I see a woman in the van. Next thing I know the guy the kid had been talking to takes two steps aside, and the woman backs the van right into the kid. Didn't hurt him too bad, just knocked him off his feet. She didn't have no running start. But I bet he came close to pissin' his pants. The man grabbed the kid by his collar and pretty much yanked him straight up off the ground."

Dittier began tapping Morgan on the shoulder. When he had Morgan's full attention, Dittier pointed his right hand at CJ. With his thumb extended skyward and his index finger pointing forward, he made the sign of a gun.

"Now, I didn't see no gun," said Morgan. "But if Dittier said there was a piece, there was. One thing for sure, that kid wasn't about to get in that van without somethin' powerful nudging him along."

"How come?" asked CJ, reaching for what was now the last pretzel in the bowl.

" 'Cause the look on his face said he was scared to death," said Morgan.

CJ looked surprised. "You were close enough to see that?"

Morgan chuckled. He started spinning the empty pretzel bowl around in a circle on the bar. "Me and the champ here could sneak in the Vatican and spy on the pope and wouldn't nobody ever know. Yeah, we was that close."

Dittier smiled, picked up the bowl, and started waving it at KK, who was halfway down the bar.

"How about a refill on the pretzels?" asked CJ.

KK walked over with a bag of pretzels. He took the bowl from Dittier, gently placed it back down on the bar, and filled it with pretzels until they spilled onto the countertop.

Dittier glanced over at Morgan. Morgan frowned. Instead of grabbing a handful of pretzels, Dittier started eating them one at a time.

Morgan, used to taking time out for Dittier, went right back to his conversation with CJ. "Like I was saying, I could see that cowboy guy's face. You were in a war, CJ. You know the kind of look I mean."

CJ nodded that he did.

"He got in the van on the side away from us. The guy who had collared him was nudgin' him along. Next I seen the woman get out of the driver's seat. She must have gone to the back of the van. After a few minutes the woman and the guy Dittier claims had the gun got out of the van on the side away from us, on the other side of the street. I never got a clear look at the man's face 'cause he was wearin' a cowboy hat tipped down real low. A couple of minutes later Dittier spotted the smoke. Seems like it wasn't but a few seconds and smoke was seepin' from every corner of the van. Then the whole thing was on fire. Dittier wanted to run up and put the fire out. I damned near had to sit on him to hold him back. The fire department was there real quick, and the cops was right on their heels. We eased back into the alley when we saw the cops, but Sergeant Dellems spotted us right off. When it comes to dealin' with cops, Dittier and me learned our lesson a long time ago. It's better to be a mistaken witness than to end up takin' the blame. So I told Dellems that when we got there the van was already on fire."

Dittier looked at Morgan as if he wanted to say *you shouldn't lie*. Then he grabbed a handful of pretzels and stuffed them in his mouth.

"Every cop's not as gullible as Dellems," said CJ.

"You and Dittier were at the front door of the murder. The cops will hound you into telling the truth because they don't want to let the murderer slip out the back."

"Maybe, maybe not," said Morgan. "The only thing for certain is that me and Dittier and the cops spend a lot of time crisscrossing these streets. Whether we meet up or not's a different story."

CJ ordered another round of drinks, hoping the alcohol would quell Morgan's sudden urge to compete with the cops. "What about the woman?" asked CJ. "Did you get a good look at her?" CJ tilted his mug sideways, pouring the beer slowly down the side in order to cut down the head.

"She was white," said Morgan, "that's all I could tell."

"And the man?" asked CJ. "Was he white too?"

"Sure was," said Morgan. "But nothing about him stood out. Just plain vanilla white."

"Anything else?" asked CJ.

Morgan eyed Dittier. CJ could tell that Morgan was hesitant about saying what was on his mind.

Dittier gave Morgan a come-clean look that said *go on, tell him the rest*. When Morgan couldn't stand Dittier's truth serum stare any longer he gulped down the rest of his drink, then said, "Dittier swears there was someone else near the van."

Dittier shook his head up and down so rapidly it looked like a spring-loaded carnival doll's.

"But I didn't see nobody else at all," protested Morgan. "To tell you the truth, though, me and Dittier was lookin' from different angles. Dittier was crouched down fooling with the front of one of the wheels on his cart just before the kid got collared and pulled inside the van. He says somebody else was standing on the sidewalk on the side of the van we couldn't see. Dittier swears he saw a pair of legs. But when the fire started, I didn't see nobody but the guy in the cowboy hat and the woman run away."

"Was your mystery person a man?" asked CJ, looking at Dittier.

Dittier nodded yes.

"You've got one hell of a set of eyes," said CJ.

Dittier smiled.

CJ ordered another beer and leaned forward against the bar in heavy thought.

"What next?" asked Morgan.

"Can you two stay low-profile for a week? Out of the way of the cops?" asked CJ.

Morgan looked at Dittier. They both laughed. "We've got spots around town the cops wouldn't dream could hold a rat, much less a man," said Morgan.

"Pick one out and hunker down tight," said CJ.

"Done," said Morgan.

CJ reached for his wallet, pulled out four twenty-dollar bills, and handed them to Morgan. "Don't use your real names at the motel tonight." Morgan immediately gave two of the bills to Dittier. "Before you take cover, let me or Julie know where you'll be," said CJ.

"Sure thing. But how come you want us to drop out of sight?" asked Morgan.

"For one thing, there's a whole lot more to that van torching than meets the eye. I don't want some gung-ho District Three cop dogging the two of you, scratching around for an ox bone and causing me to miss bagging the whole damned ox." CJ paused. Then he looked sternly at the two men. "For another—remember those legs Dittier thinks he saw—could be old Crazylegs might have seen you too."

For the first time all evening Dittier's smile disappeared.

Morgan looked at him reassuringly. He slid his unfinished drink Dittier's way. Dittier drank it down.

"Your Mr. Crazylegs can't be no bigger, dumber, or meaner than a broke-dick bull, and Dittier and me ain't never settled up but one way with a bull—on top," said Morgan, rubbing his tarnished championship bull-riding belt buckle. A moment later he handed CJ a scrap of paper with the address of their latest spot.

CJ smiled. He knew Morgan meant what he said. For the two can men, Denver's streets were just a big rodeo arena. There was no way Morgan and Dittier would ever finish second.

As the three of them packed up to leave, KK walked over to settle their tab. "Funny, seeing you here again, CJ, after just passing all evening with you the other night," he said with a wink.

"I like the ambience and the beer," said CJ, forcing back a grin. "And if anyone asks about me again, especially your new friends from the CBI, tell them I went to Arizona for my health." CJ couldn't hold back the need to laugh any longer. When he did, Dittier chimed in.

Twenty-one

Midmorning the next day, CJ sat with his feet propped up on Rosie's desk, staring at photographs of Copley and Deere, trying to imagine both of their pictures on his rogues' gallery wall. The door to Rosie's office was open, so CJ had an unobstructed view of the first repair bay. Rosie was under the hood of the Bel Air, fine-tuning the newly installed four-barrel. CJ felt as though he had been playing Simon Says and constantly taking giant steps everywhere but toward solving the Mathison murder. He knew there had to be a link between Derrick James's murder and the Grand River Tribe, but he hadn't been able to identify the thread. Before coming to the garage he had been on the phone all morning. He had called Carson Technologies first and asked to speak to Womack, hoping to zero in on any connection between Carson and Derrick James. He was put on hold and forced to listen to elevator music for a good ten minutes. When Womack finally did come on the line, he said that he had never heard of Derrick James. He told CJ to try Spence or the judge and promptly hung up. CJ tried to get in touch with Spence, and then the judge, without any luck. Half an hour later Judge Mathison returned his call, but only to read CJ the riot act when he asked about Derrick James, shouting at him to quit chasing windmills that had nothing to do with Brenda's death. When CJ told the judge that the CBI was on the case, Mathison sounded nervous, but he assured CJ that he could handle a bunch of cowboy cops. He then reminded CJ that he had exactly twelve days until his Thanksgiving deadline and that it was time to "shit or get off the pot." His remark surprised CJ, but when he followed it up with another one of his guilt-ridden summaries about why he should have paid more attention to Brenda's needs, what it was like to be a token black man in a white man's world, and how over the years he had let both Brenda and her mother down, CJ was left speechless. CJ actually wondered whether the man on the other end of the line was the same person he had talked with three weeks earlier in his office. The judge ended the conversation by saying, "Wrap this thing up by the twenty-fifth, before I have to hire the kind of people who will."

Even the deal with the renovation people had turned to mush. After CJ told Herman Currothers he wasn't going to sell, Vickers and Perez had cornered him one evening as he was leaving the office and held him hostage on his front steps for twenty minutes while they tried to convince him that selling his building would be in the best interest of them all. CJ was certain that Herman had put them up to the ambush because they descended on him five minutes after he informed Herman that he wasn't going to be part of the deal.

If a couple of gang members that Perez seemed to

bail out of jail almost weekly hadn't showed up in a lime green 1966 Impala low-rider that they had channeled and chopped to within eight inches of the ground, CJ might have had to listen to Perez and Vickers whine about his flaking out on the renovation deal for the rest of the night. But when Perez caught sight of the Impala he made a beeline for it, leaving Vickers on his own. Never one to go it alone, Vickers let CJ sidestep him and walk away.

Overnight Denver had been hit with more heavy wet snow. The city was looking more like Aspen or Vail than the Queen City of the plains and it still wasn't officially winter. The daytime high wouldn't break the teens. CJ hoped that with the kind of weather they were having, Morgan and Dittier could continue to hang tight. He knew that if he had to wait much longer for the Tribe to return from their mountain retreat, there was no way he was going to meet the judge's deadline. He could see his bonus flying away.

Disheartened by his lack of progress on the Mathison case and depressed by the cold, grim weather, CJ had come to the garage to watch Rosie fine-tune the Bel Air and to just sit and think.

The deep rich guttural sound of the Bel Air's finely tuned 289-cubic-inch V8 kicking in made CJ set Copley's and Deere's photographs aside. He got up from Rosie's desk and walked out to the garage.

"She's sounding real good," CJ said, above the engine's hum.

"Sweet as a kitten," said Rosie. He closed the hood, walked around the car, and inserted his huge frame behind the steering wheel to shut the engine down. The Bel Air sank three inches when he did.

"You want to test-drive her again?" asked Rosie.

"No," said CJ, noting that the rocker panels almost skimmed the floor. "You know I don't drive her in the snow." He ran his hand along the Chevy's rear quarter panel to feel how smooth the metal was.

"You know, Red, I keep wondering, why the shit would anyone want to trash my car, and you know what I keep coming up with in the end?" asked CJ.

"Sure don't," said Rosie, toweling the grease off his hands.

"To piss me off. That's why. Somebody's out to yank my chain," said CJ.

"Hell, I can do that by just calling you fat," said Rosie. "And why do you figure it wasn't just Razor D?"

CJ ignored Rosie's response. "I'm serious, Red. You know how I get when I'm ticked. I start thinking crooked instead of straight."

Rosie nodded his head, then turned to his tool chest and started packing away his tools. He wiped each screwdriver and every wrench down with a damp shop rag before he placed them in the chest.

CJ's eyes followed his every move. "See how you're sorting out your tools, putting each one back in its rightful place?"

Rosie stopped and gave CJ a look that said *get to the point.*

"Now, just pretend it's summer, and like every summer you're a little short-handed on help. Four or five cars hit the service islands at once and Old Man Wilhite storms in wanting you to fix another one of his weekly flats. You've got two major tune-ups on the racks and a couple more waiting outside. What do you think would happen to those tools?"

"When I was finished with them, I'd put 'em away just like I'm doing right now," said Rosie, dropping a half-inch wrench into place.

"Yeah, you would," said CJ. "But me and half of the rest of the people in the world would make a few false steps. Maybe lose the forest for the trees and give those tools there a half-assed wipedown, even mix 'em up, screw up fixing the flat, and tell people looking for tune-ups they'd have to come back. That's why they trashed my car," said CJ.

"So you'd put away greasy wrenches and screw up fixing a flat," said Rosie, punctuating the sentence with a booming laugh.

"No, to keep me from being focused, throw me off the track."

Rosie could see that CJ was serious, and he knew that if CJ was headed for another point, he'd better not laugh again. "Kind of like they say in the song, you got the right string baby, but the wrong yo-yo."

"Exactly," said CJ. "Now here's the question. How many people other than folks here on the Points would know me well enough to get me spinning in the wind like that?"

Rosie shrugged his shoulders.

CJ had already started running the numbers in his head. "Can you drop the Bel Air by my place?" he said, after a minute of name crunching. "I've got the Jeep. And I want my baby in bed and out of the cold until next spring."

"Sure, but not until Etta Lee gets back around four."

"That's good enough. I need to run over to the CU Health Sciences Center before then."

CJ threw Rosie the keys to his apartment and garage.

"Catch you later, Red," he said. "I've gotta go get focused."

Henry Bales had just taken a bite from a homemade Dagwood sandwich when CJ quietly walked up to the open doorway to his office. A quart of half-finished orange juice rested on a three-inch pile of spreadsheets and X-rays on Henry's desk. It wasn't until Henry reached for the orange juice that he noticed CJ standing in his doorway. His arm dropped to the desk.

"CJ, what are you trying to do, make me blow a mitral valve?"

CJ smiled. "Where are all your sentries, at lunch?"

"I guess," he said, looking beyond CJ out into the empty lab. "I've been in here most of the morning working on your problem, as a matter of fact." He tapped the collection of papers on his desk before he chugged another mouthful of orange juice.

"Got it all figured out?" asked CJ.

"Unfortunately, yes." Henry put the carton down and neatly folded back the spout. "They've got a hybrid all right," he said, teasing an X-ray film out from under the pile on his desk. Henry stood up and held the film up to the fluorescent lights.

"See all the black areas?" he said to CJ, pointing to several small quarter-inch-diameter black dots on the X-ray film. "Hybrid virus DNA."

"Bad news?" asked CJ, taking the film from Henry and examining it for himself.

Henry nodded yes. "A half dozen liters of the hybrid virus and your boy Deere could wipe out every cow-calf operation in the state." Henry took another swig of orange juice and looked down at the floor.

CJ knew Henry well enough to know that Henry was holding something back. "What about killing people, Henry? I need to know. I think Deere may do it just for spite."

"It all depends on how they deliver the hybrid to the cows."

"Meaning?"

"For instance, they could dump it in a few reservoirs this winter and wait for some action during the melt-off and irrigation season next spring. But that's too hit-and-miss," said Henry.

"What about palming off the killer hybrid to ranchers as a vaccine?" asked CJ.

"No way. As soon as one rancher lost a few cows the word would be out," said Henry. "And from what you've told me, no rancher in his right mind would buy anything that even smelled like it had a Tribe connection. No, there's only one sure way of killing as many people as cows."

"I'm listening," said CJ.

Henry Bales sat back down, stroked his chin, then leaned forward, elbows on his desk. "I think what they'll do is contaminate the feed."

CJ gave Henry a nod as if to say *sounds reasonable enough to me.* "But wouldn't that be pretty hard to do?"

"Maybe a hundred years ago when people like my great-grandfather were growing hay and alfalfa the best way they could, using water, the sun, and a little luck. But today, with production being the name of the game—more cows—more feed—more money—I think it would be real simple. In the ranching economy we're in now, every rancher fertilizes to beat the band. They have to make a buck. All these guys would have to do would be to bring

in some of their out-of-state connections to either sell con-
taminated hay or set up a fertilizing and weed-spraying operation in the spring. They'd have it knocked. Just offer a
cut-rate service for spraying every alfalfa field and hay
meadow they could with the hybrid, and I guarantee you
they'd kill thousands of cows and enough people to cook
up a couple of weeks' worth of lead stories on the national
news."

"Won't the virus kill the hay?"

"No. It's designed for killing animals, species like
cattle and you and me," said Henry. "It won't do a
damned thing to a plant."

"What about the people doing the contaminating?
Don't they run a risk of infecting themselves?"

"Not really. In fact, their side of the deal isn't a
whole lot different from what goes on right here in my
lab. We deal with viruses just as deadly as their hybrid
every day. The secret to not infecting yourself and not
contaminating the lab is knowing what you're doing. And
from what you've told me, the fruitcake you're after
knows what he's doing."

"Yeah, he does," said CJ, his voice trailing off in disgust. "What about the ranchers? How does the virus get
to them?"

"The same way as any infectious disease. The same
way you get everything from AIDS to the common cold:
no protection, multiple exposures, a massive viral dose,
and the next thing you know you've got either a runny
nose or you're dead. From the time the hay's cut until it
is stacked and fed, somebody's going to handle it several
times. Knowing that, I'd say the risk of contaminating
yourself without protection is pretty high."

CJ had been holding the X-ray film the entire time

Henry had been talking. He finally placed it back on Henry's desk. "Now that you've kicked me in the head a few times, tell me something good."

Henry smiled. "Time's on your side, CJ. Just like during the war. Every day you woke up still in one piece, you knew you had one less day in hell. There's no way the Grand River people could get anything this big off the ground during the winter, and come spring, in order to stay ahead of both suspicious ranchers and the law they'd need thirty or forty people spraying hay crops all around the state. From what you've said, their numbers aren't that high."

"A dozen at best. But at least one of them is sure as shit crazy," said CJ.

"Then keep them all in one place, now, during the winter, round up all the hybrid, take out Mr. Deere, and I'd say that's pretty much the end."

"I don't think they'll fold that easily," said CJ.

"Why not?" asked Henry.

"Because I think Deere's already killed to get this far."

Henry's brow wrinkled, his eyebrows arched. "Then you'd better watch yourself with him and his pack of wolves, because there may not be a back door out."

Twenty-two

CJ never left the lights on in his apartment when he wasn't home, an energy-saving dollar-wise habit his uncle had drummed into him early on. CJ could still hear the old man's voice: "Keep that goddamn Public Service Company out of my pocket." So the light streaming from the window of his back study caught CJ's attention even before the opened garage door did. At first CJ thought Rosie might have gone upstairs to use the bathroom or the phone after delivering the Bel Air. The offices downstairs were dark, and Julie's car was gone. If Rosie was running late and Julie had left, it made sense that he might have run upstairs. But when CJ saw that the garage door had been jimmied open, he knew he was wrong. CJ glanced at his watch. It was nearly five-thirty. He ran his hand across the bowed garage door latch and the splintered wood and then eased his way slowly into the garage. If somebody had touched his car, that somebody would die—slowly. As his eyes adjusted to the darkness inside, CJ told himself that before Thanksgiving, he was going to move the light switch closer to the doors. He flipped on the switch. A megaphone of warm air pushed out in front of his face. The doors to the Bel Air were closed. The car hadn't been touched. The normally un-cluttered work bench countertop next to the passenger side of the Bel Air was strewn with tools and every imag-inable form of car-care product, from paste wax to Armor All. The doors to the cabinets above and below the bench were open. CJ crouched down, reached deep into the back of one of the bottom cabinets, and pulled out a gallon paint can. The stencil on the side read "Eggshell White." The can rang hollow when CJ set it down on the concrete floor. He reached up onto the countertop for a screwdriver, popped the top on the paint can, and pulled out a snubnosed .38. CJ knew that the cylinder was full.

With his door key clenched between his teeth, CJ took the fire escape stairs up to the back exit of his apartment. All the way to the top he listened for the sound of someone inside as he followed footprints in the snow up the steps. At the top of the steps, still crouched, eye-to-eye with the back door knob, CJ listened intently for more than a minute. Finally, as gently and quietly as he could, he inserted the key into the lock. The deadbolt clicked back loudly. CJ shoved open the door. Gripping the .38 with both hands he duck-walked his way into the den. His eyes immediately went to his wall of antique li-cense plates. Every plate was in its place. CJ let out a quick sigh, then saw that the desk had been rifled and books and papers were scattered all over the room. His rocker had been flipped onto its side. The room's pocket door was open a little more than halfway. The rest of the house was dark. CJ squinted, watching for movement in the hallway ahead.

When he didn't detect any and realized that the only sound in the room was his own labored breathing after walking in a crouch for more than three minutes, he stood up, walked over to the door, and slid it all the way back into its pocket. He reached into the hallway and turned on the overhead light. The click of the switch seemed unusually loud. CJ moved slowly, gun still extended, from room to room. Every room had been searched, but the only room in real disarray was the kitchen. Bits of broken glass had been pulverized, and pie-sized fragments from plates were scattered across the countertops and on the floor. Pots, pans, and even a toaster oven littered the room. Beverage cartons were floating in the sink, bobbing in an unappetizing mixture of yesterday's leftovers, orange juice, and milk. A grapefruit half had stopped up the sink.

CJ wandered from room to room, shaking his head. He didn't think the intruders had found what they'd come after, but he couldn't be sure. He didn't decide to go downstairs to his office to take a look around until he heard a car pull into the driveway below. CJ had tucked his gun into his pocket, but when he realized that whoever had pulled into the driveway was now inside the office downstairs, he pulled the .38 back out. When he snatched open the door to his office and flipped on the light in Julie's reception area he was in a shooter's stance with his .38 aimed squarely at Sergeant Dellems's chest.

"Floyd!" screamed Dellems. "Hold your fire!"

A plainclothes detective standing just behind Dellems had his 9mm automatic out of his shoulder holster when

Dellems slammed him into the doorjamb, shouting, "Don't shoot."

"Put the goddamned gun away, CJ," ordered Dellems. Only the nearly catastrophic circumstances made him call out "CJ" instead of "Floyd."

CJ lowered the .38 onto Julie's desk. Twenty years of experience told him that no matter what might have happened in the little reception area a moment earlier, the two men standing across from him would have told a story that fit official police procedure to a tee. A story that would have played well because in the end it would always be a tale of an armed black man surprising two white cops.

The detective with Dellems had regained his balance. He didn't like being shoved into the doorjamb by another cop. He knew the situation was under control, but he also had a policeman's rule book tucked away in his head. He had to play out the string. "Ease yourself around that desk there and over here where we can see your hands." His 9mm was still trained on CJ.

CJ moved out from behind Julie's desk. "How the hell did you two get into my office?" He hoped the question would ease the tension.

Dellems looked at the detective, then at CJ. It was the kind of look that said that CJ wasn't making sense. "The front door was standing wide open," said Dellems.

CJ eyed the open door, then Dellems, and finally the detective. "How about holstering that thing. I'm the victim here," said CJ.

The detective didn't budge.

Realizing that he hadn't made his point, CJ added, "The front door was open because somebody just broke in. That must be the way they headed out. Why the hell would I leave my front door open when it's fifteen degrees outside?" CJ made one final attempt to ease the tension and get the two cops to see things his way. "Did you see anyone leaving on your way in?"

"Nope," grunted Dellems. He looked around the room. "Doesn't look like a break-in to me." He ran his fingers across the front door lock. "The lock looks fine."

"They did their damage upstairs, not down here. Now, how about that gun?" CJ said, staring the detective down.

The stoic look on the detective's face hadn't changed since he walked through the door but he finally put away his gun.

"Follow me upstairs, see for your damn self," said CJ. His hands were shaking.

"We can do that, Floyd, but we're here on other business."

"Okay," said CJ, ignoring the second part of what Dellems had just said. He turned and headed up the stairs. "Follow me, and shut the front door behind you."

CJ heard the front door slam as his foot hit the second stair. He knew that Dellems and the detective were there to fish for the real link between him and Derrick James and, if they could, stick him with killing Razor D. They were way past buying the story he had manufactured earlier for Dellems.

Back in his living room upstairs, CJ realized that he had missed the fact that his goosedown bird-hunting jacket and a couple of his old navy peacoats had been dumped in a pile in the middle of the living room floor. All of the coat pockets were turned inside out.

CJ pointed to the pile of coats to reinforce the fact

that someone had broken in. "That's just for starters. The real mess is in the back."

The two policemen followed CJ to the back of his apartment, negotiating their way around broken glass and a dented thermos that CJ had also missed on his first trip through. When they reached the kitchen the detective looked around the room and finally spoke up.

"Good thing you weren't here."

CJ was about to say, *for them or for me?* Instead he nudged the Belgian waffle iron that Mavis had given him one Christmas from the middle of the floor to one corner of the room.

Dellems watched CJ park the waffle iron in front of one of the cabinets. "You've got a mess here, all right. Nothing we can do though. This is District Five's jurisdiction. When we're done with our business, give them a call. Five-five-five, six-six-three-one. They'll send somebody out to take your statement."

CJ had the urge to shove Dellems through the wall. His apartment had been turned upside down, and he had been held at gunpoint by the very people Denver's mayor was so fond of saying were there *to serve and to protect.* To top it off, the only assistance that he had been offered was the phone number to some fat terminal-career precinct dispatcher who was supposed to remedy the whole thing. CJ's bad attitude, the one that had kept him and Mavis polarized over the years, was simmering to a boil when he suddenly remembered what Mavis had said as he was leaving the den on Fat Saturday night, and the words "Things never change" inexplicably leaped from his mouth.

"What?" asked Dellems. A look of confusion spread across his face.

Verbalizing his frustration was the vent CJ needed to keep him from pushing all the wrong buttons and perhaps ending up on the receiving end of the beating of his life.

"Nothing, just thinking out loud," said CJ.

"You know, you're even stranger than I thought," said Dellems. He sat without asking on one of the kitchen chairs. "Our business won't take long." When the detective sat as well, CJ followed suit. In the disarray of the break-in they looked like three men trapped in a buddies television beer commercial gone amok.

"Detective Fuller here is on the Derrick James case. I told him the two of you were like ebony and ivory, real good friends," said Dellems. "Even volunteered to bring him by your place here because I took your original statement." A wry smile crossed his face.

CJ eyed Fuller's bulk and wondered if Dellems had also told Fuller the pet name he had used for detectives the night of Derrick James's murder. CJ smiled at the thought, knowing full well that Dellems would never call a man the size of Fuller a dickhead to his face.

Fuller nodded at CJ as if they had just been introduced. "I understand James tried to shake you down."

Knowing where the conversation was headed, CJ decided to make the question-and-answer session brief. "I didn't kill him, don't know who would have wanted to, and don't know who did."

The expression on Fuller's face didn't change. "Did you know James was wanted in Wyoming on a couple of outstanding car theft warrants?"

"No," said CJ.

"Well, he was," said Fuller, trying to adjust his frame

to a comfortable position in an antique cane-backed chair that had never been designed to support such a load.

"Started stealing cars when he was ten. Must have had a bad seed planted early on, sort of like you. We think he was down in the Points looking to sell some dope."

"News to me," said CJ.

Fuller smiled. "Sort of ironic, he ends up buying it in a van fire. The thing I can't figure, though, is your link to a car booster. But Sergeant Dellems assures me that you'll set me straight."

"James said he knew who took a hammer to my car. That was my only reason for knowing the guy," said CJ.

"Horseshit. There's more to it than that," said Fuller. He paused for a moment. Resting his elbows on the table and cupping his head in his hands, he slid his oversized face toward CJ. "You ever hear of the Grand River Tribe?" Fuller watched for a change of expression on CJ's face. CJ didn't move a muscle. "We got a call from the Routt County sheriff the other day who says you do. And guess what, he knew your boy Derrick James. Says James worked for a burned-out old rancher named Boone Cantrell."

CJ stared directly into Fuller's eyes and said, "So?"

Fuller lost his temper with CJ's one-word response. "And—you media-loving nappy-headed nigger, if you're lying I'll find out. I'm just starting to scratch the surface here. Sooner or later I'll connect everything up and if you're the least bit in the mix, I'll fix it so your reputation is shit and you lose your goddamned bonding license. But I'm hoping you're in the shit up to your neck so I can plant your ass in Canon City till you rust." He stood up as if to punctuate what he had said.

CJ had to swallow hard to keep from going after Fuller right then. He knew that Fuller and Dellems were there to intimidate, not to search for clues. They knew that dropping by for a little chat with him wouldn't get them too far. But a little intimidation might nudge along their case.

Detective Fuller rubbed his butt as if he were trying to start up the circulation in a limb that had fallen asleep. "Do you know the two bums that saw the van fire?"

"They do odd jobs for me every now and then," said CJ.

"Know where they are now?" asked Fuller.

"No. Why don't you try calling them on their cellular phone?"

Fuller and Dellems eyed CJ as if they wanted to stomp him through the floor.

"If you're shitting us, I'll find out," said Fuller.

It was starting to sound to CJ as if *I'll find out* were the only three words Fuller knew. That told CJ that Fuller was trolling for answers he didn't have, and he was certain that at this point Fuller didn't have very much.

Fuller bent down and leaned on the kitchen table. CJ could see his holster and the butt of his gun. "I know you're holding out on me, Floyd, but everything will come out in the wash. Just remember, every man has to earn a living—every man needs a shovel in his hands." With that he turned to Dellems and said, "Let's go." But before leaving, he added, "By the way, you wouldn't know who offed Razor Dog Hicks, would you? We know you had a motive, lover boy. I'm just hoping that when we find the murder weapon, it's yours. Good thing the piece you had downstairs earlier was a .38 and not a .25, or I would have shot your black ass for resisting arrest."

Dellems stood up and stepped on what was left of a china plate. The crunch echoed under his shoe.

"It's been real," said CJ. "I'll fumigate after you've gone."

Not wanting to leave CJ with the last word, Dellems responded, "That number is 555-6631." He followed Fuller out the back way. "No need to help, we can find our way out."

CJ eased back in his chair and stared around the room. He knew that it wouldn't take Fuller too long to sniff out his connection to the Grand River Tribe, Carson Technologies, and the judge. But strangely, all he could think of was that his payday was getting closer to taking wing, and that he wanted to stomp a hole in Fuller's head. He knew that if someone had called in the CBI, sooner or later Fuller or the CBI would be back after a piece of his hide. CJ reached over for the phone to dial District Five, but before he could the phone rang. Billy DeLong was on the other end calling from Baggs. When CJ answered, "Floyd here," Billy said, "The Tribe's back home."

Twenty-three

By early the next morning Denver's week-long cold snap had broken and the temperature had warmed up to 45 degrees. CJ planned to leave for Wyoming by two o'clock. About a dozen Grand River people were back, according to Billy DeLong's second call at six. CJ figured that the Tribe's numbers had dwindled after Brenda's murder, when the less committed members realized that they were now dealing in death. CJ had paced the floor for two hours after Billy's second call, downing nearly a full pot of hazelnut decaf before he left the house.

The streets were slushy, and it seemed to CJ that every passing vehicle was aiming a mixture of salt, sand, and melting snow at the windshield of his Jeep. CJ cruised the 2600 block of Platte River Drive in search of one of Morgan and Dittier's spots. The policewoman who had come to investigate the previous night's break-in had been more interested in why there was a loaded .38 on

Julie's desk than in anything else CJ had to say. It was past midnight before CJ finished talking with her, taking inventory, and cleaning up the apartment. The police-woman was a tall, slim brunette, attractive in a woman-in-uniform kind of way. CJ wasn't surprised that a woman was on the job. He had been dealing with police-women and female bondsmen for years, but he still had a hard time adjusting to a woman as a single-duty officer, out on her own at that time of night. The fact that she was armed and probably knew how to protect herself better than CJ made him wonder if at forty-five he was too old-fashioned for the brave new world. As CJ fol-lowed the self-assured policewoman from room to room, he had tried to imagine what might have happened if Mavis had been there alone during the break-in. But he couldn't quite conjure up an image of Mavis in the apart-ment, not anymore. Mavis had been there in the past and more than once the two of them had sat on the back bal-cony after sweaty lovemaking in the warm, breezy, late-September mile-high darkness, naked as jaybirds, sipping cabernet. But not now. The song-and-dance routine that they kept going between them was their way of softening the disappointments of the past. Besides, beneath her softshoe routine with CJ and her tendency to be daddy's little girl, Mavis was as tough as nails. Anyone bold enough to break in with Mavis there alone would have tempted fate and probably met up with the other .38 Po-lice Special CJ kept on the nightstand by his bed.

Something else kept gnawing at CJ's subconscious that just wouldn't go away. Why the hell would anyone break into his house? It couldn't have been Womack or Spence looking for the missing Carson papers or the virus because they knew that if he had them he'd turn them in for the bonus. Razor D was dead, and unless he had one hell of an active ghost, he was off the list. It could have been some of the other Blades, but they'd probably prefer splattering his brains on the pavement to breaking in and trashing his house. First his car, now his house. Somebody was trying to send him a not so subtle message to back off, and the only thing convoluted enough to warrant that kind of message was the Brenda Mathison–Grand River mess. Even though it stood to reason that Copley or Deere had engineered the break-in, something still didn't fit.

The address that CJ was looking for was 2628 Platte River Drive, in what was known as the sports complex section of the city. It was a two-story flat-topped abandoned brick building that reminded CJ of a gigantic out-of-place red chicken coop. CJ got out of his Jeep and headed for the building's entrance, an arched brick doorway with a severely warped makeshift plywood door. Gang graffiti had been scrawled across the wood. CJ heard someone whisper his name as he fumbled with the twisted coat hanger that held the door shut.

"Down here. You don't want to come in that way, we got it boody-trapped," called Morgan from around the corner of the building.

CJ followed Morgan's voice. When CJ reached the northeast end of the building, Morgan pulled him around the corner, though a three-foot hole in the building wall, and inside where it was surprisingly warm. The place was an empty shell cluttered with an assortment of old-fashioned single-pedestal porcelain sinks and low boy commodes, drywall scraps, entire pallets of four- and five-inch cast iron pipe, and more than a dozen drums that had once contained ninety-weight gear oil. The corner near the hole that CJ had come in through had been partitioned off with drywall scraps into a twenty-by-twenty-foot room complete with jury-rigged overhead lights, two cots, and a mammoth Hoosier cabinet with a four-by-four-foot mirror with a single crack that formed a perfect Z. A plastic cooler that looked brand-new sat at the foot of one of the cots. Morgan's and Dittier's empty shopping carts were parked next to the cooler.

"We're in high clover till Christmas," said Morgan, waving his right arm at the surroundings like a magic wand. "An old hillbilly boy we knew from our Texas rodeoing days is selling piñon pine firewood in the yard out back. He didn't have enough sense to get him a yard that was fenced. Come dark, anybody who wanted to could just drive up and take as much wood as they want. He hired Dittier and me to look after his wood till he sells it, which probably won't be till the first of the year. The room furnishings and twenty-five bucks a week come with the deal. Can't beat that!"

"Not bad," said CJ, knowing the kinds of places that Morgan and Dittier sometimes called home.

Dittier entered the partitioned room from somewhere in the bowels of the darkened warehouse, carrying a three-foot length of one-inch copper pipe. He grabbed CJ's hand in a vise grip and pumped it for nearly thirty seconds before CJ was able to free himself and take a seat on the cooler.

"Have the cops discovered your digs?" asked CJ.

"No way," said Morgan.

"They'll be coming. SOBs caught up with me the other night," said CJ.

Dittier flopped down on the other cot. Morgan remained standing.

"I'd offer you a beer, CJ, 'cause I know that's what you drink, but all we got is Jim Beam," said Morgan.

"I'll pass," said CJ, looking around the room. The drywall had been taped and textured. The cement floor was covered with multicolored carpet remnants and 1960s-style shag throw rugs; black-and-white photos of Morgan riding two-thousand-pound bulls were thumbtacked to the walls. CJ pulled out a cheroot. Morgan followed CJ's lead and lit up a Lucky.

An odd mixture of sweet-smelling cigar and cigarette smoke filled the room. "Have you and Dittier got time to handle another gig?" asked CJ, resting back against the cot. "This one won't last much past Thanksgiving, I'm pretty sure."

Dittier nodded an animated yes before Morgan could say a thing.

CJ could sense that Morgan didn't like the fact that Dittier had said yes to the job so fast.

"We've got to be here all night and every day at noon when the Texan goes to lunch," said Morgan. "And you know me and Dittier don't take no work that separates us."

CJ nodded that he understood. "Here's the deal. I've got to leave town and I need you to stake out my place for three or four days, maybe a week. I want to know about anyone suspicious hanging around. Julie will be keeping a lookout too. You can check with her about who comes and goes so that all three of you are keeping the same score. If you see anything that doesn't look quite right, I want you to pass it on to me. I'll pay you better than the Texan. Twenty bucks a day."

"You've got yourself four more eyes," said Morgan. Dittier beamed.

"Good. You can start this afternoon. I'll be leaving by two. I'll check in with you when I get back," said CJ.

Morgan glanced over at Dittier. Dittier was lying on his back, hands behind his head. "Rodeo cowboys to private dicks. Ain't that a stretch," said Morgan.

Dittier kicked off his high-top Converse All Stars and laughed. Morgan's eyes widened as one shoe hit the floor. When the other shoe dropped, Morgan slapped his forehead with the back of his palm as if he had just remembered the most important thing in the world.

"I almost forgot about the boots," said Morgan. CJ gave him a look that clearly said *I don't know what you mean.*

"At that van burning last week, Dittier still swears that there was another person there. I thought he was seeing double until the other day when he dropped another bomb on me out of the blue while we was crushing cans at the machine on 14th. Out of nowhere Dittier lets me know this phantom man of his was wearing real fancy cowboy boots. Not any old boot, mind you, but expensive custom-made exotic-hide Luccheses. Believe me, Dittier would know. The whole time we was rodeoing, them's the only kind he'd ever wear. Dittier's seeing them boots makes me know there was another person there all right."

CJ could see a look of self-satisfaction plastered all over Dittier's face. Now there was no doubt that there had been someone else at the van burning besides the woman driver, the one man they knew of, and Derrick James. But something still puzzled CJ. It would gnaw at him the rest of the day. Had the mystery person in boots killed both Brenda Mathison and Derrick James?

Twenty-four

Currothers, Vickers, and Perez were waiting for CJ when he got back to his office. Perez and Vickers were in an animated conversation with Julie and had their backs to the door. Herman Currothers was seated in the corner by himself.

When CJ walked in, Currothers was the first one to look up.

"You're chickenshit, CJ. Chickenshit boiled down to the bottom of the pot," said Currothers.

"I love you too, Herman," said CJ. He walked straight over to Julie, interrupting Vickers and Perez, and asked for his messages.

"Other than the triumvirate here, it's been pretty quiet," said Julie.

"Sorry for butting in," CJ said to Perez and Vickers, "but I'm sort of in a hurry."

"No problem," said Perez.

Herman Currothers didn't like CJ's brush-off. "You're going to cost us, CJ, cost us big."

"How's that?" asked CJ.

"By bailing out, deciding not to sell. No matter, though, the restoration people are gonna move whether you're in or out."

"Easy come, easy go," said CJ.

"My ass," said Currothers. "I stand to lose five grand in earnest money I put up front."

CJ looked around at Perez and Vickers. "Anybody else about to lose their shirts?"

Both men answered, "No."

"You know what that tells me, Herman? It says you're either dumber than I ever thought, you paid somebody off, or you're those damned restoration people's shill."

"Think what you want. We're just here to let you know we'll be packaging the whole damn deal on our own. Old Lady Dorfmann's in too," said Herman, with a sly smile. "Sit this one out and you'll end up an island in the stream. It's only a matter of time before they force you out, and when it comes you'll get a dollar for our ten."

"I appreciate you wanting to be my guardian angel, Herman. And I'm sorry I can't run with the pack, but like I told you before, this building ain't for sale."

"You heard him," said Currothers. "He wants to sit on Delaware Street alone and stew in his own juice."

"You positive?" asked Perez.

"As I am about the sun coming up tomorrow." Since bail bondsmen needed to be located close to and visible to their main source of business, the jail, he wondered why everybody was so willing to move. Because Perez would do anything for money, his motive was easy to figure. He still couldn't figure Currothers's and Vickers's angle in the deal. But since they were white, in a white man's world, he knew they had to have something wired.

"That's it then," said Vickers. "Let's move ahead."

CJ couldn't resist aiming one last barb Herman Currothers's way. "Guess you patched up everything with the widow Dorfmann and her nephew?"

"Guess I did," said Herman.

"Beats conspiracy charges any day of the week," said CJ.

"An island, CJ, a fucking island. And eventually you'll sink," said Currothers.

"Thanks for the warning," said CJ. "I'd love to stay and chat some more, but duty calls." He walked over and opened the front door, an invitation for them to leave. "Don't spend all your money in one place."

Herman stormed out of the room. Vickers and Perez headed for the door. "Herman might be right on this one, CJ," said Perez. "It'll be tough down here all by yourself." Vickers nodded in agreement.

CJ looked across the room at Julie. She was bug-eyed, still drinking in the heated conversation.

"I'm a big boy," said CJ. "And believe it or not, I've been alone before." He smiled back at Julie as he ushered Vickers and Perez out the door.

Twenty-five

That afternoon, CJ called Judge Mathison's office to tell him that the Grand River people were back at their headquarters and that he was headed to Baggs, where he expected to have Brenda's murderer identified and jailed within the week. Instead of getting the judge, CJ connected with a bubbly administrative assistant who said the judge would be out of the office for the next two days. When she asked if there was a message, CJ said, "Tell him CJ Floyd called and that I'm about to finish up the hunt."

The Colorado regional forecast called for windy conditions in the mountains with thirty- to forty-mile-per-hour wind gusts, blowing and drifting snow, and icy and snowpacked roads. Fifty-five miles west of Denver, just outside the old mining town of Silver Plume, CJ ran headfirst into the weather. He fought treacherous road conditions for the next five hours all the way to Baggs. A trip that had been a four-hour breeze in September turned into a six-hour nightmare.

CJ made three unsuccessful starts up the driveway to Billy DeLong's with the Jeep locked in low four-wheel drive. On the fourth attempt, he got enough traction to start inching up the hill. A small ten-by-ten-foot parking space had been cleared just beyond the crest of the hill, a full twenty yards from the front steps of Billy's house. A shovel was sitting in the middle of the parking space, half buried in the snow. CJ got out of his Jeep, tossed the shovel aside, and parked. He pulled the snow shovel behind him on his way to the house, leaving a wide scar in the otherwise pristine snow. On the porch, CJ rested the shovel against the cabin and called inside for Billy.

"It's open, bring your frozen butt on in." Billy was standing at the stove cooking spaghetti in an 1880s-vintage trail-drive cast iron pot. The smell of bread baking filled the room.

"Did you find the parking space I cleared for you?" asked Billy.

"Sure did," said CJ, looking around the room for one of Billy's customary open pints. There wasn't a liquor bottle in sight, and except for a bunch of old silversmith's tools spread out on the kitchen counter, the place looked pretty neat.

"Spaghetti and biscuits, that's all I've got, but there's plenty of it, and I guarantee you it'll stick to your bones."

"Sounds good to me," said CJ. Thanks to the vestiges of Mavis's diet and rushing to get out of Denver, CJ hadn't had anything to eat all day but a bowl of raisin bran. When Mavis had served up his skimpy breakfast at Mae's she had also invited him to Thanksgiving dinner with her family. She had even said to bring along Morgan, Dittier, and Billy DeLong. Billy's spaghetti had CJ salivating, and he could almost smell Mavis's turkey and dressing.

"Looks to me like you've lost some weight," said Billy.

"A little," CJ said proudly.

"And you're just getting over a shiner," said Billy.

"Almost there," said CJ.

Billy walked over to the oven and pulled out a pan filled with a dozen piping-hot sourdough biscuits.

"Gotta serve yourself. Get a couple of plates from that cabinet above your head," said Billy.

Billy served himself first, piling his plate two inches high with spaghetti and setting three of his biscuits on top. CJ matched him biscuit for biscuit, spoon for spoon.

Billy was halfway through his spaghetti when CJ asked him if he had any beer.

"Over there in the icebox, bottom shelf," said Billy.

"How about you?" asked CJ, holding up a second beer.

"I ain't drinking right now," Billy said sheepishly.

Billy's answer startled CJ. It was hard for him to imagine Billy without a drink in his hand. "How come?"

"Don't never drink spirits from Thanksgiving to first of the year. It's one of my rules. Decided this year to start a week early because of this Grand River thing. I'm afraid we're gonna need all of our wits, banging heads with Copley and Deere. No need for liquor to interfere."

The look of surprise on CJ's face made Billy laugh. He decided it was time to clue CJ in.

"I didn't get down to the ranch today because of the weather, but the day before, the day I called you, I saw a couple of Grand River people bring in two flatbed eighteen-wheelers. Both stacked to the gills with your standard sixteen tons of hay." Billy paused to roll a forkful of spaghetti. "The guys that got out on the passenger side of the cabs were both carrying double-barreled sawed-off shotguns." Billy held up a forkful of spaghetti in the form of a toast before swallowing it down. "Figure that," he said.

CJ already had. The flatbeds had to be carrying thirty-two tons of papillomavirus-laced hay.

It looked as if Thomas Deere was out to get an early jump on spring. Thirty-two tons of hay would normally winter thirteen cows. But CJ figured that thirty-two tons of infected hay was enough to kill five hundred head in a couple of weeks, and infect a dozen or so unsuspecting ranch hands at the same time. "We need to get up early tomorrow," said CJ, washing down a biscuit with a swig of beer. "I think Deere and his people have decided to bring the mountain to Muhammad."

After their spaghetti dinner CJ lit up a Venezuelan cheroot, the kind he saved for special occasions. As the cheroot's smoke blended with the lingering smell of the freshly baked bread, CJ told Billy that it looked to him as if the man they needed to round up first was Thomas Deere. Then he told Billy about everything that had happened that he thought might be Tribe-connected since his last trip to Baggs, including the details of Derrick James's murder and the story of Dittier Atkins's phantom man in the custom-made Lucchese boots.

When CJ finished, Billy said that if they didn't want to end up like the kid in the van, they'd better figure out one hell of a plan for getting Thomas Deere away from the ranch.

"This is your neck of the woods, so I'll let you have first crack at figuring how to get him out," said CJ.

Billy spent twenty minutes cleaning up the kitchen, thinking all the while. When he had all the food refrigerated and every pot, pan, and dish put away, he turned to CJ and said, "It's elk season. That's our ticket in. But once we're in, you'll have to find our ticket out."

The next morning Billy and CJ were sitting on a hillside in a dry wash looking three hundred yards down a 15 percent grade at Grand River headquarters. It had stopped snowing, and the Wyoming sky was ice-blue clear. The temperature was 5 below. Billy and CJ were hunkered down behind a lean-to blind Billy had fabricated from corrugated tin. He had hauled it up the hillside and into the gully two weeks earlier when there were no Grand River people around. For fourteen days, Billy had parked himself behind the blind in subzero weather and heavy snows, watching for the Tribe to return. When CJ asked him why, Billy said he had chosen the two-week surveillance to serve as his annual holiday penance for drinking too much all year.

They were kneeling on a bed of frozen snow behind the blind, decked out in blaze orange hunter parkas and matching caps. Twenty yards back down the wash in a clump of Colorado blue spruce, as far as possible out of earshot of the ranch, two of Billy's quarter horses were hobbled, eating oats. Scoped and sighted Remington 30.06 rifles were scabbarded at their sides.

CJ brought a set of high-powered binoculars up to his eyes and sighted in on the ranch headquarters below. He remembered the main house as being set back about seventy-five yards from the road. Somehow it seemed further in the snow. Two hundred yards to either side of the house fence lines paralleled each other for a quarter of a mile until they dropped out of CJ's sight to the Snake River below. A poorly maintained gravel county road tied the two fence lines together and squared off the head-quarters' acreage, which CJ calculated to be twenty acres or so.

The two flatbed eighteen-wheelers that Billy had seen earlier were parked perpendicular to each other about twenty feet from the corrals. Each one was fully loaded with sixteen tons of tarp-covered hay. The only activity CJ had seen during their two hours in the blind had been a man without a coat running from the barn to the house, carrying what looked like a ten-gallon pail.

"A lot of what goes into hunting's just laying in wait," said Billy. "Let me see them binocs."

CJ handed them over. Then he reached into his coat pocket, pulled out a thermos, and poured himself a cup of coffee. Steam rose in the air.

"Want another hit?" asked CJ.

"No." said Billy. "Too much coffee and the next thing I know I have to pee. And I'm too fuckin' bundled up to pee."

CJ took a sip of the coffee that Billy had brewed. It was bitter and burned his tongue. "See anything?"

"A ranch," said Billy.

Billy's sarcasm made CJ laugh. "You know there's no reason for you to be here."

"None except to settle a minor little score," said Billy.

"If this thing gets too funky and rises to the level of the law, I'll have some real tap-dancing to do, explaining why you're out here running with a bounty hunter like me."

"Tell 'em I'm your personal valet. I came along to iron your pants." Billy let the binoculars drop around his neck. He took off his cap and rubbed his brow, then ran his hand through his thinning hair. "You know what, CJ? Deere ain't gonna be our problem. It's Copley and them yahoos with the shotguns we got to be wary of."

CJ knew Billy was right. During his two tours in Vietnam he had seen more GIs killed by kids no more than fourteen years old coming up from the bottom of sampans with AK47s than were ever killed by battalion commander types.

"We've got time on our side. Don't worry, we'll get our chance at Deere," said CJ, warming his hands over his steaming cup. CJ took another quick sip of coffee. Before he could swallow Billy had the binoculars back up. "We've got movement down there."

"Where?" asked CJ, straining to see.

"By one of the eighteen-wheelers. I'll be damned. It's Deere," said Billy.

After three murders, and five weeks, CJ was about to get his first real look at Thomas Deere. He had spent the morning freezing his ass off for three reasons. He liked to finish a job when he started one, he knew that Deere had to be the one with the Carson papers, and he wanted to collect his $10,000 from the judge.

"Someone else is headed toward him from the barn," said Billy, as he passed CJ the binoculars.

Thomas Deere was standing on the passenger side of one of the trucks, leaning against the smokestack. He was wearing a cowboy hat with a Montana block. A mop of stringy blond hair mushroomed out from under the hat and stopped just above his shoulders. CJ looked at Deere's feet. He was wearing logger's boots, the kind with stacked Cuban heels. They weren't the kind of boots Dittier had seen on the mystery man who had been at the burning van with Derrick James.

"He's wearing his hair real long these days. Other than that he looks the same," said Billy.

"Who's the other guy?" asked CJ, handing the binoculars back.

"Never seen him before." Billy kept the binoculars trained on the two men. "They're talking. That's about it," he said.

CJ glanced at his watch. They'd been there nearly two hours in the freezing cold, and all he had seen was a man carrying a pail and now two men talking beside a truck. CJ was just about to rethink the whole plan when he spotted what looked like morning fog rising in the distance over Route 9. As the fog moved toward them he realized that it was actually snow being kicked up from the highway by a convoy of trucks. By the time the first truck turned into the driveway to the ranch, CJ had counted a total of ten, all fully loaded with sixteen tons of hay. Neither Billy nor CJ said a word until the last eighteen-wheeler turned into the ranch.

Billy finally spoke up. "Somebody wants to feed a hell of a lot of cows, and you know what? I ain't spotted a cow on this place since that dead steer you and me stumbled across back in October."

CJ added up the hay tonnage in his head. One hundred sixty tons. "What'll you bet that hay's been salted with enough papillomavirus hybrid to kill a whole regiment of men and wipe out half the cattle in the state."

"Think they've got it sold?" asked Billy.

"Only one way to find out. Drop in and ask," said CJ. "But first we've gotta account for Copley, figure how to take Deere, and find us a back door out."

As the truck drivers backed their rigs into a semicircle around the corrals, CJ wondered who had helped load the 160 tons of hay and whether they had been the least bit aware of the potential risk. CJ remembered Henry Bales's warning: *Getting infected would be just like catching a cold—no protection, multiple exposures, high level doses, and BAM, you have the disease.*

Thomas Deere greeted every driver before he huddled them up and headed them toward the house. Two things stood out about the drivers. They all looked much younger than Deere, and every one of them sported shoulder-length hair.

The driver that Deere had been talking with when the convoy pulled in remained with his rig. After a while he opened the door to the cab, reached inside, and came back out with a sawed-off shotgun in his hands. CJ watched him check the gun's pump action by ejecting a shell. When the man bent down to retrieve the shell, CJ looked through his binoculars directly into the man's eyes. They reminded him of the sweltering jungles of Vietnam.

For the next eight hours Billy and CJ took turns staring down at the ranch. CJ hated waiting, but he wanted Deere and Copley as a package and he was worried that he wouldn't get his hands on the papers unless he had them both. A couple of times someone went from the house to the barn and back, but Deere never reappeared. The shotgun-toting truck driver went inside around suppertime. Before they packed up to leave in the evening twilight, Billy asked CJ what made him think the Grand

River people wouldn't just move out in the middle of the night. CJ answered before Billy finished the question. "The same thing that made a bunch of ass-kissing politicians think we could win a ground war in Vietnam. Arrogance."

Billy and CJ were back in their places a little past sunup the next day. The sky was overcast and the gravel-voiced weatherman broadcasting over the static on Billy's vacuum-tubed 1940s-style Philco radio when CJ got up had said that for the next three days the entire state of Wyoming was going to be shrouded in clouds.

Activity in the compound started earlier than the day before. By eight o'clock people were out drinking coffee and meandering in and out of the barn.

CJ sensed they were waiting for someone to tell them what to do, and when. All told he counted twelve men, ten tractor-trailer rigs, and 160 tons of hay marking time on a twenty-acre island in the snow. The break in what had become a monotonous bone-chilling two-day watch came when a one-ton extended-cab pickup with expired thirty-day Wyoming temporary tags rolled onto the grounds, and Albert Copley stepped out. CJ recognized him right away. His blond hair was closely cropped, and he looked a few pounds heavier than in his photo, but it was Copley just the same, with a diamond earring sparkling in his right ear. A few of the men who were outside greeted Copley with handshakes and high fives. Copley acknowledged them, then rushed up the stairs to the house and went inside.

CJ pulled the binoculars from around his neck and set them aside on the frozen snow.

"Ever wonder what makes people do what they do?"

asked Billy, breaking a twenty-minute silence. "Me, for instance. I didn't start drinking, I mean really drinking, till I was twenty-five. A grown man should know better. What about you? How long you been drag-assing it alone through life?"

CJ wasn't surprised that Billy sized him up so easily, but he was surprised that Billy was so quick to throw the fact up in his face.

When CJ didn't answer right away, Billy said, "No need to hold your tongue. Ain't nobody gonna hear what you say but me, the horses, and the trees, and the last two don't give a damn."

"A long time," CJ finally answered.

"I can always tell a man what's goin' it alone. Not that I'm makin' a judgment that it's good or bad. It's just a way. And it don't matter in the end. Ain't none of us leaving here except horizontal anyway. But for my money a man's always a little better off on this earth spreading himself around."

"You're sure of that?" asked CJ, hoping to cut the conversation short.

"I've done it for most of my fifty-six years. Spread myself around, that is. And the last two, sitting up here on this hill by myself have been hell to pay."

"Everybody's gotta do their thing," said CJ.

"Like them shit-asses sittin' down there?" asked Billy, pointing toward the ranch. "Bullshit. They don't give a rat's ass about nobody but themselves. All their hot air about saving the planet from overgrazing cattlemen, and protecting every damn animal in the forest, or whatever the fuck else they claim they stand for, is just a scam. I don't know what their real numbers are, maybe a thousand, maybe no more than the twelve we can see. But I can tell you this, a

third of 'em are in it for money, a third for pussy, and a
third for the excitement of holding their hobnail boot on
the neck of another human being."

CJ realized that Billy had just distilled Deere, Copley,
and the Grand River Tribe down to the opportunists that
they really were. They weren't CJ's reinvented 1960s radi-
cals, or Vietnam-era ghosts, there to rekindle nightmares
from CJ's past. All along CJ had been making the Tribe's
members into something they weren't, reconstituting
them in his mind. Maybe a few of them were the sons
and daughters of the war protesters who had left it up to
black kids like CJ to fight a white man's war. But most of
them were probably closer to roughnecks like Albert
Copley and the driver with the shotgun, than idealists
like Brenda Mathison. And most were surely closer to
Billy DeLong's definition than CJ's. Now, with Brenda
dead, they were just a bunch of losers following a crazy
man on a payback trek. Deere was using them like he
had used Brenda and in the end he would probably get
some or all of them killed or locked up for most of their
lives.

Just before noon Copley and Deere stepped out
onto the front porch. They milled around for a while
with four of the men who had driven in the big rigs.
Copley was eating a slice of pie. In between bites he
walked to the edge of the porch and looked around the
grounds as if he wasn't certain what might be lurking in
the surrounding woods. He finished his last bite of pie,
tossed the paper plate out onto the snow, and headed for
his pickup. All of the men on the porch except Deere followed him and hopped into the back of the truck. As
soon as they did, two other Tribe members left the side
entrance of the house. They split up at the corral, walk-

ing alone around the semicircle of trucks. One man climbed into the cab of the flatbed parked at the end of the corral. The other man climbed into one of the trucks in the middle.

The roar of the diesel engines turning over and the belch of black smoke rising in the air caused Billy, who later told CJ that he had only been resting his eyes, to jump straight up. CJ reached over and pulled him back down by his belt, with the instruction "Keep your orange-coated hunter's butt down here with me."

Copley was through the ranch entry in his pickup in what seemed like seconds. The two tractor-trailer rigs pulled out five minutes later. CJ reasoned that they were all going to the same place, and they weren't headed too far, or the men who climbed into the back of the pickup would surely have opted for the warmth of the eighteen-wheelers' cabs.

CJ counted up how many Tribe members were still left at the ranch. Once, then twice, and finally a third time. Each time he came up with the same number. Five. Deere, two men, one of them the shotgun-toting driver they had seen the first day, and two women he had seen briefly run in and out of the house. CJ decided the odds wouldn't get much better.

"Time to get this show on the road." CJ reached over to nudge Billy, but Billy had been calculating too. He was in an offensive lineman's crouch, duck-walking his way toward the horses.

CJ and Billy entered the Tribe's property boldly on horseback, would-be hunters looking for permission to hunt. The jarring had CJ's ribs stinging again. CJ hoped that the stocks of the two high-powered Remingtons jutting from their scabbards and their blaze orange hunter's garb would send a message that they were just good old boys out to enjoy the day tracking elk. CJ had the outstanding Montana arson warrant for Thomas Deere that Womack had given him and his .357 Magnum tucked in his coat pocket. He patted the pocket twice for good luck. Before they started down the hillside to the ranch Billy had said, "Show him that warrant and all hell's gonna break loose. I say let me rope the son of a bitch as soon as he steps outside, then drag him a couple of football fields on his face, that'll soften him up."

CJ laughed Billy off, but he was glad the old ranch foreman was there, and as they continued closing in on the house he leaned over to Billy and said, "If you get a clear chance to rope him, do it."

Billy grinned from ear to ear.

By the time they were thirty yards from the house, one of the Tribe members was standing on the porch. Billy whispered, "Familiarity is the easiest way to get a man to drop his guard. Let me talk us in."

CJ couldn't do much else but agree.

The man stood on the front porch, dressed in a checkered red and black lumber jacket and faded jeans. He looked suspiciously at Billy, then at CJ.

"Afternoon," said Billy.

"You're trespassing."

"Really?" said Billy. "I didn't realize you had posted this place. Wasn't never posted when I was foreman here. By the way, I'm Billy DeLong. Used to run this place. Me and my friend here are looking for a place to hunt."

"We don't allow hunting or anything else that gets the native wildlife killed. If you want to hunt, try another state."

"You in charge?" asked Billy.

"As far as you're concerned," said the man.

Billy looked right through him. "How about letting me hear it from Thomas Deere. If he says we can't hunt, then we'll move on."

Billy's mention of Thomas Deere caught the man off guard. Billy looked at CJ as if to say, *I told you so.* For a moment the man was speechless, a subordinate trapped between acting on his own and kicking the decision upstairs.

"Wait here," he said, as if he fully expected Billy and CJ to charge their horses at the house. He turned and disappeared inside.

Billy adjusted his weight in the saddle.

"Stay the hell on that horse," warned CJ, knowing that at any moment the situation might get so touchy that Billy's horse would have to become either a vehicle, a battering ram, or a shield.

The front door creaked open. The man who had spoken to them before walked back out, followed by Thomas Deere.

CJ stared at the bay windows on either side of the doorway trying to make out the silhouettes of people inside. He couldn't see a thing. He added up the numbers on the two sides in his head again. Two against five, with the Tribe's five including the two unarmed men standing in front of him. CJ figured that with the firepower he and Billy were packing, that pretty much evened up the odds. He hoped he hadn't miscalculated.

"Billy," said Deere, as cold as ice. He looked at CJ, without a hint of recognition in his glance.

Billy didn't answer back. Instead, he nodded and reached up as if to tip his hat.

Deere was smaller than CJ had expected. His long hair framed a chunky, aging surfer boy's face. "There's no hunting allowed here. You should know that," said Deere, looking at Billy.

"Figured there'd be no harm in askin'," said Billy.

CJ peered at the windows again, then at the corrals, and finally at the barn. He knew that he and Billy didn't have any backup, but then he was a bounty hunter and they weren't playing by big-city law enforcement rules. He'd shoot Deere if he had to, knowing that the only person he would have to answer to was CJ Floyd. He eased his hand down the stock of his Remington. His visual sweep of the grounds complete, CJ looked at Deere and said, "Sort of need to ask you something else too."

Deere had focused all of his attention on Billy, so CJ caught him by surprise. "What's that?"

"If you wouldn't mind taking a ride with us into Baggs. There's the little matter of an outstanding Montana arson warrant I've got here for your arrest."

What saved CJ from the shotgun blast that followed was Thomas Deere's eyes. His rapid glance toward the open front door an instant before the shot had CJ off his horse and on the ground before the blast peppered the horse's neck. The horse reared up, then dropped rifle side down to the ground. Before the horse had a chance to fall on him, CJ was prone, face first in the snow, with the horse between him and the house. Deere ducked inside. Billy had his horse galloping for the nearest clump of pine trees. Two more shotgun blasts filled the air. Pellets rattled the needles in the trees. CJ had his .357 Magnum out, his arm steadied on the dying horse's neck. The horse and CJ were lying in a pool of blood.

For a moment there was silence. Then, from the

Snake River side of the ranch, CJ heard a chorus of snowmobile engines revving up. A few seconds later Copley's truck turned into the drive. He was alone. He didn't see Billy in the clump of trees, but he spotted the horse and CJ right away. Copley aimed his truck straight for CJ, and Billy fired at him twice. One rifle shot shattered the back window in the truck. Copley changed course and headed for the side door of the house. Deere burst through the door holding an old-fashioned ten-gallon milk can. He threw it in the pickup bed and jumped into the cab. Copley gunned the engine, fishtailing in the snow toward the eighteen-wheelers.

CJ and Billy stayed put. CJ kept his eyes glued to the house, fully expecting the people inside to start firing on them too. The thumping in his jugular vein was fierce. When CJ saw the flatbed truck at the end of the semicircle go up in flames, he knew Thomas Deere was out to destroy something much more incriminating than an outstanding arson warrant for his arrest. The second flatbed started burning a few minutes after the first. Flames shot thirty feet into the air. There was very little smoke, just golden yellow and amber missiles shooting like rockets into the overcast Wyoming sky.

Deere and Copley continued around the arc of trucks, Deere dousing the hay with kerosene, Copley reaching out the window of the cab, lighting the fires. When the fifth truck went up in a roar, CJ could feel the searing heat.

Eighty tons of crackling hay were burning out of control when five two-man snowmobiles knifed up from the river bottom below, the only other access to the ranch.

When Copley heard the throaty roar of snowmobile

engines, he jumped from his truck, turned toward the
river, and reached into his coat pocket. CJ never saw
what he was after. One snowmobile had already stopped
twenty-five yards away from him. Before Copley's hand
was out of his pocket a man with a rifle steadied against
the rear of one of the snowmobiles dropped him in his
tracks. The crack of the rifle echoed through the surrounding woods. Copley fell face first. His box of
matches sprinkled like pickup sticks across the snow.

Thomas Deere didn't stop setting fires. He ran to the
last flatbed, ignited the hay, then disappeared between
two of the trucks. The man who had dropped Copley
like a five-point buck stepped from behind the snowmobile, and CJ realized that it was Sheriff Pritchard. The four
other snowmobiles fanned out, quickly surrounding the
house. The sheriff's snowmobile headed straight for Copley. The heat from the flames was so intense that the
truck tires were burning, leaving pools of melted snow.
The sheriff walked over to Copley, rifle extended like a
bayonet. He kicked Copley with the toe of his boot. Copley rolled onto his side and groaned.

The men in the remaining snowmobiles stormed the
house. Like Billy and CJ, they had been casing the place
for days, and had slipped in along the river bottom out
of Billy and CJ's sight. They had run the numbers too and
expected little resistance from the remaining Grand River
people inside.

CJ inched himself up on his knees. Just as he did, the
first of what would be four explosions from the hundreds
of gallons of diesel fuel sent shrapnel spinning out across
the compound like a downed helicopter's blades. CJ
jumped spread-eagled into three feet of snow. In the

chaos that followed, Thomas Deere never came back out from between the trucks.

When CJ finally stood back up he was shaking. His tongue was bone dry, his hands were numb, and his ears were filled with snow. His mind was a collection of miniature snapshots from Vietnam. The sheriff had Albert Copley propped up, the ten-gallon milk can supporting his back. No one had come back outside the house. Forty yards away, CJ heard the sound of Billy DeLong's horse trotting in. The side door of the ranch house swung open and a voice called out to Billy, "Hold your horse right there and get off." Two men, both with base-ball caps emblazoned with the letters CBI, trained their rifles Billy's way. One aimed directly at him, the other at his horse.

CJ walked toward the sheriff, kicking tire parts, a shredded seat cushion, and finally a three-foot hunk of metal out of his way. By the time he reached the sheriff, he was ankle-deep in water.

"Mr. Floyd," said Sheriff Pritchard. "I expected that sooner or later our paths would cross again." The sheriff was supporting Copley, kneeling in water halfway up his thighs. He was holding a wad of what looked like seat stuffing up to Copley's chest. All but the edges of the makeshift dressing was soaked with blood. "Help me get him to the house," said the sheriff.

CJ reached under Copley's legs into ice water and melting snow. Copley grimaced, and his head slumped back. "Lift on three," said CJ.

The sheriff nodded, still holding the makeshift dress-ing in place across Copley's chest.

"One, two, three," said CJ, lifting Copley off the

ground. The sheriff stood up at the same time. Copley
passed out.

As they sidestepped their way back toward the
house, CJ saw that one of the CBI agents had Billy De-
Long by the arm, escorting him into the house.

"Did you see him go in between those two trucks?"
asked the sheriff, just before he and CJ reached the side
door of the house.

"Yeah," said CJ, looking back on the ugly scene.
"But I don't think he found the back door out."

The first thing that surprised CJ about the inside of the
ranch house was the way it smelled. It didn't have the
barnyard smell of animals or the physical smell of working
men. On the contrary, the house was filled with the aroma
of pine needles and lavender soap. Delicate handmade cur-
tains hung at the windows, and the hardwood floors were
accented with expensive, boldly colored Navajo rugs.
Brenda Mathison's taste, thought CJ.

CJ and the sheriff laid Copley on a bed in one of the
back rooms. The sheriff called for an ambulance while CJ
watched Copley labor to breathe.

"Keep watching him," said the sheriff. "I'll be right
back."

Almost immediately four of the men who had
stormed the house earlier rushed past CJ, out the side
door, and back toward the fires.

Sheriff Pritchard came back with a man to relieve CJ.
"Let's move on out front," said the sheriff. "And by the
way, you're being detained."

"For what?" said CJ.

"For whatever I say," said the sheriff.

When CJ held out his hands to be cuffed the sheriff

said, "This ain't Denver. If need be, there'll be plenty of time for that."

CJ followed the sheriff down a short hallway to a large living room that was furnished with exquisite turn-of-the-century antiques. An ebony baby grand piano occupied the center of the room. Billy DeLong was seated at a window facing the piano. His hands were cuffed in his lap. A woman was sitting on the piano bench at right angles to Billy, her back to CJ. She wouldn't look up from the floor. Another woman and the truck driver who had been so fond of his sawed-off shotgun the day before were handcuffed to each other in the far corner of the room, flanked by two tall, ruddy-complected, broad-shouldered men. Both men were wearing black baseball caps with two-inch-high gold letters that read WBI. Only then did CJ realize that the Wyoming Bureau of Investigation was in on the bust too. The only other person in the room was another WBI agent standing a few feet to the right of the woman on the bench. He was talking rapidly into a cellular telephone. CJ could tell that he was the agent in charge.

In contrast to the ranch apocalypse outside, the inside of the house was amazingly quiet. CJ listened to a 150-year-old coffin-style German grandfather clock ticking loudly in the entryway to his left. He stopped three steps from the piano and looked over at Billy DeLong. Billy's face had a sorrowful *why me* kind of look. CJ shrugged his shoulders as if to say *I didn't know it would come to all of this.*

The Wyoming Bureau of Investigation agent put his phone down and waved the sheriff and CJ toward him. "We've got fire department backup on the way out from Baggs. Shouldn't take them more than ten minutes." He looked past CJ toward the sheriff. "I sent everybody else to the weenie roast outside."

"When it dies down maybe they'll find what's left of our boy Thomas Deere," said the sheriff. The WBI agent finally looked at CJ, giving him the kind of look an older brother would give a younger sibling. "Step over here, Mr. Floyd, and join the crowd."

CJ started around the piano toward the agent, fully expecting to finally be handcuffed along with everyone else. Just before he reached the corner of the piano bench the agent added, "Perhaps you know Ms. Holly Beckwith, here. Your friend Mr. DeLong certainly does. But he doesn't want to believe that when we swatted the house, she was lying on the floor over there with a 30.06 sticking out the window, aimed at him, ready to take off his head the first time he stuck it out from behind one of those trees." The agent pointed toward the pine trees where Billy had been hiding.

CJ looked down at Holly Beckwith. He couldn't see her face because she was still staring at the floor. He remembered how Billy's face had lit up when he mentioned Holly the first time CJ had come to Baggs. He even remembered Billy saying how much the both of them had liked their spirits.

The CBI agent eyed Holly Beckwith. "How about it, Ms. Beckwith? Are you and Mr. Floyd here friends too?"

She shifted her weight on the bench without speaking and finally lifted her head. Even without her camera and the makeup, CJ realized that the woman who had once palmed herself off as a Landmark Restoration and Preservation Society appraiser—the woman who had taken all those snapshots of his office—and the woman the agent was now calling Holly Beckwith were one and the same. All CJ could do was stare.

"Well," said the agent, breaking CJ's trance. "You two know each other?"

CJ said, "No."

His mind was racing ahead. Suddenly a huge piece of the Grand River puzzle had fallen into place. Holly Beckwith was the bridge between Brenda Mathison's killer and the Grand River Tribe and also the link between Derrick James and Razor D. CJ wanted to kick himself for not seeing the connection all along. He was hoping Holly would remain mute so that he could tie up a few loose ends and hand Brenda's killer over to the Denver cops for the judge, wrapped up neatly and tied with a bow.

Twenty-six

It was the second time in two weeks that CJ had been questioned by the police. But this time, instead of chatting over the table with a disorganized minor-leaguer like Sergeant Dellems, he spent nearly four hours in a holding cell in the Carbon County Jail in Baggs being grilled by the lead WBI agent, Sheriff Pritchard, and investigators from two states. The only time he had been allowed out of holding had been for a brief, long-distance conversation with Julie. He told her to sit tight and stay close to the phone because she might have to come bail him and Billy DeLong out of jail. As he hung up the phone, CJ noticed Boone Cantrell pacing back and forth in the lobby.

When Cantrell saw CJ, his eyes narrowed with determination. "Hope they got Copley in a hospital room with plenty of guards and lots of bars, 'cause I'll sure enough kill him for what he did to Derrick if I get the chance."

Although it was late in the game, CJ had finally made the connection between Boone Cantrell and Derrick James. Derrick James had to have been tracking the Tribe's activities for Cantrell. CJ wanted to tell Cantrell that Copley probably wasn't the man who had set Derrick up—that Copley was only a piece of a much larger puzzle and that Cantrell should hold his horses—but before he could, a CBI agent ushered CJ back for more interrogation.

He and Billy were interrogated separately by two CBI pros, a Wyoming agent, and the sheriff. When they had finished grilling him, CJ had sweat rolling down both his arms, and his T-shirt was plastered to his back. They would ask him the same questions over and over, fifteen different ways, and then repeat the original question again. What did he know about the vaccine? How did he get mixed up in this? Did he know who killed Brenda Mathison? Was he working for Carson Technologies or the judge? Had he or Billy killed Derrick James? Did he have the formula for the vaccine? Had he and his old navy buddy Henry Bales gone into the vaccine business for themselves? Between the four of them, they kept CJ's head spinning until he was almost in a trance. When they finished CJ was certain of only three things: he had just been hammered by pros; the one piece of the Grand River puzzle that they needed most, his connection to Holly Beckwith, was being overlooked; and he thought he knew for sure who had killed Brenda Mathison, Razor D, and Derrick James. CJ hoped that when they interrogated Holly Beckwith she would hold them at bay long enough for him to prove that his instincts about the killings were right.

The lead WBI agent let CJ and Billy out of their holding cells just after six-thirty. He said it was his good deed for the week. Then he added, "We're after trophy buck, not calves. Get out of here before I change my mind." By the time they'd collected their belongings it was almost seven o'clock.

On his way out CJ saw Boone Cantrell and Sheriff Pritchard talking quietly next to the stairway leading to the second floor. Cantrell looked as though he had been crying, but from a distance CJ couldn't be sure.

CJ and Billy trudged through the snow over to the B&B Motel, where Billy persuaded Ernest Devine to give them a ride back out to his place so CJ could get his Jeep. As a thank you for the favor, Billy promised to give Devine the inside scoop on what was rapidly becoming the second-biggest crime story to ever hit Baggs.

The sky was clear and the temperature had dipped into the low teens when they reached Billy's. The Big Dipper dominated the western sky. Ernest Devine pulled up right next to CJ's Jeep. CJ hopped out of the truck and into the Jeep in one rapid, fluid motion. Billy, tired of answering Devine's questions, was right behind CJ.

"Hold tight until you hear from me," said CJ as he fired up the Jeep and slammed the door.

"Been one hell of a day," said Billy, pausing to look up into the night sky.

CJ rolled down the window and called out to Billy, who was still gazing up at the stars. "Hey Billy, grab your ass and see if it's still there. If it is, thank your lucky star up there and wish me luck." CJ turned the Jeep around and nosed it down the hill toward Denver, leaving Billy feeling his buttocks with both hands and gazing into the cloudless sky.

Twenty-seven

CJ pulled up to his garage a few minutes past one. Before he opened the garage door, he made sure that his .357 was still loaded. Once the car was garaged he took the back stairs up to his apartment. He turned on one kitchen light, shed his coat, and poured himself half a glass of milk. He had finished the milk by the time he got to the bedroom. He set the alarm for 6:30 before tossing his shirt and pants in a pile on the chair and falling across the bed for what turned out to be five hours of surprisingly restful sleep.

CJ was waiting for Ricky Perez on Ricky's front porch the next morning. While he waited, CJ watched workmen stringing Christmas lights on one of the county buildings next to the jail. Perez showed up twenty minutes into CJ's wait. A downslope winter chinook had pushed the temperature into the mid-40s, a sharp contrast to the day before.

"You're too late, CJ, we've already done the deal with the preservation people. You blew your chance." Perez grinned broadly. It was a sly, self-satisfied smile.

"Like I said, easy come, easy go," said CJ, watching Perez unlock the front door.

Inside the building, the institutional smell of Lysol and cheap furniture polish hung heavily in the air.

Perez seemed oblivious to the smell. "Park it wherever you'd like. I'll put some coffee on." He stepped into a small alcove to the left of the building's massive Victorian living room and flipped on a couple of lights. "Too dark in here for my taste. I don't get that early morning sun like you do, at the end of the block. Herman's place cuts off all my light. They wouldn't let you build like that today. Easement rights and all that shit. A three-story building can sure enough block out the light."

CJ nodded affirmatively, even though he couldn't see Perez. He heard the vacuum release on a fresh can of coffee, then a refrigerator door opening and closing.

"You're gonna have to take it black. My milk is sour. Smells like hogshead cheese."

"Fine," said CJ, still unable to see Perez, talking back into the blind cul-de-sac.

"What brings you out so early, CJ? I usually don't see you on the street till after eight."

CJ heard the sound of tap water running and then the splash of water filling a glass coffee pot. "Need to tie up some loose ends," said CJ, talking to the alcove's wall.

Perez stepped out from behind the wall. The gurgling sound of water starting its trek through the coffeemaker filled the empty room.

"Any loose ends I can help you with?" asked Perez,

walking back out into the living room with a bag of potato chips.

"Maybe," said CJ.

Perez grabbed a handful of chips and offered CJ the bag.

"None for me," said CJ. "I've been cutting down on my grease."

"Forget about that," said Perez. "In fact, you're looking pretty thin. Need to do something myself." He patted his gut. "But you know how it is with kids. They leave too much junk food around. After a while you start to nibble on it, and then you're dead."

"Looking out for your kids can make you do strange things," said CJ. "Maybe even trash a man's car."

Perez looked startled.

"That's where it started, didn't it, Ricky? With Razor D and a couple of your favorite gang-bangers beating the shit out of my car? And I bet that's where you expected it to end."

Perez stopped chewing and swallowed hard. CJ watched his Adam's apple bob up and down. "Your diet must be getting to you, man. I hear people on diets can get low on protein real quick, and maybe not get enough oxygen to their brain."

"What did you think? Trashing the Bel Air would keep me off the Mathison case, and you'd have it for yourself? Was I moping around so fat and lethargic in my birthday funk that I looked that soft? Was I acting so stupid that you figured taking out my car would make me forget which way is up? Or maybe you thought I'd spend all my energy chasing after Razor D?"

"You've got it wrong, CJ."

"No, Ricky. I'm right as rain."

The coffeemaker began that final death-rattle gurgle that says the coffee's almost done.

"I couldn't stitch together all the pieces of this crazy quilt until last night, on my way home from Wyoming. You were good, Ricky. You kept me focused on Copley and Deere. Until yesterday, when I stumbled across the final thread. A lady left over from the 1960s. A wilting flower child named Holly Beckwith. She's the link between the three of us—the Grand River Tribe, you, and me. The thing I can't figure is how. I pretty much know why." CJ looked at Perez for a response. The blank expression on Perez's face had replaced his earlier sly childish grin.

"You're doing the preaching, CJ, you tell me."

"The why is easy. You did it for Uncle Sam's green. Money, Ricky. It's always been the name of your game. You'd sell the stink on shit if you figured it could turn you a buck."

"Go on," said Perez.

"The first day Womack and Spence dropped in to lay their little song-and-dance on me about finding Brenda, I hesitated taking the bait. When I didn't snap at their offer, Womack threatened that he'd use someone else. I didn't see him until that evening to say I'd take the job. True to his threat, Womack probably left my office and walked right down the street to yours, dragging Spence by the ring in his nose. What did he care whether there was one person or fifty people working the case. The judge was paying the bills."

"You're talking crazy, man. You need a shot of coffee. Maybe the caffeine will clear your head." Perez got up and walked back to the alcove. CJ heard a couple of cupboard doors open and close, then the rattle of silverware. Perez was back quickly with two steaming mugs of coffee. He wrapped one hand tightly around his mug, as if suddenly he needed to warm himself up, and handed the other mug to CJ. "I don't know your judge or any Womack or Spence."

"But you know Holly Beckwith, and she's the key. Did you know she's in jail? And that Albert Copley is probably hooked up to a respirator in a hospital in Cheyenne? And Thomas Deere. Well, they're more than likely sifting through the ashes right this minute looking for his bones," said CJ.

Perez's pre-coffee poker face suddenly turned ashen. CJ could almost see the blood drain away.

"Don't come in here accusing me of some kind of conspiracy because somebody trashed your fucking car or some bounty hunter outbid you on a job," said Perez.

"Like I said before, I know you didn't trash my car. You assigned that little task to Razor D. The problem is, there's a whole lot more to this little ditty than my car being taken to the mat. There's the matter of three murders along the way."

Perez swallowed down half a mug of piping hot coffee in three big gulps. CJ knew his esophagus must have instantly gone numb.

"The renovation deal tripped you up, Ricky. When Herman told you to get all the buildings appraised you figured you'd kill two birds with one stone, so you slipped Holly Beckwith, your ringer contact from the Tribe, in on the deal. What still puzzles me though is how you hooked up with the Tribe when I couldn't. Anyway, your flower child showed up at my place calling herself Abby Lindel, pretending to be an appraiser, snapping pictures like she was a wedding photographer for

Vogue. I didn't know who she was then, or that she was casing the place for a break-in later on. When she finally did break in, she was looking for something I didn't have."

"What?" said Perez.

"My guess is your other contact, Thomas Deere, was so paranoid he thought I might have latched on to a new protocol for making either the virus hybrid or the vaccine. He had put two and two together, and he knew I had a piece of tumor from one of his infected steers. He also had to know, from Holly Beckwith tailing me in that VW bus of theirs, that I had Henry Bales working on the papillomavirus end. But he guessed wrong when he figured that Henry and I were trying to duplicate the vaccine or his killer brew. He probably thought we might end up being the competition, when all we were really trying to do was figure out how he was gonna spread his virus around."

Perez eased back in his chair. He took a quick sip of coffee and swallowed hard. "You've gone this far, CJ, finish your fantasy out."

"The second place your little deal sprung a leak was with Derrick James. Neither you or Deere knew that Derrick was a snitch for Boone Cantrell or that in addition to being a snitch, he had the gambling bug. On one of his trips to Denver he had the misfortune of seeing Razor D break into Rosie's and go after my car. But he didn't know that Razor D saw him too. Later on, Razor D must have seen James talking to me one night at Mae's and he told you about it. You couldn't chance a thug like Razor D sniffing around your shit, so you took him out. To net it all out, I figure it like this. Maybe Womack got a little drunker than I thought he did the night he offered me the job of finding Brenda and he decided to hedge his bet by offering you the job too. You signed on and showed up at the Grand River headquarters outside of Steamboat a little ahead of both the sheriff and me. When Brenda wouldn't cooperate like a good little girl and give you the Carson papers, you probably decided to use a little force. Things got out of hand, and you ended up wrapping her neck in a barbed wire necklace that stopped her tongue from wagging for good. The thing I can't figure is how Brenda would let you get so close without knowing who the hell you were. Did you have some Grand River Tribe member running interference?"

A voice that clearly wasn't Perez's boomed from the kitchen alcove. "You're close, Mr. Floyd, but unfortunately you don't get a cigar."

Spence was standing in the alcove doorway. The first thing CJ noticed about him, after his jaw went slack, was that he was wearing lizard-skin Lucchese cowboy boots.

"For the record, Mr. Bad-Ass Bounty Hunter, we're not stupid. Brenda never saw us coming. And you're right, your friend Ricky here is the one who actually tightened the noose. I just brought along the wire. As for the James kid, I handled that myself after Holly Beckwith and Deere set him up. The skinny sad sack had figured the whole thing out even better than you. And Razor D— it didn't take but five hundred dollars to get a little gang-banging Henchman out to build his rep, to shut Razor's mouth. To tell you the truth, we were hoping you'd take the rap."

Spence noticed CJ staring at his boots. "When in Rome do as the Romans do," he said. It wasn't until Spence walked out of the shadow of the doorway that CJ saw a .357 Magnum identical to his own pointed at his chest. CJ's throat tightened. The frown on Spence's face was so intense that CJ thought his forehead muscles might snap. CJ wanted to shout *why*, but he couldn't. For some reason the only thing he could do was the same thing he did when rage engulfed him as a child. He gulped a huge breath of air until his neck quivered and held it for fifteen seconds. He let the air out slowly, as if he wanted the words to fly away. "I was hoping that somehow you were a little better than the vermin I deal with every day."

"I had hopes too," said Spence. "That Brenda would decide to come back. But I finally had to come to the realization that she wasn't mine anymore. She was just an intellectual rich bitch whore for Thomas Deere and his cult."

Jealousy was a motive CJ had considered, but the triangle had included Brenda, Copley, and Deere, not Spence. He still didn't buy jealousy as Spence's sole reason for murder. CJ made a move to get up from his chair.

"Don't do it," said Spence. "I know how to use this quite well." He glanced down at the gun.

Perez got up from his chair, walked over to one of the desks in the room, and came back with a roll of two-inch-wide filament tape. "Stand up, CJ."

CJ didn't budge.

"Do what he says, Mr. Floyd," said Spence. "I want to make this as easy on all of us as I can."

CJ decided it was time for a full-court press. "Don't peddle your love-sick bullshit on me."

Spence pulled back the hammer on the gun.

"I've heard your heartache story before, or don't you remember trying to cover your ass and Brenda's in my office. Maybe you should have been an actor instead of an engineer." Perez started wrapping CJ's wrists with tape. The sound of the tape coming off the spool reminded CJ of hot popcorn oil just as it starts to sizzle. He felt the hair on his arms pinched beneath the tape.

"Cool it, CJ," said Perez. It was a warning. The kind of warning someone gives when they know the darkest side of another person. Perez knew what Spence was capable of, and he didn't want his office to end up a bloody mess.

Spence started to babble. "I wanted her back. I even told her I would take the blame for stealing the plasmid and vaccine. But she had dropped too far off the edge. She was to the point where she actually believed that plants and little forest creatures were more important than human beings. Thomas Deere had turned her head. Everybody thought she manipulated him. Ha! It was the other way around. I thought my helping her steal the protocol for the vaccine would straighten everything out. But all it did was end up snapping an already stretched rubber band."

Perez shoved CJ back down in his chair. CJ's hands were taped behind his back. His fists hit the cushion before his butt and a sharp pain shot beneath his shoulder blades. "Save your fairy tale for someone else," said CJ, eyeing Spence with disgust. "With you and Ricky in this thing together, I've got the strangest feeling that money, and not lost love, is the real bottom line. Brenda and Deere stole a vaccine worth millions, and you weren't about to let all that fly away."

"She embarrassed me," said Spence.

"So you lost face in front of your Carson cronies.

You're telling me that was enough to make you kill someone you claimed to love. Horseshit."

Spence aimed the gun at CJ's head. "She would have cost me my reputation and my job. I showed her how to break Carson's security. When I caught up with her at that ranch house of theirs a week before Womack and I came to see you, and told her what I stood to lose, she laughed and said Deere was going to make me look like a fool. Then she called me an Uncle Tom. She wasn't my Brenda anymore. On my second trip I knew what I had to do."

CJ now understood why Spence had seemed to know Colorado's Western Slope better than he should have the first time they met. Spence had been there before. "So you had our local gang cartel broker here silence her for good," said CJ, rolling his eyes at Perez.

Beads of sweat trickled down the front of Ricky Perez's face. He started to fidget. "Let's cut the debate and move the hell out of here."

"Want to do your killing a little further from home, huh, Ricky?"

Perez cut a six-inch strip of tape and slapped it across CJ's mouth. When CJ protested with a mumble, Perez added another. CJ decided it was time to keep quiet. He looked around the room for a way out, but he had been in Perez's office often enough to know he was searching in vain.

"Head him out back to my car and stuff him in the trunk. It's the Lincoln parked next to your back steps," said Spence.

CJ realized that Spence had mapped out a plan for getting rid of him well in advance. It must have shown in CJ's eyes, because the next thing Spence said was,

"Everyone needs to plan ahead if they expect to succeed, Mr. Floyd."

"Where are we headed?" asked Perez. He grabbed CJ by the arm, leading him out back.

Spence didn't answer. He simply motioned Perez and CJ ahead of him with one hand.

The Lincoln was parked in the alley about ten feet away from the back steps. The car was black and it reminded CJ of a hearse. CJ counted the steps from the first-floor landing to the ground. There were eight. He wondered if it would be his last math problem ever. When CJ's right foot hit the ground, the trunk lid popped up. *A remote-controlled trunk lid to boot,* thought CJ. After the final step, CJ and Perez made a 180-degree turn away from the landing toward the car. CJ looked back for Spence. Spence had a cashmere topcoat draped over his shoulders, hiding the fact that he was holding a gun.

Perez nudged CJ ahead. CJ inhaled deeply, knowing there wouldn't be much air in the trunk of the car. He wanted to gulp one last mouthful of air before getting into the trunk, but he couldn't, so he inhaled deeply through his nose and thought about how much oxygen an old high school football injury that had left him with a deviated septum was going to cost him now. He was bending over, looking at the rubber molding curve its way around the bottom of the trunk, when the .357 went off. CJ spun around and dropped down on his knees. When his knees hit the ground, he knew that he hadn't been hit.

What CJ saw behind him made him promise himself that he would be sitting in the second pew at the Mount Carmel Baptist Church, the pew reserved for people recently touched by miracles, every Sunday for a month, maybe more.

Spence was struggling to keep his balance, trapped inside the loop of a rodeo lariat snugged up tight around his chest. His arms were plastered to his sides. Four feet away, on the other end of the rope, Morgan Williams was trying to squeeze Spence into the shape of an hourglass. The .357 Magnum was ten feet away, lying in the middle of an alley in an oatmeal mix of oil, salt, sand, and melted snow.

Ricky Perez was lying on the ground face up, eyes rolled back in his head. Blood was streaming down his face. Dittier Atkins straddled him. A three-foot length of two-inch copper pipe dangled loosely from Dittier's right hand.

For a big-city morning, it was morbidly quiet except for the high-pitched sound of a DC-10 gaining altitude above their heads. Dittier sidestepped his way over to CJ. He cut away the tape holding CJ's hands and pulled the tape away from CJ's mouth. CJ walked to the middle of the alley, picked up the gun, and wiped it off on his coat sleeve.

He looked down to see if Perez was still breathing and checked his pulse. "He'll live," said CJ, looking at Morgan. "Walk that rope over here to me and don't give it any slack. Then haul ass across the street to the jail and ask for a precinct duty cop. Tell them what happened and tell them CJ Floyd said get over here real fast."

Morgan walked his rope over to CJ and gave it one last tug before handing it over. He took off running. Spence stumbled toward CJ. When he saw the .357 he stumbled backward, and the slack in the rope disappeared.

CJ looked over at Dittier. The look on Dittier's face said *what's next?*

"Dittier, you did great," said CJ. "Just hang in here with me until Morgan gets back." Dittier patted the copper pipe a couple of times and smiled.

CJ spotted Morgan's and Dittier's shopping carts beneath Perez's partially enclosed back stairs. He looked up at the paint peeling off the old Painted Lady and smiled, thinking how wonderful it was that every Victorian building on the street had a storage space beneath the back stairs. A space big enough to park a car, or for street people to bed down in for the night.

Spence looked at CJ. CJ could see the amazement bubbling forth in his eyes. On the ground next to them Perez's right leg twitched, and he groaned. His arm moved in slow motion toward the four-inch gash on his head.

CJ tugged at the rope holding Spence to make sure it was still tight and aimed the gun directly at Perez's head. Then he looked back at Spence and said, "Sometimes you just have to have your people plan ahead."

Twenty-eight

Color televisions were all blaring Thanksgiving Day football in the kitchen, living room, and den of Willis Sundee's house. It was the first time in fifteen years the Broncos had played on Thanksgiving Day. Mavis was in the kitchen with her sister, preparing her special dressing. Rosie's wife, Etta Lee, was standing at the countertop behind them slicing up bananas and strawberries for a Jell-O mix that she was readying for two gigantic star-shaped molds. Kids were running from room to room.

Willis, Dittier Atkins, and Morgan Williams, freshly showered and shaved, and Roosevelt Weaks's two sons were in the living room watching the game. Morgan and the boys were debating whether or not instant replay should have been dropped. The boys were both trying to encourage Morgan to come around to their point of view.

CJ, Billy DeLong—who had driven the 270 miles from Baggs to Denver in record time for late November—and Rosie had been banished to the den by Mavis,

who told them that anyone with enough gall to eat guacamole and tortilla chips before she served her Thanksgiving meal, which had been two days in the making,
needed to be, if not out of mind, at least out of sight.

Two days had passed since Ricky Perez and Peter
Spence had been handcuffed in full view of a Channel 7
television camera and whisked across Delaware Street to
the Denver County Jail. When Morgan rushed into the jail
screaming for a cop, the Channel 7 beat reporter happened
to be on hand as well. By the time two patrol cars and six
policemen arrived in the alley behind Ricky Perez's, the
beat reporter had a camera crew rolling film. Their vulture-
like response made CJ wonder if the media shouldn't all be
deputized. For thirty-six hours, CJ, Billy, Dittier, and Morgan had become news fodder for what the Denver media
was calling the "Grand River Plot." CJ was going to be able
to claim bragging rights on Bondsman's Row for a while.
There was footage of OSHA and EPA agents in Baggs dragging canisters of virus hybrid and vaccine from a well-
equipped laboratory in the basement of the Tribe's ranch
house. There were interviews with Henry Bales, public re-
lations people from the Denver Department of Safety, and
the chiefs of both the WBI and CBI. Even Herman Currothers had a twenty-second sound bite, where he complained into a six o'clock news microphone that the
negative publicity about Perez had cost him a million-dollar
historical restoration deal. In order to save what he could
of his own ass, Perez was busy pointing the finger at
Spence for killing Derrick James and putting a contract out
on Razor D.

Four hours of that time CJ had spent in police cus-
tody under the scrutiny and pit-bull cross examination of
Detective Fuller and the CBI. CJ had been threatened

with obstructing justice, inhibiting an ongoing investigation, and operating a bonding agency with unlicensed agents. In the end only Willis Sundee's political influence had called off the law enforcement dogs.

Judge Mathison had wired CJ $10,000. "Payment for finding the scum who killed my daughter," the wire had read. The judge also offered to grease the skids so that CJ could have Spence's old job at Carson as head of security. CJ had faxed the judge an immediate response. "Thanks for the bonus, no thanks to the gig." The reply was intended to be short, sweet, and final. Carson Technologies and the judge were too cozy a duo to ever be anything more than a politically correct fit between an ambitious black man and a corporate slug. A convenient union that made CJ nervous.

Now CJ's Deer Trail plate was lying on a bed of shredded gift-wrap paper on the coffee table in front of Willis Sundee with a note from CJ that read: "Roots are as important as beans. Thanks for saving our asses from the gendarmes."

CJ and Rosie were seated on the couch together. Rosie bent across CJ and scooped a dollop of guacamole onto two restaurant-sized tortilla chips. "Hope we don't have to look at your ugly puss during any newsbreaks today," he said, looking back at CJ.

"Fifteen minutes of fame; like it or not, in America it comes to us all," CJ said with a smile.

"It's a shame about that Mathison girl, though," said Billy. "I didn't like her, but gettin' killed by a boyfriend who's missin' the batteries to his headlamp just ain't right."

CJ laughed. "Spence wasn't her boyfriend, Billy, he just wanted to be. And he didn't kill her, Perez did that.

You'd better start getting your facts straight, or you're gonna blow your time in the spotlight. Spence only killed Derrick James, the loose-cannon kid who worked for Boone Cantrell."

"That's right," said Billy. "I've got it straight now."

"Don't matter who did what to who," said Rosie. "The man is sick, killing somebody over a lousy job. Sounds like he should be working for the Postal Service to me. Now pass me some of them chips. You're hogging them all to yourself, Mr. TV Star."

CJ pushed the tortilla chips across the table toward Rosie. His face turned serious. "Relationships can be real strange beasts. You never really know what makes them tick. Spence was as sick as Thomas Deere, more concerned about his corporate image than human life. I'm beginning to wonder why we worry so much about gang-bangers like Razor D when the world's full of people like Deere and Spence."

"You ask me, I think the Mathison girl and Spence both just wanted to be white," said Rosie. "They got their highfalutin black asses all caught up in white people's things, and in the end it cost 'em big. Don't nobody I know around the Points or nowhere else that's black give a shit about cow-grazing rights or any of that other environmental shit. It's hard enough for most people around here to make ends meet."

"Maybe," said CJ. "But money and self-righteousness are powerful things. Deere wanted money and the power to have things his way and he ended up dead. Poor old Ricky Perez wanted money and he's in jail. And our boy Spence is just another black-faced killer on the six o'clock news."

"You'd think that Spence would have had more

sense than to hire a guy like Ricky Perez," said Rosie. "Hell, Ricky spent most of his life scamming—hawking stolen goods, bailing two-bit hoodlums out of jail. He ain't no more bounty hunter or a private eye than Etta Lee." They all laughed.

"Spence knew what he was doing," said CJ, grabbing several more chips. "He sized Perez up real fast. He needed a man who'd do anything for money—somebody who'd do anything he said. Turns out he had promised Perez twenty-five grand for his help before he and Womack ever came to see me. He was singing Ricky's favorite song. Ricky knew he wasn't going Christmas caroling for twenty-five grand."

Rosie nodded in agreement before asking, "Then why'd he go along with them hiring you?"

"He had to placate Womack and the judge and he thought I was just a dumb street nigger he could hold at bay," said CJ.

"Guess he was wrong," said Billy, plunging a tortilla chip into the guacamole. "You know, they didn't find much left of Thomas Deere. What they did find didn't amount to much more than a shoppin' bag full of bones. Hard to believe a man would burn himself up right before your eyes."

"Hard to believe we had Jonestown too, but we did," said CJ.

"Strange," said Rosie, polishing off the last of the chips in the bowl. He shoved the bowl toward CJ. "How about getting some more chips, CJ? You ate half the bowl. Guess you said to hell with your diet."

CJ grabbed the bowl and headed for the kitchen. His diet hadn't crossed his mind since he stood staring into the trunk of Spence's car. Things desert your mind when you don't know if you'll live another ten minutes.

All the way to the kitchen Rosie's two grandkids circled CJ, tugging at his pants, saying, "Uncle CJ, get us some chips too, get us some chips too." CJ promised he would deliver them a secret stash, but they couldn't tell Mavis, and they headed back into one of the bedrooms to wait for his return.

"Back for more?" said Mavis as CJ entered the kitchen. CJ could feel the warm glow in the room.

"Keep it up, and you'll be back topping off the scales," said Mavis.

"It's for Rosie and Billy, not me," said CJ.

Mavis eyed him suspiciously. "Etta, hand me those chips over there." Etta Lee passed the tortilla chips over to Mavis, then went back to check on her candied yams.

Mavis emptied the chips into the bowl. "Did you see what Billy DeLong brought me? He said it was for having him here for Thanksgiving dinner." Mavis crunched up the empty tortilla bag and tossed it in the trash can under the sink.

"No," said CJ. "Let me have a look."

Mavis reached up to a cache of recipe books and pulled out a small white box with a silver bow. She lifted the top off but held the box toward her so CJ couldn't see what was inside.

"Go ahead, let me see," said CJ.

Mavis reached inside and pulled out a delicate handmade turquoise and silver hatband. Each piece of turquoise had been carved into the shape of an animal: an antelope, a deer, a fox; and each piece of silver had been hammered into the shape of a leaf. Mavis handed the hatband to CJ.

"Pretty," he said, surprised at the weight. "Did Billy make it himself?"

"Sure did," said Mavis. "He said it took him almost a year to get it right. I think he might have made it for that woman Holly Beckwith, the one you said is going to tell the tale that puts Perez and Spence away."

"Have you got a hat for it?" asked CJ.

"No, I don't," said Mavis.

CJ looked around the room, inhaling the rich aroma of turkey and dressing, homemade rolls, and sweet potato pie. A loud cheer burst from the living room and the den at the same time. He knew the Broncos had just scored. CJ suddenly felt the familiarity of home.

"How about tomorrow you and me go out together and find you the proper hat?"

Mavis turned the hatband around slowly in her hand. She hesitated before saying, "Okay." But she couldn't resist adding, "What brought that on?"

"Nothing in particular," said CJ. "Let's just say I'm on a brand-new diet." He watched as Mavis gently placed the hatband back inside the box.